The Road to Bethany

An Idyllic 1940s Irish Historical Fiction Novel

ORLA KELLY
PUBLISHING

Danny Dunne

978-1-915502-23-0

Orla Kelly Publishing
27 Kilbrody, Mount Oval,
Rochestown,
Cork,
Ireland

To all those who are near and dear to me

From every house the neighbours met,
The streets were fill'd with joyful sound,
A solemn gladness even crown'd
The purple brows of Olivet.

Behold a man raised up by Christ!
The rest remaineth unreveal'd:
He told it not; or something seal'd
The lips of that Evangelist.

—Lord Alfred Tennyson, *The Raising of Lazarus*

Contents

Author's Note

I don't think anyone will ever forget the COVID-19 years that isolated us from the world for so long. This story grew wings during that time. It was based on an idea I'd been putting together some years earlier but had left on the long finger for quite a while.

This book tells the story of a people who lived ordinary, quiet lives. They had a certain degree of education that they left behind at the end of primary school. Further education was the privilege of those who could afford it. Secondary education in the 1940s had to be paid for. It would not be available free to everyone until 1967.

These people, even though they had a limited education, were highly educated in many other ways. They were full of the lore, heritage, stories, religious beliefs and practices they lived as part of their everyday existence. They had a deep, profound Christian faith that directed their lives and nurtured a deep spirituality. Coupled with this were a series of ancient customs of pagan origin, rooted in a far-off Celtic past, which were now embedded in that deep Christian faith. They were a gentle folk who helped, cared for, and shared with others in their parish community.

They lived off the fruits of their labours, moving with the seasons, growing and harvesting as well as caring for their animals.

It sounds like an idyllic world, but deep down, there was great poverty, hardship, and illness as well as a high mortality rate among infants in large families. TB was rampant and out of control.

It was a period in Irish history, during World War II, known here as the Emergency. Even though the war didn't reach our shores, there was rationing and food shortages as well as compulsory tillage to keep the people fed. This is a childhood story, a recollection of times now long gone.

It was into this strange world that young Margaret Kerr, a refugee from London, found herself immersed. Leaving the war behind her, she learns to embrace and love this place. We see it through her eyes. Older generations today, who lived through those times, knew people like John, Martha, Maureen, and Bartley. They were a happy and contented people, whose philosophy in life would spill onto Margaret through time.

I cannot finish this note without mentioning a few people. The dedication to this book includes all those who are dear to me. I'm a Westmeath man, a Midlander, a Lakelander, and these are my people. What better place to set this story than my home area in a fictitious parish near Mullingar.

I would like to thank Orla, my publisher, for this book. Her professionalism knows no bounds. I cannot forget Rachel, my editor, for her time and patience with me to see this project through.

Will there be another chance to see Margaret at Bethany? When you read the story, you'll find out.

Danny Dunne

March 1, 2023

Part 1
The Blitz

Chapter 1

My memories begin in early childhood, somewhere in there where the world was easy-going and your whole life was regulated for you, breakfast, school, trips to the park, the cinema, a show in the city, or that annual trip to the seaside at Margate. All the world was a donkey ride on the sand, and plenty of fun.

I was nine years old when I had the first real trauma in my life. Father came home from work and said he might enlist in the army. We had recently been on holiday in Margate, and I would soon be returning to school after the summer break. I remember the night we sat at the radio and listened to Prime Minister Neville Chamberlain break the terrible news to us.

'I am speaking to you from the Cabinet Room at Ten Downing Street. This morning the British Ambassador in Berlin, Nevile Henderson, handed the German government a final note stating that unless we heard from them by eleven o'clock that they were prepared at once to withdraw their troops from Poland, a state of war would exist between us.

'I have to tell you now that no such undertaking has been received, and that consequently this country is at war with Germany . . .'

I sat by the fireside, and the faces of my parents shone silent and wan in the firelight. I knew that whatever happened, things would never be the same again.

'We'll be all right,' said Father. 'We'll stick together. Hitler won't show his nose on my front door.'

'Don't say things like that, dear,' Mother replied. 'Don't frighten little Margaret.'

Nana was sitting by the fire, her knitting needles going, and I knew she didn't want to believe it was happening all over again.

'We came through it in 1918,' she said. 'Stop worrying and carry on as normal. Life must go on, Germans or no Germans. Your father, John Kerr, weathered the trenches, vermin, bullets, the lot. What did he get? The bleedin' flu in the spring of 1919 and left you without a father. What did he get for it all? Sweet nothing.'

'Don't talk like that in front of the little one,' said Father.

'Well, she must know the truth,' said Nana. 'At the end of the day, we'll get nothing, only heartache and trouble. Believe you me, that is all we'll get. So the first thing we should do is stop worrying. No one will give us thanks for it, not the king, not the prime minister, not even those who come after us.'

Mother told me to go to the kitchen and fetch the jar of sweets we'd brought from Margate. She spoke in her soft Irish accent, which she'd never lost.

I brought the jar back into the room where they sat. Father stood at the window, gazing across the city of his childhood. I didn't know what he was thinking about, but Mother seemed to. She sat silently embroidering the altar cloth for Father Ryan's mission fund. She had to have them done by the end of October.

Eating some of the sweets brought a little reprieve from the tension. I tried to forget about tomorrow and all it might bring.

Mother changed the subject and spoke of home. Father soon left and went down to the local.

Nana sighed when he was gone. She and Mother exchanged glances, and Mother began to cry.

'Don't do that, child. For Margaret's sake, don't do it.'

'It's all right, Mother,' I said, trying to comfort her. 'I'm here, and I'll look after you.'

'I know that, pet,' she answered, and she kissed me.

'You know what you should do if he joins up?' said Nana.

'Please don't start arranging our lives for us now . . .'

'I'm not arranging anything for you at all. You must face up to the fact that it could be dangerous here.'

'And where do you think we should go?'

'Go back to Ireland. It will be safer there. Take Margaret with you.'

'I'm not leaving you, not tomorrow, never!'

'I'll manage all right. I managed long before *you* came along, even though you've been a godsend all these years. But at my time of life, there's no point in me changing. I'm staying here, and even if Hitler comes at me with a firing squad, I'm not going anywhere.'

'Don't talk like that, Nana,' said Mother, and she began crying again.

I took her hand. 'Mother, what is a firing squad?'

'I told you not to say things like that in front of the little one,' she pleaded. 'You will frighten her.'

'Have you even considered going back, then?' asked Nana.

'Too many memories,' Mother said. 'I want to escape the past, not return to it.'

'Don't rule it out, anyway. You never know, you might have to go back there someday.'

'I won't leave you,' said Mother. 'You are *my* mother now, and I owe you so much.'

Nana continued knitting, but she smiled over her glasses at Mother.

*****

My mother was born Kitty Costello, near Mullingar in 1905. Her father was a solicitor who had a practice in the town. In 1919, when she was fourteen years old, her mother died of the flu, and her father sent her to Dublin to live with an old maiden aunt in Rathmines. There she continued her secondary studies and went to work in the civil service in the new Free State.

One day, as she was looking in a shop window on Grafton Street, a young man tapped her on the shoulder and handed her the scarf she had just dropped. She knew from his accent that he was English. He asked her to go for a walk with him down O'Connell Street. So as not to be rude, she accepted his invitation and went with him.

That young man was my father, John Kerr. He was a student studying English and mathematics at Trinity College. He was staying with Irish relatives who lived in Rathfarnham.

To make a long story short, she fell in love with him, and she took him home one weekend to visit her father. He was too busy in his practice to take much notice of the young man and sent her packing to her uncle John, her father's brother, out in the country. He lived on a farm near one of the lakes. He was a bachelor. His two sisters, who also had never married, lived with him. It was a mystery to Mother as to why they stayed together and were content to do so. But this was something I was to find out later, when fate decided that we spend the war years with them.

Their farm was a home from home for Mother whenever she returned from Dublin.

From the snippets of history I'd managed to gather from Mother over the years, the Costello family had a very colourful past. In the days following the Cromwellian settlement in Ireland, the Costellos had been dispossessed of their lands, and their estates were given over as payment to soldiers and adventurers who supported Cromwell, who then settled in the area. The Costellos were scattered to the four winds, but some of their flock remained and in time managed to make a living, surviving many generations until the middle of the nineteenth century, when Mother's grandfather began a successful hardware business in the town. But challenging times came their way also, and they sold out. Mother's father was one of the lucky ones; he was educated during the good times and went to college, becoming a highly successful solicitor. But the younger members of his family, his brother John and his sisters Maureen and Martha, were left high and dry without a proper education, as they had to leave school at twelve years of age.

To provide for them, their father bought a farm when all the debts were paid, and this was to be their home for the rest of their days. Ironically, the farm had been part of the Costello holdings before the Cromwellian settlement, and moving to this place was a bittersweet moment in a time of great distress in their lives. The loss of their business saw John's parents to an early grave, but the three siblings worked well together, and the farm thrived.

On Father's early visits to the farm, he discovered that Uncle John had a nickname. It stemmed from the great flu of 1919, which John had been lucky to survive. Neither of his sisters caught the virus, and it was through their care that he struggled back, taking many weeks to recover fully. From then on, local people christened the farm *Bethany* and Uncle John *Lazarus*. Uncle John paid little heed to such gibing, but he was a little amused to be compared to someone Jesus had raised from the dead.

Uncle John and his sisters treated Father with suspicion at first and told Mother that she should have chosen a good Catholic man rather than this strange Protestant Englishman. Mother was not at all perturbed by such remarks, as she believed Uncle John was too provincial in his attitudes and that if you were to believe all he said, you wouldn't do anything, go anywhere, or even leave the parish. This was the world Uncle John lived in.

Before long, her father died in a tragic boating accident on the lake and she just wanted to get away from it all. When she went to London, she decided she would never return to Ireland. It had too many sad memories for her. Coupled with that, she chose to ignore Uncle John's remarks about marrying a Protestant man, but when she approached the local parish priest to arrange her wedding, he couldn't see fit to give his blessing to a mixed marriage, so they settled for a civil marriage in London. Mother agreed to this if Father allowed any children born to them to be brought up in the Catholic faith. Despite her disappointment with the clergy at home, she was deeply rooted in her faith. This did not faze Father in the least, or Nana, for that matter. Father's mother felt she had more important things to worry her.

'Who cares what faith they're baptised into?' she said. 'They're still baptised.'

Nana and Mother bonded very quickly. Nana didn't go to church very often herself, but she reminded Mother every Sunday not to forget to go to mass.

They had a great understanding of each other, and Mother entered a happy phase in her married life.

Uncle John and his sisters were now her only contacts back home. It must have been at least fifteen years since she had been home. All of that had happened so long ago.

My early childhood, then, was a happy and secure one, until Mr Hitler decided that London was someday soon going to be his.

*****

When the school term began, everyone was talking about the war. I expected great armies to storm into our school and take us away, but nothing happened. The crows made a racket in the trees outside, and distant dogs barked in small urban gardens.

I saw Felicity at break time, and she was all excited about the whole affair. Her mum declared if there was any danger, she was heading north to Scotland where her relatives lived.

I wondered what would happen to us. Miss Scott told us to pray that Jerry would stay away and leave our green and peaceful shores alone.

School continued as normal. There was the regular hum of traffic on the street outside, and for the moment, I forgot all about it. I was more concerned with trying to establish whether long division was a punishment put on poor children or whether I was just stupid not to be able to work them out for myself.

We ran through the playground. The leaves on the trees were beginning to fade, telling us autumn had arrived. Some had fallen with the wind the night before, but we ignored their presence and kicked them aside as we sought each other out in our varied games.

I was good at skipping, and I spent a lot of time in the centre between two girls, as I could jump the longest without tripping on the rope. Felicity envied me so much for this, but she admired my stamina. She was not as strong as me, and she was ill quite often. I thought that maybe if she did move to Scotland, the air there would be much better for her health.

The bell called us in, and we assembled at our respective classroom doors. My classmates and I waited for Miss Scott to return from her lunch to unlock the door for us.

There was a scuffle at the end of the queue; two girls were fighting hand to hand. It was Michelle Hornby and Gerta Gruber.

Miss Scott arrived at a scene of chaos. She rushed in and separated the two girls. With a loud clap of her hands and a great roar, she exclaimed, 'Silence!'

We returned mutely to our places in the queue. She turned to the girls, shouting, 'What is the meaning of this outburst?'

There was silence from the two, but Gerta was crying.

'Who is responsible for this? If you do not own up, the whole class will be punished.'

We protested our innocence and urged Michelle to speak up. Eventually, under duress, she did as we asked.

'I called her names, Miss!'

'You know that calling names is akin to the devil's handiwork.'

'Yes, Miss!' she answered. 'I'm sorry.'

'What names were you using, girl?'

Michelle refused to answer and turned to Gerta.

'What did she say to you?'

'She called me a Nazi bitch,' sobbed Gerta.

'Right. I'll deal with this as soon as possible. Into class with the lot of you.'

We filed in past her and sat quietly in our places. Gerta and Michelle stood outside until they were ordered in.

Gerta's mother was English, but her father was German. He had been a British citizen for many years, and he owned a jeweller's shop on our street. We knew in our hearts that what Michelle had said was not true.

Mr Gruber was not a Nazi supporter. Quite the opposite; they were of the Jewish faith and lived a quiet and private life close to our place.

'Do you realise the cruel things you've said?' asked Miss Scott.

'Yes, Miss!'

'You have got to realise that Gerta is a British citizen, just like you. You will kindly apologise right now.'

'I'm sorry, Gerta,' said Michelle.

'It's all right!' said Gerta. 'Let's forget about it.'

'Now, Michelle, would you go to the headmistress and tell her everything you did. You must never say such things again.'

Michelle turned without saying anything and left the room. Miss Scott then faced us all and gave us a lecture on kindness and how to treat others with respect.

'Times are hard and cruel. These are dark days. We must be careful what we say and do. We must be watchful. You never know from what corner the enemy will be lurking. We must keep our thoughts to ourselves, regardless of what we might think. You never know the day or the hour the enemy will pounce, or who is working for them. There will be difficult days ahead, so beware. Your enemy is never the most obvious person around you. You will meet him on the street, and you might not know him. If you give away any information, it could help the enemy get a foothold in our beautiful country. Be careful, girls; that's all I have to say.' She sat down, and class resumed.

I was frightened, and all I was afraid of was that I might wet my underclothes. I asked to be excused. As I headed to the toilet, I met Michelle returning from the headmistress's office. She was in tears, and she carried a letter – a note for her parents, obviously.

I went to the toilet and shut myself in. I could hear noises. I listened and waited. I could hear a grating sound down the pipes, and then the noise of something tapping. I had often heard it before, water rushing through the pipes, causing them to rock gently so that they tapped against the wall. But today the sound was more sinister.

I felt as if I'd been sitting on the toilet all day. I half pulled my clothes on and ran from the place. The enemy was coming, and children were their target. As soon as the children felt pain from torture, they would give away every scrap of information.

I sat down in my desk, glad to be back again, but I watched the door all afternoon, hoping that the enemy would stay away. When the evening bell rang, I gathered my things quickly and ran through the playground.

Mother was waiting for me. She smiled her usual smile, and I knew everything was fine. We walked home together, and she told me she had a letter from Uncle John in Ireland.

*****

After dinner, she showed me the letter. I sat down to read it, and when I had finished, I asked her to read it to me again.

Father was in his study, preparing work for school. At times like this, we dared not disturb him. Nana sat quietly in her chair, knitting. She had large quantities of double knitting wool, and I knew she was preparing to clothe us in warm woollies for the winter. But this winter might be exceptional, so there was an extra rush on. She had all her patterns laid out, but she never consulted them. She was an expert at gauging size as well as the content of wool required for any one garment, whether it be for a child or an adult or a small infant. Even in her ageing years, her hands were strong and agile, and her work provided great therapy, keeping her mind alert.

Just as Mother was about to reread the letter to me, there was a knock on the door, and she answered it. It was Derek, one of Father's teaching colleagues from school. They shared the teaching of English, so he was often a visitor to our house. Father and Derek would often spend late into the night in the study, talking and smoking. Next morning Mother would have to open the windows to relieve the room of the smell of smoke. Whenever Mother protested that the smoke remained on everything, Father would complain that smoking was one of the few creature comforts he had in life. Mother would always reply, 'Lucky you!'

'It's cold out tonight,' said Derek. 'Rather a good nip in the air.'

'Winter is fast approaching,' answered Mother.

'Indeed. It could be a long winter, by the looks of things,' said Derek.

'Please God it won't,' sighed Mother.

'Don't worry, old girl. With a nice little Irish prayer like that, nothing will happen to you,' he joked.

'I hope you're right. It's a big worry now.'

'Trust my judgement – Jerry won't put a foot on good old England.'

Mother took his coat and scarf and hung them in the hall. She offered to bring him in to sit at the fire. He declined the offer but asked if he could be excused and whether he could seek out his usual haunt.

'You know where it is,' said Mother. 'You must have a path worn there by now.'

'There's only one thing on our minds tonight . . .'

'Please don't talk about it,' said Mother. 'I don't want to know.'

She opened the door and let him in. I could hear the hum of voices inside. Then she and I went back to the warm fire so I could hear her read the letter.

> *Dear Kitty,*
>
> *It's been such a long time since we heard from you. We often wonder how life is with you. We are all fine this end and we can make ends meet. It's not younger we're getting, and I feel the years are creeping up on us.*
>
> *We often think about you and your family and wonder would we ever see you again. We offer the rosary every night for your safety; what with talk of war, no one is safe anymore. They are preparing here, all right. If the Germans come, we would not even stand a chance against them.*

Maybe it is safer here. They say that de Valera will have nothing to do with the war if it comes, and in that case, they might stay away.

The reason I write this letter to you is that if times get bad in London, there will always be a place for you and your family here.

Maureen and Martha wonder all the time how little Margaret is. She is probably a big girl by now. The nights are lonely here, but occasionally a few neighbours drop in. Whenever a cow calves, there is a glut of milk, so it's an excuse for someone to call if they are short of any.

At this stage, girl, I think it is time to sign off. I plead with you that if things get worse out there, come over here, and we will look after you all. For the moment, God go with you, and keep away from danger.

Your Uncle John

There was a tear in Mother's eye when she read the letter, and I knew that deep down inside, she longed for that place again. She would go were it not that there was nothing there for her, only the memories and her sad losses of childhood.

She folded the letter, placed it back in the envelope, and put it on the mantelpiece behind the orange delft dog.

She sat with her embroidery, and I resumed reading my book at the table. There was complete silence but for the hum of deep men's voices coming from the study across the hall and the gentle click of Nana's knitting needles. I knew Nana was keeping a watchful eye on Mother, and she waited for her moment.

'You could go, you know,' she said softly. 'Don't let me hold you back.'

'I'm not going. How can we? Margaret needs to go to school. John has his teaching job. There is this house, and I'd never leave you on your own.'

'Leave me on my own,' laughed Nana. 'I have been on my own all my life. I brought my son up in hard times, and he turned out to be a good man. Then he got a lovely wife, and they have a beautiful daughter. What more do I want? But there is danger, love. I fear for your safety, for all your safety. I am an old woman, I've had a good life, and I have no regrets. I don't want to lose those I care for. I would prefer to see you safe somewhere.'

'For the moment, we're all right,' said Mother. 'I'm not going to panic, and we're not going to leave you.'

They continued talking for a while, weighing the pros and cons of moving to a safer haven, and as the night wore on, I lost them in their conversation, as my book seemed more interesting.

Then the study door opened, and Father emerged. I could hear him and Derek talk in a low whisper. Derek put on his coat and left. Father came to the fire and stood with his pipe in his hand as clouds of smoke carried and dispersed on the ceiling.

'Is there something wrong?' asked Nana.

'I don't know,' he replied.

'Derek left rather early,' said Nana.

'He has enlisted in the army.'

'Oh!' said Mother. She put her embroidery down and looked him straight in the face. 'Where does that leave you, then?'

'I don't know.' He tapped his pipe on the hob and tossed the ashes into the fire. Then he spoke again.

'I suppose, as he is joining up, then I must do the same. There is no way out of this one. We need to fight for king and country.'

He left the room and returned to the study, shutting the door behind him. A few minutes later Mother followed him, and I could hear them talk quietly. Nana remained silent, but I could see the silent tears in her wrinkled old eyes. Finally, she told me to go to the kitchen for a glass of milk, and I went upstairs to bed, wondering what was going to happen next.

Chapter 2

After Christmas, Father left. He'd enlisted at Halloween and was told to report to the barracks early in the new year. He made us all promise that if anything happened in the city, we were to take the boat to Ireland. It seemed the right thing to do, but Mother insisted we were going to stay. She wouldn't leave Nana behind on her own.

'We have a good strong house, and we'll be safe here,' she sobbed at the station as we said farewell to him.

'Bricks and mortar won't stop a German bomb,' said Father. 'Look what happened at that airfield the other night.'

'I know we'll be all right,' said Mother. 'So don't worry.'

He stooped down to my level and held me in a tight grip.

'You be good, young lady, and take care of your mother.'

'And don't forget Nana!' I retorted.

'Especially Nana. She will need a lot of care, you know.'

'Don't forget to write, Father, and tell me about all the things you see.'

'Well, whatever faraway Kent has to offer should be a great thing, and I'll tell you all about it.'

I kissed him, and I could feel all the sadness of his parting. It was the first time in our lives that we'd ever been separated, and it was the first sense of great loss I'd ever had. He took Mother in his arms then, and they said farewell silently with their embrace. I joined them and held them close together as the train began to make headway from the station. He jumped on board and stood waving out the window at us. We watched as the train disappeared in the January fog, and when we turned to go, Mother was crying. She took me by the hand and told me we were going for a cup of coffee.

We sat in a small café near the station, and I gazed out the window at the changing city, a city at war. There were signs advertising *The Wizard of Oz.* But dispersed among them all were pictures cautioning us about spreading rumours and advising us to conserve food. There were posters encouraging young women to join the Wrens, and I felt that if I were old enough, that was what I would do to help the war effort.

I drank a cup of hot tea, and Mother ordered some muffins. We had more than enough, and when we were finished, Mother put the last two muffins in her bag.

'Our contribution to the war effort,' she said. 'Waste not, want not. We'll follow the crows for it someday.'

'What do you mean by that?' I asked.

'It's an old Irish saying. In Ireland there is a lot of countryside, and whenever there are scraps of food thrown out, the crows fly down from the trees and snatch it away very quickly. So if we waste too much, we might have to follow the crows for it.'

In response to that, I took a paper bag I had in my pocket and emptied the sugar bowl into it. It was full of perfect white cubes of sugar. I put it in my pocket and smiled at Mother.

'We might have to follow the crows for that too,' I laughed.

'Margaret! That was a dreadful thing to do.'

'You paid for them, Mother, so you are entitled to bring them.'

'I just hope no one has seen you. Sugar will be in short supply.'

Mother paid for our snack, and we were just going out the door when a waiter saw the empty sugar bowl. He shouted after us to come back. We didn't heed his call and both ran as fast as we could.

When we got home, Nana was sitting in her corner, and the fire was a welcome retreat from the cold. We brewed up tea again, and Mother told her about Father's farewell.

Nana gazed into the flames. 'It's the same thing all over again. My man went away, and I lost him too. I only hope I don't lose my own little boy as well.'

'Don't say that, Nana. He'll be back.'

'I hope so, love. I only hope so.'

To change the subject, Mother told her about the muffins and the sugar, and Mother's comment was that "this young lady" would be a survivor.

That was my intention. I was determined to survive, whether Hitler liked it or not.

*****

The year moved slowly on, and the war had not directly affected us. Food was rationed, and there were long queues. It meant that Mother was away from home more often and I had to care for Nana.

Father was home at Easter, and he showed us photographs taken with his comrades in uniform. To Mother's relief, he had been told that he was too old for active service and had health issues besides, so he would best serve his country by spending his time in an office pushing a pen.

Nana was thrilled with the news, knowing that he would return someday, when the war was over. She hoped and prayed it wouldn't be too long.

There was talk of airfields being bombed and great devastation all over England, but we had seen nothing.

It was a beautiful, hot summer, and we decided to stay where we were. I found the whole place closing in on us with the constant sound of aircraft. I knew it had to be our boys on manoeuvre, because if there was a Jerry attack, we would be warned in advance.

In August, we heard the rumble of bombs falling on airfields to the south, and one night the sky lit up as fires raged many miles away.

Then, on September 7, the London Blitz began. The raids that had been taking place on airfields and other military bases had eased. Bombs fell all over London, and Buckingham Palace suffered a hit on the thirteenth. On the fourteenth of September, the German bombers were successful in their raids on southern England. Because of the state of the airfields following attacks, there was little resistance to the raids. On September 15, two major raids on London were suppressed by the Royal Air Force.

When we heard the bombs for the first time, we hid under the stairs. We thought it would be safe there. But we were told by the authorities that it was too dangerous to stay inside the house.

People began making their way to the nearest shelters. They flocked in large numbers to the Underground stations, much to the annoyance of the authorities. But the Underground was to prove a welcome place right through the Blitz.

Mother slept with me at night. I had wakened many times over the past few months with nightmares. The stability of my life was being eroded by the war, and now that Father was gone, I feared he might never return.

One day while we were at school, we were made to wear gas masks as a training exercise in case there was a gas attack. I could barely see the blackboard, let alone hear the teacher speak through her mask. The gas mask was contained in a small box with a strap, which we were to wear over our shoulder and take with us to school every day, or anywhere we might be travelling in the city. I was terrified inside that mask, and suddenly I knew how a horse must feel when blinkers were put on it. I felt I was a creature from another world, and they were such ugly-looking things. I was glad when the exercise was over.

As the days and weeks passed, my friends began to leave. The government established Operation Pied Piper in 1939, where countless people, mainly children, were evacuated to safer havens in the country. In June 1940, for fear of invasion by sea, evacuations took place from coastal towns and cities in the south of England.

I felt lonely and alone as they began to go, for I knew I would never see some of them again. On many occasions I came home from school crying, and Mother would hold me close to her. There was relief from my anxiety when another letter arrived from Uncle John in Ireland, and the question of whether we should leave or stay reared its head once again.

Nana declared as always that she was staying put, as Mother wanted her to come with us. So, when she refused to budge, there was no question about it: Mother wasn't going to leave either. But things were about to change fast.

The last few nights had been quiet, but one night we were once more wakened by the sound of the moaning minnies. They were the air raid sirens used to warn people to seek shelter from the bombs falling on the city. They had been part of our lives since late summer, and it had become routine to leave and go to the shelter.

We returned that night to find that our house had been looted. Father's books were thrown everywhere, and the silver cups Nana had kept from her early married life were gone. Granddad had won them for playing cricket, and she had treasured them. This upset her gravely, and she declared she would never leave the house again. Mother put her to bed, and she was unwell for a few days.

Mother feared that when the next raid came, she would have to get Nana out, as the bombs were coming ever so much closer.

She arranged for Felicity's mother, Berna, to help if it was required, so I was sent away to her house in the early evening. If there was a raid, I would go to the shelter with Felicity and her mum and return home with Mother when danger had passed. I was glad to have a friend to hang on to, and I knew that without me as a burden, Mother would persuade Nana to leave.

Felicity and I played snakes and ladders all during the early evening, and she told me that her mother was preparing for them to move to Scotland.

Then quite suddenly, the sirens began to roar, and we were ready to go. I wore a heavy overcoat and beret. I carried a patchwork rug that Nana had knitted. It had no specific pattern; it was a way she had of using up old ends of wool by knitting little six-inch squares and sewing them together.

Berna held us tightly by the hands out in the darkness of the streets. We could hear the rumble of bombs as if it were a thunder-and-lightning storm. At first, it seemed far away. Then suddenly there was a deafening explosion that sent us all crashing to the ground. I began to scream, but it was lost in the confusion and noise that followed as people rushed to the shelter underground. We had just arrived when the terrible rain of bombs began in earnest.

From deep in the bowels of the earth where we had found refuge, we could hear nothing, only a rumble here and there, and occasionally the interior of the shelter shook as nearly direct hits exploded over our heads.

I wiped my tears of terror away with Nana's rug. Berna wrapped my badly cut knee with a handkerchief. I was so overwhelmed with fear, I could hear nothing nor feel the pain of the gash in my knee. Then a nurse arrived to tend to those with minor cuts and abrasions, and she began to bandage my knee properly.

I shouted as loud as I could through the throng. 'Where's my mother?'

'Take it easy, love,' said the nurse. She was young, and she smelled of nice perfume. She smiled at me as she worked to try to reassure me that Mother was safe.

'Did you lose your mother?' she asked.

'No, I came with Felicity and Berna,' I sobbed. 'Mother was bringing Nana with her. She is old, and she is slow. I don't see them anywhere.'

'What's your mother's name?'

'Kitty!'

'And her second name?'

'Kitty Kerr!'

The nurse stood up and called out through the crowd for silence.

'Is there a Kitty Kerr here, by any chance?' Other nurses and personnel called farther down the line with the same request. But there was no response. Kitty Kerr was not in the shelter.

'She has more than likely gone to another shelter nearby. You'll see; you'll find her in the morning.'

'We'll just have to wait till we get the all clear,' said Berna. 'Take it easy, love, and try to get some sleep.'

I tried calling Mother's name again, but I was hoarse from crying and my voice was lost in the hum of people talking. I watched through the low light for her face to appear with Nana's, but as the night wore on, there was no sign of her.

People coughed, children whimpered, and someone somewhere consoled a crying baby. No one talked, and there was little to amuse us as we all waited in fear of what was happening above us.

Suddenly, a little small woman jumped up and shouted in her best Cockney accent, 'Oi've just 'ad enough of this. 'Ow about a song. Come on, ducks!'

She was smiling down into my face, but I wouldn't answer her.

'She's lost her mother! She's out there somewhere,' said Berna.

So the woman began to sing herself, and as the song progressed, others joined in.

Don't put your daughter on the stage, Mrs Worthington
Don't put you daughter on the stage . . .

A few people stood up and danced where they stood, and sleepy children began laughing. The nurse who'd dressed my knee came to me again and said, 'Don't worry, little girl, you'll find your mother all right.'

Berna held me tight to her. Through all of this, Felicity was calm and quiet. But she was lucky to have her mother with her, and through the noise and melee, she had fallen asleep. I was the one who couldn't sleep. I was so worried about my mother and my nana.

If only Father were here, he would have gone back to the house to find them and bring them safely here. I had visions of Mother huddling under the stairs, as we had done on other occasions when the bombing was somewhat distant from us. Maybe she had remained with Nana, who had refused to budge. Worse still, they might be stuck in an alleyway or a doorway. There was also the possibility that they had gotten lost on the dark streets in the mayhem and confusion and Nana had not been able to go any farther.

The Cockney woman threw a stole around her shoulders and began to sing again.

It's a long way to Tipperary

It's a long way to go

It's a long way to Tipperary

To the sweetest girl I know . . .

Just as soon as she finished singing, the sirens blared again, giving the all clear.

The rumble and thunder overhead had ceased.

The crowd moved slowly and sleepily from the shelter up into the city streets. I thought it must be early morning, we had been down below so long.

Then, when the light met us, I was certain it must be midday. But I was wrong. The whole street was on fire. Buildings were collapsing and crumbling in the great heat, and we were directed away from it. I wanted to go straight on in the direction of our house, but a policeman turned us away.

'Where do you want to go?' he asked.

'Cavewell Street,' shouted Berna.

'Don't even go there,' he answered.

'Why?'

'It's just a heap of rubble. If anyone was still there, they wouldn't have made it out alive. They wouldn't have had a hope. It suffered a direct hit.'

I began to scream again, and Berna dragged me away.

'Come along, Margaret. If your mum and your nana made it safely out of there, they might have headed for my place. So come on, stop screaming and crying; let's get out of here. There's nothing we can do till morning.'

We made our way towards Felicity's house; through dark alleyways and streets I didn't know. We had to make a detour round the bombed area till we came close to her home. There was a clear dividing line in the bombing. The Germans had found their targets with precision. As our eyes adjusted to the darkness, we left the sounds of war behind, and I was so relieved when we found the front door of their house.

With the vibrations and roaring of bombs some streets away, the house was in quite good condition, except for the fanlight over the door.

We stepped through the broken glass, and Berna lit a candle. The fire in the grate was still lit. She stoked it up and boiled a kettle on it, as the gas was turned off. The mains had been destroyed in the bombing.

I was shaking, and the hot cocoa made me calm down a little.

'If your mother is all right, she'll find you,' said Berna. 'If she doesn't turn up tonight, I'll go to the police station in the morning to see if I can find out anything.'

'Come to my room tonight,' said Felicity. 'You can sleep in my bed.'

'You are all so kind,' I sobbed.

'Kindness is not the word, love. Only too glad to help in these hard times,' said Berna.

I didn't sleep for a while, and when I did, I could hear the bombs falling. I woke up a few times to passing noises in the street outside – the bell of a fire engine or people talking. Then, before dawn, I could hear the harsh sound of the Cockney woman going home. She was still singing. It was her way of dealing with the terror of the times. Music and song soothed her soul.

I woke at ten o'clock, and Felicity was already up. She was making toast downstairs with a long fork, holding the bread into the open flames of the fire. I could smell the toast as I got up. She made some for both of us. Her mum had left earlier to go to the police station.

Felicity tried to cheer me up by telling me stories she had read from her books and showing me her collection of cigarette cards. I tried to keep my bright side out by pretending to show some interest in what she was saying and doing. The cigarette cards showed pictures of famous film stars, and there was a little summary of their lives and film careers on the back. The smiling faces indicated that the war was a long way away from them. But I was to learn later that many of the stars had joined the army and fought bravely for their country. Some of them were decorated for valour as well. Others travelled the war zones and entertained the troops.

But here in this little house in London, I waited to see what fate lay ahead of me. Mother should have done what Uncle John had said and taken the boat to Ireland. Even if Nana protested and screamed over it, she would have been safe.

When we were finished with the cards, we sat the rest of the morning looking out into the street and watching everyone coming and going. Life went on as normal despite the tragic events of the night before. Occasionally, people went past displaying wounds and injuries from the bombing. They were just superficial injuries, of course, not like those of the seriously injured in hospital or those of people who had lost their lives. But the people going past that morning were already putting the terror of the previous night behind them, and nothing was going to stop them from carrying on with their lives.

At about eleven o'clock, we saw Berna running through the crowds towards the house, and we raced out into the street to meet her.

'Margaret!' she shouted. 'I've found her!'

'Where is she?'

'She's all right, love.'

'Where is she?' I asked again.

'She's in hospital. She will be simply fine.'

'Where's Nana?'

She stooped down and took my hand. She squeezed it tight.

'I'm sorry, love . . .'

'What happened to her?' I screamed.

'She's dead, love.'

She held me close to her, and I began to cry.

'Come along inside, and I'll tell you all about it.'

*****

Mother had persuaded Nana to go with her to the shelter when the first bomb fell. The vibrations sent ornaments crashing from the mantelpiece and plaster falling from the ceiling. With the dust bleeding into the air in the room, Nana began coughing. She decided it was time to go out into the hall and under the stairs. But having reached the hall, Mother made her put on her coat.

By now, the bombs were whistling all round them, and Mother knew that before long, our house would be hit as well.

'I'd prefer to go to my bed,' grumbled Nana. 'What is it worth to me, leaving this house I have lived in all my life? If they want to bomb it, let them go ahead and do so.'

'I'm not staying here with you,' exclaimed Mother. 'If we both stay, we'll be killed. It's not worth the risk.'

Nana made no more protests but went slowly into the noisy street with Mother.

Bombs were dropping all round them, and they could feel on occasion the heat from the strikes. But this didn't deter them. They kept going, following the route Mother knew to the safety of the bomb shelter. The darkness of night had gone, and searchlights reached like great arms into the night sky. It was a veritable fireworks display, but no one was staying to watch.

They couldn't move very fast, as Nana was slow on her feet, holding tightly to her walking stick to give her support. Mother tried to keep a step ahead of her to prevent her from tripping over fallen masonry and bricks. Fire engines roared past and turned into other streets. Several fires weren't being tended to at all.

Then Nana began to feel tired and wanted to rest. Mother told her she would have plenty of time to rest when they got to the shelter, but still she protested. So they decided to take a chance and sit in the darkness of a doorstep.

Looking farther up the street, Mother could see a woman trying to loosen the wheel of a pram from a piece of iron railing. Overhead, the building was being consumed by flames, and soon the outward wall would collapse. Mother knew she needed to get the mother and child away from the building very quickly. As the fire rapidly progressed, the intensity of the heat grew. Mother called to the woman to grab her baby and get out of there, but the woman couldn't hear her.

Mother told Nana to stay where she was and ran up the street to the woman's assistance. There was no hope of releasing the wheel, given the way it was caught in the railing. Mother began roaring at the woman to take her baby and run, pointing to the building close to her, which was on the verge of collapse. The woman immediately understood, and she grabbed the baby and ran.

It was then that it happened. Mother had time only to look across at Nana before the bomb struck. A great light flashed before her, and she knew no more till she woke up in hospital.

She had a broken arm and some superficial head injuries from the blast, which had thrown her across the street. Had she been ten or twelve feet closer, she would have had no hope. The woman with the young baby had just made it to safety. Luckily for her, the burning building did not collapse, and shortly after that the bombing stopped.

They found Nana's body in the rubble of the bombed house. She never knew what had happened to her, as she was killed instantly.

*****

Berna took me to see Mother later that day. She was still in shock. The doctor told her that she would be fine but that she would need great care.

Father was contacted, and he arrived home the next day to arrange for a funeral. It was a very sad time in our lives. We knew that things would never be the same again. Our main concern now was to bury Nana.

We had no house. We too had suffered a direct hit. There was nothing left. The bricks lay there crumbled and broken, with the bay window looking upwards towards the sky, a reminder of the happy home it had once been.

After a day or so, I gave up crying, and I decided there and then that I'd done enough of it to last a lifetime. We had nothing left in the whole world and nowhere to go. Father couldn't stay very long, and when the funeral was over, he was given two days to return to his barracks.

It was then that Mother decided there was no way out for us but to go to Ireland and stay with Uncle John and his two sisters. She thought a safe haven in Dairy Hill was the best choice for us. I too had had enough of the war; I just wanted to get away from it all. There was no going back to our little house ever again.

Part 2
Dairy Hill Farm

Chapter 3

In November 1940, we arrived in Dublin to a peaceful city busily going about its daily routine, but without the hustle and bustle of London. The first thing I noticed was the absence or scarcity of motor cars. Trams trundled through the centre of the city, slowly but surely reaching their destinations, as people waited patiently for them to take them home or to work, depending on which way they were going.

When we got to the station, we had a two-hour wait for the train, which was heading for Galway. Mother took me in for a cup of coffee, and she warned me not to take any of the sugar, as there was an emergency here also, and commodities like sugar might not be as readily available.

Mother had been a little weepy since we left, as we'd said farewell to Father not knowing whether we'd ever see him again. He had made all the arrangements for us, and after a long train journey, we'd boarded the boat at Liverpool, setting out across the Irish sea into the black November night.

But the early-morning sunshine of Dublin welcomed us, and I didn't feel lonely in such a strange place. In fact, it was just like coming home. Mother had told me so many stories about Dublin and Mullingar that I knew every brick and hill on my journey.

The train was comfortable, and it wasn't long before we were out in the open countryside. The morning yielded a laughing frost across the quiet little hills and hummocks. A canal ran alongside the railway for most of the journey, and it was extremely quiet everywhere.

Cattle sought the shelter of the ditches, where the frost had not permeated, to try to find grass that had not been frozen, and occasionally a lone farmer waved from his field as the train crossed through his land. Sometimes the driver sounded the whistle in response to the gesture. The journey was easy, and the train stopped quietly at a few stations along the way.

When we reached the town, it happened very suddenly. I could see that here, unlike London, there was a distinct dividing line between the country and the town.

The train ground to a halt with a hiss, and we immediately stepped out. Mother looked up and down through the smoke and the steam to see if there were any familiar faces. She was still wearing a sling, as her arm had not yet set correctly. She dropped the single case she was carrying and ran into the arms of a tall man with silvery grey hair and a moustache to match. He was in his midfifties, and he was a healthy- and fit-looking man. It was Uncle John. There were tears and embraces, and I knew by the way Mother was laughing through her tears that she was coming home after a long absence.

'You haven't changed a bit,' he exclaimed. 'We thought we'd never see you again.'

'You are a sight for sore eyes, John Costello,' she laughed, coughing and holding back the tears.

'Now you need a good rest, girl, with all that you've been through. Don't let me hear another word. Where's this baby you're supposed to have?'

He turned to me. He stepped back as if surprised. 'Are you telling me lies, Kitty? I don't see any baby.'

'She's no baby.' Mother smiled. 'She's quite grown-up now.'

'I don't believe you,' he exclaimed. 'Well, I will have to take my hat off to such a fine young lady.' He did just that and bowed to me as if I were the Queen of Sheba. I went really shy and hung my head.

'Don't tell me you're going all bashful and quiet, now, are you? I don't think any Costello was ever shy.'

'No, I'm not!' I exclaimed with a little giggle.

'Well, thanks be to the Lord God for that.'

He was down on one knee and imploring, his eyes to heaven. I liked him from the start, and when I smiled at him, he swept me up in his arms, which took me by surprise. I screamed with laughter as he did so. I knew he was a man who liked children, and I could see a great happiness in his face. He was young once more and delighted in something new to look forward to. He had a distinct country smell, of animals, stale milk, and tobacco. It wasn't a revolting smell, but whenever I moved around on the farm in the next few years, I always knew when Uncle John was coming and where he had been.

He turned back to Mother, and seeing her arm in a sling, he said, 'Look, alannah, a few weeks rest and the girls will have you as right as rain.' 'The girls' were Aunt Maureen and Aunt Martha. They were both much older than their brother, as he was the youngest of the family. To him, they would never grow old, no more than he would himself.

'It must have been a shocking time for you all,' he said.

'It was awful,' said Mother. 'I could do nothing to help Nana. I'd left her for a few moments to help a mother and baby in distress when it happened.'

He put his arm around her shoulders. 'There, there. If you hadn't done that, you would have both been killed. You wouldn't be standing here telling me all about it, and this little girl would be as good as an orphan. Thank God for small mercies. Now stop crying and come with me. You can tell us all about it when you've rested and are in better health. By the looks of you, you'd make a good pull through for a darning needle.'

Mother laughed through her tears, coming to herself again. Uncle John grabbed our two cases and made his way out of the cold, grey station.

By now, the frost had eased, and there was a hint of warmth in the sun. Outside the station, there were no cars at all but rather horses and donkeys tethered to carts and traps.

Uncle John had a dark-green trap, and he opened the back door, throwing the cases inside. He hoisted me up in his arms and told me to sit at the front. He helped Mother as well, but I was surprised to see that she automatically put her foot on the stirruplike step and pulled herself in using her good arm, with a little help from Uncle John. When we were settled inside, he made us put some colourful Foxford rugs around us, saying it was a good four miles out into the country and we'd be frozen cold by the time we got to the farm.

'What's the name of the farm?' I asked.

'It's in the townland of Carrickloman, and the farm was always known as Dairy Hill Farm.'

'I thought it was called Bethany,' I said.

I didn't realise that Bethany was the nickname given to it by the local people, more in jest than anything else.

'Margaret!' Mother exclaimed. 'Don't be so cheeky. Apologise to Uncle John at once.'

'I'm sorry!' I replied, hanging my head in shame.

Then he started to laugh.

'Leave the lassie alone, will you, Kitty? Isn't she right? Sure, I'm known as Lazarus. I could be called worse. Not only that, I live with Mary and Martha. Weren't they friends of Jesus? Isn't it great to be a friend of Jesus?'

'But I thought Maureen was her name,' I said, 'and not Mary.'

'Well, girl, Maureen is another name for Mary. It means little Mary, and you will see for yourself how small little Mary is.'

Mother started to giggle to herself. I didn't know why, but Uncle John winked at her as he eased the trap out of the station and down the town.

'I think Bethany is a lovely name,' I said. 'Do you mind if I call the farm Bethany?'

'Call it what you like, love,' he laughed. 'As long as it's not too early in the morning.'

Mother started giggling again, but it would take me a while to understand Uncle John's wit and his jokes. There was often a hidden meaning in the things he said, and I came to learn during those years how he put together beautiful plays on words. Whatever little education he and his sister had received, it was put to good use with such an excellent command of English.

There was a fair in the town that day, and animals were everywhere. Men stood in groups, buying and selling cattle and sheep. There were pigs also, corralled on carts or kept in pens constructed to keep them from running riot around the town. A smell of animal dung hung in the air. I didn't know how the people of the town could put up with it. But then I realised why there were so few cars on the streets of Dublin. These days, due to the war and the shortage of fuel for cars, it was mostly horse traffic.

People were buying and selling goods in the market square. I could see women with buckets of eggs as well as butter and vegetables. For the townspeople, this was their only source of such commodities, as they were hard to come by. Eggs were especially valuable, as the season dictated that it was time for Christmas baking, especially making cakes.

After we made our way down the town, past the courthouse and the county hall, we left it all behind as we went under the railway bridge on the gravel road leading into the winter countryside.

'Have you many animals on the farm?' I asked.

'I have a good lot,' Uncle John said. 'You'll meet them all in due course. Now, let me introduce you to the first resident of Bethany – Dairy Hill Farm.' With a gentle tap on the back of the animal, he introduced me to him.

'This is Bobby, and a right cantankerous devil he can be.'

'Is he a pony?' I asked.

'No, he's a jennet.'

'What's that?' I exclaimed, and Mother smiled to herself. It was great to see her cheering up, and it made me happy too. I smiled along with her as I listened to Uncle John.

'That's a good question. I often ask myself the same thing. He's neither one thing nor another. He's not a donkey and he's not a horse. He's kind of half in between.'

'What do you mean by that?' I asked.

'Well, give it time, girl. When you see Mother Nature working on the farm, you might be shocked at first, but you'll learn, and when you do, you'll know what life is about. There might be many an awkward question which you'd need to ask your mother, and eventually you'll find that you're an expert, just as much as the rest of us.'

Tears ran down Mother's face from laughing as Uncle John said this, and all I wanted to do was meet Mother Nature face-to-face to ask her all these awkward questions. I wondered what she looked like. Was she like a fairy godmother waving a magic wand, or was she some sort of kind witch? I'd never seen any Mother Natures in London. Were they found in Ireland only?

When I saw Mother drying away her tears of laughter, it was a great change from the sadness of the past few weeks.

'You never lost it, John Costello. You never lost it,' she exclaimed.

Leaving the busy town behind, we made our way for the open country. The road was rough and gravelled, and the low light reflected in the potholes, mirroring it back into our faces. There was a dead look everywhere. The leaves had fallen from the trees and were now a wet, decaying mass along the grass verge. In places, great beech trees from each side of the road met overhead, covering it in a gloomy canopy. Jackdaws were roosting in great numbers high up there, and they made such noise.

Wherever there were great trees like this, the road served to divide two estates, and sometimes it was possible to see the big houses through the trees. They were connected to the main road by tree-lined avenues. The high stone walls were a giveaway too, and each entrance was guarded by a gate-lodge.

It felt cold under the beeches, and I was glad to get away from the constant noise of the jackdaws in the high treetops.

Slowly we eased our way into open country, where there was little traffic to be seen but for the odd cart or trap making for the fair in town.

Uncle John had a kind word for everyone he met, telling them about his relatives, refugees from the London Blitz. This embarrassed Mother.

Our arrival to the farm caused more curiosity among the country folk than anything else.

Finally, we reached Dairy Hill. The farm itself had a gravelled avenue just like the road. There were several beeches too.

'You have trees as well,' I said, 'but they're not as big as the ones we saw coming from the town.'

'They are exactly forty years old,' said Uncle John. 'They were placed there to celebrate the coming of a new century. They were planted in 1900. That's how old they are.'

The farmhouse was a big, grey-slated building, gloomy in appearance, very different from the bright-red brick buildings of the city. I was to learn as well that houses were built with local materials. The stone used to build this farmhouse had come from a quarry on Uncle John's neighbour's land about a hundred years previously. The local stone was grey limestone. As a result, the buildings blended into the landscape, and I was seeing it now at its gloomiest in winter. A stone wall sealed off an area to the front of the house. I was also to learn later that this was to provide a little flower garden for the two aunts. Flowers would not survive around a farm if they weren't protected from hungry, grazing animals.

Uncle John drew Bobby to a halt at the back door. The yard was like a courtyard, surrounded on three sides by three large sheds, with an open gateway leading to the fields and the rest of the farm. At this point, all that bothered me was the distinct smell of animal dung, which pervaded the air. I didn't think I could stick this for very long.

Aunt Martha and Aunt Maureen came running out to meet us.

'You all got here,' exclaimed Martha as she embraced Mother.

'You're welcome back,' cried Maureen, who was in fact quite tall. I didn't think she was small at all. Uncle John got everything wrong. In time, I would come to realise that when Uncle John said one thing, he meant another.

I was swept down off the trap by Maureen. She smelled of flour and raw potatoes. They both brought me by the hand into the house, and we were directed into the parlour. A warm turf fire glowed in the hearth, and we were made to sit down to warm ourselves after the cold journey on the trap. The aunts began fussing around us with cups of tea and cakes. Mother was handed something in a glass. It wasn't meant for children, and I was given more tea.

The aunts talked quite a lot, and it was hard to get a word in edgeways. I was hungry, and the cakes tasted quite good. The parlour was cosy, and I looked around at all the old, framed pictures. Some of them were photographs; others were of the Holy Family; and another was of a man with his head turned sideways. I was later to learn that it was Pádraig Pearse, one of the leaders of the Easter Rising in Dublin in 1916.

But the journey had taken its toll on me, and I gently slipped away into sleep. I can't remember much of what happened after that, but when I woke up, Mother was going to bed.

We were in a different room. There was a small metal fireplace, and the fire glowed. There was no electricity in the house. A little oil lamp stood on a three-legged table by the window. The warm yellow glow shone softly around the room, giving just enough light for us to get ready for bed.

I said nothing to Mother and kept my eyes closed, pretending to be asleep. I was in a single bed, and Mother had another one close to me. When she was ready for bed, she turned the light wick down low so that if I happened to waken in this strange room during the night, I wouldn't be afraid.

The wind howled, and the rain beat heavily on the windowpanes. The curtains waved gently from a draught, but the place was warm. I felt safe. There were going to be no bombs tonight. I had found refuge. I thought of Jesus, who'd visited Lazarus in Bethany, and how it was a place of peace for him. I said a little prayer that we would be safe here, but I said a special prayer every night over the next few years to protect Father, wherever he was.

Feeling happy in myself, I settled back to sleep once more, and again I dreamt of Father. If only he were here, my whole world would be perfect again.

*****

But dreams don't last forever, and morning comes. I would like to have slept on but for the fact that a cock crowed out on the farm. It was after seven a.m., just as there was a hint of first light. I could hear Uncle John stir in his bedroom, and then the two aunts. They went quietly with a whisper and carried their lamps in the semidarkness down the stairs to the kitchen. I could hear metal banging and bolts being drawn back.

When the people of the house stirred, so did the animals. Cows lowed in the shed, requesting to be milked and released out into the pastures. Then I could hear a young calf call for its feed, and it was then that I decided to get up and see what was going on in the world.

Mother slept on, and I didn't disturb her. I dressed quietly in the darkness and made my way downstairs. The hall at the bottom of the stairs led straight to the kitchen. I was hardly down when Maureen pulled me along to the table for some breakfast.

'You poor starved girl, you haven't eaten a morsel of food for two days. Now you will have to eat a good feed this morning.'

'I'm not hungry, really,' I protested.

'Nonsense! Enough of that. Young girls like you should have great appetites, and if you want to eat, don't be shy in this house. There's always plenty.'

As she said this, she placed a great big bowl in front of me, then scooped out two or three large wooden spoonfuls of porridge from an iron pot on the open fire and dropped them in the middle of the bowl. When I saw the porridge, it reminded me of Oliver Twist. I couldn't for the life of me see why he ever asked for more. He must have been very hungry. For a start, I didn't like the look of it, and whatever hunger pangs had come over me were now fast fading away.

I didn't want to refuse. We were guests of these nice people, and why should I be rude? Maureen then began to pour lashings of cold milk on the porridge, with a little sugar. I could see she was sparing the sugar, and for good reason; it was rationed during these times. She mixed it all together into a gruel. By the time she had finished, it didn't look too bad at all, so I decided to try some of it at least.

I ate every morsel in the bowl. It was quite pleasant to taste, and I didn't realise how hungry I was until I began eating.

This was to become my regular breakfast every morning, and I grew to like it. Mother was surprised to hear later that I had eaten a bowl of porridge without complaint. It was something she declared *she* could not do at all. But then, Mother had never had a great appetite. Uncle John told me I had quite a lot of Costello blood in me and that was the reason for my healthy cravings.

While I was eating, Martha came from the shed outside with a bucket of turf and stoked the fire. A big black kettle was boiling, as it was sitting on some of the embers from the day's previous fire. They were quickly brought to a greater flame with small sticks and twigs, which Maureen called cipeens. One little job I was given over the few years I stayed there was to gather cipeens from the ditches and hedgerows and have them ready for the morning. Some days they were wet, and they weren't dry the next day, resulting in a slow take with the fire and a long wait for a boiled kettle. So I used to gather buckets of them and store them in the shed beside the turf and timber, and by the time they were used, they had become crispy dry. The aunts declared that they didn't know how they had ever done without me, and this made me feel good.

Next, there was a pot of tea made in a large brown delft teapot, and it was placed in the middle of the table on a matching round delft stand. I knew by the look of it that it was old, and a few chips had broken off it over the years. But this didn't take away from its usefulness; it had served them well over time. Maureen apologised to me for making the tea so weak, as it was rationed these days, and the half pound had to last the week. I didn't mind in the least.

Martha was much quieter and had very little to say. She smiled at me every time she passed the table. Then she began cooking eggs on the pan with slices of bacon. Soon there was a big fry in front of me, and it smelled heavenly. The bacon was quite salty, but it was their own, home cured, and that was all that mattered. There were three slices of fried brown bread on the plate, and I finished it all with great difficulty.

Then Uncle John arrived with a bucket of milk and strained it into a cold crock in the dairy, a large room off the kitchen near the back door. His breakfast was ready too, and he sat across the great big table from me. He took off his wide-brimmed hat and rolled up the sleeves of his shirt.

'She's a great lassie,' said Maureen. 'She has a great appetite, you know.'

'Well, busy people on the farm need plenty to eat, and it can get quite cold here in the winter, not like the big city. So you will want to eat well, girl.'

'I'll try,' I replied.

'Anyway, you have a busy day ahead of you,' said Uncle John. 'I want to introduce you to all the gang.'

'What gang?' I asked.

'All the animals,' he laughed. 'As soon as I'm finished, we'll feed the calf. It's only a week old.'

'Was that him I heard this morning?' I asked.

'It's a heifer,' he replied. 'She's a lady. I'm going to keep her. When she's grown up, she'll make a grand cow. She's a red shorthorn, and if she takes after her mother, she'll be a great milker. We're so lucky. You see, her mother will milk right through the winter, and in the spring when she's gone dry, the other three cows will give milk right through the summer.'

I thought he'd never finish his breakfast, I was so anxious to see the little calf. Before he went out, he poured half the milk from the bucket into another one and brought it with him.

'You see, I had to take the calf from the cow a day after it was born, and now she's able to drink from a bucket on her own. I had to train her to drink by getting her to suck my finger while pushing her head down into the bucket.'

Before I went out with Uncle John, Maureen came running with a new pair of Wellington boots for me.

'You can't go out in the winter weather in soft city shoes; you'll get pneumonia. I bought these for you last week in town, and I hope they're the right size for you.'

'Thank you very much,' I said. I tried them on, and they were just a size too big for me.

'That's good,' she said. 'You will grow into them.'

Martha returned from the parlour with a pair of blue hand-knitted socks.

'Put these on,' she said. 'In that way, your feet won't be flopping around in those old boots.'

My feet felt quite warm and comfortable. After putting on my heavy coat and hat, I was ready to meet the day.

As Uncle John went across the rough stone yard, he took great long steps, and I half ran after him, feeling the weight of my new Wellingtons on my feet. Everywhere was wet from the rain, and I could feel the mud squeeze underfoot. There was a red dawn, and the black clouds were clearing.

As Uncle John opened the door of the shed, I said, 'That's cruel. You should have left her with her mother.'

'There are many things that seem cruel on a farm. Never get too attached to an animal unless you're going to keep it. It makes parting with them easier. You see, a cow forgets very quickly, and she has already forgotten about her calf. She's more worried at night to get inside for a feed of hay. She's fond of her comforts. In a few weeks, the calf will be out in the field with her, and she won't even recognise her. The only mother the little calf has now is me, or Martha or Maureen. It comes to whoever feeds it.'

The little calf came running to us, and I bent down and hugged it. I received a little puck from it, as it tried to feed from me. It was very hungry.

'Give her your finger,' said Uncle John.

'I will not,' I said. 'She will probably bite it off.'

'She won't bite. If she bit her real mother, she wouldn't let her drink her milk and she'd knock her to the ground with a kick.'

42

Reluctantly, I gave the calf my long finger, and she calmed down as she began to suck it. I could barely feel her milk teeth, but she sucked away using her tongue. After a short while, I was nervous no longer. It wasn't too bad at all. She was a beautiful little animal, innocent in her own little way, helpless and depending on Uncle John to keep her alive. When I withdrew my finger from her mouth, Uncle John gave me a handful of sweet-smelling hay to wipe the wet stickiness from the calf's mouth off my hand.

Then he took her head and shoved it down into the bucket. The calf started to shake her tail as she began to drink the milk. She was contented to get the feed she had long waited for.

'You'll have to give her a name,' he said.

I thought for a moment, and I remembered the mournful way she'd called early in the morning. She was like an alarm, sounding us out of bed, just like a siren.

'I'll call her Minnie,' I laughed. 'Moaning Minnie!'

Uncle John took her by the ears and pushed her back as we edged our way out the door.

'Right you are so! We will call her Moaning Minnie, and I don't want to hear any more moans out of her until she's hungry again. She'll lie down now and have a sleep. Come on and help me put the cows out in the field.'

He told me to run up the haggard and open the wooden gate into the field. The haggard was the place where the ricks of hay were kept, and as I ran past them, they seemed huge. One of them had a large slice cut out of it. As the hay was needed, Uncle John cut it away with a hay knife. It kept the rest of the rick intact, preventing it from blowing away in a storm as well as allowing the rainwater to run off without penetrating deep down into the much drier, sweeter hay.

I opened the gate and watched the four cows move slowly from the shed up the haggard to the field. They paid no heed of me but ambled slowly out the gate into the browning aftergrass, content to spend the day grazing to their hearts' content. Each of them was heavily in calf, except for Minnie's mother, and the first would calve after Christmas, early in the new year.

Then Uncle John brought me to see the workhorses. He had three of them.

Paddy was the oldest, and he was semiretired. Uncle John could never part with him but let him spend his days lazing in the fields. He had worked hard in troubled times, and he deserved this restful period at the end of his life. But since the war began, Paddy had been taken out of retirement for heavy work, such as ploughing and sowing. It was difficult to hire or borrow horses for such work.

Whenever Uncle John went out into the fields, Old Paddy would walk slowly to him, looking for a treat. It might be an apple or a slice of bread, but Paddy always demanded his wages.

Today was no exception, and Paddy nuzzled Uncle John as he spoke quietly to him. Then Uncle John hugged the old horse. He patted him on the head and rubbed his mane as he ate the slice of bread. This was when Paddy played his usual trick. Uncle John knew it was going to happen; it was always the same. The horse knocked his master's hat off.

Then Uncle John picked up the hat and pretended to hit Paddy with it. Paddy gave a little snort and trotted slowly away. I knew by the horse's attitude that he always got the last laugh.

'Get along, you lazy, good-for-nothing animal,' Uncle John joked. 'I should have sent you to the glue factory years ago.'

He straightened his hat and put it back on his head as Paddy bowed up and down some distance away.

'I love that auld fella,' said Uncle John. 'We are a long time together. Come on, and we'll meet the young ones.'

The other horses were like twins. They were black, with two streaks of white on their foreheads. The mare was quieter, and she was in foal. The colt was her son, and he looked just like her. He was smaller, but through time, he'd be as big as his mother.

'I call her Magic, she's so black,' said Uncle John, 'and the young fella is Moonlight. I call him Moonlight because he was born one moonlit night before Easter last year. He is destined to take over Paddy's work, give him another while.'

'I thought Paddy was retired.'

'He is, but I'm afraid come spring he'll have to go back in harness to plough the fields. It wouldn't be fair on Magic when she's carrying another foal. She'll be quite close to having it by then.'

'Is Paddy the father?'

'No, he's not. He's a gelding.'

'What's a gelding?'

'It's hard to explain. Sometimes Mother Nature must intervene. They had to do something to Paddy so he could not be a father but could spend his working days doing the heavy farmwork.'

'I still don't understand.'

Uncle John was beginning to tie himself in knots. He finished this conversation by saying, 'I told you that Mother Nature works in strange ways. Now when you are a little older, your mother will have a long chat with you someday about all that. In the meantime, just enjoy all these new things you're seeing and learning and take it all one step at a time.'

Later that night I told Mother all that Uncle John had said, and she pointed out that he was a man with wisdom beyond his years. He wouldn't tell me any lies, and he felt I wasn't ready yet for some of this information. Then Mother revealed that she totally agreed with Uncle John.

I was still concerned for old Paddy, and I asked Uncle John more questions about him.

'Will it be hard on Paddy if he has to go back into the fields again?'

'He worked the fields last year. He was tired after all the work was done, and I decided to let him rest. But then I gave Magic on loan to another farmer, and lo and behold, guess what, she decided she was going to have a foal. So Paddy must give it a go for another season. My neighbour

Bartley will lend me a horse to be his teammate. But with the war and the Emergency here, there is a great demand for horses during this time, to work in the fields. The government has asked us to grow extra crops to help keep enough food on the tables, as there's little food coming into the country. We must do it whether we like it or not.'

'Don't worry, I'll help you,' I said.

'You are a good girl, Margaret. Now come on and I'll introduce you to the great-granddaddy of them all. I keep him a good distance from the house.'

'Is it another horse?'

'Not at all!' he laughed. 'But he eats like one.'

We returned to the haggard again and went to a large shed, set away from all the rest. The door faced away from the house. It was divided in two, like a horse stable. The top half could be opened to allow people to look in at the animals. Despite what Uncle John had said, I was sure it was going to be another horse.

'This is Murphy,' said Uncle John, 'and a right lazy devil he is, except when Moll is with him.'

I peered across the half door, and I knew the smell that met me was not that of horses. It was a pungent, stifling odour, and I was introduced to a great big boar. I'd never realised that a pig could grow so big. He looked up at me through two small beady eyes, smelling the air as he did so. Obviously, he wasn't too happy with what he saw. He grunted and turned his back to me, showing me his tail, which was curled up over his back, revealing a very dirty rear end.

Uncle John opened the door and beckoned me to follow him. Murphy paid not the slightest heed to his intruders but continued poking through the straw in front of him. There was a door leading to another cubicle in the shed. Uncle John pulled back the bolt on the inside of the door, and we looked across at Murphy's wife, Moll. She was a sow. She had another fine, fat pig with her, and I asked Uncle John what his name was.

'He has no name,' he replied. 'As I told you before, if you're not keeping them, don't get too attached. I sold all his brothers and sisters last month. He was the strongest and the fattest of them.'

'Will you sell him too?'

'I'm afraid not. He will do nicely for the Christmas dinner, along with a fine fat goose.'

'You mean you're going to kill him!' I choked.

'It's part of life, love. He's our food, and he will provide us with meat for most of the winter.'

He knew that I didn't want to hear this. It was lovely to see all the animals, but this was the first one I'd found under a sentence of death, and I just wanted to get away from the place.

I was nearly in tears, and Uncle John knew that he shouldn't have told me all this. It was too much, too quick. But then he was glad that I knew. Life was hard, and I'd have to face up to Mother Nature and her strange ways.

'Will you kill him yourself?'

'I never do it. Jimmy Kiernan is doing it for me in early December. You see, girl, I'm a big softie too. I try not to become attached to them, but it's hard. That's why I put Moll in with him. He'll have company for that last two weeks of his life. Then I'll put her back with Murphy again, and she will have more little pigs – or young bonhams, we call them – sometime next year. You'll be fascinated to see them all when they arrive.'

'I don't know,' I said, 'especially when they have all this facing them.'

'Don't fret your little heart over it now. The farm will take getting used to, and I'll guarantee you that within a few short months, I'll have made a fine country woman out of you.'

Chapter 4

Later that day it grew quite cold, and having seen everything on the farm, from the machinery to the animals and finally the fowl, I decided I'd had enough. Just like the pig, there was the old gander and his wife, with twelve offspring. The young birds were destined for the Christmas table at Bethany as well as a few other houses in the area where geese were not kept. By the time I had seen them, it didn't come as much of a shock, as I was used to seeing the goose being prepared for Christmas.

Finally, I'd better not forget Sam, the border collie. Uncle John had him shut into a small shed near the gate, strategically located, as Sam could sound the alarm by barking if anyone came to the gate at night. The callers were usually neighbours dropping in for a chat or a game of cards. It was a local custom, and it happened during the winter months, when the nights were long, dark, and cold. In summer, the long days meant longer hours working out on the land, and there was little time for socializing. Uncle John had forgotten to let Sam out that morning, as he was so busy showing me around. It was only when Sam began to bark in the shed that Uncle John thought about him. He let the dog out, and Sam was just too friendly for words, looking for attention anywhere he could find it.

At four thirty, the lamps were lit. Maureen went around the house with a taper from the fire and lit each one on the wall, teasing the wick just to the right flame. Then when the glass globe went back on the lamp, the flame did not flicker but remained steady, throwing the low light to the far corners of the kitchen.

When tea was over, Martha called everyone to say the rosary. Mother had told me about her father saying the rosary when she was young. It was an important prayer time in the day, when everyone knelt and prayed the five decades as well as the litany. Each person took a chair to kneel at for the duration of the prayers. Mother asked me to kneel, but she remained seated when the prayers began. Martha led the prayers, and each person recited a decade. Mother asked me to recite the last decade, but I had no beads for counting each Hail Mary, so I counted them on my fingers. This was done every night after tea, and if there were any visitors, they joined in as well.

When the prayers finished, I sat up on the chair, but everyone remained on their knees, praying silently. Mother told me that they were saying their night prayers and that if I wished, I could do mine at this time rather than before getting into bed. At home in London, Mother did not say the rosary, as Father was Church of England, though she and I went to mass on Sunday while Father stayed at home. He went to church occasionally, but Nana had stopped going some time before, since she was not able to walk very far. Once a month, Father had brought her to church in a taxi, and any Sunday Mother and I went to mass, Nana told us to pray for her while we were there.

When the rosary was finished, Martha made Mother sit in the armchair by the fire to rest. She then placed a big glass lamp in the centre of the table.

'Will you help us to get the Christmas pudding ready?' asked Maureen.

'But Christmas is not for weeks yet,' I said.

'I know, love, but you must give the pudding time to mature, and that's why we're doing it now. It's always the start of getting things ready for Christmas. Then there will be the cake baking, the salting of the pig, the cleaning of the house, the pictures, the furniture, the shopping, the holly. You could go on forever naming the things that need to be done, so we must start somewhere.'

Soon the whole process began. I was given the job of cutting up the suet into very thin pieces. I didn't like the job, but I wanted to help in any case. Martha began shredding white bread into crumbs. She was none too pleased that the flour used in the bread was not as good as what they'd used before the war.

'We're very lucky to get any fruit at all this year,' she said.

'If the war continues,' said Mother, 'you might not get any next year.'

'You might!' said Maureen. 'If you are prepared to pay dear for it. There are right gombeen men going around selling stuff like this for three prices. I don't know where they get it, but if people are desperate enough to get what they want, they'd sell their mothers to pay for it.'

'I hope you don't sell *my* mother,' I retorted.

They all began to laugh at what I had just said, then Martha explained what she meant. 'Not at all, love; it is only a figure of speech. People would part with something very precious to get some of the goods that are scarce these days.'

When all the ingredients were placed in the large crock, there was a beautiful aroma of spices in the air. Maureen filled a jug of porter from the half barrel in the dairy, to bind and further flavour the mixture. From this large jug, she filled a pint glass with the liquid and left it on the dresser.

When Uncle John came in from the yard, he decided it was time to sit down and enjoy his glass of porter.

I didn't know what the stuff was, and I asked if I could have some.

'Certainly not!' said Mother. 'It does not befit a young lady to drink porter, and don't ever let me hear tell of you doing so.'

Uncle John took the glass from the dresser and sat down by the fire opposite Mother, to savour and enjoy one of the creature comforts he had in life.

Then we were all asked to stir the mixture. In doing so, it was a tradition to make a wish. I closed my eyes and contemplated what I wanted my wish to be. It was obvious what I wanted. I wished that the war would end, and that Father would return to us and take us back to London. I knew that Mother's wish was the same, but I didn't know what the other three wished for. I had a guess that they wished we could stay for a very long time.

Then Martha covered the mixture with a white muslin cloth and left it to mature overnight in the scullery. I helped them tidy the table. As they wiped it clean with a damp cloth, they told me to leave the jug by the porter barrel under the table in the dairy. As I carried it out, I discovered that there was still some porter left in it. It was at least a quarter full.

Then, of course, curiosity got the better of me. If Mother *had* told me to taste it, I might not have been interested at all, but temptation was something I could not resist.

I put the jug to my head and drank the contents down. There was still some left, as I was unable to finish it all. It had a bitter, pungent taste. I felt it was nothing to write home about. I couldn't understand why Mother was making such a fuss about it. If a lady wanted to drink it, I didn't see why not. I felt it would not do me any harm. But that was the naivety of childhood. I didn't know that alcohol could, in fact, ruin a person's life.

I returned to the kitchen and sat on the corner stool next to the fire. I wasn't sure whether I felt guilty or not. Then I hiccupped.

'Eating too many raisins,' said Mother. 'I hope they don't make you sick.'

'I'm sorry!' I said. I hadn't the words out of my mouth when the kitchen and the lamplight began to swim around me. Uncle John saw me in time as I began to fall over. He grabbed me and held me still.

'I think it's time for bed now, lassie!'

'The poor little pet is all in,' said Maureen. 'She's had a very long, busy day.'

'I'll carry you up the stairs and leave you at your bed,' said Uncle John.

I was glad he did, as I was not able to put a leg under me. Mother told me she'd be up in a few minutes to check on me, after she finished her cup of tea.

The light was already lit in the room, and Uncle John placed me on the bed. It was then he started laughing.

'You are a right young lady.' He giggled as he said it. 'If your mother finds out that you drank from the jug of porter, she'd tear her hair out.'

'How do you know?' I stammered.

'I am a man who has seen a great lot of this world, and I know the symptoms when someone is drunk. Wasn't I often that way myself?'

'Please don't tell Mother!' I pleaded.

'I'll say nothing,' he said, 'but remember, don't do it again. If she gets the smell of porter off you, she'll think it's me. That's why I carried you up the stairs.'

'Thank you, Uncle John,' I said, and without thinking, I threw my arms around his neck and gave him a big hug. He gave another little giggle as I did so, and I knew he was wishing I were the daughter he never had.

'Let this be *our* secret,' he said, and he winked at me as Mother entered the room to see if I was in bed.

*****

Next morning, Mother asked Uncle John to drive her to the village on some business. She didn't tell me what it was, and I didn't ask. I'd always been told that children didn't ask questions unless it was something to do with learning, or literature, or seeking information about the world. Whatever business grown-ups had remained their secret, unless they were prepared to tell you themselves. Uncle John looked at me as she spoke softly to him, and Maureen helped her on with her coat.

There was a chill in the air as Bobby trotted down the short avenue to the gate. Uncle John had to get down off the trap to open it. It was a double iron gate, and it needed repair, something he'd meant to do for a long time, but he kept putting it on the long finger, as there were more important things to be done on the farm. He even remarked on occasion that he'd get the blacksmith to make a brand-new gate whenever he could afford it. He declared that someday it would just collapse from old age.

When they had gone out of sight, I went back inside to see what the two aunts were doing. Maureen was washing clothes in a great tin bath by the back door, so that whatever steam there was would be wafted outside. The back door remained open all the time, even on this cold day in November. It faced east, and was sheltered from the prevailing westerlies, which raged across the Atlantic for most of the year. Instead, there was a cool, gentle breeze moving inwards, ensuring that the fire on the hearth roared up the chimney, keeping a great pot of water on the boil most of the time while the washing was going on.

There wasn't anything interesting about washing clothes, so I decided to watch Martha bake bread. She knew I was curious, and she threw a small piece of dough on a plate and told me to make a little cake of my own.

'I'll put it on the griddle later,' she said, 'and you can have it in the evening.'

I wasn't long kneading it out on some flour, to prevent it from sticking to the plate, and when it was done, I said, 'Now I'm ready!'

'Not quite yet,' said Martha. 'Can't you see you have to put a cross on it?'

'Why must I do that?' I asked.

'Bread is holy,' she answered. 'Our good Lord broke bread for us, and then died on a cross. Therefore, you must bless the bread with a cross.'

This I did, and left it ready for baking. I wandered around the kitchen, looking at this and that, asking questions about their uses – the churn, the butter pats, the crocks, saucepans of various shapes and sizes, and the colander, to name but a few.

I'd sat down again, wondering what to do next, when Maureen, who was still busy washing clothes by the kitchen door, said, 'Why don't you take yourself off down the boreen to the lake field? You never saw the lake yet.'

'I didn't know that the land went all the way to the lake,' I said.

'It doesn't,' she replied. 'Hegarty's land begins at the end of the boreen, and his fields take you right to the lake shore. John has a boathouse there. He shares it with Bartley. His father and himself built it after the Great War, to give themselves a bit of peace and quiet of a summer evening or a Sunday afternoon. You will see their boats if you go down there. Now, keep to the right towards the lake. Stay away from Bartley Hegarty's quarry; it's a dangerous place.'

'Be very careful at the lake too,' said Martha, 'and don't fall in. It can be a treacherous spot, that lake. Ghosts have settled in the water there, and several people have drowned over the years. Their bodies were never seen again.'

'Not alone that, they say that if you drown and the pike get you, they tear you apart,' said Maureen. 'And your remains settle in the mud at the bottom, giving you a watery grave.'

'I won't go close to the edge,' I said. 'I'll be careful.'

'Why not bring Sam with you?' said Martha. 'A dog is always a great help. He'll stay with you, and if he comes home alone, it gives a message that there could be something wrong. Sam is only dying to go for a walk with people.'

'What if he doesn't want to go with me?' I asked.

'He'll go with you, all right,' said Martha. 'He'd go with the pooca.'

'What's that?"

'That's another story for one of those long nights during winter, when there's nothing to do but sit by a warm fire,' said Maureen.

'Remember, you must be back within two hours. It shouldn't take you long to get there,' said Martha.

When I went outside, I called Sam. He came running to me from up the back of the farm somewhere, silently, without barking and wagging his tail, as if he were the answer to every girl's dream.

I told him to follow me, and he knew what I wanted him to do. We crossed the field that ran between the avenue and the boreen. In fact, it was the eastern boundary to the farm. It was easy to cross the fence at this time of year, as there was no leaf cover on the ditch, and Sam knew where to go.

The boreen was dark and overhung with trees. I was to learn later that the Land Commission had constructed it at the early part of the century, after purchasing a section of the Johnson estate, to allow local farmers access to the lands allocated to them. Uncle John's father had added ten acres to his holding at that time and paid back for it over many years.

The boreen led most of the way to the lake shore. Hegarty's field began at the end of the boreen. Here there was a spring well and some barrels, providing a local supply of water for cattle. It meant an extra trip from your field each day with your animals if they needed to drink. Uncle John didn't use this well, as he had water already on his land, but Bartley Hegarty made use of it. There was no access for cattle to the lake, as the shore itself was common land right round its boundary. Bartley had the quarry as well, which was just a short field from his house. It was fenced off on three sides, allowing access for drinking at the front, where the water was shallow and safe.

The boreen was gloomy and damp, the long-covered gravel underfoot smeared with a few inches of mud churned up over the years by endless cattle trips to the water barrels.

I felt quite nervous on my own, in a very strange place with no people around. It was lonely and frightening, but I knew I would need to get used to it as time went on. I expected it would take me many weeks to settle into the ways of country life and its loneliness. I wanted to turn back a few times, but I was driven on by determination and the never-changing friendship of Sam, who ran about twenty yards ahead of me, sniffing the dead undergrowth in the ditch. Every so often, he'd turn back to see if I was following. I felt that he knew I was in unfamiliar territory and he was making sure I was safe. Looking back now on that day, I know I might not have made the journey to the lake if it were not for Sam.

I continued onwards till I came to the end of the boreen and the spring well. I climbed the gate into the field, and there it was before me, fresh and blowing right up to the shore.

I ran through the dead grass, which still had a hint of frost at midday, and the mud cleared from my boots as I did so. As I approached the lake, the breeze grew greater, and my hair blew in all directions. I pulled my woollen cap tighter down over my ears and yelped with excitement.

The field fringed a large wooded area along the shore, which came to a V at the corner of the field, extending into an area of fifty or sixty acres. I knew it was somewhere I could explore later, but I wasn't going to go beyond the territory mapped out for me by the two aunts today.

I crossed the fence and ran to the shore, listening to the lapping of the waves and the blowing of the wind, clearing my head and ears of the vulgar, frightening sounds of war. This was peace, and it made me squeal with excitement. I rummaged through the shingle and threw stones into the water.

Here on the shore, it was like a little beach. The water was shallow and lapped against the shingle that divided the water from the land. There was no way I could fall headlong into a deep, dangerous abyss, as documented by my two great-aunts. I realised then that they were scaring me enough to ensure that I didn't do something stupid that would lure me into deep waters. I was not going to tempt fate in any way, or even allow water to flow in over the top of my Wellingtons.

Sam knew I was playing some sort of game and ran into the cold waves to retrieve the stone I had thrown. Then he dipped his nose down and came running back to me, shaking himself as he approached, leaving the stone at my feet. When I threw it again, away he went. Then I thought to myself that he might get ill if I allowed him into the water at this time of the year, so I called a halt there and then.

It was then that I saw the boathouse. It was a few hundred yards up the shore and hidden from view by the beginnings of the wood. It was a low shed, really, covered with rusting galvanise and built of mass concrete. Its front door opened out in an archway to the lake, and I was later to discover that it looked like a large mouth drinking from the water. It was possible to row your boat into the house and berth it against a small cement dock. For most of the time during the summer, Uncle John left his chained to the dock and floating in the shelter of the shed. In winter he dragged it farther in on the ledge and left it lying upside down, to prevent any damage from high winds.

There was a small back door to the shed, which he kept locked always, as it was impossible to get in from the lake side unless you were a good swimmer. There was a small porthole on the outside door, and I could see in. I could see two upturned boats resting for the winter. The lake breeze blew back at me through the little hole, telling me I was not welcome here. That didn't disturb me one bit, as I was to make many a trip to the shore over the next few years.

Having seen all I was going to see, I turned tail for home, calling Sam to lead the way, and I felt as I crossed over that field that I had been here many times before. I could feel that the place was growing on me.

As I was crossing the gate to the boreen, Sam gave a little yelp and ran towards the well. I jumped down and turned to look behind me. There was a man standing by the water barrels with a bucket in his hand, obviously filling them for the animals to drink that evening. He had a large cap down over his forehead and wore a once-brown overcoat, now weathered and torn from constant use on the farm. Hay seedlings hung like confetti over his shoulders, and the legs of his trousers were stuffed into his leather boots. A large piece of thick twine was wrapped two or three times around his coat to keep it buttoned, as there were no buttons left on the front of the coat at all. He had a black beard, a few days old. His last shave had been on Saturday night in preparation for Sunday mass. This was normal practise in the country, whereas Father shaved every morning at the mirror in the kitchen, ensuring that he was spick-and-span before going to school.

The stranger looked older than he really was. He was in his mid to late thirties. If he were cleaned up and shaved, he'd be quite a handsome man.

I stood fixed to the spot for a few moments, wondering whether I should run or not. When Sam did not kick up a fuss but sat wagging his tail staring up into the man's face as he patted the top of his head and rubbed his ears, I knew he must be all right, and I waited for him to speak.

'Good girl!' the man said, then spat on the ground. 'You must be the young one from London?'

'My name is Margaret Kerr.'

'Don't worry, I know who you are, all right, and I want to welcome you to these parts. My name is Bartley Hegarty.'

He stepped forward and grabbed my hand, shaking it, and then put his hand back in his pocket again.

'Is it not strange for a little girl like you to come from the big city to poor people like us?'

'They are not poor people,' I said. 'Everyone has a house and food on the table.'

'Well, anyway, we are rough-and-ready. And you will have to take us as you meet us. How long are you staying with us?'

'I don't know. We have no home in London. It was bombed, so we will stay if Uncle John lets us, or maybe until the war is over.'

'What'll happen if Hitler comes here?' he asked. 'Where would you go then?'

'I don't know,' I replied. 'I only hope he doesn't.'

'Ah, you see, girl; Hitler will lave us alone. We didn't go out to fight him at all, and de Valera said he would not take hand, act, or part in it. So you're quite safe here.'

'I hope so.'

'Indeed, you are quite safe, with auld Lazarus down there. He'll look after you, all right.'

'Does everyone around here call him Lazarus?'

'Indeed they do. When he got that flu, they thought he was going to die. But he was a strong man. Many is the one who got it and didn't survive. But John Costello did. Sure, he went to the jaws of death, and it's only for the love and care of his two sisters that he lived. They used to sit up at night with him, and during those weeks when he was recovering, they'd carry him out on fine days and put him sitting on a chair. It was during the late spring, and he was kept in that room close to the kitchen. They thought he'd never get his strength back again, but survive he did, and to this day, he has been a very fit and well man. The two girls had settled in there on the farm after a few adventures of their own, and they decided that they'd live together, if the good Lord allowed them, and they'd never marry. They are still there, getting older and wiser, but as good-natured and kind neighbours you wouldn't find between here and Timbuktu."

'Was it after that he built the boathouse?'

'It was! My father and him built it in the summer of 1920, and it has stood the test of time since. John and I go out on the water every summer to land the pike.'

'I could stay talking to you all day,' I said, 'but the two aunts will be worrying if I'm not back in two hours in time for dinner.'

'Sure, I will not delay you, girl. It was nice to meet you. I hope you will call with John to see me sometime.'

'I will. Goodbye.'

Then I ran.

*****

When I got home, Martha had three great brown cakes on the dresser, wrapped in tea towels to cool, and a small one no bigger than a large bun on a plate for me. I was ravenous, but she wouldn't let me eat it then, as it would spoil my dinner. She had a large pot of stew simmering on a crane over the fire, and the aroma of the bread and the stew were making my hunger pangs worse.

She gave me a large cake of carbolic soap and sent me out to the pump to wash my hands for dinner. In London, Mother would pour a kettle of hot water into the sink so I could wash. If I needed a bath, she'd light the water geyser upstairs, which was fed from the gas mains. I had not a clue yet as to how I was going to have a bath here.

I was to find out on Saturday night, when the great tin bath Maureen was using to wash the clothes was brought up to our bedroom and filled with basins of hot and cold water from the kitchen. I realised then that if I were lucky, I'd get a bath once a week.

I didn't complain about having to wash outside at the pump, as I knew things were done differently here and their world had not yet caught up with the lifestyle we enjoyed over in London. It would be selfish of me to do so, as they had given us shelter and refuge out of the goodness of their hearts. Mother had warned me to say nothing if things went wrong or did not go the way we expected them to, as we could easily outstay our welcome and find that we had nowhere else to go.

Just as I was finishing, Sam gave a little yelp, and I could see Uncle John and Mother returning in the trap from the village. She was very cold, and Martha made her sit by the fire and gave her a hot cup of soup, straight from the stew pot.

'I don't know how I will ever repay your kindness,' said Mother. 'You are so good.' Then she began crying again, and both aunts ran to console her. She was only now letting go of the grief she'd held back from the events in London, and when she now had time to think about it all, it began flowing from her like a deluge. I know now that this was good for her, as she was no longer bottling things up inside. In my childish world, I didn't understand, as I was on another journey, coming to terms with the culture shock the move from London had brought to me. I had known nothing else in my few short years, but this was the lifestyle that Mother had left behind her, and coming back again wasn't such a big deal to her. In fact, the security and comfort it brought her began to help her cope with all she had suffered.

While all this drama with Mother was playing out, Uncle John said little, but he winked at me and said, 'I'm sure you'd like a good feed, girl; you're starving with the hunger.'

'I *am* starving,' I said. 'I went way down the boreen to the lake, and I'm not long back.'

Through her tears, Mother chastised me for being so forward, and when she heard I'd been away on an adventure of my own, she continued, 'What's that I hear about you wandering down the fields?'

'She went at our suggestion,' said Martha. 'Sure hasn't she to get used to living around here? And what better way than to go for a walk to the lake.'

'Sam came with me, and we met a man called Bartley. He was nice, but he could do with a wash.'

'Margaret!' Mother shouted at me. 'I'm really getting cross with you.'

'Will you stop that, Kitty?' said Maureen. 'Doesn't the truth come from the mouths of babes?'

'Yes!' said Martha. 'Children and fools tell the truth.'

'What Bartley needs,' said Uncle John, 'is a good woman to take over his life and to care for him as well.'

'Just the way Aunt Maureen and Martha care for you, Uncle John.'

'Out of the mouths of babes,' said Maureen, and they all broke out in peals of laughter. It cheered Mother up, as she laughed through her tears, and she began eating the soup she was given.

'Now will you all stop fooling around?' said Martha. 'We want to get on with the dinner.'

Finally, everyone settled down to eat, and Mother joined them at the table. I knew that something else bothered her as well. I was to learn later that the local GP, Dr Daly, whom she had just visited, had told her to leave the plaster on her arm for another fortnight. She still felt she was a great burden on everyone.

When Maureen made a pot of tea after dinner, Mother made an announcement that concerned me.

'By the way, Margaret, I went to the convent in the village this morning, and I met the Reverend Mother. I have enrolled you in the primary school beginning next week, the first week of December.'

'Mother,' I protested. 'I don't want to go there.'

'Now, I don't want to hear another word from you. What is to become of you if you don't get a proper education? You won't get an education in this godforsaken place—'

She stopped midsentence, knowing she had said the wrong thing. Uncle John's moustache was moving back and forth again. I knew he was enjoying it all.

'I'm so sorry,' continued Mother. 'I didn't mean it that way. I meant that there was no place here for her to learn unless she went to school in the village.'

'Don't worry, girl,' said Maureen. 'God forsook this place ages ago.'

Then they all laughed again, and when Mother saw how lightly they were all taking it, she continued, 'How can you learn anything on a farm? You need school, and discipline. Another few weeks roaming around the fields and you'd end up a useless article.'

'But Uncle John can teach me. He knows everything.'

'Yeah! A right bit of a know-all,' he laughed.

'Please be serious, Uncle John. She is going, and that is that. You will be starting in Sister Bernadette's class.'

'A nun. I will be going to a nun!'

'That's right, and I hope she puts plenty of manners on you.'

'There's nothing wrong with nuns,' laughed Martha. 'They are human beings just like us. They are great people, giving their lives to serving God.'

'Look,' said Maureen. 'This tea will be cold if we don't drink it, and you can eat your little cake. I'll put plenty of gooseberry jam on it.'

'No thank you,' I said. 'I'm not hungry anymore.'

Then a thought struck me.

'Mam, how am I to get there? Will I have to walk the four miles into the village?'

'It might do you good,' she retorted. Mother was very much under the weather this evening. She'd normally never speak to me like that. My young mind knew deep down that she was grieving and that tomorrow she would have cheered up again. She needed to get to bed early and rest.

Then Uncle John spoke up with a proper answer to my question. 'That brings me to something else,' he said. 'Can you ride a bicycle?'

'No, I can't,' I answered.

'You will have to learn fast, then, and I will have to teach you. I went and bought you a second-hand one in the village.'

My eyes lit up with excitement, and I jumped from my chair. I threw my arms around his neck and began smothering him with hugs.

'First of all, you will have to finish your tea and cake,' said Martha.

'And what about your manners?' asked Mother.

'Oh yes!' I exclaimed.

I began hugging him and kissing him again, showering blessings and thanks and praises on the best granduncle I'd ever known. I knew he was enjoying my excitement more than anything else.

'You'll want to get on and finish that tea and cake,' he said. 'That bike is out there covered up on the trap, and we might get a little bit of training on it before darkness begins to fall.'

When I had finished, he brought me to the trap to show me the bike. And so began my first lessons, the rudiments of learning how to cycle.

Chapter 5

The following Monday morning, I set out reluctantly for the village to attend the convent school. I was nervous riding the bicycle on my own for the first time. Uncle John had spent three days with me, teaching me how to ride. He'd held the bike the first few times while I stood on the pedals, and my best attempts were made going down the small hill to the road. I fell many times, but after the first day, I could ride the bike standing on the pedals. He left me practising all the next day, and whenever mealtime came around, it was a welcome reprieve.

On the third day, he adjusted the saddle and left it low enough for my short legs to reach the pedals and make a complete revolution on the freewheel. I found this frightening at first, as it compelled me to use the brakes more rather than tearing my shoe along the gravel avenue. He warned me not to pull the front brake suddenly, or I'd end up going head over heels on the road.

By the evening of the third day, I wasn't afraid anymore, and when I put the bike away, I fell into bed, so tired that I heard nothing until about eleven o'clock the next day, which was Saturday.

On Sunday, we went to early mass in the village on the trap. It was a heavy load for Bobby carrying all five of us, but Uncle John knew how to manage him. The two aunts were dressed all in black, their coats reaching down to their ankles, and their long black stockings ensured that there was no other colour to be seen. They each had a black hat, which they carried with them, and they wore their heavy shawls while travelling. When they got to the church, they put their hats on for mass, securing them on their heads with hatpins that threaded through their hair and prevented the hats from being blown away with the wind.

Mother made sure my head was covered as well, as it wasn't respectful for a lady to appear in the church without a hat. Men had to do the opposite and take their hats off. Uncle John wore a bright, clean, black, wide-brimmed hat, just like his everyday one, and he looked a different man when he was cleaned and shaved. I wanted to go with him, but Mother said he was going into the men's side and I had to go with her and the aunts into the women's side.

Before going into mass, Uncle John showed me where the convent was, and the school was next door, close to the road. He introduced me to Billy Bryce, who lived opposite the church. Billy was the man who rang the church bell to call people to mass, as well as at twelve noon and six p.m. to remind everyone to pray the Angelus. Uncle John told me to leave my bike at Billy's place when I went to school rather than leaving it on the school grounds, and said he'd take care of it for me during the day.

The convent was a big grey building about seventy years old. A large white statue of St Joseph stood in an alcove in the centre of the building, at the top of the third story. The school nearby had huge windows and had been built at the end of the nineteenth century. The windows were high up, so it was impossible for the pupils to be distracted by looking out at people passing. Their purpose was to flood the rooms with as much light as possible so as to encourage the learning process. This was what was facing me, and I didn't like the thoughts of it one bit.

I set off that morning in December just as the sky was reddening for dawn, thus giving myself plenty of time to get there. The two aunts had packed a lunch of brown bread and jam for me, as well as a bottle of fresh milk from the cow. The bottle felt slightly warm as I put it into my bag. I knew that by the time I got to drink its contents, it would be quite cold. I had no books with me, but I knew that the nuns would soon make sure I was well kitted out for the class. I carried a pen, a pencil, and a writing copy as well as a jotter, just in case I had nothing to write on the first day.

It was a cold morning, with white frost everywhere, and my breath condensed into steam in the cold air, as if I were a fiery dragon breathing smoke. There were icy patches on the road, and Uncle John came with me as far as the battered old gates at the road. Mother kissed me goodbye and waved at me from the kitchen door, and before I knew it, I was out in a lonely, frosty world on my own.

I could see the lake to my right, but it was lost in a half mist rising out of the water as some lonely water birds called far away through the haze. The dead leaves crunched like burnt toast under the tyres of the bike. I was afraid they would puncture. I needed to take care where I rode it, as Uncle John had said that tyres and tubes for bikes were a scarce commodity these days. I was allowed ride the bike only to school and at home, or for any emergency that might occur.

I thought that the journey would take all day, but it wasn't long before I saw the spires of the two churches rise above the frost and the mist, and I knew I was coming to my journey's end.

The village was alive with children. The boys were heading to their school at one end of the village, and the girls filtered past the church onto the convent school grounds. By now the light was much stronger, and I could see it was going to be a fine, though cool, winter day.

Billy Bryce was standing waiting, looking across the half door, and I could see that he had a warm fire glowing on the hearth.

'Lave it in the shed over there, girl,' he said, 'and I'll mind it for you.'

'Thank you very much,' I answered, taking my bag with me. 'I'll see you later this evening.'

'Think nothing of it, love.'

I was noticed the moment I entered the village, and I knew they would all know who I was. I was the refugee from the war. I had seen and heard the bombs fall, and I had lost my home in the Blitz. I knew what was going through their heads.

They avoided me and didn't speak. When I entered the playground, most of them were playing rhyme or skipping games, and I stood away some distance from them with my back to a stone wall. I watched their games and made not the slightest remark in response to all their staring. There were prying eyes everywhere.

I knew it wasn't their fault. It was seldom they had a stranger among them, and they didn't know how to deal with it. I was to be feared, at least for the moment, or until such time as they found the courage to make friends.

I was enjoying the game one of the groups of smaller girls was playing. They formed a ring with one girl in the centre, on her hunkers, with her head buried in her hands and her eyes closed. They joined hands just like in 'Ring a Ring a' Rosie' and moved clockwise in a circle, chanting:

Little Sally Saucer

Sitting in the water

Rise up, Sally

Turn to the east

Turn to the west

Turn to the little one

You love best

As they recited this, the child rose slowly, keeping her eyes closed, and began reaching out to grab hold of one of the children in the circle. When she succeeded, the child who was caught became Little Sally Saucer, and the game began again. I smiled for a moment, and it was a while before I noticed another girl, much the same age as me, standing near me.

For all the world, she was not unlike Felicity, whom I had left behind in London, so I thought she might be friendly enough. Then she spoke.

'Can you speak English?'

'Of course I can,' I said in my best London accent.

She turned to the other girls and smiled, then looked back to me. 'I thought you were a foreigner!'

'What do you mean by that?'

'Well, like the French or Spanish. We wouldn't understand your language.'

'I can understand you, all right,' I said, 'but Mother can speak a little French, you know. She teaches me some words now and then.'

'Well, what words do you know?'

'*Bonjour, mademoiselle.*'

'What does that mean?'

'*Hello, young lady.* And if you were married, you would say, *Bonjour, madame.*'

'Janey Mac! I did not know that. Would you teach me some French words?'

'I will, but I'll need help with the Irish language. I was told I'd have to learn that.'

'Don't worry about that at all. Sister Bernadette is very good at the Irish; she'll do a good job on you.'

'By the way, my name is Margaret Kerr.'

'I'm Sheila Bryce.'

'Are you related to the man at the church?'

'He's my uncle. I live in a house on the road as you go to the town. Billy lives in the village. He rings the bell for the priest.'

Just then a nun appeared at the door, ringing a different bell, and the girls scattered to various lines, according to whatever class they were in.

'What class are you going to?' asked Sheila.

'It's fourth class,' I answered.

'Well, then, stay with me, and I will take you to Sister Bernadette's class.'

When our turn came, we marched down a long corridor, which smelled of damp. There was grey wainscoting on the ground up to just above my height, and the walls were painted with a sickly cream paint. There was nothing pleasant about it. A large statue of the Blessed Virgin stood on a tall pedestal at the end of the corridor, and a few withering flowers had been placed at her feet. I think they may have been chrysanthemums. I came to learn afterwards that the convent gardener grew some in the big greenhouse and they were in bloom for Christmas every year, at a time when there were few or no flowers to be got.

Before entering the classroom, we hung our coats on a row of hangers outside the door. A warm fire glowed in the grate. The room was a dark place but for the high windows. The wainscoting was brown to match the desks, and a few sticks of furniture made up the classroom. The higher part of the wall was painted a creamy white, not much different from the colour in the corridor. The shelves contained a few dozen books, which were tired looking from overuse and would more than likely soon need replacing. There was a smaller statue of the Blessed Virgin in the window. She stood on the world with a serpent crushed beneath her feet. There were no flowers here, but some of the children had made some from bits of coloured paper and feathers, tying them together with thin, rusty wire and standing them in a bowl. A great big map of Ireland adorned the wall, depicting the counties and provinces, which were written in Irish. There was no sign of England next to it.

Sheila asked me to sit beside her, as she sat on her own at the back of the room. Every other child had a companion to sit with, but Sheila hadn't.

There was total silence when we sat down, and each child took out a table book. Then Sister Bernadette entered and closed the door quickly behind her. With that, the whole class stood up. She seemed to glide across the floor to her desk, as I couldn't see her feet move in the long habit she wore. All that was visible was her young white face, and she smiled at us before beginning.

She spoke a greeting in Irish to the class, and they all responded. She began with a litany of prayers, some of which I had never heard before, and after what seemed like an age, she spoke again in Irish, and everyone sat down.

She wrote the day and date on the blackboard and delightedly informed us of the number of days there were till Christmas. Then, turning around again, she saw me sitting at the back of the class.

'Would the new girl please stand up?'

I did as I was told.

'What is your name, child?'

'Margaret Kerr, Sister.'

'I believe you are from London.'

'Yes, Sister.'

'You see, girls, Margaret is a refugee, and a refugee is a person who must flee from the terrors of war. They are in danger of being killed by some stupid, silly leader who murders many people because he is greedy and wants power. Soon we will be talking about the birth of Jesus and how he was a refugee. He, too, had to flee into Egypt for fear he might be killed at the hands of King Herod. I'm sure Margaret will be able to tell us all that has happened to her.'

'Yes, Sister. I was very frightened.'

'You wouldn't mind coming up to my desk and telling your story? You see, children, there is a lot to be learned from other people's experiences, and if you listen, you might learn something new. Come up here, child, and stand beside me.'

I did as she asked and stood beside her. I could feel the warm glow of the fire on the backs of my legs. She sat down on a chair and handed the floor over to me.

I gazed around the room, and I could see, for the first time, the sea of faces of girls who were my age. Some were very neat and trim, and I knew they came from homes where there was plenty of food and clothes were cleaned regularly. Others looked thin, their hair in need of a wash and their clothes a bit threadbare, patched in places, more than likely hand-me-downs from older sisters. I didn't know how these other classmates viewed the world or what their level of understanding was, as some of them would never have moved far outside the village in their lives.

I began by talking about my life, my parents, my nana, and Father going off to war. I told them about the bombings, the moaning minnies, and how Nana had been killed. Then I told them about losing our house in the Blitz and how we had to come to live at Dairy Hill Farm. I didn't use the pet name Bethany, as everyone called it Dairy Hill.

It took a good half hour to tell my story, and in the middle of it all, Reverend Mother entered, and Sister Bernadette signalled to her to sit and listen to my tale. The girls were listening carefully, and I could see Sheila smiling through it all.

When I was finished, Reverend Mother came forward and took my hand to welcome me. Then, turning to the children, she said, 'Now, girls, it makes us all appreciate the home we come from, our parents, and the peace we still have in our land. Sister Bernadette, will you lead them off in a verse of "Faith of Our Fathers"?'

They all stood up and began to sing:

Faith of our fathers, living still
In spite of dungeon, fire, and sword
Oh, how our hearts beat high with joy
Whene'er we hear that glorious Word!
Faith of our fathers, holy faith!
We will be true to thee till death
We will be true to thee till death

When they had finished, Reverend Mother left, and Sister Bernadette spoke to me quietly before I returned to my desk.

'Are you happy to sit beside that little girl at the back of the class?'

'Yes, Sister, I don't mind. Why, what's the problem?'

I looked down at Sheila, and I could tell she knew that Sister Bernadette was talking about her. She hung her head low.

'That little girl is quite ill at times; just be aware of that.'

'I don't mind, Sister!'

'That's quite all right,' she said, and told me to sit down.

When I reached my desk, Sheila was still hanging her head, and I could see tears falling on the brown desk in front of her.

'It's all right,' I whispered, but she turned her head away and gazed into her table book, pretending to be learning her tables.

For the rest of the day, Sheila kept away from me, as the other girls wanted to know what the bombs looked like. Had I been injured? Had I seen my nana being killed? Between answering their questions and trying to stave off their too-familiar friendships, I couldn't get near Sheila, and she stayed away.

When we were going home that evening, Sister Bernadette called me to one side and said, 'Listen, child, I asked you that question this morning about Sheila Bryce not because I wanted to be cruel to her, but one must be practical. You see, Sheila has tuberculosis. The other children don't want to sit beside her for fear they might contract the disease too. I just wanted to tell you in case you would have some dread of getting it yourself.'

'Thank you very much, Sister, but I'm not afraid of sitting beside her. I had a friend in my class in London who was often ill like that, and I wasn't afraid to sit beside her.'

'Well, talk it over with your mother, and if she says it's all right, then I'll leave you sitting with her. In fact, she could do with your company.'

By the time I left the convent school, all the other children were gone. I collected my bike at Billy Bryce's shed and headed for home.

Just outside the village, I caught up with Sheila. When she saw me coming, she kept walking faster.

'Sheila, I want to talk to you,' I said.

'Go away, please. You don't want to be my friend, just like the rest of them.'

'I do! I still want to sit with you.' She kept walking away, and I climbed down off the bike to keep pace with her.

'Sheila, I know you have TB,' I shouted. She turned around and dropped her bag.

'Who told you?' she exclaimed through more tears.

'Sister Bernadette,' I answered softly. 'She wasn't being mean telling me. Because you're ill, she was afraid I might get ill too. The other children aren't being mean to you either. They're afraid. I'm not afraid. I will still be sitting with you tomorrow. Sister Bernadette is a kind lady, you know. She's glad that I've made friends with you.'

'You're not afraid of getting it yourself, are you?'

'I'm not! I don't want to even think about it. I just want to be your friend. I'll walk with you, if you like.'

Then she smiled, and I knew that she was happy for the first time in a long time. I took her bag from her and hung it on the handlebars of the bike, on the opposite side from mine, and I walked her home in the cold, dark, cloudy December evening.

*****

That night as I sat by the table at the fire in the half light of the oil lamp, doing my homework, Martha and Maureen began preparing to make the first of the Christmas cakes. There were four plum puddings hanging up in the scullery, wrapped in cloth. They had been boiling for hours the day after they were made, and I was told there would be plum pudding until after St Brigid's Day.

I was glad my first day of school was over and Mother was happy, as she had received a letter from Father telling her where he was stationed. There was a fear that if the letters got into the wrong hands, it could give important information to the enemy, so he had made his location known in code. She didn't know if she'd ever get a letter through to him, but she'd try.

She was proud of me for saying I'd continue sitting with Sheila at school.

Then Uncle John told me about Sheila's family.

'God help them,' he said. 'The father has TB as well as two of the children. There are three children in the family. Mr Bryce and the boy, Conor, have it. He is away working, but he has spent a lot of time in a sanatorium in Dublin. Poor Sheila might end up there too if she gets any worse. No one knows when that silent killer will attack; give it time and it will take them. As far as I'm concerned, it's a plague that has hit this great and holy land of ours.'

'Will I ever get it?' I asked.

'I don't think so. If you eat well, wrap up from the cold, say your prayers. Don't get wet. If you stay healthy, you'll be all right. If you haven't got it before now, you will never get it.'

'Uncle John, you should have been a doctor,' teased Mother.

'A doctor of nothing – jack-of-all-trades and master of none,' he answered jokingly. But my thinking on the matter was quite serious, and I passed off their gibing.

'The other children treat her as if she were a leper,' I said.

'They're afraid,' said Mother. 'It's not that they want to treat her that way; they're afraid they might get it too. They see no other way of dealing with it, and that comes from their parents as well. It's called ignorance. A little bit of education can help people a lot, to make them more aware and understanding in the world. That's why I want you to have a good education.'

'I'm not afraid,' I answered, 'but I'm wondering if there is any other way I can help her and her family.'

'You show good example, and it will cure some of them of their ignorance. As I have pointed out already, they are being told by their parents as well to keep their distance. People have a great fear of the disease, and it is hard to blame them.'

'You are a very considerate and kind little girl,' said Maureen. 'Don't you agree, Kitty?'

'I do indeed, Maureen. I'm very proud of her.'

I gave a little smile as they said this and continued with my homework. When I was finished, Mother told me it was time for bed. It had been a long day, and I had to face that journey once again.

Before I went to bed, Uncle John called me to one side and, changing the subject completely, said, 'By the way, Margaret, we are killing the pig on Friday.'

A shiver ran down my spine. It was something I did not want to hear about.

'I'm afraid I won't be here,' I said. 'I hope it will be all over before I come home from school.'

*****

Sheila was glad the next day when I sat beside her in her desk. I was given the details of my uniform, which the two aunts had decided they'd make for me on the Singer sewing machine. I mixed well with the children, and I was soon picking up the odd word of Irish. I was happy to be there, but I knew there was always the fear of being punished for gross misbehaviour, and Reverend Mother had a cane in her office, which she used on occasion. These were the things the children told me, and it put the heart crossways in me when they recounted occasions when they'd been punished. I decided that at all costs, I'd do my best to avoid such an event. But it wouldn't be long before I felt the sting of that cane on my hands. It happened the day the pig was killed.

*****

Jimmy Kiernan had arrived early, just before I went to school, and when I came down to eat my breakfast, he was sitting at the table eating his. His cap rested on his knee, and he talked nonstop about the weather, the war, and the rationing. I shook hands with him, but I did not bid him welcome.

'You're a murderer,' I said, 'killing that poor pig.'

With that, he exploded with laughter, and Mother, who was horrified, made me apologise.

'Well, if I were to be accused of the murder of every animal I slaughtered down the years, I'd be hung, drawn, and quartered long ago,'

'What does that mean?'

'Don't ask too many questions,' said Mother. 'Don't delay eating your breakfast, or you will be late for school.'

The two aunts laughed, and when Uncle John came in, he too had to share in the comedy. I was not impressed with their humour. I didn't think it was funny, and I had the feeling that it was going to be one of those days. I didn't finish my breakfast but left in a huff and set out for the village in the cold, wet, westerly wind on a dark and unpleasant morning.

At school, things progressed normally, and I was coming to grips with everything. At break time it happened.

Sheila and I were playing tip and tig. Whenever I tipped her, she'd run after me and then tip me. I didn't want to run her too much, as I knew she wouldn't be able and would tire all too soon. I could run forever, but not so Sheila. So we rested every so often, and when we were ready, we'd run again. She was delighted to have somebody as a friend, and for her, it was ever so special – that I, being a stranger from another country, had made friends with little Sheila Bryce.

Just before break ended, we were running around the school when Sheila collided with another girl. Their heads banged together, and they fell headlong on the yard. With that, the other girl began screaming, drawing everyone's attention to her. They all gathered around her, but nobody went to assist Sheila.

'Excuse me,' I shouted, 'but Sheila is hurt too.'

I picked her up, and she had a big black bump on her forehead.

'It was her fault anyway,' said the other girl. 'She wasn't looking where she was going.'

'That's not fair,' I replied. 'It was an accident. It could happen to anyone.'

'She shouldn't be here anyway; she should be locked up in a great big hospital with all that TB.'

'How cruel of you,' I screamed. 'I have a good mind to give you a good thump.'

'I wouldn't do that if I were you,' said one of the girls. 'Her daddy is Dr Daly. That's Carmel Daly.'

'She should be kinder to others if she's the doctor's daughter.'

'Why don't you go back to London?' said Carmel. 'Maybe a bomb will fall on *you* and take that other one with you.'

I said nothing but gave her a shove, and she fell into the arms of another girl. During all of this, some of the other girls tended to Sheila. One of them held a cold stone to the bump on her forehead, and the swelling was going down. I was glad to see this, as the girls were beginning to listen to me; it was because of the things I'd seen, which were sad and terrifying, that they were beginning to care for others too.

Then the bell rang, and we ran to our various lines.

About ten minutes later, the classroom door opened, and Reverend Mother entered. She looked none too happy, and then she stood in front of the class.

'Would Margaret Kerr please stand up.'

A shiver ran down my spine, and I did as she asked me.

'Would you follow me to my office right now.'

I left my place, excusing myself from Sister Bernadette, and followed her down the long, dark corridor to her office.

When I went inside, Carmel Daly, who was in fifth class, was sitting by the small fire, drinking a mug of cocoa. Reverend Mother made me stand by the door, and she sat at her desk.

'I would like to know what the meaning of this outburst was outside.'

'It was an accident, Sister; they didn't see each other.'

'That is not what I meant. You pushed this girl, and if it were not for the quickness of her friends, she'd be lying on the ground injured.'

'I'm sorry for that, Reverend Mother,' I said, 'but she deserved it. She said that Sheila should be locked up in a great big hospital with her TB.'

'Did you say that?' asked Reverend Mother.

'I didn't, Reverend Mother. I wouldn't say such a thing.'

'You little vixen,' I shouted. 'Other people heard you say it. Ask them; they will tell you.'

'Don't you tell me what to do, and hold your tongue, young lady,' said Reverend Mother.

I paid little attention to her. Turning to Carmel again, I began shouting. 'You upset Sheila very much. Don't be telling lies. You will go to hell if you tell lies.'

'Stop right now,' shouted the nun, banging a cane on her desk. She'd had it hidden behind her somewhere. I jumped with fright, and I could see Carmel jump as well.

'Listen here to me now; it's your word against Carmel's.' Turning to Carmel, she continued, 'Have you finished your cocoa, dear?'

'Yes, Reverend Mother,' she replied.

'You may return to class, then. I will sort this problem out.'

Carmel left quietly, and it was then that Reverend Mother came from behind her desk with the cane.

'Now, my dear, I regret having to do this, but you must learn to control your temper. I feel sorry for you. I believe your father is not of the same persuasion as us. He's Protestant, isn't he?'

'What has that got to do with it?' I sniffed through my tears.

'Quite a lot. You must really know that only Catholics will go to heaven. But don't worry. I'll pray for him.'

With that, she took my right hand and brought the cane down twice on it. I froze on the spot. I would not give her the satisfaction of knowing she was hurting me to the core. Then she did the same to my left hand, and the hurt was even greater the second time around.

'Do not let me hear tell of you doing such a thing ever again to the child of a very respected citizen of our parish. Dr Daly is very good to our school and contributes generously to the parish.'

Even though I was so young, ten years old, I understood that the issue wasn't the rights of individuals, but money talked. Reverend Mother answered it all for me herself. Carmel mattered a lot to the nuns, as she was an important source of revenue to the convent. Little Sheila was of no importance, a quiet, diseased little waif from a three-bedroomed cottage on the side of the road.

Whatever it took, I was going to stand by Sheila, and Reverend Mother wouldn't faze me.

She then hushed me out of the room, and I returned to my class. I entered as bravely and quietly as I could and sat beside Sheila. Sister Bernadette knew what had taken place and that Carmel Daly had abused her place of privilege. But being a young nun, having been fully professed only this year, she knew her status in the convent hierarchy meant that she had to keep to her vows of obedience and not challenge the authority of the Reverend Mother.

When we were getting ready to leave that evening, she put a stick of Peggy's leg into Sheila's bag and another in mine. Smiling at us, she told Sheila to rest well over the weekend and to take care of herself.

As we left, Reverend Mother stood at the school door with her arms folded. She didn't speak as we passed her by but stood with a stern look on her face, watching after us. She knew she was wrong in doing what she did. She was aware that Sister Bernadette would tell the other young nuns what had happened, but she would deal with that if they said anything. She would have to stand by the words she had used, as she had to keep on the side of the good doctor. Carmel had the makings of a fine boarding pupil in two years, when she graduated from primary school to the secondary school, and she was scholarship material.

Sheila was all apologies for what had happened, but I was glad I had stood up for her. She kept saying that I was her best friend and that I'd have to come see her someday – her mammy would be delighted. But I didn't give her an answer. I was now worried sick about Father. What would happen to him if he were killed?

*****

When I got home, the kitchen looked like a morgue. Martha was stirring pig's blood in a bucket and adding spices and other ingredients to it to make black pudding. The table was covered in animal offal, including the liver, heart, kidneys, and other organs. The pig's carcass was hanging in the shed, and Jimmy was preparing to carve it up into sections.

Mother had removed herself to the fire in the parlour, and she was writing Christmas cards. She was completely unperturbed by the whole affair. Maureen went to give me my dinner, but I threw my schoolbag on the chair by the parlour fire and ran out into the fading light. I knew the operation was just complete, and as I ran into the haggard, I was still haunted by the corpse of the pig hanging in the shed. Uncle John and Jimmy Kiernan were washing their hands and arms in the cold water at the pump with carbolic soap. Uncle John called after me, and I didn't answer. Sam ran with me, and as I passed the pigsty, Moll and Murphy seemed quite unperturbed by the loss of their son.

I ran into the darkening field, and the first friend to greet me was old Paddy. He stood his ground, as he usually did, and I embraced him, crying into his soft, hairy mane. He stood quite still and rigid where he was, and I knew he was aware that I was upset. I could now see why Uncle John loved him so. My hands were sore and marked by the force of the cane, but it didn't bother me that much. I stood there for the best part of ten minutes or so, feeling the comfort and gentleness of the great strong horse. Then I felt a hand on my shoulder. It was Uncle John.

He pulled me around to him and took my hands. He felt their scorching hotness, and I winced as he pressed them gently. He then opened them out, and I could see anger grow on his face.

'Tell me, who did this to you?' he asked.

'It's all right, Uncle John. It was just a misunderstanding.'

'I don't care,' he bellowed. 'Nobody has a right to do this to a small child.'

'It was a mistake. Just forget about it.'

'I won't forget about it. Nobody does a thing like this to John Costello, or anyone belonging to him, and gets away with it. Now who was it? Come on, out with it!'

Paddy seemed a bit distressed when Uncle John raised his voice and trotted away a few paces. Uncle John kept shaking me, wondering why I wasn't telling him.

'Uncle John!' I screamed. 'Don't do anything, please. I still must go to school there. If you say anything to Reverend Mother, it will be worse for me.'

'Come on, tell me what happened. I know you wouldn't do anything wrong.'

'That's just it; I did nothing wrong. I tried to protect poor Sheila from Carmel Daly, and Reverend Mother took sides with Carmel, just because her dad gives money to the nuns.'

'I might have known. She's a right auld snob, that one. Don't worry, someday she too must meet her Maker.'

He took me in his arms, and I cried into his grubby old farm coat.

'Come on now, it's all right. This house will always be a safe place for you.'

'Oh, Uncle John,' I sobbed. 'When is Father coming back? Then everything will be all right.'

'He'll return someday, don't worry.'

*****

That night I had a nightmare. There were bodies everywhere, and limbs. When I looked closely, they were pigs' limbs, and Father was calling me to save him. I screamed and woke up. I was in a cold sweat, and Mother was there to console me. She gave me a drink of water.

It was then that I asked her about Father.

'Mother will Father go to hell?'

'My goodness, why do you say such things?'

'Reverend Mother told me that Father, being a Protestant, was doomed to go to hell.'

'Isn't she a meddling old bitch!'

'She said that only Catholics can go to heaven.'

'What makes her think such things? Is she an expert on such matters? How do we know whether *we* will ever get to heaven or not, let alone Protestants, Jews, or any other religion, for that matter? We can only go to heaven by the life we live, not by what religion we belong to. Your father is a very good Christian, and I would say he's closer to God than miss meddling Reverend Mother. I don't see why your father should not get to heaven. If I had thought such things, I would have still married him. I chose him because he was a kind, gentle, and loving man. He has great respect for me, and he has never hurt or harmed anyone in his life. So if anyone deserves to go to heaven, then he does.'

'I wonder, will he come back someday?'

'Please God he will,' said Mother. 'All we can do is pray for his safe return.'

Part 3
Christmas 1940

Chapter 6

Soon I left that incident all behind me, and life continued as normal. The other girls knew it had not been my fault, and so did Reverend Mother. I tried to give her a wide berth and kept out of her way as much as possible. But my encounters with her didn't stop there, as I remained her little scapegoat in the scheme of things over the next few weeks.

Then Sheila didn't turn up for school a few days later, and I was told she was ill. She would reappear again in the new year when the school opened after the Christmas holidays. This was normal practise for her, and as a result, she kept falling behind in her work at school. Sister Bernadette understood this and gave her as much help as she could. I had promised to pay her a visit as well, so I waited until the Christmas holiday arrived before venturing to see her.

Meanwhile, the Christmas preparations continued. The pig was salted and cured. The carcass was divided into segments and stored away in the cool room near the back door. This was a very cold room in the winter, but in summer it was quite the opposite, and when it was cleaned out at the end of spring, it often served as a sleeping place for journeyman workers, who travelled from place to place, helping with the sowing and harvesting.

At times, the cattle jobbers stayed in it as well. These were the men who helped take cattle from town to town to sell them at fairs, and several farmers in the area would enlist their help. They were also known as drovers. But their services were needed badly during the war years, when it was difficult to transport cattle from fair to fair. When life began to return to normal after the war, the work of the drover was no longer needed, as farmers began transporting their cattle to fairs and marts using lorries.

When all this fuss and hullabaloo had passed, we set out for town one Saturday near Christmas to do some Christmas shopping. The term the aunts used for this event was *to bring home the Christmas*. Maureen and Mother stayed at home, and Martha decided to do the buying. While she tripped up and down the town, Uncle John went into a public house for a few pints of stout.

As we were shopping, she seemed to need everything, from needles to an anchor. The list was endless: new oilcloths for the table and mantel, salt, flour, minerals, whiskey, sauces, sugar, tea, whatever her ration tokens would allow. She was happy that she would have enough to last until early in the new year. She didn't even entertain getting more stout, as the barrel contained enough to keep Uncle John going through the festive season. She bought four big red candles and told me that it was my job to get them ready on Christmas Eve.

It would have been impossible for us to take everything home, so we arranged for a delivery to be made with a horse-drawn van on Monday. I had a few shillings with me, and I asked Martha to help me buy something for Sheila. We settled upon a little mother-of-pearl pendant on a chain. We saw it in a shop window, and the lady in the shop placed it in a little box and wrapped it with brown paper.

Then I was deposited with Uncle John in the pub. Mother had told me that a public house was no place for a young lady, if I had to spend some time with Uncle John. It must have been prearranged, as I was taken into the snug, where there were other women relaxing. The landlady fussed over me and brought me a hot cup of cocoa and a little plate of ham sandwiches. Uncle John remained in the bar. He was only in the next room.

When Martha returned, she joined me in the snug. She had other parcels with her, which she kept a tight hold of, and she did not tell me what was in them.

Finally, when Uncle John was ready, we set out for home. I knew by his manner that he was a bit under the weather, as he'd had too much to drink, and he left it to Bobby to navigate. The old jennet was so used to the journey that he knew the way. Martha just held on to the reins, and the animal brought us slowly there.

When we got home, it was teatime, but Uncle John fell asleep in the soft chair by the fire. Maureen had the evening chores done, the animals fed, and the cow milked. She even unyoked the jennet and let him out into the field. Mother was able to get the tea ready. I was glad to see that she was coming back to herself and she would be much happier at Christmas, even though Father was far away from us.

*****

Two days before Christmas Eve, I cycled all the way to Sheila's house near the village to see how she was. She and her family lived in a small three-bedroomed cottage just off the main road.

Mrs Bryce greeted me and made excuses for the state of the house. The whole family lived in a small kitchen, with an open fire, and depended on the wages the father, Fintan, earned as a gardener at the Johnson estate. Even though he carried TB, he was able to work and earn a living, and the work he was assigned was never too taxing. Whatever he earned managed to keep the wolf from the door, with a little help from his own vegetable plot at the back of the house. Sheila's brother, Conor, who was fifteen years old, had the disease, but it was also taking its toll on Sheila.

She was in bed when I called. She shared her room with her sister, Eileen, who was sixteen years old.

Sheila was sitting up in her bed, reading a book, and she was ever so excited to see me when I entered. She was pale, and her face was thinner. I sat down beside her, and she said, 'How is that auld battle-axe of a Reverend Mother?'

'She's fine,' I said. 'She knows she was wrong in doing what she did, and she knows that *I* know too. She just keeps out of my way. I do the same thing; I keep out of her way as well.'

'That's the way to keep her,' laughed Sheila. Changing the subject, she said, 'I suppose you will have a great Christmas down on the farm.'

'I don't really know. Father won't be there. We had a Christmas card from him, but it was posted here in Ireland. I'd say someone he knew who was coming here for Christmas brought it for him and posted it.'

'I just wish it were spring again,' said Sheila. 'Flowers, the leaves, the trees . . . and I love the birds. I feed them in the winter all the time, and they never leave the place. I love the lake shore too. It makes me feel good and clean inside, and I would just love to dance all day.'

'Whenever the spring comes,' I said, 'I'll take you down to the shore, and we'll have a picnic there.'

'Would you really?' she asked excitedly. 'I'm feeling better already.'

'What are you getting from Father Christmas?' I asked.

'Who's he?'

'I mean Santa Claus. In England we call him Father Christmas.'

'I don't know if he'll come to our house at all. We have little money, and with Dad being out of work a few times this year because he was sick, we couldn't save any money. Mam has selected a chicken from the back of the house for the dinner. She's getting old and didn't lay any eggs this year.'

I was horrified when I heard this; they would not have enough for one dinner, let alone two, by killing a farm chicken. My heart went out to Sheila and to the whole family, and I knew I'd have to do something.

Then I reached into my pocket and took out the little brown packet that had been wrapped by the lady in the shop in town, and I gave it to her.

'This is a little present for you for Christmas,' I said.

She squealed with excitement, then remembered something.

'I haven't anything got for you,' she said.

'You're my friend. Isn't that enough? You made me welcome when nobody else did.'

'Oh, thank you very much,' she said excitedly. 'May I open it now?'

'Of course, go ahead!'

She opened it to reveal the little gold chain with the mother-of-pearl pendant on it. It was the most beautiful thing she had ever seen in her whole life, and there were tears of joy in her eyes.

There was a little card along with the gift. It was one I'd made myself, with a pencil drawing of old Paddy out in the field. On the back, I had written:

For my best friend Sheila in Ireland

Thank you

Margaret

Sheila said, 'I'm going to keep this pendant. If ever I feel I need you, will you come to me if I send it to you?'

'I will!' I answered.

'No matter where you are in the world?'

'I promise I will come to you.'

'You're a very good friend, Margaret.'

I thought it was a very strange thing to say. But as I grew to know her, I realised that Sheila was a special little girl with little gifts and talents that hid away her illness. It was as if she knew what life was dealing out for her, and this was her way of staying connected with me.

I stayed sitting on the bed beside her, and soon she fell asleep. The excitement was too much for her.

Mrs Bryce could hear the whole conversation from the kitchen, and when I left the room, she was sitting at the table with tears in her eyes. She went over and closed the door and spoke to me in a whisper, just in case Sheila would hear what she was saying.

'You have made her Christmas, Margaret. Thank you very much. She is so happy. You have made me happy, and wait till I tell her father and the rest of the family; it will make their Christmas happy too.'

I knew by the way she was speaking that Christmas was going to be a lean affair at their little cottage. As I waved goodbye to Mrs Bryce, she told me that I was welcome in their home at any time; I didn't even have to ask.

But the poverty of their little place upset me, and I was glad to return to the farm.

At tea that evening, Mother wondered why I was so quiet. She hoped I wasn't getting ill. She didn't want to see me sick for Christmas.

'I'm fine, Mother,' I said. 'I'm just a little sad.'

'Why are you sad? Is it that you miss Father?'

'I do miss him. I miss him all the time. But it's something else.'

'What is it, alannah? Go on, tell me!'

Then I burst into tears. She beckoned me to come to her, and I put my arms around her neck and cried into her shoulders. When I composed myself, I sat beside her and said, 'Sheila's house is a very sad place. I didn't know what poverty meant till I went there. They have very little for Christmas, and I don't even think Father Christmas will visit them.'

'It's all right, love. You shouldn't go there if it's upsetting you.'

'Oh, but I am going back there. It made Sheila very happy that I called.' I was beginning to gather my thoughts together. I had a question to ask Uncle John, and I was a little apprehensive in asking him. As I finished my tea, and just before everyone knelt for the rosary, I put it to him.

'Uncle John, you wouldn't give me a present of one of the geese you've kept for after Christmas?'

All eyes were focused on me, and the aunts who had said nothing during all this time looked on with amused expressions on their faces. I think they knew why I was doing this.

Uncle John had a fair idea where my request was leading. Amused, he put a spanner in the works. 'I couldn't give you that goose as a present. Isn't she already dead and plucked and hanging along with the poor pig in the cold room?'

'I know that!' I said. 'That's why I want it.'

'Margaret, what is wrong with you?' said Mother. 'Will you stop beating around the bush and get to the point?'

'The Bryces have very little for Christmas. They're going to kill a chicken. That won't be enough for a family.'

'I didn't realise they were that badly off,' said Martha.

'You see, Mr Bryce works at Johnsons' as a gardener, and there was no money a few times during the year, as he was sick. It's probably that TB he has.'

'There is only one problem there, girl,' said Uncle John.

'What's that?' asked Mother.

'If I went down to their house in the morning with that goose, Fintan Bryce would say it was charity and throw it back in my face. They are proud people, you know.'

There was silence for a few moments as we thought things over, and then I stood up.

'I know how we'll do it!' I was all excited and began dancing around the kitchen.

'Margaret, will you stop making an exhibition of yourself?' shouted Mother.

'Tomorrow evening is Christmas Eve. After dark, we'll take Bobby and the trap out, and we'll drive down near the house. If we go too near, they might hear us. We can leave it in a box at the door.'

'Clever girl!' said Maureen.

Uncle John made no reply to that, but taking his big blue striped mug in his hand, he swallowed the last of his tea and winked at me with his left eye as well as with his moustache.

Next day, the two aunts got a large cardboard box from the shed. After wrapping the goose in newspaper, they placed it in the bottom of the box. The goose had been cleaned out and was ready for the oven. Martha had made some stuffing and wrapped it in butter paper, ready to go inside the bird. They put one of the red candles in as well, a Christmas cake, a plum pudding, a baby Powers whiskey, and a box of sweets. With all this inside, the box was quite heavy.

When we were ready to go after dark, Uncle John asked Mother to go with us, as he would need some help with the box. Her plaster had been removed the day before, and it was better to her than any Christmas present, as it meant she had completely left the war behind her. Her arm would be quite weak for a while, but she was recovering well, and I think Uncle John reasoned that asking her to help might boost her confidence again.

Reluctantly, she decided to go, and we moved quietly in the darkness towards the village.

It was a pitch-black night, but Bobby could smell his way. As we passed each house and little cottage along the road, candles glowed in windows everywhere. It was something new to me, but Uncle John said it was a tradition in Ireland to light candles in the windows on Christmas Eve, to show Mary and Joseph the way to Bethlehem on their journey. Then he said we should not delay, as he had a job for me to do when we got back home.

We stopped a few hundred yards from the cottage and faced Bobby for home. Uncle John tied him to a tree, and then he and Mother carried the box between them to the cottage while I followed along. The place was very quiet; luckily for us, the Bryces had no dog. The gate was open, and Uncle John and Mother let the box down gently at the door.

Returning to the gate again, we could hear the soft murmur of prayers inside – the rosary was being said. The Bryces were at the end of the litany. Soon the whisper of prayers stopped, and we knew that someone would come out to get a breath of fresh air. We moved into the gloom on the grass verge, feeling our way through the darkness. When we were at a safe distance away, we stood and listened for a few minutes. It was Conor Bryce who opened the door, and he began shouting and cheering at the top of his voice. Mrs Bryce dragged the box inside, assisted by Conor. The door closed, and after about a minute, there arose a great cheer inside. My work was done, and I knew they had accepted their little gift.

By then we were at the back of the trap, and Uncle John led Bobby along the road in the grass margin to drown out the sound of the wheels and the jennet's hooves.

I was glad when we got home. The goose was being prepared for the pot oven. The aroma of stuffing pervaded the whole house, and the plum pudding was given another boil in the skillet hanging on the crane.

The three candles were ready on the parlour table. I had placed them in large, two-pound jam pots earlier in the day and filled the pots with gravel to keep them in place. The outsides of the jars were covered with coloured tissue paper that had been wrapped around new clothes after purchase.

Then Martha sat me down on the chair by the fire in the parlour and began telling me about some little Christmas traditions she wanted fulfilled. This was the beginning of my journey with the two great-aunts. Their lives were so full of the traditions and customs they'd grown up with. Over the next few years, I was to learn from them many stories and customs that filled their lives from year to year. Tonight, on Christmas Eve, two of these customs were introduced to me, and *I* was to be the centre of their little ceremony.

Uncle John had told me out in the darkness about the Christmas candle and the tradition it held of showing Mary and Joseph the way to Bethlehem. Martha told me that it was my job, as the youngest person in the house, to place the candles in the window. There were tears in her eyes as she spoke, and being a religious person, Martha was extremely happy this year.

'It's been a long time since there was a little child in our house to do this job, and we are blessed this Christmas to have you here, Margaret, and your mother as well. When she was a little girl, she did the same job you're doing, and now it's your turn tonight.'

She carried one of the candles to the kitchen, and putting a little stool just under the window, she asked me to stand on it. She handed me the candle, putting her hand firmly underneath the decorated jam pot. She held it along with me, and I let it down gently in the centre of the window. The light gave a little flicker now and then, disturbed by a soft, frosty breeze when the door opened.

It would be lit every night during the Christmas season, and the last candle was left aside to be used for the New Year. We left the second candle in the parlour window. The lace curtains were pulled back, and the candle sat in the centre. This window faced the road, and it looked like a little star from the distance.

'There's one final task for you,' said Martha.

'What's that?' I asked.

'It's your job to place the infant Jesus in the crib.'

Maureen had prepared it a few days beforehand. They had a large wooden box, which had been painted a dull grey some years previously. It was covered in ivy and berried holly with a little silver star made from card and tinsel. The statues were about ten inches high and made from alabaster. The crib was sitting on the large sideboard in the parlour. From constant use over the years, some of the paint on the garments of the figures was fading, and little chips had flaked away, exposing the white alabaster underneath. Mary and Joseph stood on a bed of straw, staring down at an empty manger. Three shepherds stood to one side, one carrying a lamb on his shoulders, and the donkey and cow were lying down on the other side, facing the manger as well. Each figure stood in prayerful supplication to an infant who was not there. Now that was about to change.

Martha opened a door in the bottom of the sideboard, and taking the little lone infant, she kissed it and blessed herself. She handed it to all present, and they did the same. Uncle John took his hat off before kissing the little figure of the infant. Then it was handed to me, and when I had finished blessing myself, I placed it in the little manger. The whole scene was now complete, and the crib would sit quietly on the sideboard until after the Feast of the Epiphany on the sixth of January.

Mother sat at the fire and looked on with a tearful smile, thinking about the few times she'd spent Christmas here, before her father died tragically. They had stayed for Christmas here each year, and when she had moved to Dublin, this little custom had not been observed in her mother's sister's house.

We sat for a few moments looking on, and a thought struck me: Why were so many dreadful things happening in the world tonight? Jesus had been born into the world to save us from sin, and we were welcoming him into our homes, but in distant parts of the world, there was sadness and death. Then Martha summed up the reason the crib was there.

'It is to remind us that he is God's son, and anytime you pass it by, say a little prayer. I have great faith in prayer.'

So, everything was ready for Christmas. The house was spotless and tidy and the pictures were clean, capped with sprigs of holly, and bedecked with plenty of red berries. I could see from the expression on my aunts' and uncle's faces that they were so happy tonight. It cheered Mother up as well, as her thoughts were usually on Father, who was so far away from us.

Uncle John sat in the corner, drinking a mug of black porter from the half barrel in the dairy. He winked at me when he took his first sip, and it left a white mark on the bottom of his moustache.

Tea was late as a result of the preparations, but when it was over, Mother told me that it was long past my bedtime and it was time to go. She came with me. There was a small fire in our bedroom, and the place was warm.

'I hope Father is safe tonight,' I said.

'Please God he is. Just remember him in your prayers.'

She tucked me in and smiled at me as she kissed me good night.

'I hope Father Christmas brings you a nice little present. You are a very kind little girl; do you know that?'

She kissed me on the forehead as she said this, but before she left the room, the glow from the fire and the excitement Christmas was bringing me were too much, and I fell asleep.

*****

Christmas day came all too quickly, and I woke to a dark frosty morning, as we all went to early mass in the trap. There was no sign of dawn yet, and I wondered what the great man with the red coat and white beard had brought me. Mother insisted we wait to find out till we'd had our breakfast after mass, saying that the birth of our Saviour was the most important event in our lives that day.

It was a hard, white frost, and we wrapped rugs around us to keep the biting cold away. Bobby was none too happy to be on the road so early, as Uncle John had kept him in the shed overnight so he would be ready for the road in the morning. He showed his anger every so often by kicking his heels back at the front of the trap. Uncle John chastised him by drawing on the reins rather quickly, and he'd canter into a trot.

I was starving with the hunger. We'd been fasting since the night before to receive Holy Communion this morning, and I dreamed of a large mug of soup from Martha's stew, to keep the frost away.

We said very little, as we were more concerned about getting there on time. Candles still burned in the windows of some of the houses and cottages. As we headed down the avenue to our left towards the town about a mile away, we could see the lights of the big house, the Johnson estate. Every window in the place was lit up.

'There was probably a party there last night,' said Uncle John, 'and there'll be another one tomorrow if the hunt takes place there.'

'He must be rich,' I said.

'So well he can. Didn't his ancestors before him soak every penny out of the poor people to keep themselves and their troop of servants happy.'

'But he gave employment,' said Mother.

'It was pittance, slave labour, just about kept the wolf from the door.'

'Anyway, the man who is there now is a good man,' said Martha.

'And his wife is a lady. So sad her health has failed her in recent years,' said Maureen.

'Yeah, but it takes a long time for old wounds to heal,' said Uncle John. 'He wouldn't be there today if it weren't for the fact that his father gave refuge to our lads on the run during the Troubles.'

'There you are,' said Mother. 'He is a born Irishman.'

'Maybe,' said Uncle John, 'but it's hard to forget.'

'Don't be so uncharitable,' said Martha. 'And this is Christmas morning, peace on earth to men of goodwill. When you go to the altar, say a prayer for the man and his family.'

Uncle John muttered something under his breath and begged Bobby to go a little faster, and it wasn't long before we reached the village.

The church was dark, with several candles clinging to the walls on each side on sconces attached to hold them in place. The altar was aglow with candles, which reflected downwards into the nave. The crib was nearly life size, standing to the right of the altar and close to the rails in the front. The statues were old and could do with a coat of paint.

It was a long mass, and I thought I'd never get to have a bite to eat, warm up, and open my present.

When we were coming out the church door, someone tapped Uncle John on the shoulder. It was a man with a dark cap and black coat.

'Was it you, John Costello, who was responsible for leaving that box of goods at my door last night?' It was Fintan Bryce, Sheila's father.

'I won't tell you a lie, Fintan. I did.'

'I am not too happy about it, but then, I can do nothing about it now; my children have smiles on their faces this morning. That is so nice to see, but I'm not a charity case.'

'There are two things I want to say to you, Fintan. It wasn't my idea, you know; it was this little girl here who has opened our hearts this Christmas. She is responsible for it. She has seen so much war and heartbreak; she knows when it's time to share with others. So *do not* be angry with her or me.'

'You are a good-hearted little girl,' he said, 'and you have made my little girl so happy as well. But unfortunately, I will not be able to repay you for all this.'

'That brings me to the second point I want to make,' said Uncle John. 'It is not charity, Fintan. It's being a neighbour. But neighbours help one another. You're not getting away that easy. I have a small job for you to do for me later in the new year, around mid-March, when there's a brighter day to work, and if you are strong enough to go ahead with it.'

'What's that?' asked Fintan.

'My two sisters have a flower garden at the front of the house, and it needs a complete overhaul. It's getting overgrown in places, and some of the flowers are choking others. I want you to do something with it in your own time.'

'I'll do it with a heart and a half, some Saturday. Thank you both very much, and have a very happy Christmas.'

'Now will you go home, Fintan, and enjoy yourself? It's Christmas, and we should think of everyone at this time.'

'Thank you all so much. I will never forget your kindness.'

When he had gone, Uncle John turned to us all as we stood at the waiting trap, and he mopped his brow.

'Thank goodness for that,' he said. 'He could have just taken it the other way and thrown it back at us, but when he heard it was *your* idea and that he'd have to work for the gift, it was a horse of a different colour.'

At home, when breakfast was over and the animals had been tended to, we retired to the parlour, and the presents were opened.

Father Christmas was kind to me. I got a doll. I was so glad, as I'd lost Mollie in the bombing, along with any other toy I had. Martha had a new knitted hat for me as well as a beautiful blue rosary beads to use at night when we knelt in prayer. Maureen gave me new gloves. Uncle John gave me a brush-and-comb set in a brown leather case. I could not imagine him going into a shop to buy them. I knew he'd had help in that field.

'Now you can admire yourself anytime you want,' he laughed.

My presents consisted of things I'd made myself. I gave Mother a little bag I'd made by sewing two handkerchiefs together. It was to keep all her own handkerchiefs in. She kissed me and told me she'd treasure it always.

I'd painted a tobacco tin blue and written Uncle John's name on it. It was for him to tip his pipe ashes into when he was finished, so as not to see them scattered all around the hearth on the ground. From him, I received a beardy hug that left a red mark on my face for a while.

Finally, I gave my two great-aunts a supply of mints. They were always eating them as they worked, and I knew they were glad to get them.

When this was all over, Mother produced another parcel.

'This came in the post recently, while you were at school. Again, it was posted in Ireland. It came the same day as Father's Christmas card.'

I squealed with excitement and tore open the brown paper. There was a bottle of perfume for Mother, and some photographs of Father in uniform, and then there was a fancy-coloured box with my name on it.

'It's really beautiful,' I said. 'It must be a jewellery box.'

There was a little catch on the lid, and when I released it, I got the fright of my life. Up sprung a long clown with a laughing face. It scared the living daylights out of me. It was a jack-in-the-box. Inside was a little note with just the words:

Have a good laugh, Margaret

Happy Christmas

Father

I put it standing on the parlour table, and then I began to cry. Mother joined me, and the whole morning ended with the aunts consoling her and Uncle John consoling me.

By nightfall I was exhausted, what with all the food and the excitement of the presents that I had not expected to get.

Uncle John had invited Bartley Hegarty over to join us for the dinner, and the two of them spent the evening sipping punch. Uncle John spent the whole time telling Bartley it was time he found a wife; he wasn't getting any younger. Bartley told Uncle John he was a fine example of Irish wedded manhood himself. They joked and bantered with each other, and I realised it was often the topic of conversation with them. But Uncle John was being serious behind all the jests. It would do Bartley good to have a reason to keep his farm going and to try to make a family for himself. He had stayed with his parents all his life. They'd been in their early forties when they married, and Bartley was their only child. When they'd died a few years back, he had continued running the farm alone. He came to Bethany at Christmas for his dinner, and he joined my uncle and aunts on several Sundays during the year as well.

It ended up that the two men were in no condition to tend to the animals but fell asleep each side of the fire in the parlour, as they had become quite inebriated as the day wore on. Bartley's farm animals were all dry stock and were out in the fields, savouring the aftergrass. As a result, he stayed the night and did not waken till the morning.

Martha, Maureen, and I tended to the animals. I felt important being given a little responsibility. I dished out hay to the cows and shut in the hens. I fed Sam, and he went into his little shed for the night. Martha checked on Bobby and the horses, and Maureen milked the cow.

A thought struck me as I was doing the chores: if Father had been in the company of the men inside, would he be drunk as well? I'd never seen Father drunk in my life.

Chapter 7

The wren-boys arrived early next morning when breakfast was just over. I'd never in all my days seen such a band of happy-go-lucky, colourful people. Their presence was heralded by Sam barking in the yard. As they banged on the door, a voice outside shouted, 'Good people within, may we come in?'

'Why do you want to do so?' shouted Maureen.

Then a man stepped inside, all wrapped in straw, with a woven hat of the same make. His face was blackened with coal, polish, or maybe a cork charred in the fire. I was horrified when I saw what he carried. He had a piece of furze bush in his hand with a little dead wren dangling from the end of it. He stood before the fire and began to chant:

The wren! The wren!

The king of all birds

On Stephen's Day

He was caught in the furze

Although he was little

His family was great

Rise up, good Lady, and give us a trate

As I went out with my hat so tall

I saw a wren upon the wall

I took a stick and knocked it down

I brought it into Mullingar town

So up with the kittle

And down with the pan

And give us a penny to bury the wran

I dipped his head in a barrel of beer

I wish you a merry Christmas and a happy New Year

He finished by staring into my face in a menacing, clownlike fashion, and I returned his gaze by shouting back at him at the top of my voice.

'You're a right cruel monster you are, killing a poor little bird like that.'

With that, the man opened his mouth in a sinister, manic laugh. He clapped his hands, and the music of an accordion sounded outside the door.

In a matter of seconds, the kitchen was invaded by about ten people with accordions, a fiddle, spoons, and a drumlike instrument being beaten with a stick to the rhythm of the music. I was to learn later from Maureen that it was called a bodhrán. It was made from wood and goatskin. Again, I was annoyed to realise that a poor goat had had to die to make that instrument. But Maureen said that at least the animal's spirit was forever part of the music.

The wren-boys were dressed in an array of rags, coats, streamers, and straw, with upturned hats and blackened or coloured faces.

The music was loud and cheerful, and I thought they might lift the roof off. One of the troupe grabbed hold of Martha and danced around the floor with her. Then to my horror, Mother was on the floor as well. They danced a half set, and I'd never known that Mother could dance like that. What would Father say?

While this was going on, Maureen was filling mugs with porter from the half barrel. She handed mugs around to all the musicians, and as each received one, the music slowed down and stopped for a few minutes. But one man continued playing a lively tune, and I asked Uncle John what it was called.

Taking the pipe from his mouth, he said it was called 'The Boys of the Blue Hill'. Then the smoke from his pipe wafted higher to the ceiling as he clapped in time to the music.

Then, just as quickly as it had begun, the music stopped as each of the musicians savoured his mug of stout. One of the troupe was a boy about twelve years old. He was at the table, drinking a mug of lemonade and eating a slice of cake that Martha had given him. Then the man holding the dead wren, the master of ceremonies, turned to the young boy and chanted, 'Come on, Shawnie, how's about a song?'

With that, the youth stood up and left his half-eaten slice of cake on the plate. He had a soft, soprano voice for one so young, and the kitchen fell silent as he sang. The fiddle caught his melody and key and accompanied him quietly in the background.

> *'Tis the last rose of summer left blooming alone*
> *All her lovely companions are faded and gone*
> *No flower of her kindred, no rosebud is nigh*
> *To reflect back her blushes or give sigh for sigh*
>
> *I'll not leave thee, thou lone one, to pine on the stem*
> *Since the lovely are sleeping, go sleep now with them*
> *Thus kindly I scatter thy leaves o'er the bed*
> *Where thy mates of the garden lie scentless and dead*

The boy continued his soft lament from verse to verse, and later in the day, Martha told me it had been written by an Irish poet called Thomas Moore in memory of his wife, who had died young. I was amazed that one minute everyone was dancing around the kitchen and the next the music was sad, just at the drop of a hat. I thought it was very beautiful, but I wondered what was going to happen next.

When the crowd applauded the young boy for his song, Maureen was still handing around slices of cake and plum pudding to those who were drinking their stout. They weren't ready to continue with their revelry.

Then, just like the jack-in-the-box the day before, I received another shock. The master of ceremonies put his furze bush down on the table and swooped me up in his arms.

'How's about a song from this little girl?'

'No thank you!' I protested.

Before I knew it, I was standing on a chair looking down at everyone.

'Aw, come on, it's Stephen's Day. Every little girl knows a song. Don't let Shawnie beat you in that one.'

'I don't know any song!' I protested again.

'But you do, dear,' said Mother. 'Remember the one you sang last year for your school Christmas concert?'

For once, I wished that Mother would keep her mouth shut. I did not want to sing. But the man was standing beside me, and he wasn't letting me go till I obliged with a song. There was no way out.

I didn't know how these people would react to an English folk song, but I decided to give it a go. I held my breath, cleared my throat, and then I began to sing.

On Richmond Hill there lives a lass

More bright than Mayday morn

Whose charms all other maids' surpass

A rose without a thorn

This lass so neat with smile so sweet

Has won my right goodwill

I'd crowns resign to call thee mine

Sweet lass of Richmond Hill . . .

They listened intently, and when I finished, they all cheered, and someone let out the loudest wolf whistle I'd ever heard. I was swept back on the floor again. Then the man shoved something into my hand. When I looked, it was a two-shilling piece, which everyone called a florin. I'd gotten paid for my singing.

'Now, good ladies and gentlemen,' said the master of ceremonies. 'We must bid you goodbye to bring the message elsewhere. Good day to you all, God bless you all, and have a happy and healthy New Year.'

He held the furze bush aloft, and they marched and danced out into the yard. As the last person left, he showed Martha a sweet can, and she threw several coins into it, which rattled and jingled as he danced out the door. The music continued down the avenue, and when they reached the road, they boarded several traps and proceeded to the next house.

Martha stood with me and watched as they went. I was curious about the whole pageant, and I asked Martha about it.

'There is an old story about St Stephen, the first Christian martyr,' she said. 'It was shortly after Jesus died on the cross. He was one of his disciples, and those who followed his message were in danger of death. It is said that Stephen was chased by several men, who wanted to kill him. He sought shelter inside some furze bushes. He thought they wouldn't search in there, as furze bushes are so thorny. But a little wren flew out of the bush, and the men decided to search in that place. They found poor Stephen hiding, and they took him and stoned him to death.'

'So that's why they kill the little wren? The poor little thing.'

'It's an old tradition,' said Martha. 'It's hard to break with tradition.'

When I went back inside, Maureen was sitting by the fire. 'I'm not able for this anymore,' she said. 'I'm getting too old.'

'They'd lift your heart though, wouldn't they?' said Martha.

'Mother!' I exclaimed. 'I never knew you could dance like that.'

'I did once, love, but I thought I had forgotten how.'

'Who taught you, then?'

'It doesn't matter. It was a long time ago. I didn't think myself that I'd remember.'

'It's like this,' said Maureen. 'They say that it's like learning to walk, or run, or swim maybe: once you know how, you will never forget.'

Then the day's chores began again, and I went upstairs to play with my new presents. Mother was standing at a basin of water at the table downstairs peeling potatoes, humming some soft tune to herself.

*****

The following afternoon, when dinner was over, I decided to take a walk to the lake again. I put on my Wellingtons and headed down the boreen. I didn't bring Sam with me, as he was down the fields with Uncle John. I wasn't afraid this time, and I wondered if I would meet up with Bartley Hegarty again. But he was nowhere to be seen. He was still celebrating Christmas and sleeping it all away.

It was an intensely quiet world today, with a slight to sharp north-easterly breeze. I pulled the woollen cap down over my ears, and the mittens I wore kept my hands warm.

There wasn't a sound anywhere, except for the odd low of a cow or a dog's bark in a far-off farmyard.

When I got to the lake shore, four swans were bobbing and dipping in the water a few hundred yards out, oblivious to me or to anything else, knowing that they were quite safe where they were. Nobody was going to touch them there. I stood watching them and then went for a walk down the shore to see if I could pick up anything or see anything out of the ordinary.

I left the boathouse behind me and continued down to where the wood began to stretch to the shoreline. The breeze carried into the wood, making a continuous noise in the trees that drowned out the lapping of small waves on the shore.

I stood, throwing small stones into the water, trying to see if I could throw them any farther each time, but my throwing distance had a lot to be desired.

Suddenly, I thought I could hear a whimper. I threw another stone. Had I heard it again? I held my breath to see if I could distinguish any noise above the sound of my breathing.

Then it happened once more. Someone was calling for help. It came from the nearby wood.

'Hello!' I shouted, to see if anyone would answer me.

A voice called faintly, 'Over here!'

I followed the sound of the call into the wood, taking the path and moving slowly into the black low light of a winter woodland. As the sound of the lake moved away from me, I could hear the voices of the wood more clearly. There was a constant whimpering sound coming to me, and soon I could see a foxhound sitting by a beech tree. By its side lay something black. I was afraid that the dog might growl or bark at me, but as I approached, it came running with its big red tongue sticking far out of its mouth and wagging its tail. I stroked its head, and it whimpered again.

I approached the dark object on the ground, and when I adjusted my vision to the woodland light, I could see that it was a person lying on the ground in a bed of wet, dead leaves.

I ran to the spot where the person lay, and I could see that it was an elderly man, in his early seventies. He was wearing riding gear. His thick curled hair was white, and he was older than he looked. He had fallen from his horse and was lying there, blood trickling down his face.

I was frightened at first and wanted to run, but the man gave a moan.

'Are you all right?' I shouted.

He turned over on his back and seemed to be coming to himself again.

'Who are you? Are you hurt?'

The man looked up and, seeing me, began to babble something in a foreign language I couldn't understand.

'Can you speak English?' I shouted.

He spoke again in a language I wasn't sure of, but then I heard him use the word *kinder*. I recognised it as the German word for child. *Oh my God*, I thought, *have the Nazis arrived? Did they get here unknown to us?*

It was then that I decided to run.

The man called after me. 'No! No! No! Please, little girl, don't go away. Help me, please. I beg you.'

I was standing at the lake shore, wondering what to do next, when I saw a beautiful black hunting horse wading through the shallow shingle farther up the shore. It was saddled and kitted out for riding, and its reins dangled out in front of it. I followed it, and it gave a slight snort as I approached, and then it neighed. I came to it slowly, and I soon realised it was in fact a quiet animal, and I took the dangling reins gently. As I gave it a gentle tug, it followed me into the wood.

When I reached the spot where the man lay, I realised he was in a lot of pain. He had dragged himself up into a sitting position, with his back to a tree. Then he spoke in English again.

'You did not run away after all. I thought I frightened you. I'm sorry.' He had very good English, but he spoke with a German accent.

'Are you a Nazi?' I asked.

Then he began to laugh, and as he did so, he tried moving his injured leg, and he cried out in pain.

'Now you see what you did,' he groaned.

'I'm sorry, I didn't mean to—'

'I'm only joking, little girl; you made me laugh, and I'm in great pain.'

'You are a German, aren't you?'

'That is true, I am German. But I am not a Nazi. I am Irish too; my mother was Irish. I hate the bastards, what they have done to my country.'

'I don't know what to do or where to get help,' I said.

'If I can get back up on my horse, I need to get back to the Johnson place. I'm staying there. But I think my ankle is broken.'

'Let me help!'

He was in great pain as he took my hand, and he told me to bring the horse closer to him. Pulling on the reins, he used the strength of the horse to pull himself up, standing on his good leg. Then, holding on to the saddle and using the brute force of his upper arms, he pulled himself high enough to allow his good foot to catch the stirrup, and he rolled onto the horse's back.

'You speak English very well,' I said.

'I have lived in England for many years, but I come from Bavaria. My late wife was English. I went back to Bavaria when she died, but I had to leave Germany and take my grandson with me to safety.'

He was in great pain and was finding it difficult to manage the horse. He leaned forward, holding the animal's mane, and I took the reins to lead him out of the wood. He talked to me a little as we went along, and I asked him many questions.

'What is your name?' I asked.

'Manfred Von Gebler. And you are?'

'Margaret Kerr, from London. I am a refugee too. I stay with Uncle John at Dairy Hill Farm.' Then I thought to myself that if he was a spy, I was giving away too much information.

But then he said, 'Yes, I know Dairy Hill Farm. I'm staying at the Johnson place. Peter Johnson is my brother-in-law.'

'Do you mind if I take you to Uncle John? The Johnsons' might be too far to go for me, and they're expecting me at home shortly. Uncle John will get you home the rest of the way.'

'I will let you do whatever you wish. I am in great pain, and you are so good to help me.'

Now the problem was, how was I going to get him out of here? If I went back to the gate leading to the boreen, I know I couldn't open it, as it was locked with a padlock. I wouldn't be able to break it.

'Is there any way out of here?' I asked.

'If you follow the woodland path, it will take you to a gate, and from that field it will take you to the road.' For someone from another country, he was familiar with the territory. He slumped forward on the horse, wincing with pain, and I knew it was up to me to get him safely home.

I led the animal deeper into the wood, not knowing where I was going. If I got lost in here, it could be next day before I was found. I was a little bit scared, unsure of the geography of the countryside. If what he had said was true, then I was fine.

The foxhound trotted just a short distance ahead of us, his tail dancing as it pointed upwards to the sky. He paid little or no attention to me but seemed to know the path.

Soon I could see daylight through the trees as the edge of the wood came in sight. There *was* a gate, just as the man had said there was, and it was secured with strong bull wire. I knew I could open it, but I had to tether the horse to a post nearby first, as I had to use my two hands.

When I got us all through, I had to tether the horse again. The man pointed across the field to another gate. I followed his directions till we reached that gate, and this time it had a bolt that glided across easily. I led them through. This field went to the road, and there was another gate, which was open. There were no animals in the field, so there was no urgency with the gate. There was a fine crop of green aftergrass there, and I learned later that it was being kept till the new year to allow dry stock to graze.

When I took the horse through on to the road, I turned and closed the gate, just in case any stray animals ventured in there.

It was about a half mile to the avenue. When we came to our farm, Bartley Hegarty had arrived. His bike was at the gate leading into the yard. He was still celebrating Christmas with Uncle John in the parlour. I led the horse into the yard and began shouting for help.

Maureen was the first to carry the news to Uncle John that there was an injured German man on a horse outside.

When Mother heard this, a great anger rose inside her. What was a German doing here in this place? Whatever frenzy or madness gripped her, all that pent-up anger and grief over losing Nana and our home exploded inside, and she saw a chance to seek revenge. Before I knew it, she had gone to the press in the scullery, and she arrived outside pointing Uncle John's rifle at Manfred Von Gebler. The poor man gasped when he saw what she was doing, and I began to scream.

'Mother! Stop, put it away.'

'You Germans killed my mother-in-law, and you destroyed my house, my life, my family. You all deserve to die.' She was shaking with fear, and the gun was directed straight at the man's head.

'I am no Nazi, dear lady. They destroyed my country too. I have lost my beautiful Germany.'

'You are all tarred with one stick, and if I can shoot every German I meet, I will.'

With that, Manfred fainted and slumped gently off the horse. I pulled the animal away and tied it to the gate. Mother was still pointing the gun at him, and I screamed at her to stop.

'He is a refugee, Mother, just like us. Please don't do it.' But Uncle John just stepped quietly into the yard and took hold of the rifle, pointing it away in the other direction.

She released it slowly into his hands, and he said, 'You should have loaded it first Kitty. Look!' He pointed it skyward, and then there was an unmerciful bang as it went off.

The horse jumped and whinnied in fright but could not escape, as I had him well tied to the gate. Sam went running to hide in his little shed, while the foxhound ran to where the horse stood.

'Good God, who loaded that?' he bellowed.

'I did!' shouted Mother, who was in tears.

'Jesus, Kitty, you could have been up for murder.'

'How could you do this, Margaret, bringing this man home?'

She ran into the house, and I could hear her sobbing loudly in the parlour. Her pent-up anger was being released in one great outburst once again, and at the moment, Manfred was the object of her rage. It would not last long indeed, for when she had stopped crying, she returned to the kitchen.

Soon, Manfred was sitting on the chair by the fire, his ankle raised on a stool. Uncle John and Bartley had helped him in from the yard. Maureen was gently washing his forehead with hot water and Dettol, as he had a deep gash in it. She had given him a cup of sweet milky tea, as he was in shock, more from the fright with the gun than the accident in the woods. Uncle John had dispatched Bartley to Johnsons' to get Peter to come with his car and take the man to hospital.

'Sure, isn't he the poor German man who had to flee his country,' said Maureen. 'He had to leave everything behind him as well.'

'I am so sorry to intrude on you kind people,' he said.

'Will you whisht, man,' said Martha. 'You're safe now.'

'She's a good little lady. She saved my life,' he said, shaking his finger kindly at me. Uncle John gave me a hug and sat me on his knee.

'Nothing exciting ever happened around here, Margaret, until you came,' he laughed.

Mother was sitting at the end of the table, drinking a cup of tea to calm her nerves.

'I am so sorry for that outburst. I could have killed you. Please forgive me,' she sobbed.

'We are all truly angry people. I left Germany, my country, too. I took my grandson to stay with my brother-in-law, Peter Johnson. Then the Irish government put me in prison for a while; they thought I was a spy. But Peter fixed everything up, and I am safe here, and so is my grandson.'

'I really am so sorry too,' said Mother. 'We lost everything in the blitz, and my mother-in-law was killed. I have kept all that anger inside me, and you were the one who had to suffer. Please forgive me.'

The man didn't answer, and I knew he was in great pain with his leg. He lay back and rested, and it wasn't long before we heard the engine of a car rev at the back door.

Immediately, a blond-haired boy of about thirteen bursts in, shouting, 'Grossvater! Grossvater! Where is he?'

Then he began shouting something in German and shaking Manfred. The old man looked up at him and said, 'Es ist in ordnung, mein Junge,' which I later discovered meant *It's all right, my boy*. As he said it, he gently stroked the boy's golden curls.

When the boy calmed down, he turned to all present and said, 'Forgive me, good people, for shouting. I thought my grandfather was dying. I can see he has been well taken care of.' He had perfect English. There was a hint of an English accent to it as well.

Then Peter stood in the doorway, wearing knee-breeches and a tweed coat and cap. Jokingly, he said, 'I say he has taken refuge in the house of Lazarus.'

He was probably in his midfifties. When he took off his cap, I could see he was going bald. His hair was longer on one side, and it was trained across the top of his head to hide the bald patch, giving the impression that he had more hair on top than he really did.

'Good God, does the thieving landlord seek refuge in my house as well?' said Uncle John.

'Still living back in the days of the land wars, John, I see,' said Peter, with a smirk on his face. I gathered from the tone of their voices that this was a way of life with the two of them, rather than a feeling of hatred.

'Someday, some well-deserving people will get *your* place,' said Uncle John.

'Do you ever give up, John Costello? This is the 1904s, and we have a greater enemy on our doorstep.'

'He's too near, as far as I'm concerned,' laughed Uncle John, winking at me. I didn't really know what he meant by that, but later I realised he was referring to Peter as his enemy.

'If Hitler came up this avenue, John, I suppose you'd give him refuge too?'

'Yeah, but he might get to your place first, and see the fine house and all that land. So he would have no need to go any further.'

In an angry outburst, Maureen put a stop to their charade. 'Will you stop, for heaven's sake? Go and help this poor man. Can't you see he's in great pain? Such talk I never heard from two grown men, and it the Christmas season. You ought to be ashamed of yourselves.'

The three men carried Manfred out to the car. They left him lying on the back seat and closed the door. His grandson got in beside him and smiled out at me when he saw me standing at the door. Then Bartley caught the foxhound and deposited him in the boot of the car. The animal was quiet and made not the slightest whimper when he was plunged into the darkness.

'By the way,' said Peter, 'is this the young lady who saved my brother-in-law today?' He approached me, and stooping down on one knee, he took my hand and kissed it. I blushed. It was something I had seen only in the movies, where men in long tails and top hats kissed beautiful ladies wearing fine dresses and long white gloves.

'Listen, my dear little girl,' he said softly, 'if you ever need any help, just give me a call. I mean that. It is a very special thing you did today.'

'Thank you, sir,' I answered. Mother smiled approvingly and held my hand.

'Farewell, everyone, and thank you,' he shouted, just like a theatre actor making his final exit.

But Uncle John called after him. 'By the way, I see you haven't used up all the gallons of petrol you've been storing in that big shed up at your place. If the army knew that, they'd be after you.'

'I'll come to you for advice when they do,' Peter laughed. 'I'm sure the black marketeer will supply you with tobacco the same way he supplied me with petrol.'

Both men laughed, and the exhaust fumes from the car filled the air with pungent smoke as it turned and headed out the avenue. Bartley followed them on his bike, leading the horse by the reins. As the bike moved on, the horse trotted beside him, and soon the place was quiet again.

I turned to Uncle John. 'Do you speak to him like that all the time?'

'It's a way of life, girl. I've been speaking like that to him ever since he was knee-high to a grasshopper. We have never shaken hands or agreed with one another, and I suppose I never will. It's something we both must live with, as well as agree to differ too.'

'You should not be so cruel to him. He's a nice man.'

'Oh, you're just standing up for him because he spoke nice and cooed to you and kissed your hand,' he joked.

'I am not!' I protested. 'I just like him, that's all.'

'Anyway, so much is happening so quick around here and it's been exciting for us all, I think we still have a big lump of a goose to tackle and leave nothing but the bones. Could you see that Bartley Hegarty was starving and he'll eat us out of house and home when he gets back?'

*****

A few days later, I had a visitor. It was Manfred Von Gebler's grandson. He cycled up the avenue, and taking his cap off, he told Mother his name. Mother knew who he was, but he introduced himself to be polite. She brought him in, and Uncle John welcomed him. He spoke in a quiet tone, and he was a perfect gentleman. It was far easier to understand his English than his grandfather's, and he sat on the soft chair on one side of the parlour fire. I sat on the other one.

I was uncomfortable. I had never spoken to a boy of his age before. He had a nice soft face, and his skin was slightly pale in colour. Mother sat with us and listened as she knitted. Knitting was helping her to get strength back in her arm.

Uncle John was away out in one of the sheds, mending some pieces of harness, while the aunts were busy cutting Christmas cake and opening another bottle of red lemonade for our guest.

'I came to thank you for saving my grandfather's life. It means so much to me, you know.'

'I just happened to find him,' I said modestly. 'How is he now?'

'He is in hospital. He will be fine. His ankle is badly broken, and it will take a long while for it to set.'

'At least he will make a full recovery,' said Mother. 'He is lucky he wasn't killed off that horse.'

'You see, my grandfather is all I've got now. My father and mother made us leave Germany just before the war. They were to follow us later, but it was too late; they could not get out. When they did not support Hitler, they were taken away. Mother is Peter Johnson's sister. My parents met in England, but they lived for some years here.'

'I see now why you're English is so good,' said Mother.

'You see, Papa would not side with the Nazis, and they made it difficult for him. I do not know if they are alive or dead.'

'I'm so sorry,' said Mother. 'And I nearly killed your poor grandfather. How will you ever forgive me?'

'Do not worry, dear lady; we all have a lot to be angry about. I miss my parents very much, but I do not cry. I was made to join Hitler's youth movement. It was cruel, and they tell you that German boys never cry. Papa stopped me from going to them and made Grandfather take me out by train one night. I was halfway to Ireland before I knew it.'

'Do you ever want to go back?' asked Mother.

'I want to return to the Germany my papa and my grandfather knew. It's a very beautiful country, and it makes me sad to hear about the terrible things that are happening there, and what is happening all over Europe. Every summer there was a festival in our village, and Papa could dance. They all dressed in their lederhosen, and they sang and danced. The men would drink their beer, and everyone was very happy. The mountains were alive with summer, and it was beautiful. It was a lovely time, just coming into the autumn, and the harvest ready to be saved. Then it all changed. The nightmare began, and here I am, in a strange country.'

'Please God you will return there again someday,' said Mother, 'and the mountains will still be there, as beautiful as ever.'

He sipped some lemonade from his glass and said nothing. I knew he too was feeling lonely for the places he loved and the childhood and memories that had been snatched away from him by war. Then Maureen shoved a plate of Christmas cake under his nose, and he was very polite, taking a small piece.

'Why don't you come to visit us more?' asked Mother.

'I must return to school in Dublin tomorrow, and I will not be back till Easter. Grandfather said that I must study hard; that whenever there's a new Germany, it will need young, well-educated people to build it up again. That is what I want for my homeland. Peter Johnson has given us refuge. Grandfather helps him with the horses for a small wage, and he pays for my education as well. He is such a kind and generous uncle.'

When he had finished eating, he suddenly excused himself and thanked us again for saving his grandfather's life. Turning to Mother, he said, 'If the Nazis do ever come, dear lady, please make sure to have more than one gun ready.'

Mother laughed and gave him a hug.

Then, turning to me, he said, 'Will you walk with me to the gate, Margaret?'

I looked at Mother in wild surprise. I had never walked with a boy before, let alone talked with one. Mother knew I was taken aback by this request. Looking at me in amusement, she said, 'It is quite all right to walk with this young man. He won't bite. You can take a stroll down the avenue if you wish.'

As he was leaving, Mother said, 'I'm sorry, I have forgotten what your name is again.'

'It's Fritz,' he answered.

'My name is Kitty,' she replied. 'These kind ladies are Maureen and Martha, and the man of the house, his name is John.'

'Thank you very much, Kitty,' he said, and putting on his cap, he took his bicycle, which had been resting by the wall. Sam wagged his tail, and Fritz rubbed the top of his head.

I walked slowly down the avenue, and it was then that the snow began to fall. He stopped in his tracks and watched the first flakes flitter and flow gently to the ground.

'It snows at Christmas at home,' he said, 'and we go skiing up in the mountains.'

'I'd love to ski. Someday I will get you to teach me to ski.'

'Whenever the war is over, you must come to Germany, and I'll teach you. I owe a lot to you for saving my grandfather.'

'I only found him by accident.'

'I know that, but you *did* find him, and for a very young girl, you were brave, and you were not afraid to help him. I will never forget that of you.'

I knew that day that I had made another friend. Over the next few years, Fritz was to become a special part of my life, and I'd learn more about his parents and their links with Ireland.

By the time we reached the end of the avenue, the snow was quickly covering the ground, and wherever we walked, we made tracks everywhere. I leaned against one of the broken-down gates and watched him go. He waved from the corner, and all that remained were the snakelike tracks the bicycle wheels left on the thin carpet of snow.

Part 4
Buttermilk and Butter Cake

Chapter 8

The Christmas season ended, and I went back to school, cycling on dark mornings on the rickety gravel road, trying to avoid potholes as well as fresh cowpats in places where farmers had to take their animals back and forth each day to their fields.

When I reached the school the first morning, I discovered that Sheila had not returned after Christmas. No one knew anything about her. The girls in my class were all talk about what they'd done during the festive season, and this was what occupied us as we sat on benches in the shelter, as it was raining heavily. Some had heard about me rescuing Manfred Von Gebler near the lake shore and wanted to know all about it.

Carmel Daly, who abandoned the company of her own class, decided to listen to ours. I thought it strange that this was a regular occurrence; she was being excluded by the other girls in her class. It didn't seem to bother her, as she spent most of her time playing with all the girls in fourth class. She too listened carefully when my friends asked me about Manfred.

Then, out of the blue, she spoke up.

'Nobody asked me where I was.'

All the girls turned to her, as if drawn by a magnet, and I was left standing alone.

It turned out Carmel had gone to Dublin during the Christmas season and had been to the Theatre Royal. Not alone that, she'd gone to the cinema and seen Clark Gable.

'Clark Gable!' some of them sighed.

'You saw him in the street!'

'No, you silly girl. I saw him in *Gone with the Wind*.'

'What's *Gone with the Wind*?' asked one girl. 'Is it about a storm?'

'Really, you provincials are so ignorant of the real world. I have to teach you so much.'

My thinking about Carmel was that she looked down on everyone, which was something her classmates couldn't handle, and as a result she found herself out on a limb. Nobody wanted to be friends with her.

Then she gave a rather sly sort of smile and said, 'Now gather round, and I will tell you all about it. Miss Prim and Proper over there can tell you all about her Nazi friends later, if she wishes.'

Why had she said this? I couldn't understand why she was so mean. She gave me a cynical smile, and I sat at the other end of the bench, staring at the large raindrops falling on the puddles in the schoolyard. My thoughts were on Sheila. I hadn't seen her since before Christmas. Maybe I should have gone to see her for the New Year. It was such a pity that more of her classmates didn't go to see her, knowing that she wasn't very well. Again, it was all down to ignorance and fear, which kept everyone away.

As I gathered my coat around me to keep me warm, the girls came flocking back, as *Gone with the Wind* was alien to their world. Their minds were fixed on Fritz. He was somebody real. He was a German.

'Did he wear a uniform?'

'Was he cross looking?'

'Did he speak any English?'

I laughed with them and explained his story to them. Carmel was none too pleased and sat some distance away, listening. I didn't realise she was going to cause trouble once again.

*****

Billy Bryce came out to meet me when I went to collect my bike from the shed. He first wished me a happy New Year. Fintan had called to him on Christmas morning and invited him to join the family for dinner. There was so little they had, and yet they were ready to share with others. It seemed, then, that Billy would have had no Christmas dinner if it hadn't been for his brother Fintan.

'Sheila told me that if I saw you, she wants to see you.'

'Is she still ill?' I asked.

'She has her good days, but she's lonely. None of her friends call to see her.'

'I'll call on my way home,' I said.

'Good girl! I knew you would.'

I left the village as quickly as I could and made my way to their little cottage. The heavy rain had cleared, and a blue sky peered through breaking clouds. The road was very wet, and my legs were spattered with splashes from the puddles.

The gate was closed, and Mrs Bryce could see me through the kitchen window. She came running to meet me with open arms, showering blessings of thanksgiving on me for being an angel of mercy at Christmas. Sheila was sitting on an armchair by the fire. She was alone. Mrs Bryce was frying a big pan of sliced potatoes on the open fire. She had mixed onions through them, and the smell was delicious.

'Look!' said Sheila. 'I'm still wearing it.' She was talking about the mother-of-pearl pendant I'd given her at Christmas.

'It looks really good on you.'

'I missed you. I thought I'd see you during the Christmas.'

'I'm sorry, but so much happened that the time just slipped by.' Then I told her about the wren-boys, Fritz, and the rescue of Manfred from the lake shore.

She was so excited by it all that I could see colour coming back into her cheeks again.

'I'd love to be you,' she sighed. Then she began to cry.

'Now, don't start doing that, little one,' said her mother. 'I want you to get well again.'

'But I'm not getting well, Mammy.'

'When the spring days come after the feast of S. Brigid, and it's only a few weeks away, you'll be much stronger. Wait till you see. While Margaret is here now, I want you to eat a bit and make you strong again.'

I put my arm around her shoulder, and I could feel her shoulder blades through her thin flesh.

'I didn't mean to upset you,' I said. 'I'll go if you want me to.'

'Please don't go,' she pleaded through her tears, holding on to my coat. 'It's just that your life is just one great big adventure.'

'We can have adventures together,' I said, 'if you try harder and eat better.'

'Spring is so far away,' she said.

'It's only a few weeks, and I want you back beside me. I need someone to keep Carmel Daly away. She is such a snob, you know.'

Then I told her about Clark Gable, and how the other girls had left Carmel and wanted to know all about Fritz.

After a few more laughs, she went silent, and I said, 'I really want you to try hard and get your strength back. There is a reason I tell you this.'

'What's that?'

'Remember I told you I'd take you to the lake some fine day when spring comes?'

'Oh, I'd really love that.'

'I want you to promise me.'

'I promise!'

'I will take you there at Easter, if I haven't returned to England.'

'Please don't go before that,' she said. 'I remember last summer, Daddy took us all on a picnic one day, and we sat near your uncle John's boathouse. There were swans on the water. It was a breezy day, and the sun was shining, and there were lovely white clouds floating across. I lay down on the ground and looked up. I felt I wanted to float away on a cloud and see the world. I wanted to look down on the village, and then the town, and away across the Irish Sea. I didn't want it to stop. I wanted it to go on forever and ever. I wish I could do that again.'

'I want you to promise me that come St Brigid's Day, you will be back at school, and I promise *you* that we will go to the lake together at Easter.'

She promised me, once again, that she would do her level best.

Then her mother put a plate of fried potatoes and onions in front of her, and I left her eating.

Mrs Bryce came to the gate with me, and taking my hand, she said, 'You know, little girl, that you have a heart as good as any Costello. The blessings of God on you.'

I waved goodbye to her and headed home. Night was falling fast. Uncle John was waiting at the avenue gate for me. He'd begun to worry, as I was a little on the late side. I told him where I'd been, and he understood.

While he was waiting for me, he'd been taking down the old, battered gates. I knew he was thinking of getting them repaired at some stage, maybe when the Emergency was over. Now such work would not get priority, but he was thinking ahead to the spring and another year of sowing and harvesting. The gates were a bit of an eyesore now, and he was taking them down to put in the shed.

*****

Next day during Irish class, Reverend Mother entered. She had both her hands tucked into the arms of her habit, and when she glanced across her glasses, we knew there was trouble. She stood behind Sister Bernadette's desk and stared at all of us. We wondered what was going to happen next.

'Would Margaret Kerr please stand up.'

My legs went to jelly, and I did as she asked. She floated over to my desk and stood looking down at me.

'Would you go and wait outside my office door?'

'Yes, Sister,' I answered, and left quietly.

Five minutes later she emerged from the classroom. Taking a bundle of keys from inside her habit, she opened the door. She told me to enter and stand facing her desk. She sat herself down and stared at me over the top of her glasses.

'When you came to this school, young lady, I thought you were very brave, having experienced the war and all its horrors. I admired you for it, even though I have had to take you in hand and show you that life is quite a serious place. Not alone that, I have said before that you are a lucky girl to be born a Catholic, but unfortunately, your father is not so lucky, in that he will not have the privilege of going to heaven.'

'Reverend Mother, my father is a good Christian,' I exclaimed, but she was back just as quick with an answer.

'That may be, child, but he is not a good Catholic, and only Catholics can enter heaven. Now let that be the end of it. I pray every day that he will see things our way and that he will become a Catholic, for your sake and your mother's. But that is not the reason I brought you down here. It is another matter altogether. In fact, it is quite a serious one, and if the proper authorities got to hear about it, it could put you and your family in danger.'

I hadn't a clue what she was talking about, and I began to shiver with fright. She got up from her desk and stood looking out the window for a few moments. Then, turning around, she said, 'It has come to my notice that you are consorting with the enemy and helping the Nazis.'

'You mean Manfred Von Gebler,' I said.

'Yes, well, that's what he calls himself, anyway.'

'He is a refugee, and so is his grandson. They are staying with Peter Johnson.'

'Yes indeed. Another Nazi, if you ask me, giving refuge to people like that. Why, not that many years ago, his ancestors before him were throwing innocent people out of their homes and burning their houses to make way for fat cattle in their fields. If he isn't a Nazi, then nobody is. Someday they will murder us all in our beds.'

'Mr Von Gebler's son and daughter-in-law are in prison in Germany because they wouldn't support Hitler. Manfred escaped with his grandson and is working at Peter Johnson's place. Peter's sister is married to Mr Von Gebler's son. They are staying there till the war is over.'

'You seem to know a lot about them, then. Where did you hear all this?'

'Fritz told me.'

'And who is Fritz, then?'

'He's Manfred's grandson.'

'And fraternizing with young boys too, I see. What will your mother say?'

'Sister, please stop this. Please!' I burst into tears and wanted to run from the room. But I wasn't going to let her get the satisfaction of seeing me doing it.

'Oh, crocodile tears, I see! Now you listen to me, young lady. I order you to keep away from them. They are a bad influence on you as well as the innocent young girls of the village. Some of them are afraid to sleep at night now.'

I knew there and then that *some of them* was in fact Carmel Daly and no one else. It was her fault for saying such things.

'Now, you must know also that it is quite improper for a young lady like you to walk down the road with a boy. There might be an excuse for any local innocent lad from the area, but if that boy is a German, well, that is something else. Someday he will draw out a gun and shoot you or murder you all in your sleep.'

'But Mother said that it is all right for me to do so,' I sobbed.

'Now you see, they are beginning to have an influence on her as well.'

Rather than argue with her anymore, I decided that enough was enough. I left the office quietly, and I wanted to run away. But if I did that, I might be considered a coward. I returned to class wondering what to do about the whole thing.

I was reluctant to eat my dinner, and Mother wondered why. She knew there was something wrong.

I could cope with Reverend Mother condemning my father to hell. I had resigned myself to the fact that she wasn't God and was in no position to pass judgement on others. But her Nazi invasion outburst was the last straw.

When I told Mother what had happened, she broke into convulsions laughing, as did the aunts, who were pottering around as usual. When Uncle John was told the story, he said nothing, but lit his pipe and laughed silently to himself, sending the usual cloud of smoke to the ceiling. Then he declared, 'You know what, wouldn't it look great if the whole lot of us went up to the convent door, pulled the bell, and demanded to see the Reverend Mother? Then when she appeared, we'd just step forward together, raise our hands in salute in front of us, and shout at the top of our voices, "Heil Hitler!" That would put the wind up her sails, now, wouldn't it?'

I went to bed with a vision of Reverend Mother fainting on the steps of the convent door. But that wasn't the end of the matter.

*****

It happened the next day. There was a knock on the classroom door, and one of the pupils answered it. It was one of the girls from sixth class, and she stood at Sister Bernadette's desk.

'Excuse me, Sister,' she said, 'but Reverend Mother wants Margaret Kerr in her office.'

All eyes focused on me, and this time I wondered what was bothering her. She was hardly going to throw it all back at me again about my father and making friends with the Von Geblers.

I knocked gently on the office door, which was open just a crack, and she told me to enter. My heart began to pound with fright when I saw who was there. It was Father O'Reilly.

'You may close the door, child,' she said softly, 'and you may stand in front of my desk. Now, stand still and put your hands behind your back.'

She spoke to the priest immediately, explaining about my background, my family, Uncle John, my mother, and all those who lived at Dairy Hill.

Reverend Mother had come to the convent about one year before, having been requested to supervise and govern the sisters following the death of Mother Bernardine. She was totally unaware that Father O'Reilly knew the ins and outs of most families in the community, and there was a smirk on his face as she spoke.

She gave an account of our encounter with the Blitz in London and our passage to Ireland to escape the war. She left no stone unturned, and she had my every movement since my arrival on the tip of her tongue, ending with the rescue of Manfred Von Gebler at the lake shore and how we, the residents of Dairy Hill, were consorting with the enemy.

The priest wore a wry smile through this, and I didn't have any fear or worry inside me. I could tell he didn't view the case in the same light as Reverend Mother.

'I must say, that's a remarkable story indeed, and I want to thank you, Reverend Mother, for telling me all about this little girl.'

I knew deep down that he knew every detail of our adventures over the past few months. There were no secrets in the little parishes of Ireland, and whatever news there was that was out of the ordinary, it spread quicker than any newspaper or radio broadcast.

He stood up from where he was sitting and said, 'Indeed, I must shake her hand too, for all the good things she has done.'

He gave my hand a good, warm-hearted shake and sat down again.

'Sorry, what is your name again, little girl?' he asked.

'Margaret Kerr, Father.'

'Well, Margaret, I'd say you're tired standing there like that. Why don't you sit down and rest the auld bones?' I glanced over at Reverend Mother, and she indicated with her eyes peering over her glasses that I should do what the priest had asked. I sat down on a high-backed chair with a soft red velvet seat, and I could feel my legs were shaking still. But after a minute or two, I began to relax.

'Excuse me, Father, but what is the meaning of this?' Reverend Mother exclaimed.

'Is there something wrong, Reverend Mother?' he asked.

'I asked you in here to talk to this young lady about the virtues of keeping good company, as well as keeping the enemy from the gate.'

'What enemy are you talking about?' he asked abruptly, raising his voice a little.

'Nazis!' she answered crossly. 'Can't you see they are everywhere? That German man and his grandson, staying with that Nazi supporter Johnson – God only knows what is happening up there at that place!'

'Tell me this and tell me no more, where are you getting your information from? Do you mean that kind gentleman we see riding Johnson's horses? He's working there, and he's not interfering with any person. He is a refugee too, from the war.'

'We must be so careful, Father—'

He stopped her in her tracks. Pointing a finger at her, he said, 'Well, to put you at ease, Reverend Mother, Manfred Von Gebler sits in the third seat from the front on the men's side of the church every Sunday morning and goes to Holy Communion. He's a good Christian and a good Catholic. You're doing the man a grave injustice by spreading stories about him.'

'Excuse me, Father, I wouldn't do such an unchristian thing.'

'Think about it, Reverend Mother. If you were a good Christian, you'd be a little bit more charitable towards this little girl, and the other refugees from the war. This little girl here is the unsung hero of the village, and I cannot allow you treat her in this way.'

He then turned to me and said, 'Margaret, if John Costello and his two generous and good-hearted sisters knew you were being treated like this, and they such good Christian people, they'd be very sad indeed.'

'You see, Father, I didn't know—'

'You didn't know,' he interrupted, raising his voice. 'Why didn't you know? Wherever you're getting your information from is not correct, and in these sad times, we must be careful how we spread rumour and innuendo. I think this little girl deserves an apology for being treated like this.'

'Are you here to pass judgement on *me* and my work in this parish, Father, or who gave you authority to do so?'

'If you cannot accept my advice, then I could always refer you to the bishop.'

She stared him straight in the face, and without even the slightest expression of fright or surprise, she stood up, came over to where I sat, and took my hand.

'Margaret Kerr,' she said softly, 'please accept my apology for treating you in this way. I'm sorry, and I humbly beg your forgiveness. All I can do for you is pray for your family's safety, and that your father will return home to you. His welfare is in God's hands, and I'll pray for him every day.'

'Thank you, Reverend Mother, but you didn't have to do that.'

'It's done, child, and it would be unchristian of me not to do so.' Then, turning to the priest, she begged to be excused and left the room.

I was alone with him in the parlour, and he sat down opposite me in Reverend Mother's chair, leaning on her desk. Then he sat back and folded his hands behind his head with his arms bent in the shape of an angel's wings. He said nothing for a few moments, and then he spoke.

'You see, I know what you have been up to in these parts.' He sighed. 'And I must say that I never saw as happy a family as the Bryces during the Christmas season. I believe you were the angel that brought Christmas to their door.'

'It wasn't completely my idea, Father; it was Uncle John and Maureen and Martha as well as Mother.'

'I'm not surprised,' he laughed. 'Now, any child who is so kind-hearted could never have a sin on her soul. Didn't I really put the wind up on poor Reverend Mother?'

'You shouldn't have done that, Father.'

'Don't worry about her; she's as tough as auld boots. It will take more than that to furl that lady. In her own odd way, she's doing her best, but she often gets things wrong. Now, not a word to anyone, do you hear? Reverend

Mother has a job to do too, and it wouldn't do to have her a subject of ridicule in the parish.'

'Yes, Father, and thank you for believing me,' I replied.

Changing the subject, he said, 'By the way, tell John Costello that there's a card game in Hennigans next Friday night, if he's interested.'

'I will, Father,' I replied. 'Now may I be excused?'

He gave me a nod and a wink, and I left. As I went out the door, he was searching in a drawer in the desk, saying quietly to himself, 'Now where does she keep those peppermints?'

*****

That finished Reverend Mother's tormenting of me. I heard some time later that she had gone to visit Manfred Von Gebler and apologised to him as well as Peter Johnson. She knew that people in the parish were talking, and it was best to clear the air.

Peter Johnson was amused at the apology. It was the first time that a nun from the convent had ever put a foot inside his door. She too would become a friend of the family, and Peter even supported the convent when there was need to raise funds for improvements there.

Every morning when I went into school, Reverend Mother spoke to me politely if she was standing at the door, and I did likewise.

But there was another mystery I wished to solve. I wanted to get inside Carmel Daly's head and bring her along. I had begun to realise that she was in fact a very lonely girl.

But it would take a long time before I managed that.

Chapter 9

Slowly, the days of winter passed, and the evenings began to grow a cock-step longer every day. I found myself out on the farm with Uncle John till after six o'clock, feeding the calf and giving fodder to the rest of the animals. Grass was getting scarce in the fields, and the cattle were calling at dusk to be fed with hay, which was thrown across the fence into the field to them. Minnie was no longer moaning in the mornings, as she was now able to eat some hay and wasn't as hungry as she used to be. She was growing fast, and Uncle John said he would let her out into the haggard after St Brigid's Day. Soon three other calves would arrive, and they too would need to be fed.

The first of them to arrive was a bull calf that I christened Danny, but Uncle John said he'd be fattened and sold at the fair in about two years' time. I gave the calf that name because Uncle John was always humming a song called 'The 'Derry Air', which Mother said was also called 'Danny Boy'.

In the evening time, Uncle John encouraged me to help him milk a cow, and after a few attempts, I began to master it. But to make it easier for me, I was given Snowdrop. She was a quiet animal, and she'd stand in the manger chewing her cud while I was milking her. She was snow white, just like the snowdrop, the first flower of spring. I'd always believed that spring didn't begin until the first of March, but Martha thought differently.

'The old people, those who went before us, always said that spring began the day we celebrated the Feast of St Brigid.'

On the eve of the saint's feast, she went down the fields with me, and she brought a great big sheep shears with her. It was a dangerous-looking thing. For all the world it looked like a giant scissors with large blades.

I carried a small sack for her, and she wanted me to help her gather rushes in a field known as *the bottoms*. It was wet and boggy and not well drained. It was pock-marked with cattle tracks that were filled with water, and you had to take careful steps, as you could easily step out of your

Wellington if it got bogged down in the mud. But Martha knew the safe places to go, and she cautiously brought me with her.

'Now look for the lush green rushes, not the thin, spindly, pale-green ones. They are no good for weaving into breedoges.'

'What are they?' I asked.

'I will show you tonight when I will teach you how to make one. Let us not delay, as I want to beat the fast-falling darkness, and there's also a fog rising. I don't want to end up on a fairy's pass and get lost out in the fields for the night.'

A shiver ran down my spine as she said this, and it scared me a little. I would make sure to ask her later what this was all about.

To cap it all, there was a sharp yelping sound coming from across the field towards the lake. It scared me a little, as it came to my hearing out of the fog and the darkening light.

'Don't worry, child, it's not a banshee.'

'A banshee! What is that? These fields are getting stranger and stranger.'

'Another story for another time. It's just a fox calling. It's one of the sounds of the country.'

Then she began cutting the thick green rushes and threw them in bunches into the bag. I held it for her, which made it easier for her to gather them.

'Many hands make light work,' she said.

It didn't take long to gather the rushes, and soon we were making our way home. The light from the kitchen was like a dark star in the distance, but it showed the way home for us. I didn't want to be out in the darkness, not knowing where to go.

The kitchen was warm when we got home. The chores were nearly done, and Uncle John had milked Snowdrop for me. It was nice to be in out of the dark foggy January night.

*****

When the kitchen was cleaned up after tea and after the rosary had been said, Martha and Maureen began to make their breedoges, or St Brigid's crosses. I didn't realise what they were till the aunts began making them.

I was not happy when I saw the result. It looked like a swastika, but Martha rebuked me and told me it was the sacred emblem of one of the greatest of Irish saints. Then Maureen's story began.

'Brigid was one of us. She was of the country, just like us. She came from County Louth, and she built her monastery in Kildare. She went to the king of Leinster one day and asked him for a piece of land to build her monastery on. The king asked her how much land she needed, and she told him that all she wanted was as much as her cloak could cover. She spread it outward, and a miracle happened. It began to grow and spread until it covered the plains of Kildare. The king, being a noble man, was obliged, then, to keep his promise.'

'Is this true?' I asked.

'Believe what you want to believe,' said Maureen. 'The old people would swear by it.'

The aunts wove the crosses and tied them with thin twine. They then trimmed the ends and left them in a row on the table. Then Martha continued with another story.

'One day, Brigid went to visit an old man she knew. He was a pagan and did not believe in God. When she got to his little house, she found the man in his bed, and he was dying. He was afraid of dying, but Brigid began to tell him about Jesus and how he died on the cross to save our souls. As she spoke to him, she picked up rushes, which had covered the floor, and began weaving them the way we are doing it now, and she explained to him how Jesus was nailed to the cross and had great suffering. The old man died in peace, having heard about Jesus.'

I sat and listened to the aunts as they worked and told stories. Mother was quiet. She too was reliving those tales, which they had told her years before. Then, when I turned around to look at her, Mother was making the crosses as well.

'May I make one?' I asked.

'Let me show you,' said Mother. So I spent the rest of the evening making crosses, and soon there was a heap of them on the table.

'What are you going to do with them all?' I asked.

'We are going to give them to all the neighbours,' said Maureen, 'and there will be one hung at the altar in each house. And if they have not got an altar, they will hang one on the back of a picture. The breedoges will protect the home from fire. By the end of the year, they turn brown and begin to fall apart, so we make new ones for the Feast of Brigid.'

I wasn't finished asking questions, and I had a few more to ask before I went to bed.

'Aunt Martha, what is a fairy's pass?'

'I knew I had something else to tell you. I nearly forgot.'

She took up the poker and stirred the coals in the fireplace. Pulling the crane around, she hung a kettle of water to boil over the flames so I could have a cup of tea before bed. Then she answered my question.

'It is dangerous to be out in the fields at night. A person can be led astray in the darkness, especially if there is fog. You can forget where you're going. I know of a man who was lost one night, and he kept arriving at this road. He knew he was lost and had found a fairy's pass. He could not get onto this road, as there was a high ditch and he could not cross it. He kept walking and could not get out of the field. After a few hours, he grew weary, and he wanted to die. That is how he felt. A great hunger and tiredness came over him. He sat down on a stone and began to pray. Then, soon, he could see a light in the distance, and he followed it. When he got close to the light, he called out, and a voice answered him. It was his neighbour, who came searching for him when his wife raised the alarm. When he reached the neighbour, whatever spell the night had on him went away, and he knew how to get home. The road he kept coming to was the river, and he was lucky he could not cross it.'

Then the kettle began to boil, and Maureen made tea. Mother told me to hurry with my tea, as it was time for bed. But I had one more question to be answered.

'Aunt Martha, what is a banshee?'

'She is a fairy woman. She foretells of a death in a family. She comes crying in the night, and if you hear her, you know that someone close to you, someone you cherish, has died. If you do not know then whether they have died or not, you will find out in a very short while.'

'Have you ever heard her?'

'I did,' said Maureen. 'I heard her the night before your grandad died on the lake many years ago.'

This statement took Mother by surprise, and she scolded Maureen for saying it. 'Will you stop that now, Maureen, and don't be giving us a fright? You never told *me* that, you know, and after all these years you come out with it now.'

'It was a long time ago, and I couldn't tell you then, but you should know and so should Margaret. She has a very curious mind, and she should know these things. Now don't be upsetting yourself; a little knowledge won't go astray.'

Mother said no more, but Martha, who had paid little or no attention to the conversation, continued with her knowledge of the banshee.

'If you can see the banshee, she is an old woman dressed in black, with exceptionally long hair, a pale, gaunt face, and dark-red eyes. As she wails or keens over the person who is dead or dying, she combs her hair. My father told me about a friend of his who had a few people over to his little house one winter night to play cards, and when they were playing late into the night, a banshee began wailing and crying at the window. One brave man opened the window, and lo and behold, he snatched the comb out of her hand. As quick as he did, her wailing and crying became a frenzy of screaming, and there was a fear that she would knock the little house down. One of his friends told him to give it back, and just as he was about to do it, the man of the house roared at him to stop. He gave him the tongs from the fire and told him to hold it with the tongs and carefully hand it to her. The man did as he was asked, and the banshee snatched it, disappearing into the night, wailing and screaming across the bogs. When they looked at the tongs, the man had only half of it left in his hands.'

I could feel myself shiver as she said this, and as she ended her story, she said, 'And you can write under that.'

'You have never changed, Martha,' said Mother. 'So full of your stories, even after all these years.'

When I got my mug of weak milky tea and a slice of currant bread and butter, I went to bed. The stories of Brigid, the fairy's pass, and the banshee were still on my mind, as was my father. I don't think I was long asleep when my dreams made me hear a banshee. It scared the living daylights out of me, and my world changed to a letter coming from the postman with bad news about Father. Mother was reading it, and she began weeping and crying. Father was dead.

I woke in a cold sweat, crying out, and Mother was there, comforting me.

'It's only a nightmare,' she said. 'What's the matter?'

'I could hear a banshee, and we got bad news about Father. You were crying, and I began to scream.'

'I don't know what I will do with those two ladies and their stories. They're just filling your head with nonsense. Now go to sleep and forget about all those silly banshees.'

I fell asleep, but as the months and years rolled on, I was to be captivated more and more by Martha and Maureen as they told their stories.

*****

The spring days progressed slowly and brightened. There was hope in the air, and snowdrops laughed at me each evening as I cycled up the avenue from the road. They grew on each side on the grass verge. I did not delay in eating my dinner and doing my homework, as I felt very important being able to help with the chores outside. I knew when I could hear the cows lowing at the field gate above the haggard that Snowdrop and her three other friends were waiting to be milked.

Uncle John spent quite a lot of time down the fields, mending ditches and leaving fences secured for the coming season. When he saw I had the cows in, tied in their mangers and eating a bounty of hay, he'd shove his hat back on his head and say, 'I don't know how I ever managed without you, Margaret.'

I took a white enamel bucket and sat on a little stool to milk Snowdrop. As each milking began, it was a noisy affair, with the rattle of milk in the pail, but after a few minutes, when it began to fill, a great white froth gathered on the top, just like a pint of stout, and the sound of the milk grew almost to a silence as it hit the pure white froth below.

Uncle John sat next to me and began to sing.

I'll take you home again, Kathleen
Across the ocean wild and wide
To where your heart has ever been
Since first you were my bonny bride . . .

He maintained that singing to the cows soothed them, helping them to relax and release their udders full of milk. In fact, experience had told him that they gave a greater and richer supply of creamy milk.

When I was finished, I presented the bucket to Maureen in the scullery, and she strained it through a strainer with two or three layers of muslin to clean the milk. She then set aside so much for the house and so much for the calves. The milk sat and cooled in a large crock, and after a few hours, when the cream came to the surface, she skimmed it and transferred it to another bowl. She gathered it morning and night, and when the large bowl or crock was full, it was time to make butter.

The churn was brought onto the kitchen table, and the first thing she did was scald the inside with boiling water and place a bucket on a chair under the churn. She pulled a little wooden stopper at the bottom and caught the water, which was then thrown out. There were little wooden paddles as well, which were used to shape the butter, and they too were scalded and placed to one side. Then she filled the churn with the sour cream, and when all was ready, the churning began.

We took turns at turning the handle. This made the separator inside turn like a water mill and batter the cream. It began to separate the water from the cream, and soon it became beautiful yellow butter.

The job took the best part of half an hour, and we all continued to take turns at turning the handle. The churning finished when the separator felt heavy with each turn of the handle. When you looked in, great big lumps of butter floated on top of the buttermilk and clung to the paddles of the separator.

A bucket or pail was placed on the chair beside the table once more, and when the little stopper was pulled, the buttermilk began to flow and fill the bucket. At this stage, if Uncle John was around, he'd take a large mug from the dresser, dip it in the buttermilk, and drink every drop of it. He always maintained that it was very good for the thirst on a hot summer day. I didn't like its bitter taste, but everyone sampled it at each churning, and even Mother tried it on occasion.

The buttermilk was used for baking brown bread and was always kept in a crock in the scullery for each day's baking. Sometimes, especially in summer, there was such a glut of buttermilk that it was mixed with whole cooked potatoes and other leftovers from the house and given to Murphy and Moll. They liked it so much that they even buried their trotters in the mixture, standing in it till it was all gone.

Then the butter was scooped out onto the lid of the churn. Salt was added, and the butter paddles were used to beat it into shape. It was squeezed and kneaded to remove any excess buttermilk from it, then teased into useable blocks. It was then placed on a plate, covered with muslin, and left in the scullery.

If there were visitors coming, Martha's job was to put some into little wooden moulds that shaped it into what looked like little flowers or leaves, then arrange them in her best glass butter dish and place it on the table beside the little bowls of jam. Sometimes during the spring or summer, churning was done quite often, and the excess butter was sold along with eggs at the market in the town. Martha also had a few good neighbours with whom she shared some of the excess farm produce.

*****

It was an afternoon just before Easter when I was sent off to Bartley Hegarty's house with a can of buttermilk and a lump of butter sailing on top of it. He lived alone, and there was little likelihood that he would marry. Now in his late thirties, his prospects of finding a wife were slim. He was past the stage of socializing at the local dances or even going to the pictures. I knew all about him now, as he was a constant visitor to Dairy Hill. Uncle John treated him as his right-hand man in times of emergency, along with Jimmy Kiernan. Jimmy was not one of my favourite people, not that he ever did anything wrong but for the fact that he slaughtered the animals on all the local farms.

Bartley's house was a two-storey farmhouse, not as big as Dairy Hill, and it could do with a good coat of paint on the windows.

He saw me coming and opened the half door to let me in. A big tomcat ran out the door just ahead of me, and when I got inside, there was a white she-cat playing with four kittens. Two of them were white and the others were tortoiseshell, just like the tomcat who'd run out the door. It was easy to establish, then, who the father was; using Uncle John's expression, Mother Nature was busy on this farm as well. The kittens were quite wild and ran for shelter under the large chaise longue on one side of the fire.

I entered a dark, dingy little kitchen. The chimney needed some cleaning, as all the smoke didn't make its way upwards from the open fire but filled the whole place and leaked out through the top half of the door. I left the can on the table and sat down on the chaise longue, which was covered by a soft brown leatherette. It had plenty of scratches on it from countless generations of cats playing and sharpening their claws on it. When I turned around, the big she-cat jumped up on my knee and began to purr. I stroked her gently, and she crouched to a forward position and settled down, glad to get away from her kittens, even for a little while.

The walls of the kitchen were painted a glossy green up halfway, and the rest were a creamy white distemper, which was cracking in places. The green colour was used everywhere in people's homes – in kitchens, on doors, gutters, gates, barns, and sometimes even on windowsills. Uncle John called it churchyard green, as it was used on church gates as well as those leading into graveyards. The great advantage of this green paint was that a fresh coat every year kept the place looking bright and cheerful. But it had been several years since Bartley had painted *his* house, and now the green was becoming darker and darker because of the smoke.

'Put that auld cat down off your knee, girl,' said Bartley.

'She's all right,' I said. 'She's happy!'

'She'll ruin your lovely coat; she's losing her hair.'

He shooed the cat down off my knee and ran to get a clothes brush. I brushed the cat fur away and sat down again.

'Would you like a sup of tay and a bit of butter cake, then?'

'Yes, please,' I replied. I had never heard of butter cake before. This was going to be a surprise. But my excitement waned very quickly when he produced two slices of brown bread with butter on it, cut into neat little fingers. This was called butter cake. When Father made tea for me sometimes in the morning and cut the bread up in slices like this, he called them soldiers, as they were lined up as if marching into battle.

So as not to disappoint Bartley, I had three pieces of the bread, and it tasted quite good. Then, looking around at the untidiness of the house, I turned to him and said, 'Bartley, did you ever think of getting married?'

'I did once, but that was a long time ago. I never talk about it.'

'I'm sorry. I didn't mean to pry.'

'It's all right, alannah. I can tell *you* about it, but I don't tell very many people. She was a local girl, you see, and she lived near the town. She was ambitious, and she wanted to go to America. We even got engaged. She went to America ahead of me. I was to follow her, but my mother died, and there was no one to look after the farm. My father was still alive. He was getting old. He was years older than my mother. I thought he wouldn't live too long after her. She said she'd wait for me. But I was wrong about my father. The years began to slip by, then one day a letter came from her, telling me that she was getting married to an American man. She sent me back the ring, and I still have it.'

He got up from the chair he was sitting on and went over to the dresser. He took down a little wallet from the top shelf and took out the gold engagement ring the woman had returned. It had a beautiful little white diamond in the centre. I looked closely at it, and as I was handing it back to him, I could see a tear in the corner of his eye. He placed it back in the little wallet and returned it to the top of the dresser.

'I'm sorry,' I said.

'It's all right, girl. My father lived for ten years after my mother, and I'm glad I didn't go off and leave him alone. He wasn't lonely at the end of his days.'

'Are *you* lonely now?' I asked.

'It's hard to know what loneliness is about. I don't feel alone when the hens come cackling to the door, or the kittens are playing, or the dog is chasing a rabbit. You're happy when you see things happen. But it's an empty place inside you, without the company of people. That's why I visit other people a lot. John Costello and the girls are the best neighbours ever.'

'Did you never think of getting married again?' I asked.

'I did indeed, but I'm afraid time has passed me by. I wouldn't be a good catch for a young girl nowadays.'

'You're a very kind man,' I said.

'And you are a very good little girl. Now before you go, I want to show you something outside. It doesn't happen very often, but you're lucky to be here to see it.'

He brought me out to a shed at the back of the house and opened the door into one of the stables. I could hear gentle whimpering as I entered the darkened shed. In one of the mangers, lying on a bed of straw, was a border collie just like Sam, and she wagged her tail when she saw us. She was lying on her side, suckling six little puppies almost identical to their mother. My heart melted when I saw them.

'This is Maggie. She's a very quiet auld girl. She is getting too old to have pups now, so I want to have one of her female pups to keep her line going. Would you like to hold one?'

'Yes, please!'

'Well, pick one and take it in your arms.' I stooped down, and Maggie wagged her tail as I picked up one of the little puppies.

'They have just opened their eyes,' said Bartley. 'You won't feel till they'll be running around.'

I held the little animal cradled in my arms and gently rubbed its black-and-white coat. It was a little male dog, and it whimpered and cried because it had been taken from its mother.

'Don't cry, little one,' I said, and I gave it a gentle kiss on the top of the head. It was a beautiful moment for me, as I had never held a little animal so young before. It was one of those experiences that made my coming to Ireland so worthwhile.

'He is beautiful. He's just perfect.'

'I want you to give him a name.'

'His name is Shep,' I answered.

'Shep it is, then.' Bartley took the puppy in his big, gentle, but weather-worn hands, and he pointed out that one of his paws was black. None of the others had a black paw.

'Now I know which one is Shep,' he said. He handed the puppy back to me, and I kissed it again and let him down beside his mother. He pushed his way through the heap of black-and-white moving bodies of his siblings and began to feed from his mother again.

'Thank you for showing me the puppies. It has made me so happy.'

'You are very welcome, little girl. Now, there's a little bit of advice I want to give you. You heard me tell you all that happened to me. The day will come and you will be a young woman, and you will meet a suitable young man.'

'I will not,' I joked. 'I'm never getting married. I don't want a man.'

'Well, the time will come when you will, and if you meet a suitable young man, hold on to him for dear life. Don't let him go. Don't leave it too long before you decide to marry. Think of that can of buttermilk you brought me. You know that long churning makes for bad butter.'

I didn't understand what he meant, but Maureen explained it to me that evening at tea.

'If you leave something too long, like an engagement, there is a strong likelihood that the wedding will never take place, the same as if you overchurn the butter, it melts and falls apart.'

This was something I would always remember. But I felt sorry for Bartley, and I chastised Uncle John for poking fun at him now and then. He just smirked at me and asked me if anything else happened at Bartley's. I told everyone about the cat and the wild kittens, and I finished with Maggie and her puppies.

'Did you hold any of them?' asked Maureen.

'I did!' I answered. 'He was beautiful.'

'That's good,' said Uncle John. 'You picked a little male dog.'

'Did you give it a name?' asked Martha.

'I called him Shep.'

'That's a proper name for a male dog,' said Uncle John. 'So you named him, then.'

'Yes, I did!'

'Remember what I told you about animals on the farm if they're not going to stay.'

'Yes, I do. Bartley wants to keep one of the puppies to replace Maggie, as she is getting old.' Then I thought again about what Bartley had said.

'Wait a minute. Bartley wants to keep one of the female dogs.'

'John Costello, what are you up to?' said Mother.

'Shep is going to be your dog, Margaret.'

I screamed with delight and ran to him, hugging him and kissing him.

'Stop! Stop, will you, and don't kill me.'

Mother looked on in dismay. She wasn't too happy about this.

'No, she is not getting a dog,' said Mother. 'How are we going to take a dog back to England with us, especially a big dog like a border collie? It's just not going to happen. Now, Margaret Kerr, get that idea out of your head right now.'

'Mother, no!' I protested. 'He's so beautiful, and I have given him a name. He has to stay.'

'Now, Kitty, you're getting the wrong end of the stick altogether. Sam is getting old, and we need another dog here for rounding up the cattle. I'm giving the care of this dog over to Margaret, if she stays here with us, and it looks like you and she will be here for another long while. This little dog will need care and minding while it's still a pup. Then in a few months, I will be training it, as it will be following what Sam's doing. Now don't spoil things on me now. Margaret has a big job ahead of her.'

I turned to Mother and saw that her angry face had turned to a smile, and I hugged her. I think she was remembering similar times in her childhood too, and now it was my turn.

'Bartley will bring that little dog over here when it's time for him to leave his mother,' said Uncle John. 'It will be in about ten or eleven weeks, and you can spend the summer caring for him.'

I was so happy going to bed that night. I thought it had been such a perfect day, and I only wished for the time to come when Bartley came with the little dog for me to care for.

But events would throw this happy time into the background as another crisis loomed at Bethany, Dairy Hill Farm.

Part 5
Old Paddy

Chapter 10

Magic was due to foal around the middle of April, which meant that old Paddy was put back in harness again, to plough the fields for the spring sowing. He was partnered with an ageing horse belonging to Bartley.

It was going to be a busy time, as there was compulsory tillage to be sown as well. This directive from the government – introduced in 1940 and finished in 1948 – was an emergency request to ensure that there was enough food to feed everyone during these troubled times. Each farmer was obliged to set aside one-tenth of their farm acreage for the purpose and instructed to sow one or two cereal crops. Wheat was the main crop sown, as it was used to provide flour for bread making. Uncle John had to set aside eight acres. As well as oats, he had to grow wheat, both crops in equal measure. This extra pressure from the government meant he was greatly concerned about doing things right and ensuring the crops were in on time. The sowing of the cereal crops was scheduled to follow the sowing of the potato crop. Because of this, he hoped the weather would hold out for a few days till the work was done.

Mother and I decided to help him sow the potato field. I dropped the potatoes in the drills from a bucket. Uncle John had spent a long while slicing the seed in two, making sure there were eyes on each half tuber, which would grow and sprout into new plants in the ground. He left them in the shed for a few days, so that the wounds created by the cutting would callus and protect the tuber from decaying.

He had been ploughing the land that had been cultivated the year before, and he was following a field of oats with potatoes and returning the oats to the potato field of the previous year. The wheat crop was going into a fresh new field set aside for the job. Paddy and his team-mate sailed through the ploughing, and we began to sow the potatoes on a Friday. I was given the day off school to lend a hand, as it would take about two days to finish the job.

It was a good, dry spring day, with a strong, harsh wind from the east. The grass in the headlands was crisp and would burn like thatch if it caught fire. Uncle John had made a few trips to the field, bringing seed potatoes, buckets, spades, forks, and finally, Mother and me. I was surprised to see Mother volunteer to help, but she insisted that it was the least she could do for the war effort. The aunts took care of things at home and prepared the dinner. They would fetch us home later by ringing a big handbell from the yard at one o'clock. I was wrapped well in a coat and scarf, and after a little teaching from Uncle John on the rudiments of sowing potatoes, I became an expert craftsman at this back-breaking job. Mother helped me for a while until I was seven or eight drills ahead, and then, taking a fork, she began to help Uncle John spread the dung over the potatoes in the drills. He had spent two days prior to the sowing taking cartloads of dung from the heaps in the farmyard, left over after housing the cows at night during the winter. The mixture of straw, urine, and cow dung had blended into a foul-smelling brown mass, and when he began to fork deep into the piles, they were steaming with heat, as it was breaking down into a dark compost, which could be used even in the vegetable and flower garden. He spread the dung in heaps at intervals along the drills, ready for covering over the newly sown potatoes. Whenever I came to a heap, I left two or three tubers together, so that they could be dropped in the furrow when the heap was spread in the drills.

It wasn't long until I met the brick wall, just like a long-distance runner. My back began to ache. I was glad when I was so many drills ahead and when Bartley joined us just after twelve midday, I knew I had to keep working to stay ahead. Mother returned, and began dropping potatoes again, to take the strain off me. But I didn't mind in the least. My thoughts were on the little puppy Shep, who was going to become part of the farm in several weeks. I imagined him racing around just like Sam, and we were running through the long grass or the falling leaves.

At one o'clock, I could hear the bell ringing down in the farmyard, and it was time to go for dinner. We were all starving with the hunger.

'Nothing like a spring day like that,' said Uncle John, 'to give everyone a good appetite. It did you well, Kitty, to get out. There's a fine colour coming in your cheeks.'

The potatoes were piping hot. The aunts had hungry-gap kale cooked and cut up in a dish, along with great slices of bacon and home-made butter. We washed it all down with mugs of fresh milk, and to finish, we drank mugs of tea and slices of currant cake. Martha declared that it was the last of the currants from Christmas. She didn't know when she'd ever get any again. She also reused the tea leaves from the breakfast by stewing them in the teapot on a few coals on the hearth. She wanted to stretch the rationed tea as far as it would go.

When we returned to the fields, I felt like falling asleep. At around four o'clock, Uncle John declared that we had enough drills sown for the day and he was ready to close them in. So it was time to relax for me, and the afternoon was warmer than the morning. I climbed up on the cart and wrapped a few sacks around me.

Mother and Bartley were covering the last few drills with dung halfway across the field. All I could hear was the jingle of the horses' harness and Uncle John's soft voice as he directed the team up and down the drills. I faded into a relaxing sleep, resting my aching muscles from stooping and bending my back all day. Soon the sounds of the field and the voices talking faded into my subconscious, until suddenly I was awakened by what sounded like a scream.

It was Mother.

I jumped up, and she was running to Uncle John. He stood in the field, transfixed at what lay before him. Paddy was lying in the drills, snorting. He seemed as if he were moaning. He had fallen before the plough. There was a look of fright and horror on Uncle John's face, and he tried to get to the horse, who was thrashing his legs and hooves, attempting to get up again. The other horse was agitated as well, and Uncle John released him quickly, letting him run away down the field.

'He might have a broken hip,' said Bartley. 'I'll go for Jimmy Kiernan.' As quick as lightning, Bartley was gone, and Mother held Uncle John. She was crying. I didn't know whether to cry or scream.

'Don't worry, Uncle John, he'll be all right,' said Mother.

He was nodding his head silently. Then, after a short while, Paddy calmed down, exhausted from his wriggling and thrashing. He bent down and rubbed his head gently.

'Please be all right, my auld friend,' Uncle John said.

'Don't upset yourself,' said Mother.

'Listen, Kitty, I want to be alone with him.'

Mother took me away a safe distance, and we stood watching. I began to cry, knowing that Paddy would never get up again. Then when Jimmy Kiernan arrived with Bartley, followed by Maureen and Martha, I failed to notice that Bartley was carrying Uncle John's rifle. They all stood some yards away, watching, as Jimmy examined the old horse.

'I was such a fool to put him back in harness again,' bellowed Uncle John, as Jimmy's eyes told him there was no hope.

'He was just too old for this work, John; it couldn't be helped, with this auld war and all that it has brought into our lives. You had to take the old boy back to the land.'

Then Martha said in a quiet whisper, 'Jesus, Mary, and Joseph, if that animal dies, it will kill John Costello as well.'

By now we were all in tears, and Jimmy came over to get the gun.

'Maybe you should all go,' said Jimmy. 'You'd need to get the little girl out of here.'

But Uncle John was hot on his heels, saying, 'Listen, let you all go.'

'No! I'll stay with you, John,' said Jimmy.

'I said, all of you go,' Uncle John shouted in a sad but angry voice. 'I'll do it. I want to be alone with him. He was my friend, and I want to say goodbye alone. Now go!'

We began to move away and head down the fields home. But Maureen stood her ground and called after Uncle John, 'Let someone stay with you, and don't do anything stupid.'

'Go home, woman, and get the cows in. I'll be there later.'

Then we turned and moved slowly out of the field, leading Bobby and the cart, and headed for the farmhouse. When we were closing the haggard gate, a shot rang out across the countryside, followed by another, and it startled all the neighbouring crows, as they flew out of every tree around, cawing and making an unmerciful sound everywhere.

Mother held me, and I had no control of my crying, just like when Nana had been killed. She brought me in and made me take a drink of cool spring water from the enamel bucket in the scullery. The two aunts were silent, as Jimmy and Bartley helped with the evening chores.

Half an hour later, Uncle John returned. His eyes were red, and he flung the gun in the corner. He didn't speak but went to the parlour, and we could hear the key turning in the door.

'He'll be as drunk as auld boots for days now, wait till you see,' said Maureen.

'It will be the death of him,' said Martha. 'I have never seen him like that ever since our parents died. That old horse was here for more than twenty years.'

'What about the potatoes and the corn?' said Mother. 'We'll have to get those in, won't we?'

'I don't know what we'll do,' said Martha. 'God in heaven only knows.'

But I had other ideas.

*****

As Jimmy Kiernan and Bartley did the evening chores, I had my tea. I didn't feel like eating. But I knew there was someone who might be able to help us. There were fourteen drills of potatoes in the field uncovered, and if they weren't closed within a few days, the crows would have a jolly old time and the crop would be ruined. My thoughts returned to Christmas, when Peter Johnson had kissed my hand and told me that if I ever needed any help, he would do his best for me. I went to Mother and told her what I wanted to do.

'You know,' she said, 'it's worth a try. Why don't you get up on your bicycle and cycle up that far? If he has forgotten about his promise, don't say anything, but come home again as quick as you can. Don't delay, as it will be dark in about two hours.'

She came to the gate with me and waved me off. We didn't tell Martha or Maureen, for fear they might tell Uncle John.

'Be sure and be home again before dark, young lady,' she said again, and stood watching me make my way. I had become quite competent on the bike by now, and she knew I would be all right. It was a fine but blustery evening, and I didn't feel the mile-long journey to the Johnson place.

It was a great big Georgian house, hidden among mighty oak, chestnut, beech, and lime trees. The avenue was covered in small, tiny stones of a uniform nature, not like the rough gravel roads, and it was easy to cycle on, as the stones had become compressed into the avenue by countless wheels, mainly car tracks. There was a strong metal fence on each side of the avenue to hold back horses and other farm animals. I was greeted by a beautiful black stallion, who trotted along with me inside the fence as the avenue rose towards the house. Then his journey ended abruptly, as he was met by what looked like a high wall. But it was a bank dividing the parkland on a higher level, rising towards the house. When you stood in front of the building, it seemed as if the parkland continued as far as the eye could see. But it was divided by this hidden bank, which I later learned was known as a *ha-ha*. It was a feature of large country houses, as it kept the animals a safe distance from the place yet still in plain view of their owners.

When I reached the front, the avenue divided into a very wide driveway centred by a large round box-knot bed. This was to allow coaches, traps, cars, or any other large transport vehicle to turn around and stop at the front doorsteps. Peter's car was parked at the bottom of the steps, and the great grey house loomed over me like a big dark castle in the fairy tales Mother read to me when I was younger. I knew that invited guests always went to the hall door and that everyone else, including the servants, used the service entrance at the back.

I left my bike lying against a great stone lion, two of which guarded the steps leading up to the front door. Its great big mouth was open, and I reached up and placed my hand inside it, between large stone teeth.

I climbed the steps to the door, and I pulled a big brass knob to ring the bell. I couldn't hear a sound within, as the bell rang in the servants' area in the bowels of the house down in the basement. It would be a while before it was answered, I thought.

Someone came to the door after about two minutes. A servant girl stood before me in cap and apron. She spoke gently to me. I told her who I was and that I wanted to speak to Mr Peter Johnson.

'Excuse me for one minute,' she said. She was a woman in her late twenties with a bright cheerful face. She was the sort of person who was always busy and enjoyed being so. She left me standing in the front hall, waiting.

She returned a few minutes later and, smiling at me, said, 'Mr Johnson is out on the land somewhere. He should be back for tea in about half an hour. I'm on my own tonight, as Jordan the butler and the other three house staff have the evening off and are gone to the Coliseum Cinema in the town. Come with me.'

She led me through the great hall, and I was amazed at the ambience of the place. It had a great winding stair leading upward into the heart of the house. It was decorated with red velvet curtains and beautiful Turkish rugs on the floor. Great big paintings of past Johnsons stared down from the walls, keeping watch over their territory. Were these some of the people who had been responsible for staking claim to the Costello lands? This was still part of Uncle John's thinking, and in fact, even though it seemed as if it were some form of banter between two people from childhood, the land and its ownership still formed part of the folklore of each family and was still embedded in their psyche. The dispossessed still had dreams of getting their lands back, but laws, time, and a new nation had left such pipe dreams a distant memory and people moved on, leaving the past behind.

I followed the woman down the long hall. She opened a great oak door and announced me as Miss Margaret Kerr. She stood back to let me in, and when I entered, I was so glad to see familiar faces. Fritz Von Gebler was standing at an open fire, and his grandfather was seated in a soft chair to the left of the large marble fireplace. There was another middle-aged lady, very beautiful, sitting knitting. She didn't raise her head, but her knitting was just a continuous long piece of cloth, just like a scarf, with different colours added on. It was Georgina Johnson, Peter's wife. She was in a world of her own. I didn't realise then that she needed constant care; her mind had been gone for quite some time. Following the death of their only son when he was nine years old, she'd left the world behind her and lived somewhere in a limbo place, interacting with reality in little snatches, and at times her mind was back somewhere in a distant and lost childhood. Peter cared for her very well, and this evening she had been left in the care of Manfred and Fritz, while some of the house staff had a night off.

Manfred stood up, cheered, and welcomed me.

'Wilkomen, mein Kind,' he exclaimed.

I knew what he meant and replied, 'Danke, mein Herr.'

Then in English, he said, 'You speak German, do you?'

'No, I don't, but there were German friends back in London, and I picked a few words up from them.'

'I'm delighted to see you,' said Fritz.

'I thought you were at school in Dublin,' I said.

'I got pleurisy, and I was sent home. Dr Daly has been caring for me. I won't be returning to school till after Easter. I'm much better now.'

Then Georgina lifted her head and beckoned me over. She looked around as if she wanted to tell me a secret.

'You know, little girl,' she whispered. 'The Dilly men are coming to take me away.'

'Where are they?' I asked.

'Someone from her childhood,' said Fritz. 'When she saw you, she thinks she's a little girl again.'

'Listen, Emily,' she said to me. 'Let's play cat's cradle.' Her voice was the voice of a queen. She was someone who had been reared by a governess and spent the rest of her childhood at some school in England.

'I can!' I replied.

She took a long piece of wool and tied both ends together, weaving it between her fingers to make a cat's cradle. She held it up to me, and I took it from her onto my fingers, preserving the cradle effect. Then I returned it to her hands. When she handed it back again, I lost control of it, and the cradle fell apart.

'I won! I won!' she shouted. Then, returning to her knitting, she began singing.

Flow gently, sweet Afton
Among thy green braes
Flow gently, I'll sing thee
A song in thy praise . . .

She continued singing the song for a few moments, and then setting down her knitting, she hummed the tune quietly to herself.

'You are a busy young lady,' said Manfred.

'Yes, sir,' I replied.

Then he said something in German to his grandson, and Fritz looked a little alarmed.

'Grossvater, bitte hör auf damit,' exclaimed Fritz. I believe he was chastising his grandfather for saying whatever he had. Then he explained it to me.

'I'm sorry, Margaret,' said Manfred. 'What I was saying was that you look a bit like a worker just in from the fields.'

'I have done just that,' I replied, 'but things have gone horribly wrong.'

'What has happened?' asked Fritz.

Before I could answer them, I burst into tears. There was shock written on both their faces, and then Georgina shouted, 'Put that cat out, Bertha, quick. It's going to have kittens.'

'Don't mind her,' said Fritz. 'The noise she hears is a cat to her. Your crying has distracted her.'

'Get the brush, you foolish girl,' she shouted, 'before it gets sick all over my aspidistras.'

My tears began to fade as the poor lady continued shouting and making no sense. I realised I had to stop, as she kept poking under the chair with a walking stick, trying to put an imaginary cat out. Then she drew the stick out to hit a large green glass vase on top of a what-not, but Fritz grabbed it and said, 'It is all right, dear lady, the cat has gone. Give me the stick, and I will mind it for you. Now why don't you go back to your knitting? You still have a lot of that scarf to do.'

She sat back in the chair and resumed her work. Fritz was a very gentle youth, and his kind words settled her down.

When things had calmed, I told them what had happened during the day and how I had now come to Peter, looking for help. I said I had Mother's approval to come and I was not to be too late.

'I'll fetch Peter,' said Fritz. 'Do you want to come with me?'

'Yes, please!' I answered.

He led the way, taking long steps and I walked after him in a half trot. I knew by his haste that he didn't want to delay me. We went quickly through the house, down a servant's stairway, to the kitchen, with its great stone-paved floor and a large table in the middle. The lady who answered the door was having her tea, and she stood up.

'Excuse me, Master Fritz,' she said. 'I'm just having my tea.'

'I'm sorry, Esther,' he answered, 'but I want to find Peter. This is Margaret Kerr.'

'Pleased to meet you, Margaret,' she said.

'You know, she is a wonderful cook as well as housekeeper,' said Fritz. 'It would be my dream to take her back to Germany with me and keep her forever. Esther Kerrigan is the best cook in all of Ireland.'

'Now don't flatter me now, young master. You foreigners have a great way with the ladies.'

'Now, now!' teased Fritz.

'Will you get out of my kitchen, you young scoundrel, or I'll get the back of my hand to you.' Jokingly, she made as if to chase after him, but he ran for the back door, and I followed quickly.

We waved goodbye to her, as I followed him out the door, and we entered a cobbled courtyard together, with horse stables all around. We walked through the courtyard under an archway in the stables to a laurel walk leading to a walled garden. There was every sign that the gardeners had been working. There was no sign of Sheila's father, as it was well past quitting time.

The path led eventually to the parkland I had just come through up the avenue, and in the distance, I could see the horses that had followed me till they came to the ha-ha ditch. It was now invisible to the naked eye, and the rolling green parkland, decked with fine mature trees, stretched away into the sunset.

Darkness was coming fast. There was a paddock close by, and Peter was riding a tall brown horse, jumping fences there. He saw us coming and dismounted close to us. He was wearing riding breeches and a black coat and riding hat. The horse was a bit frisky, and Peter tied him to a post. When we were well clear of the animal, he spoke.

'What is my young heroine doing here?'

'I'm sorry, sir,' I said, 'but I'm coming to ask you for help. You told me to call on you anytime.'

'Come along then, young lady, and tell me everything. Fritz, will you tend to the horse and put her back in the stable? Let us walk back to the house, and you can fill me in.'

I followed him through the laurels and did as he asked.

*****

Meanwhile, Mother was getting worried at home because I had not returned, and she had to tell the aunts quietly what was happening. She decided to walk down the avenue again to the road and wait. If I didn't arrive in the next twenty minutes, she was going to start walking till she came to Johnsons. The sun had gone down in a blaze of red, with a little darkened cloud dotting the sky here and there in the twilight. It would be a good day again tomorrow.

Then she could hear the noise of an engine in the distance, and soon the headlights of a car loomed through the fading light. It slowed down near the avenue and pulled up just beside Mother. Peter had decided to leave me home safe.

'Oh, you are such a kind man,' said Mother. 'I was getting so worried.'

'Think nothing of it,' he said. 'This is such a brave lady, you know, facing out into the evening dusk.'

'She told you what happened,' said Mother.

'Every clear and sad detail. Don't worry; when my workmen arrive in the morning, I will divert a few of them in this direction for the day. I don't like doing this tillage myself either, none of us do, but that's life now. But we will kill two birds with the one stone; we will finish the potatoes, and between us we will get those cereals planted at my place as well as yours. I am sure the men will be glad of a bite to eat at some part of the day.'

'Oh, thank you very much. John has lost the head completely over the old horse. I often wonder why he ever started farming, as he gets so attached to some of these animals.'

'It's the sign of a good heart and a good soul,' Peter said, 'even though he still has this past grudge of land loss and deprivation. He is a lucky man to have such a fine place as this.'

'I keep telling him that,' I said.

'Now, Margaret, I'll get Fritz to take your bicycle back in the morning. No one will take it during the night.'

'Thank you, sir,' I said.

'Would you like me to take you up the rest of the way home?'

'No, thank you all the same,' said Mother. 'I don't want John to know what's happening. He will be faced with it in the morning, and if he does any whining, just ignore him.'

'That's fine. Sorry, I have forgotten your name.'

'I'm Kitty.'

'All right, see you in the morning, Kitty.'

I got out of the car, and Peter switched the lights off as he turned it around to face for home so that they didn't reflect up to the farmhouse. Uncle John might see him and become suspicious.

Mother put her arms around me as we walked up the avenue together. 'You feel cold, pet. I hope you don't get a chill or a cold.'

'I'm fine. I just had a little adventure this evening.'

'It's a fine place, isn't it?'

'It is indeed, but it's a sad place. His wife is not well, and she lives in another world.'

It was then that Mother told me what had happened to Peter and Georgina's child. He'd contracted meningitis and died. Peter was a dedicated and loving husband, having cared for Georgina all these years. 'I really don't know what's going to happen to that place in years to come. He's a lonely man, and I'd say he's glad to have his relatives staying with him.'

I thought about Peter and how he was perceived in the community. There were those who regarded him highly, and he commanded great respect from them. There were others who saw him as an opportunist, especially during these times, and there were stories of goods being smuggled and of contraband petrol being stored in the farm buildings. He was colourful and kind, and yet there was a hint of shadiness to his character. But his neighbourliness shone through, and it was this that people liked.

*****

Next morning, we were awakened early by Sam barking as if the whole German army had appeared out of the bushes. I ran to the window, and there was a great commotion on the avenue. Peter Johnson's car drove slowly in front of a flotilla of horses, carts, ploughs, and harrows. I screamed with delight when I saw it. I called Mother. She threw on her dressing gown, and we made our way down the stairs quickly.

Maureen stood in amazement at the back door, while Martha kept banging on the parlour door to waken Uncle John. He had not emerged from the evening before.

'Come out quickly, will you, John Costello? Help has arrived to sow the crops. Stop brooding in there and come out.'

When the Johnson car pulled up at the back door, Fritz followed behind, riding my bike. He smiled when he saw me. Peter stood as leader of all he possessed, and Maureen welcomed him.

'Thank you very much for your help,' she said.

'You can thank my little heroine over there,' he said, smiling. 'Only too glad to help.'

'Would you like a sup of tay before you start?' she asked.

'On the contrary, dear lady, when I have everything working and going well, I must leave you and tend to my own affairs. Bloody awful about the horse, isn't it?'

'He's lying up there in the drills,' said Maureen.

'We'll move him out of the way, don't worry.'

'Be careful with him, won't you?'

'But sure he's dead, isn't he? What harm can befall him now?'

'If you damage a bone in his body, I'll break every bone in yours.' It was Uncle John who spoke. He was standing inside the door, and he emerged tattered, dishevelled, and worn out from lack of sleep. His eyes were red from a night of whiskey drinking.

'If it isn't the landlord himself,' said Peter.

'Landlord, me eye. They are a dying breed, and they can't die half quick enough.'

'Well, just point the way, good man, and I'll do the rest,' said Peter.

'You know the way; do you not remember? Isn't this land part of what your ancestors took from us years ago?'

I didn't like what Uncle John was saying. I felt he was being ungrateful and cruel to Peter, who seemed to ignore the jibes and insults, but I'd say deep down he was sad to hear such taunts.

'Isn't he very kind, coming to help like that?' I said to Uncle John.

'I wonder who's responsible for this,' he growled, showing me more of the whites of his eyes than anything else. I blushed, held down my head, and said no more. The Johnson party began to move slowly into the haggard and headed for the fields.

'Will you not come with us?' asked Peter, 'You've had a hard time last night, and some fresh air will clear your head.'

'I'll leave you to it, Peter Johnson. I can only say I appreciate what you're doing, and I say thank you, but I can't bring myself to shake your hand.'

'That's a start, John. Go ahead and sleep it all off. With all you've had last night, it might take a week to clear your head.'

Uncle John followed Peter's suggestion with a wry smile and his usual cutting remark.

'At least it's drowning out the smell of all that petrol in your shed. If you're not careful enough, someone might set a match to it some night.'

Peter didn't answer, but the four men helping him chuckled quietly to themselves and continued their journey. Fritz went to follow them, but I called him back.

'Can't you stay a while?' I said. 'We're just going to have breakfast.'

He smiled, thanked us, and followed us into the house.

Uncle John said nothing to anyone but went quietly upstairs to bed. Maureen followed him and began banging on his bedroom door.

'What are you giving up for now?' she shouted.

'Will you go away, woman, and leave me alone?'

'They need you out in the fields. The crops must be sown. If you don't get the compulsory tillage in, the inspector will be around, and he will take the land off you to do it. Then you will have reason to moan about landlords and land wars. That was auld God's time, John Costello. Those days are long gone, and they are not coming back, thanks be to the Lord God. Now get out of that bed and go help that good man.'

'Are you finished?' he shouted.

'I'll not stop until you come out of there.'

'You can stand there till Tibb's Eve. You'll probably die roaring.'

'You are an ungrateful whelp, John Costello, you are just that.'

He made no answer, and after a few minutes, she came back down the stairs, crying into her apron. Martha went to her to comfort her.

'I don't know what we'll do about that man,' sobbed Maureen. 'He'll take to that bed, and the devil and his angels won't move him.'

'It's all right,' said Martha. 'We can only pray for him. When he's finished sulking, he'll come out.'

*****

Fritz stayed for the day, and after breakfast, we went to the fields to check on the work. I wasn't allowed help this time, but Fritz and I looked on at what was being done. Bartley had joined the gang in the meantime, and the working men knew him too; I believe they had grown up together and gone to school in the village.

They progressed quietly, and at a swift pace. Paddy's body had been moved to the corner of the field, and Fritz told me that Peter had ordered a cart to take it away.

Later that afternoon, I cried a soft tear when I saw the great body on the back of a big cart, covered with a large piece of tarpaulin. When I looked up at Uncle John's bedroom window, the curtain was pulled back, and he was watching his old friend on his last journey. This was his final goodbye.

It was only then that I really understood his words and his wisdom about getting too friendly with animals on the farm. There was really no point in doing so unless you were going to keep them, and Paddy was one of the greatest losses he'd ever suffered.

Meanwhile, back in the fields, Martha took control and guided the men to another field, which had already been ploughed. It now had to be harrowed and softened to make way for oats, and the last one at the edge of the farm was given over to the compulsory tillage.

While Fritz and I wandered the fields, following the workmen, Martha returned to the house to prepare some dinner for them, with Mother and Maureen. Bartley called me over and said, 'Why don't you take this young man over to my place and show him Shep and the other pups? They are growing fast. I'll be handing him over to your care, girl, before too long.'

I jumped to the idea, and we skipped across the fields to the boreen and followed the laneway to Bartley's place. There was little to be heard, as Bartley had dry stock and they were out in the fields. He didn't grow any crops, but he had given over a field to the compulsory tillage, and it was already sown.

I found the stable where the puppies were, and when Maggie heard us coming, she jumped the half door and came bounding to meet us. Fritz rubbed her ears for her, and when we gazed across the half door, six little fat black-and-white fur balls were whimpering and sniffing around the stable. We went in and closed the door behind us. Maggie went to her nest, and they all followed her, climbing all over her. She lay down to let them feed and, reaching her head over to some of them, began licking them.

'They are beautiful,' said Fritz. 'They really are.'

'Uncle John is taking one of them, and I was asked to pick it out and name it.'

'Which one is it?'

I scanned the moving mass of whimpering black and white and found little Shep. He began crying when I picked him up, and I held him close to my face. He gave a shrill little bark, and I took him and laid him in my folded arm. He liked the feel of my woollen jumper, and he nestled in to fall asleep. I stroked him gently as he did so.

Fritz picked one also, a little female, and she snuggled up too in the warmth of his arm. Maggie looked on approvingly. She knew we didn't pose any threat to her little offspring.

We sat down on some clean straw in the corner of the shed, watching Maggie care for her little family, and I got a closer look at Fritz. He had a long, gaunt, pale face, and there was a wheeze in his breathing. He wore a scarf around his neck, and I knew he was only just moving out into the world again after his illness.

'I know you've been very sick,' I said, 'but is there any more news about your family?'

'I have heard nothing since Christmas. Grandfather tells me lots of things. There are not many people coming for refuge in Ireland. We are a lucky few, I suppose. It is because of the Irish government.'

'Why is that?'

'Ireland does not support the war. It is neutral. Mr de Valera intends to keep it that way, so that it would give Hitler no reason to come here. There are lots of Jewish people getting out of Germany and the other countries Hitler has invaded. They say those who are left behind are being put away in some form of camps. They do not know much about these places yet. I think my parents might be in one of them, as they would be seen as enemies of Germany.'

'How come you and your grandfather managed to get here?'

'I am actually an Irish citizen. I was born here. My parents were here when the Irish government were building a large hydro-electric power station on the River Shannon. My father was an engineer on the project. I was born during that time, so I have an Irish passport now. I have a German one too, but Papa sent my birth certificate to the Irish government, and they issued me a passport to come here.'

'What about your grandfather? How did he manage to get out?'

'Again, it was Peter. He knows a lot of important people. There is a government minister who sought refuge in Johnsons' during the War of Independence. He was a soldier then, fighting for the cause, and Peter's father smuggled him out of the country for a while. Now he is a government minister, and Peter took advantage of this fact, and Grandfather has an Irish passport too. My mother was waiting to get a new passport from Ireland. Peter was trying to get one for my father too, but they never arrived. We were sent on ahead. As far as I know, they have never received them. They were to follow us. But now they have just disappeared.

'When we got here, Grandfather was sent to a place called the Curragh for a short while till all his papers were checked and verified. Peter is such a good man. My mother is his sister, and he is doing his best to have her and Papa found in Germany and to get them out. So far, they haven't heard anything.'

'You were very lucky, then.'

'I thank God for that. But there are a lot of people who were not so lucky, and we will not know anything about them till the war is over. The British government have taken in many refugees, and Grandfather said that there are some of them in Northern Ireland too.'

'I hate this war, Fritz, I really do.'

'Oh, I nearly forgot.' He put the little puppy back with his mother, and reaching into the deep pocket of his coat, he produced a large brown paper sugar bag.

'This will cheer you up!'

'What is it?' I asked.

'You will see.'

He took little Shep from me and placed him back in the care of his mother, and she began licking the top of his head. I stood up and surveyed the paper bag before I opened it.

'Grandfather made it for you.'

I opened it to find a little wooden carved squirrel, holding an acorn in its front paws. It was beautifully finished, and its big bushy tail swirled up its back and curled backwards above its head. It was finished in a brown shiny varnish, and it was about six inches tall.

'It's so beautiful,' I said.

'It is a little Easter present for you. I could not get you any chocolate.'

'Oh, this is just fabulous, thank you.' I threw my arms around him and gave him a hug. When I looked up at him, he was blushing. I had taken him by surprise and embarrassed him.

'I'm sorry I have nothing for you.'

To make light of his embarrassment, he said, 'That's no problem. A hug will do just fine.'

Then I hugged him again, and we started laughing. It was moments like this that made us forget the war.

By the time dinner was prepared, we were back in the farmhouse kitchen, ready to eat a meal fit for a king. Fritz and I waited till the men had finished, and when they had gone back to the fields, we sat down with Mother and the aunts. Maureen was still upset over Uncle John, but Martha, as ever, trusted in God and prayer to solve her problems.

When I showed Mother what Fritz had given me, she showered him with blessings for what he had done, and said to thank Manfred for making it.

'Grandfather is a very good craftsman,' said Fritz. 'We make a lot of little pieces like that where we live.'

'He should do some of that work here,' said Martha. 'That's a God-given gift, and he should use it.'

Maureen had tried to encourage Uncle John to come down for some dinner, but he refused and would not answer the door. We felt that he had given up on the world on account of old Paddy.

But there were two events that would take him back to recovery.

*****

Fritz went back to school after Easter, and he gave me his address so I could write to him. He wrote back to me as well. He was looking forward to the summer holidays so he could be back with his grandfather again. He was still hopeful that his parents would be found. I knew he was lonely, and he was glad to have someone who'd seen the tragedy of war and would understand. Mother teased me about having a boyfriend, and I scolded her for even suggesting such a thing. We were simply good friends.

But Fritz wasn't the only one who was lonely. I had been visiting Sheila on my way from school, and she remained sitting at the fire each day with a rug around her. She was not eating very well, and anytime I called, she made a very special effort to please me. I intended to keep my promise to her and take her to the lake. I had planned to do it during the Easter holidays, but she had not been well enough to go. I didn't know how I would get her there, but I'd think of something.

I mentioned it to Fritz in one of my letters, and when he wrote back, he told me to leave it to him. He would be back at the end of June, and he'd organise something for me.

Uncle John remained in his room. Martha and Maureen kept pleading with him to come out, and Mother said under her breath that he was now behaving like a bold child.

After mass on Sunday, I was sitting on the wall at the gate, writing one of my letters to Fritz, when Bartley arrived on his bike. He was all decked out for fishing. The day was fine, and he was ready to go. I knew that this was a ploy to get Uncle John to quit his sulking and come out of his room.

He had fishing rods and other tackle in a special green canvas bag. He was wearing a brand-new pair of black leather boots. I admired them as he rested his bike against the wall, and for something to say, I said they were a nice pair of boots.

'I got them from the LDF.'

The LDF was the Local Defence Force. They were civilians trained by the Army to protect the country against invasion. They were trained in the tactics of war and went on manoeuvres regularly.

I knew it wasn't just the idea of army life that had brought Bartley into it but also the fact that he was able to get new tyres and tubes for his bike. They were only available to people in the LDF, as a mode of transport was important to them.

'Is that man still in his room?' he asked.

'He is,' I replied.

'Don't worry, girl, I'll soon shift him. This isn't the first time he did this, you know, but I'll put the wind up his sails.'

By Wednesday of the previous week, Peter Johnson's men had finished. He came in person to the fields to ensure that they had left everything just as they'd found it.

As they made their way out through the yard onto the avenue, the aunts showered blessings on him and his men. He took his hat off to them as if he were an actor taking a bow at the end of a theatrical performance. I thanked him most sincerely. He bowed to me as well and continued down the avenue, driving his big car.

'A bit of a show-off,' said Mother.

'If you ask me, it's all a show on the outside,' said Martha. 'He has had such a tragic life. It goes so hard on him watching poor Georgina, the way she is. She is really lost to him, and he is still so dedicated and in love with her. It is such a tragedy, God help him.'

'It's hard on us all, this war,' said Mother. 'Our lives are so uncertain from day to day. I often wonder have we any tomorrow at all.'

'Don't despair, love,' said Martha. 'The good Lord looks after his own.'

As the Johnson party left the avenue, the farmwork continued, and I began to wonder what I'd say to Fritz in the letter I was going to write to him. But Bartley's intervention on Sunday gave me plenty to write about. I was just about to begin the letter when he arrived, and I folded it and put it away. I followed him into the kitchen to see what he was going to do.

He walked in and spoke to the women. Martha opened the door to the hall, and he went quickly up the stairs. He began banging on Uncle John's door, determined not to stop until he got an answer.

'Go away, woman,' came the voice from within.

'Call me a woman, now, would you?' shouted Bartley.

'What the hell do *you* want?'

'I want you to come out and come with me.'

'Where?'

'To the lake.'

'For what?'

'What do you think we do at this time of the year?'

'Will you go away?'

'No, I won't. I'll sit here all day, and all night if I must. I'll annoy and pester you until you give in.'

'Please yourself so.'

'All right, but I didn't tell you about the boat.'

'What about it?' asked Uncle John.

Bartley winked at Martha and me. We were standing at the bottom of the stairs looking on. He kept banging on the door.

'What about the boat?' Uncle John asked again.

'The boathouse was broken into, and I think someone was tampering with the boat.'

'The cross of Christ on it anyway,' roared Uncle John. 'First the horse, and now this.'

'Let me in, and I'll tell you all about it.'

There was silence for what seemed like an age, but it was only a few minutes. Then we heard the floorboards creaking in the bedroom and the key turned in the lock. Bartley went inside and closed the door behind him.

We went back to the kitchen and sat around the table waiting. Half an hour later, Bartley emerged and came down the stairs.

'Get me some hot water in a tin basin,' he said. 'He's going to shave.'

'Thanks be to God,' said Maureen. 'He's beginning to come to his senses when he's doing that. John takes everything to heart; you know he was always a bit of a softie. He did the same, you know, after the death of each of our parents, and it took Bartley's father to coax him out eventually.'

'No wonder they call him Lazarus,' said Martha with a wry smile on her face. 'It's as if he dies and comes back to life again.'

'I never thought of it like that before,' said Mother.

Then there was a flurry of activity in the kitchen. There was such a hustle and bustle throughout the house. The tin basin was retrieved from under the table in the dairy, Uncle John's cut-throat razor was sharpened on the leather strap hanging from the side of the dresser, and all was handed to Bartley, along with a towel and John's shaving cup and lathering soap, as he reentered the bedroom.

At least another half hour went by before the door opened again, and the two men emerged. We stood at the bottom of the stairs, wondering what to say and what to do. Uncle John was dressed in clean clothes, with a smooth, clean-shaven face, carrying his heavy coat in his arms. He stood at the top of the stairs looking down at us.

'What the hell are you all gaping at?' he growled. 'Have you seen an apparition or something?'

'Well, you might just say that,' said Martha wryly, with a smirk on her face, referring to her earlier comment about Lazarus rising from the dead. We all scampered in every direction, pretending not to notice trying to look as if we were busy doing something.

When Uncle John reached the bottom of the stairs, he turned to Maureen. 'Where's me pipe and tobacco?'

It was then that Mother realised that he had been away in his bedroom for so long and hadn't had a smoke of his pipe. It was one of life's guilty pleasures, and he'd managed to live without it. But Martha declared that it would have done him good, as he hadn't stopped smoking for Lent this year, and she thought it was a bit selfish that he hadn't.

Maureen must have anticipated what he was going to say next, as she handed his pipe and tobacco to him immediately.

'Go easy on it,' she said, 'as it is running low in the shops.'

'There's plenty there,' he said, 'if you know where to get it.'

Then he turned to me with what seemed an angry glare in his eyes. Now I knew I was going to get a right telling off for fetching Peter Johnson against his wishes. But I knew Mother would defend what I had done, as she agreed wholeheartedly with what had taken place. I held my head low, waiting for a barrage of abuse, and was ready to burst into tears.

'I want to have a serious talk with you, young lady.'

'Yes, Uncle John,' I said, swallowing something that seemed to stick in my throat. 'I'm sorry!'

'What are you sorry for? I only want you to help carry the big catch of fish we're going to bring home today.'

With that, he laughed, and I ran into his arms, and I knew he was coming back to us. He went down on one knee, giving me a big bear hug, and I felt that if life had given him the chance, he would have been the greatest father in the world. He stood up then and declared that there was never a sup of tay in the house when he wanted it.

Again there were busy feet, and we all sat down to our Sunday dinner, ever grateful to Bartley for getting him out of the room.

In the afternoon, the three of us set out for the lake, and when we reached the boathouse, Uncle John saw that the place had not been interfered with and the boat was in perfect condition, ready for the water.

'What's all this about, Bartley?' he said, winking at me. 'Why were you telling me all these lies about the boat and the boathouse?'

'Lies have often saved people's lives,' said Bartley, 'and that's all I'm going to say about it.'

Being the strongest of the three of us, he reminded me of St Peter pushing the boat out into the water on our way to find the catch of a lifetime.

*****

Two nights later, Maureen called to me. It was just approaching dawn. I sat up in bed, frightened, and she said that everything was fine.

'Go for Jimmy Kiernan,' she said. 'Magic is going to foal.'

'It's dark!' I said.

'You will have to go, dear,' said Mother. 'You will be quick on your bicycle. Anyway, dawn is approaching, and there will be lots of light in a matter of minutes.' I dressed quickly and found my bike in the shed. Uncle John and Martha were in the stable with the horse.

I did not delay. I soon found myself out on the road on a frosty spring morning, seeking to find the man who butchered all the animals. Now he was coming to save a life and to help bring a new little one into the world.

The fields were white with frost, but now, at the end of April, the frost burned off just after sunrise, as the local people would say.

Jimmy heard me coming, and it was his dog who rose the alarm. It too was a border collie, and he looked familiar. He had a black paw, just like little Shep. Mother Nature was working, it seemed, between all the local dogs too.

'Whisht, Rover!' he said, and threw the dog a large crust of bread to quieten him down.

'You don't have to tell me what's wrong, girl,' he said. 'Come on, let's get moving.'

We cycled quickly back to the farm, and I found myself working harder to keep up with this big, strong, fit man. Everyone was waiting anxiously for our return.

Mother ordered me immediately into the house, but Uncle John intervened and said, 'Remember, Kitty, Mother Nature is working here this morning. It will do her no harm. She's a growing, sensible girl.'

I was glad I was allowed to stay. The foal was born easy enough in the end. She would have managed on her own, but Uncle John was just being extra careful, as he didn't want to lose another animal if there were any complications.

It was a little black colt, with a star in the middle of his forehead. For all the world, it was Paddy all over again. But Paddy was not this little animal's father. I learned afterwards it was a stallion at the Johnson place. We stood there in amazement as Uncle John rubbed him down with straw as he struggled to stand and seek his mother's milk. There were tears in his eyes as I heard him say 'Paddy!' repeatedly.

Mother sent me back to bed for an hour. I slept. When I woke, it was after ten o'clock, and she decided to give me the day off school. When I went out again into the bright morning sunshine, Magic was allowed into the paddock with her little foal trotting after her. Uncle John was leaning over the gate. I knew he was pleased with the result.

'Can I give him a name?' I asked.

'I think I know it already,' he said.

'What about Paddy?'

'That's the right name for him all right. Paddy it is!' he replied.

Part 6
The May Bush

Chapter 11

As May approached, Martha declared that there was a lot of work to be done to prepare for the month of Our Lady. There were times during the spring and summer when Martha disappeared to the fields, and she walked quietly in circles with her rosary beads in her hand, praying. I found it curious, and I said nothing for a while, until I went to her one day and asked her why she was praying like this.

She put her finger to her lips and said quietly, 'Just go back to the house, love. This is my special time with God.'

I let her be, and returning to the house, I asked Maureen why her sister did what she was doing.

'I can tell you why she does it. It was a long time ago. Martha entered a convent to become a nun. She decided to do this because she wanted to give her life to serve God. She became a postulant and prepared to take her final vows to spend the rest of her life as a nun.'

'What's a postulant?'

'She's a person learning and preparing for her mission, through prayer and good works and living a life of poverty, chastity, and obedience.'

I wasn't sure what all this was about, but I knew it meant Martha was going to spend her life away from her family and dedicate it to the service of God.

'Why did she not stay, then?'

'She wasn't too young when she entered, and she had spent her life on the farm here. Then John got the Spanish flu. It was shortly before she was to make her final vows. She asked the bishop if she could return home to help care for him, as quite a lot of people were dying because of that epidemic. She wanted to be with him, her only brother. It happened very quickly, and it wasn't long till she was back here among us. With her return and through her gentle care, John recovered from the flu. She said it was like Lazarus returning from the grave. She decided not to take her final vows, and because of that, we stayed together. John was so grateful to be alive, and the good Lord has looked after us ever since.'

'Why does she go out into the fields to pray, walking in circles?'

'I think you ask too many questions,' said Mother.

'Leave the child alone, Kitty. She is interested in learning, and keep her that way.'

Then Maureen turned to me and proceeded to tell me why Martha walked around in circles.

'You see, Martha has still given her life to God. She walks in circles praying, as it was part of life in the convent. Our home, if you notice, is full of prayer. We say the rosary every night. The Sacred Heart light is kept lit on the little altar in the kitchen, and Martha has a fine statue of Our Lady on top of the chest of drawers in the bedroom. She blesses everything with a prayer, and she never says anything bad about anyone.'

*****

As the first of May approached, Martha asked me if I would help her with the May bush. It was something she had done every year since she was a little girl. She got John to go down the fields and cut a sceach.

'What's a sceach?' I asked.

'It's a blackthorn tree, and its flowers are out now. It makes a lovely May bush. The only problem is, it has thorns that would go to the bone, and it must be handled with care. That's why I get John to get it for me.'

May eve was a beautiful, cool, but sunny evening. The trees were bursting into leaf, and spring flowers bloomed everywhere, the first forage for bees, who had been very active all day. As the sun was setting that evening, Martha remarked, 'There'll be a heavy dew in the morning. That means only one thing, young lady.'

'What's that?'

'You must get up before dawn and wash your face with the cold dew. It will ensure you have a wonderful complexion for the rest of the year.'

'You won't have any pimples or spots,' said Mother.

'How do you know all this, Mother?'

'They gave me all that information too, when I was a young girl.'

'Margaret doesn't need to wash her face in the dew,' said Martha.

'Will you be washing your faces in the dew?' I asked both aunts.

'We're too old to have nice complexions at this stage in our lives,' said Maureen. 'And indeed, you don't need to either, you are so young, and you have such a pretty face too.'

Uncle John was sitting by the fire, smoking his pipe and listening to the whole conversation.

'I don't agree with that,' he said. 'If you saw her this morning before she went to school, sitting there at the table with a face on her like a thunderclap, you'd think differently.'

'Uncle John!' I exclaimed, making to hit him, but he grabbed me and started tickling me, and I had to make a hasty escape.

Mother came with Martha, Maureen, and me to gather flowers in the fields for the May bush. The little foal was skipping around his mother in the paddock as she grazed contentedly in the approaching twilight. I was sent off to gather bunches of daisies, while Mother and Maureen searched the ditches and headlands for primroses and violets.

Martha thought she might find some lilac, but I pointed out the first hawthorn flowers, which were in bud, and she exclaimed in a rather alarmed voice, 'They may be beautiful, but it's bad luck to take the flowers into the house. The fairies charm them, and if you look into that far field there, there's a lone hawthorn bush growing there. It's very old. If you find one standing alone like that, it's a fairy tree. We just leave it alone, and we won't cut it down. I read in a magazine once that Joseph of Arimathea, who was Jesus' granduncle, made a trip to England when Jesus was a boy. He used to trade with the people of Cornwall, who were great tin miners. They say that Jesus was with him once, and they went to where the later holy Abbey of Glastonbury was. Joseph brought back with him a cup that he traded with the people. When Jesus died on the cross, Joseph is supposed to have collected some of Jesus' blood in the cup. He brought it back to England and hid it near Glastonbury. To this day, it has never been found. But he was an old man, and he carried a staff to help him along. It is said that he planted his staff in the ground, and from it grew a hawthorn tree. It grew there for hundreds of years, and when the monastery was destroyed in the sixteenth century, the tree was cut down, but some local people stole pieces of it and planted them secretly. They are still to be found at Glastonbury, and not alone that, they flower twice a year, at Christmas and at Easter.'

As the sun went down, the flowers were all tied in bunches and attached to the blooming blackthorn that Uncle John had placed in the middle of the hedge. I was asked to do one more job, which was to make a series of daisy chains, and they were draped over the bush as well.

As we went inside, Martha produced another handful of daisies and asked me to make one more. As Maureen stoked the fire to make some tea, Martha took me to the bedroom, and she made me stand on a chair so that I could drape the daisy chain around the Virgin Mary's neck.

*****

I was up at the crack of dawn, and there was a white frost. I couldn't find dew anywhere. Maureen told me to look close to the trees in the headlands. The frost at this time of the year stayed away from there, as the grass was protected by the trees. The sun had not yet appeared, and I found some heavy dew. I knelt and washed my face with the wet dew. It was freezing cold, and my hands were falling off me.

I ran back to the farmhouse and dried my hands and face in the kitchen.

'I hope you don't get your death of cold,' said Mother.

I went to the shed to milk Snowdrop. Her milk was beginning to dwindle, as she was in calf again. Uncle John and Bartley had brought her to visit a bull at another farm back in March. It was an aspect of Mother Nature I was not yet allowed to witness.

Before I went to the house, Martha met me at the cow shed door with an egg cup. She scooped some of the milk from the bucket and threw it as high as she could over the lintel.

'The good Lord will protect our cows and give us plentiful supply for the rest of the year.'

With my head full of folk tales and May bushes, I ate my breakfast and cycled to school in the beautiful May sunshine. Nature was fully awake, as the buds were bursting forth on the trees. Rabbits scurried across the road in front of me, and the birds were busy building nests. Just like the evening before, I was seeing life in a way I had never seen it in London, and it made me smile, as it brought comfort to me, away from the bad things that had happened.

When I got to the school, there was another surprise that brought a smile to my face.

*****

Sheila had returned after a long absence. She ran to me when she saw me, and she cheered up no end. She knew that she was behind in her schoolwork, but I promised to help her more, and I told her about the little puppy, Shep, who was due at the farm any day.

Sheila was much stronger now, and there was better colour in her cheeks. Sister Bernadette brought her up to the top of the class, and I joined her. Sister Bernadette knew she would need a lot of help and wanted to keep an eye on her. The other girls in the class welcomed her as well, and I knew that my friendship with her had awakened in them something to help get rid of their fears. At playtime, she was included in the games, but when I looked over at the older fifth-class girls, Carmel was sitting on the long form in the colonnade, reading a book. She was still being excluded by her class.

I went to her and asked her if she wanted to join us, but she looked up at me and said, 'I don't play with smaller children.'

I left her to her book, realising that there was something very lonely about this girl. I just couldn't understand her. She had everything she'd ever needed, and yet she was so unhappy. So much so that it rubbed off on her classmates and she found herself all alone. It would take a long while before I found out what was bothering her.

When we were leaving school that evening, Sheila told me she wanted to show me something. It was a big secret.

'What is it?' I asked.

'I'm not telling you; it's a surprise. I think you'll like it.'

I knew I had to be prepared for disappointment, and regardless show her that I was surprised and pleased at what I saw.

I walked my bike with her on the short journey out of the village. She looked happy and well as the sun shone in her long, fair hair.

'I want to show you something at our house,' she said.

'Don't be teasing me, Sheila,' I grumbled. 'Go on, tell me!'

'No, I won't,' she laughed, and skipped along the road in front of me.

Her mother met us at the gate, and opened it to let us in.

'You are very welcome again, Margaret. I could hear you both laughing and talking, coming along the road, and it was a lovely sound to hear.'

'Thank you, Mrs Bryce,' I answered.

'Mammy, I want to show Margaret my little friend out in the garden.'

'Well, don't frighten it,' Mrs Bryce said.

I followed Sheila to the small garden at the back of the little cottage, which was being prepared for a main crop of potatoes and some vegetables. She told me to stand at the garden gate and not to make much noise. She waited in the middle of the garden, among all the soft ground that was being dug by her father in the evenings when he came home from Johnsons'. She held up her hand with her palm extended upwards and began calling.

'Come on! Come on! Come here, little one!' Then she gave a little whistle and called again. After a minute or so, a little bird fluttered out of the hedge and landed on the palm of her hand.

'Now come on over, Margaret, and don't make too much noise.'

'Hello, little one!' Sheila said. 'This is my friend Margaret.'

When I got close enough, I saw it was a little robin. It then flew from her hand and perched on the garden gate. Sheila put her hand in her pocket and took out a handful of bread crumbs. The little bird flew back again, lit on her hands, and began pecking away at the crumbs.

'How do you *do* that?' I asked in a whisper. 'It's so beautiful. She trusts you so much.'

'Now walk slowly with me. I want to show you something else.'

I followed her to the hedge as the little bird flew away and landed on the garden gate again. Sheila pulled the branches of the hedge back and said, 'Now look in, and don't touch anything.'

I peered into the darkened light in the centre of the hedge to see a nest with five little eggs.

'Oh, Sheila! This is just magic,' I said.

'I must get her back now,' she said.

She let the branches back gently to their normal state and began calling again. We moved away from the hedge, and the little robin flew back to its nest and the five little eggs. After a few minutes, Sheila took me back quietly to the spot where the nest was, and we peered in silently again. The robin was snug and safe on her nest now. She knew we were looking at her, but she had no fear at all.

When we turned around again, Mrs Bryce was standing at the gate, smiling across at us.

Over the next week or two, I called every day, going from school, and Sheila kept me up to date as to what was happening with the robin and her eggs. Then one morning in class, she whispered across to me, 'They're here! They were born last night. They are all well.'

When we went into the garden that afternoon, we had to watch and wait as the little robin flew in and out of the nest, busy feeding her hungry little brood. The baby birds chirped loudly when she returned each time with food, and went quiet when she left. With a window of only a few minutes before the mother robin returned, Sheila pulled the branches back, and there they were, five little naked bodies with big beaks, wriggling and writhing with their bills wide open to any movement they detected. Then when nothing happened, they went quiet, but when Sheila gave a little whistle, they opened their mouths, bold and wide, in anticipation of food.

We watched them grow each day, and within a few short weeks, they fledged and flew. They remained in the garden for a while, as their mother brought some food to them, but then they began foraging, searching the vegetable plot for insects, grubs, and worms. By late summer they were gone to find a new territory for themselves.

The aunts and Mother listened with intent each evening when I gave them a progress report on Sheila's little brood of robins in the garden.

'She has a gift,' said Maureen.

'Aye!' said Martha. 'It is an angel's gift.'

'Only special people can do that,' said Maureen. 'You see how St Brigid could tame animals, even wolves.'

'And don't forget St Francis and St Kevin. The birds all flocked to them,' said Martha.

'It's a gift from God,' said Maureen. 'When I was going to school, the nuns told us a story about St Colm, and he lived in a place called Terryglass. The birds used to land on his arms. When his friend and teacher St Finian was dying, he wanted Colm to be with him when he died, and Colm came to him as a dove, flying.'

Then Martha told a beautiful tale about a saint named Mochua who lived in Ireland in early Christian times. Martha had been told the story by her grandmother when she was only a little girl.

'He was a friend of the great saint of Iona in Scotland whose name was Colmcille. His name meant that he was known as the dove of the Church. In Scotland they call him Columba. One day he received a letter from Mochua. He was sad, as he had suffered a great loss.'

Then I was all ears, as I knew it would be another of Martha's tales told from the depths of her ancient wisdom. I was not disappointed.

'Mochua had three pets, and he loved them very much. He had no worldly wealth, and he lived a very simple life as a monk. His three pets were a cock, a mouse, and a fly. He spent long days working, studying, and praying. As a monk, he had to rise from his bed a few times in the night to pray. The cock crowed at the exact times he needed to rise from his bed. As well as that, he had a lot of study, reading, and writing to do, and if he began to nod off at his table in his little cell, the mouse would nibble at his ear to waken him again. The fly, on the other hand, followed the lines he was reading on the page, and whenever he left his cell to pray, the fly waited at the spot where he stopped reading till he returned. Mochua was a very happy man with his three pets.

'But animals, unlike humans, have a very short life. In fact, a fly's life lasts for only one summer. So each of the pets in turn passed away. The cock was the last one to go. Mochua, in his sadness, wrote to St Colmcille to tell him of his great loss.

'Colmcille wrote back to him and said, "Sadness comes from being rich. You were rich when you had your three little friends. Do not grieve for them, but be happy to have known them."'

I thought there was a great lesson to learn from that story, and that Martha was quietly passing a message to Uncle John. The sadness he publicly displayed at losing old Paddy meant that he was rich for having the beautiful memories of his old friend. He was quietly listening as he sat beside the fire and smoked his pipe, and when I looked over at him, he looked back with a tearful but happy smile.

With such a story, I felt that I too was rich to have experienced being so close to nature. The stories, tales, history, and legends told by my two great-aunts, sitting by the fire, would be forever etched in my memory.

There was a great innocence and security at times like this during those years. I realised that someday in the future, though I did not know how long it would be, I would have to leave all this behind. I would need to take stock and remember the words of St Colmcille. I was rich. When it was all gone, I would still have the memories, and not only that, I would still be rich.

*****

During those years, animals were so much a part of my life. Earlier in the spring I had been sent to Bartley's house to deliver some buttermilk and some butter, but unbeknownst to me, Uncle John had arranged with Bartley to show me Maggie and her litter of puppies. Uncle John preferred the border collie; according to him, they were among the cleverest of animals. The puppy I named that day, Shep, was to become another member of the band of four-legged creatures at Dairy Hill.

I didn't realise that Sheila was to display her giftedness again before too long.

When I returned from school one evening at the end of June, Bartley had arrived. Again unbeknownst to me, he had brought the little puppy with him. He carried him in the inside pocket of his old grey coat, with Shep's little head peeping out from behind the lapel. He was whimpering and sad, having been taken from his mother for the first time. He had grown fat from all the feeding his mother had given him.

When Bartley placed him down on the kitchen floor, the first thing he did was leave a large lake all over the cement.

'If he pisses any more,' said Uncle John, 'we might just call him Killarney, he'd leave so many lakes about the place.'

'Uncle John, please!' said Mother. 'Just mind what language you use around here.'

There was a round of laughter in the kitchen, and I took the little fellow up in my arms. He nestled into the warmth of my cardigan and fell asleep. I was so happy to hold him. But Mother was not long in bringing me back to my senses.

'Bartley Hegarty, look what you've done this evening! I will get nothing done now. She has homework to do, and she must eat her dinner. Not alone that, she must help with the milking.'

'Well, isn't she the little dog's mother now?' he said.

'Have you nothing better to do, have you?'

'Bartley, come on and I'll show you how the foal is doing,' said Uncle John. 'When you're on the same floor as a houseful of women, it can be dangerous sometimes.'

Mother went to hit him with the tea towel, but the two men hightailed it out the door to the paddock and freedom.

'Listen, alannah,' said Maureen. 'I'll put him in a box of straw I've prepared in the scullery. He might go to sleep.'

She lay him gently in the box, and after a short while, he was silent.

But that wasn't the end of it. When he awoke, the whimpering began again, and Maureen thought he might be hungry. She prepared a little plate of milk with some soft bread broken up in it. He ate about half of it, and I took him outside, where he again left a lake on the dry gravel, and not only that, he left another job too.

He sniffed around the place, just as dogs do, and when Sam arrived from his little shed at the gate, he was none too happy with the new arrival. Shep began running after him and pulling at his tail, but old Sam turned around and snapped at him. The little dog yelped and came back to me. I picked him up and began petting him.

Over the next few days, Sam kept his distance from him, and if the little dog approached him, he growled back. He was master of his territory, and he was not happy with this new whippersnapper on his doorstep.

That first night, just as we were settling down to sleep, the little dog began howling from the scullery, and there was no sign of him stopping. I wanted to go down to him and pick him up, or even take him to my bed, but Mother would not hear of it. Eventually, I could hear a stir, and Uncle John went grumbling down the stairs.

'What must a person do to get a good night's sleep around here?'

I wanted to follow him, but Mother said, 'No! Go to sleep now. You have school in the morning.'

I could hear Uncle John taking the little dog outside somewhere, and the whimpering continued for a long time in one of the stables, but it was faint and in the distance. Eventually the world fell silent, and the little dog fell asleep from exhaustion.

This pattern continued for two or three days, and I kept telling Sheila at school about Shep. I was wondering if the little pet would ever settle down.

Then Sheila spoke.

'Your Uncle John called yesterday evening to see Dad. He is under a promise to tidy up the flower garden on Saturday for your two aunts. May I come over with him? I would like to see the little dog too.'

'That would be a great idea,' I said, and I looked forward to the day.

They arrived at about nine on Saturday morning. Fintan brought Sheila on the carrier of his bike. She was sitting on the back, holding on to the saddle behind her father, and her two legs were stretched out, just in case she caught her feet in the spokes of the wheels. She was cold and sore from the three-mile journey, and Mother brought her in to the fire and made her stay in until the day warmed up a bit.

We sat chatting to each other, and she had the little puppy on her knee. He had cried a lot the previous night and was now asleep, exhausted after keeping the world awake for so long.

'Well, he can't spend his days in the house,' said Maureen. 'He's going to be a working dog, and he will stay outside on the farm and sleep in the shed at night. You don't want to make an ashy pet out of him and have him under our feet all the time.'

'He's just a baby, really,' I said.

'I know what we'll do with him,' said Mother. 'We'll make your bed out in the shed with him, and that will be the solution to all our problems.'

When Mother spoke like this, I knew she meant the opposite. The dog was staying outside, regardless of my pleas and complaints.

The only one I could think of who might help was Sam, but he kept growling and snarling at the little dog. But what happened next has never failed to amaze me, even to this day.

'He's lonely!' said Sheila, 'He was taken away from all his family. He hasn't found a new family yet. We're all just humans. He needs to have a friend.'

When we went out at about eleven o'clock, we took the little dog with us, and he toddled after us down to the paddock to see little Paddy the foal. He had just had a feed from his mother. There was froth around his mouth, and by now he was no longer shy. He came running to the gate, followed by his mother. We spent a little time with him, and then we went to see how Fintan was doing.

Uncle John was with him, giving him a hand, as there was a lot of weeding and cleaning to do. Some of the herbaceous perennials were taking over the flower beds and needed thinning. Uncle John did some of the deep digging, as Fintan was able to do only light work. Sam was with them and sat on Uncle John's coat, preening himself. He paid little attention to us, but when the little dog came close to him, he began to growl.

Sheila stooped down to him and said, 'Shh, Sam! It's all right.' She held the little dog in one arm. She rubbed Sam's head and began to calm him down.

'It's all right, Sam. You're his daddy now, and he needs you.' She took the little dog and held him down close to the old dog. Sam made to growl again, but Sheila shook her finger and said, 'No, Sam!'

He stopped growling, and as Sheila held the little dog close but at a safe distance from Sam, he began to smell him.

'Good man, Sam!' she said. He began to wag his tail in approval, and what happened next was unbelievable. He started licking the little dog on the head.

Sheila let Shep down on the ground. Sam stood licking the little fellow, and Shep moved closer to the old dog. Sam lay back down again on Uncle John's coat, and the little dog curled up beside him. In a few minutes, they were both asleep.

'They're friends now,' said Sheila.

'How did you *do* that?' said Uncle John.

'I just told Sam to behave himself and be a good daddy.'

'But you didn't say that,' said Uncle John.

'You don't have to. He understood what I meant.'

'That's our Sheila,' said Fintan. 'She has a way with them.'

We left the two men working and went off to explore the fields and gather flowers. The sun shone that afternoon, and I had to go a little easier than usual, as Sheila couldn't move as quickly as me.

When we returned to the farmyard, Shep was following Sam everywhere, and the old dog stopped every so often and sniffed him all over.

That night, when I went to put Shep in the shed, I couldn't find him anywhere. I called for him, but he hadn't yet latched on to his name. The sun was going down, and I was afraid he'd get lost out in the fields and end up being taken by a fox. He was still very young. I called Mother, and we began searching for him in the sheds and stables.

When Uncle John arrived back on the trap after leaving Sheila and Fintan home, he found us in a blind panic looking for the little dog.

'Have you looked in all the sheds?' he asked.

'Everywhere!' I said.

'Where's Sam?'

'He must be in his shed,' said Maureen.

'Well, see if he's gone in for the night.'

When I looked into Sam's shed, he was lying flat on his bed of straw, and the little dog was tucked up fast asleep, lying close to him.

Uncle John was so pleased with this, as he knew that Shep would follow everything Sam did. It would make his training easier.

Chapter 12

In July 1941, we were busy making hay. The school had just closed for the holidays. I was happy with the fine weather, and I had a good appetite. I had lost the pale colours of city life, which had given way to a red, rosy complexion and the benefits of good, wholesome food. But when I looked in the mirror, my face was covered in freckles. I wasn't too happy about this, but Maureen said they were a sign of beauty. Uncle John, on the other hand, had his usual amusing take on the subject, and declared that every time I farted, a freckle grew. He had me in stitches laughing as a result.

But there was a cloud on our joy that day as we were making hay. Mother had received a letter from Father. We hadn't heard from him for a long time, and the letter stated that he had been drafted to North Africa. He couldn't disclose in the letter where he was destined to go, for fear it might fall into the wrong hands.

Mother wept all morning, and to keep her mind off things, Uncle John handed her a two-grained fork and told her to help turn the hay.

He was back to his old self again. He looked across the ditch occasionally at Moonlight, who grazed contentedly by himself, and Magic moved slowly along the ditch, followed by little Paddy the foal, who was now beginning to grow quite fast as well.

Bobby showed his contempt every so often by turning his back and kicking his heels at them. Magic was not having any of it, and she chased after him, bowing her head and nuzzling him in the backside as she did so. Then he retreated to a quiet corner, afraid of what the proud mother might do to him.

Mother wanted to be alone, and Uncle John told me quietly to leave her be.

'She's lonely,' he said. 'She misses her man, and it can be worse than death, you know. If he were dead, at least you'd know there was no coming back. But she doesn't know what to do.'

'I hope she'll be all right; I don't want to lose her too.'

'Give her a few days, and we'll see her back to her old self again. Remember, she was like that at Christmas when the parcel arrived. She got over it soon enough. The women will be on with the tea in a few minutes, and that should brighten her up as well.'

Sam was sniffing through the heaps of drying grass; it was full of frogs and field mice. Shep was following what he was doing, and occasionally he pounced on something and began nibbling at it and giving his little puppy bark. It was usually a beetle or some other insect, such as a moth, emerging from beneath the drying meadow.

Then the tea arrived, and we leaned against cocks of hay and ate to our hearts' content. There were great wedges of rhubarb tart, sweetened, not with the normal sugar but icing sugar instead. There was some of it left over from Christmas in the cupboard in the kitchen, and it was beginning to get damp. The top of the tarts did not have that beautiful brown lustre but were darker in colour on account of the black flour.

We were used to the black bread at this stage. The flour was made at home from Irish wheat. At the time, it was regarded as of poor quality, not like the clear white imported flour. In fact, however, it was more nutritious and healthier than the highly refined flour.

Mother was hungry, and she cheered up somewhat.

'You're getting sunburnt,' said Maureen. 'Maybe you've had enough for today, alannah.'

'I'll finish my tea, and then I'll go,' said Mother.

'I thought Bartley was to give you a hand today,' said Martha.

'That's right,' said Uncle John. 'It's not like him to let us down.'

'I'll call to him on my way back,' said Mother, 'and tell him that you need him urgently.'

So Mother returned to the farmhouse, making a diversion through the fields to Hegarty's place. We resumed turning the hay. One half of the field was in cocks; this half had been cut three days beforehand with the mowing machine. Jimmy Kiernan had borrowed one from a local farm along with two horses, as Uncle John did not yet take Moonlight and Magic out to work together.

For some time now in the mornings, I'd been awakened by the corncrakes from early dawn until the sun was high in the sky, and then again in the evening until after dark. Since the meadow was cut, they had moved on to another farm, and the calling had ceased. It could be annoying at times, especially when you were trying to sleep.

Out of the blue, help arrived. It was Fritz. I ran to him, and I could see that his golden hair had become even more blond with the bleaching the sun was giving it.

'I came to help,' he said.

'Good lad,' said Uncle John. 'You're a good strong young fellow, and it will make things easier for us.'

I tried my best to follow and keep up with him at turning the hay, but he proved too much, and I knew he was teasing me. He moved quickly around the field and began to catch up with me again. It annoyed me that I was not as strong as him, so when he was passing me by, I stuck out my foot and tripped him.

He fell headlong on the fresh-drying hay, and I could hear him swear and curse in German. I didn't know what it meant. I started laughing at him, and he jumped from where he stood and threw me down on the hay, covering me with it. I began screaming with glee, and Uncle John chuckled to himself. Then I grabbed a dead thistle, and the thorns embedded in my fingers. I cried out, and Fritz stopped his antics straightaway.

'I'm sorry,' he said. 'I didn't mean to hurt you.'

'My fingers. They're all thorns.'

'Show me.'

I climbed out of the nest of fresh hay, and he took my hand.

'Don't worry, I can see them all.' He tugged gently at the small, needlelike thorns, and one by one, he got them out.

'I'm sorry,' he said again.

'Yeah, you should be,' I grumbled, 'you big bully.'

'I'm no bully,' he protested.

'Oh yes you are,' I jeered. 'Bully, bully, bully!' I started laughing, and then I ran down the field. He ran after me. Down the rows of dried hay I ran, and he tried to catch me, but every so often I doubled back, and he had to slow down, turn around, and pick up speed again.

We were heading for the gap when suddenly he stopped and shouted in German for me to stay quiet.

'Ruhig, bitte! Ruhig, bitte!' he exclaimed. Then I could hear it. Someone was calling from the back of the fields towards Hegarty's place. It was Mother. We crossed into the fields beyond our boundary and ran to her. She was in a panic.

'Fritz, will you get Peter Johnson to take the car to Hegarty's house? Bartley's very ill. I think he might be dying. He needs to be taken to hospital immediately.'

Fritz began to run, and I shouted after him, 'Take my bike. You'll be quicker.'

He didn't delay, and he made his way hastily back to the big house to fetch Peter Johnson on another mercy mission.

*****

Bartley nearly died in the next few days. It was appendicitis. He was curled up in pain on the chaise longue in his kitchen when Mother found him. He had been like that for a day or more and wasn't able to get any help.

His appendix burst when he was on the operating table, and they thought he might not pull through. But to make a long story short, he *did* survive, and as he lay recovering in hospital, he worried about his farm and the animals. But Uncle John, Mother, and I kept a close eye on things for him, as most of his animals were dry stock, and they were quite content grazing the summer pastures.

One evening Uncle John was in town, and he went over to the hospital to see him. He discovered that Bartley had an unlikely visitor. It was Esther Kerrigan, the cook from Johnsons'. Peter had asked her to call on Bartley on her day off to see how he was recovering. Peter was in Dublin these days on family business.

Georgina was getting more difficult to care for at home. A week or two earlier, she had sneaked out in the night, and she was nowhere to be seen the next morning.

A search of the countryside began, but it was called off after some hours when Fintan Bryce found her sitting outside his gate in the early hours of the morning. She was cold and very confused. Mrs Bryce took her in to the heat of the fire and gave her some warm tea while Fintan went to fetch Peter. She was taken to hospital, and it was while she was there that Peter was advised to place her somewhere safe and secure. He chose a convent in Dublin, where the nuns had a nursing home for people like Georgina. It was a sad day for him, as he was totally dedicated to her, and it broke his heart to have to place her in care. It was while he was in Dublin for a few days, staying close to the nursing home to see how Georgina settled in, that Esther rang him and told him about Bartley.

Esther brought the patient some nice fancy buns she had made from white flour, which was still to be got at Johnsons'. John knew that Bartley felt uneasy with his female visitor, but when he left the hospital, he offered to give her a lift home on the trap. He tied her bike to the back and left her at the gate-lodge before travelling the rest of the way home himself.

I am not sure what conversation took place that evening on the journey home from the hospital, but when Uncle John told us all about Esther's visit, there was a wry smirk on his face.

'What are you trying to do, Uncle John?' asked Mother.

He blew a large cloud of smoke after inhaling from his pipe, and it soared upwards to the ceiling.

'Maybe I'm testing fate,' he said, again with that smirk on his face.

'What have you gone and told her?' asked Martha. 'Can you not leave well alone?'

'I'm just testing the water. Maybe this is the moment, a turning point in this man's life. God knows he needs a break. He's been so good to his parents, life has left him behind.'

'I just hope you haven't bitten off more than you can chew,' said Mother. 'And on top of that, don't lose the friendship of a very good neighbour.'

He continued to blow smoke to the ceiling. 'We'll see. It might be the best thing that has ever happened to the man.'

A few days later, word reached us that Bartley would soon be coming home, and Mother and I decided to go to the farmhouse and tidy things up for him so as to have it a little presentable when he returned. When we got there, Maggie came running to us, followed by three fast-growing puppies, who were too full of friendship and wagging tails. There was a bicycle propped at the door, and it wasn't Bartley's.

Mother called out at the door and knocked to see who was there. Esther Kerrigan met us. She was wearing a bib fastened around her waist and a scarf wrapped around her head as if she were a pirate.

'What are you doing?' asked Mother.

'Just lending a hand. This man needs someone to take care of him.'

Mother agreed with her, and then Esther said, 'Stay and give me a hand. It would make things a lot easier, and believe you me, with the state of this place, this fellow needs a woman badly.'

Without any further ado, Mother had a scarf tied around her head as well, and an intensive spring clean began, even though it was July. Esther worked quickly, and it was difficult to keep up with her. By the time we were finished, the place was spick-and-span. Not only that, she had doused the kitchen and bedrooms with DDT to get rid of all the insect life that had abounded there. Looking back now, many years later, I know it was lucky Bartley wasn't poisoned by the stuff, considering it was banned worldwide by the 1980s.

Meanwhile, Bartley got the shock of his life when he returned home and saw what Esther had done.

'I don't need a woman to clean my house.'

'But look at what she's done,' said Uncle John. 'She's even got rid of all the insects.'

'I used a natural way to get rid of all the insects before she came about the place,' growled Bartley. 'They're called spiders and cobwebs. The place used to be full of them, but now there's not a trace of one.'

'You have a fine, clean, well-kept house,' said Uncle John. 'What more can you wish for?'

'I'm very grateful indeed,' said Bartley, 'but I'm wondering what I'm letting myself in for. What in the honour of all that is holy is going to happen to me next?'

Uncle John smiled, and I knew he was saying to himself, *Time will tell.*

*****

Fritz arrived one afternoon towards the end of July with a small pony and sidecar. It wasn't unlike the Bianconi sidecars that were common in Ireland in the nineteenth century, but a small jaunting car. When I saw some of them many years later visiting Killarney on holiday, they brought me back to that day, which was a very happy one, as unbeknownst to us, we would see changes in the years that followed.

It was a quiet little pony called Nell, and Fritz told me that Peter used to take Georgina out on trips to the lake and village in their younger days, when she was in better health. The sidecar had lain abandoned for some time, and it needed repair. His grandfather had taken on work like this of late, and this was his pride and joy. The sidecar was now tastefully restored and roadworthy.

Word had got around the area that there was a German man repairing carts and coaches at Johnsons'. This had brought plenty of work his way, as there had been a huge increase in horse traffic again due to the Emergency. Carts and traps that had lain forgotten in sheds and barns with the advent of the motor car were being dusted down and taken to him for repair. Manfred was glad of the work, as it helped pay for his and his grandson's keep, and he didn't want to be depending on the kind nature of Fritz's uncle Peter.

I gave a little gasp of delight when I saw the whole outfit and Fritz tied the pony to the gate.

'I'm here to collect you,' he said. 'We will take Sheila to the lake.'

'That's a fabulous idea,' I said excitedly, and I ran to call Mother from the shed. She was collecting eggs from the hens.

'Wait now, we'll have to take something with us for a picnic,' I said.

'Don't worry,' he laughed. 'I have come prepared.' There was a basket tied with leather straps to the back of the sidecar, filled with all sorts of goodies ready for a day out.

'Esther did it. She is a very nice lady. She says that the only way to a man's heart is through his stomach.'

'She's right, you know,' said Mother. 'That's something we have discovered of late.'

'What do you mean?'

'Let's leave that for the moment, and time will tell.'

'I'd say a young fellow like you is hard to feed,' joked Maureen.

'You might as well be throwing biscuits to a bear,' said Martha.

'Or haws into a barrel,' continued Maureen.

'I'm sorry, I do not understand,' said Fritz.

'Don't worry, lad,' laughed Mother. 'Someday you will. Now away with you both, and behave yourself, madam.'

'Yes, Mother!' I cheered, and ran to kiss her.

I sat up beside Fritz on the sidecar, and the little pony edged her way gently down the avenue and onto the main road. It was a fine, sunny day and a beautiful place. It was a moment I wanted to last forever.

The summer was at its peak of growth, and there was a hint of a turn in the season, telling us that autumn was on its way before too long. For us, the war was a million miles away. Here I was, in the care of a gentle young boy from another country. He, just like me, was lost in a strange place too, and he was glad that we shared something in common.

When Sheila saw us coming, her face lit up, and she called her mother. She was sitting making chains with buttercup flowers, as the spring daisies had long passed. I could see that her strength had returned with the summer. I hoped it would stay.

She was speechless, and her mother made her take her coat with her, in case she got cold.

'Don't be late,' her mother called. 'I don't want you to be out when the night air is falling.'

'We'll be back at about six or seven o'clock,' said Fritz. 'And don't worry, I'll take good care of her.'

Sheila sat beside me on the side seats, and Fritz sat up in front, driving the pony. We talked, laughed, and sang songs.

Fritz could sing very well, but whenever he struck up a tune, it was in German, and Sheila began giggling. I'd then give her a dig in the ribs, and she'd hold her mouth, lest she offend Fritz. But he didn't mind in the least; he wanted to act the clown to impress us both.

'Why don't you sing something together?' he asked.

'All right,' said Sheila. She looked at me. 'Remember "Molly Malone"?'

'Let's do that so,' I said. It was a song Sister Bernadette had taught us. We both started after the count of three.

'One, two, three, go!'

> *In Dublin's fair city*
>
> *Where the girls are so pretty*
>
> *I first set my eyes on sweet Molly Malone*

As she wheeled her wheelbarrow

Through streets broad and narrow

Crying cockles and muscles

Alive, alive-o . . .

After the first verse, Fritz joined in on the chorus. Then he asked us to sing it again.

Thus we made our way through the boreen, past Hegarty's, and down the field to the lake. The padlock was off the gate during the summer, as there was a common right-of-way to the shore for people who wanted to fish, swim, or just relax and have a picnic. He took us through the woods on the path where I'd brought his grandfather to safety, and we stopped close to the water's edge.

Sheila jumped and ran to the shore as Fritz and I watched her. She reached down and picked up some of the shingle that fringed the water's edge, and she threw handfuls into the air and more into the water. The disturbance she made upset a flock of water hens feeding in the nearby reedbeds. They fled to safety by practically running across the water, flapping their wings to give them buoyancy just above the surface. Meanwhile, Fritz untied the pony, tied her to a tree, and let her graze quietly in the shade.

Sheila turned to us, and the laughing smile on her face said everything.

'This is great,' she said. 'This is freedom. I just hope today will last forever.'

'Take it easy,' I said. 'Remember, don't overdo things, now.'

'I'm fine,' she answered. 'I've waited all year for this day.'

'Well, first things first,' said Fritz. 'I'm starving with the hunger, and I think we should eat.'

He unfastened the basket from the back of the sidecar and placed it on a soft cushion of white flowering clover near the shoreline. It was like opening a great big treasure chest. He set out a blue-and-white gingham cloth on the grass and arranged everything for us. There were salad and cheese sandwiches, bars of chocolate, which were such a treat, and a large can of milk and some cups with which to drink it. At the bottom was a beautiful trifle in a great glass bowl. Beside it were some dishes and spoons. It felt like Christmas in July as Sheila and I looked on in amazement.

'Where did all this come from?' I asked.

'Grandfather wants to say thank you. He will never stop thanking you for what you did at Christmas.'

'He is so kind,' I said. 'Hasn't he done enough already?'

'As long as it pleases him to do so, I won't stop him,' said Fritz.

'I must thank him myself. What will Uncle John say when he hears all this?'

'Don't mind what he says. Peter said his bark is bigger than his bite. I don't understand what some of these English phrases mean. I thought he was talking about a dog.'

Sheila and I laughed together at what Fritz had said. He just smiled at us and continued with his conversation.

'As well as that, Peter is ever so thankful to your mother and father, Sheila, for caring for Georgina when she got lost. Esther made all this, and said you were not to be shy but eat everything up. She doesn't want to see a morsel of it left.'

'I don't think she need worry,' said Sheila.

'Now, will you all please say nothing, just sit down and eat? I am starving, you know,' he grumbled.

'I know that,' I giggled. 'Haven't you said so already?'

We made a fair assault on the food, and we left some for later as well. We each had a fine helping of the trifle, and later we attacked it again. Esther indeed need not have worried; Fritz was returning with a basket containing only cups, spoons, dishes, a can, and an empty trifle bowl.

I wanted to do nothing that afternoon but lie on the grass and face upwards, gazing into the clear blue sky. It was such a shade of blue, and I knew that somewhere just hundreds of miles away, that beautiful blue was being assaulted by rockets, bombs, and aeroplanes in bloody battle.

Sheila lay beside me, and Fritz had taken himself off for a walk along the shoreline. He spent his time skimming flat stones along the surface of the water. He knew that this day was for Sheila, and he wanted to give her as much space as he could. He was fulfilling a promise he'd made to me earlier in the year, when he'd asked me to leave it to him to arrange something for her.

She was still giddy, and she giggled every so often.

'Why do you giggle so much, Sheila?'

'I'm happy, just like those white clouds that are coming across now. They are never the same twice. They are all the time changing. Remember last winter, I told you that I wanted to sail away on a cloud and see the world?'

'But you can't sail on a cloud,' I said.

'I know that, but sure is it no harm to dream? I have had nothing all year but my dreams, and I wished and prayed that one of them would happen. You and Fritz made that come true for me today.'

'I don't make dreams come true,' I said. 'I'm your friend. I only want to help.'

'Then believe in me,' she said. 'I just want to sail away on a cloud. It will never happen, but we could share a dream. Someday I will go away. I know I will, and I don't want to be lonely.'

'You will never be lonely, Sheila.'

'No, not when I have you. You see, if ever I go away, I would like to be just like a daffodil in spring. I will bend with the wind and fade away as the summer comes, happy just to have lived.'

I knew by the way she was speaking that this was not a child the same age as me. She was an adult. She had grown up and lived her life very quickly. I felt I wanted to weep for her, but this was her day, and she was so happy.

'Don't look so sad,' she said. 'Can't you see I'm happy? When you are near, it makes me so cheerful. I've never had a sister my age. My only sister is all grown up, and she doesn't have time to spend with me. So I could never share secrets with her the way I can share them with you.'

'Have you any deep, dark secrets, then?' I asked.

'No, I haven't,' she laughed. 'That's where you come in. You're the one who tells me everything.' She was right in saying this, as I spent the next half hour telling her about Bartley, and how Esther Kerrigan had walked into his life. She sat giggling away on the grass, and she wanted more and more.

Then late into the afternoon, when she was beginning to get tired, she went quiet. After a short while, she said, 'Won't you keep your promise?'

'I will,' I said. 'Just send me the message whenever you need me.'

Then she jumped up and ran along the shore, leaving me to ponder all she had said. I knew she was gathering the last minutes of the day and wanted to hold on to them. She wrapped a scarf around her neck, and she faced into the wind, looking across the lake to the far shore.

Fritz returned and sat down beside me.

'She's happy,' he said.

'I know, but she's sad as well.'

'We should go soon.'

'Let's just wait a few more minutes,' I said. 'She'd like that.'

We waited another half hour, and as evening approached, I thought of Sheila's mother saying she didn't want her out when the night air was beginning to fall. We gathered everything up and turned for home, and Sheila went silent. When we left her back in her mother's care, she turned to me with tearful eyes and said, 'Thank you both. I will never forget this day.'

*****

Bartley arrived on Sunday morning all dressed up. He didn't know what to say. In one breath, he was angry. He didn't want a woman to be part of his life. On the other hand, there was a great change in him.

'You're a new man, Bartley,' said Uncle John.

'Will you whisht! I blame you for this.'

'What had I to do with it?'

'For one thing, what did you say to that woman when you gave her a lift home from the hospital?'

'What *would* I tell her, man? I'd never say anything only the truth.'

'If I know you, John Costello, you told her the height of lies. I'm heart scalded with her. She's down every evening with bottles of beef tea, hot Bovril, and other little titbits to give me back my strength. What does she want, a weight lifter or a boxer or something? God knows I'm no Jack Dempsey or Jesse Owens. All I want is a quiet life.'

'Well, do you want a bit of advice, then?' asked Uncle John.

'No, I want no advice from anyone. I went to Jimmy Kiernan, and he told me to tell her to go away and get lost.'

'And did you?'

'I did!'

'What happened then?'

'She started to cry and go all weepy and told me that I was an ungrateful hound. She had been so kind to me, and was this the way I was going to pay her back?'

'What did you say to her then?'

'I told her I was sorry, that I didn't mean it, and she went all lovey-dovey. God, I can't shake her off.'

Uncle John winked at me, sitting in the background, and continued filling his pipe.

'Maybe you shouldn't shake her off. She's a good woman, and a kind one at that. Keep in with her. Buy her a box of chocolates and bring her to the pictures.'

'Well, her bike is punctured, and she has to borrow one from one of the other workers at Johnsons'.'

'Now, someone in your position might be able to get a tyre and tube for her bike from the LDF. You know, it might be just as good as a box of chocolates or a bunch of flowers.'

'I never thought of that before,' said Bartley. 'Maybe I will, then.'

Part 7
The Blue Enamel Teapot

Chapter 13

Life moves on and time passes by when you're enjoying yourself. For all I knew, there had been no life before coming to the farm, and I was really enjoying it all. I settled back to school in the autumn and progressed well into fifth class with Sister Philomena. There had been no word from Father in months, and Mother maintained that as each day went by, no news was good news. I knew she missed him, and as life became rather boring on the farm during the day, she decided to get a job.

If Father had been with us and had been working here, she might not have been allowed to accept employment, but when she went for an interview at the grocer shop in the village, there seemed to be no problem, and she got a job there. Another bike was purchased, and she cycled to school with me each morning. In the afternoon I returned home alone, as she didn't quit until the shop closed around seven in the evening. During the dark nights of deep winter, Uncle John got Bobby ready for the road and collected her from the shop. This she was glad of, as if it were raining, she could at least haul a rubber mac over her on the journey home.

Sheila returned to school in September, and she moved into fifth class with me. Reverend Mother wanted her to remain in fourth, but her mother felt that if this happened, she would be forever in that class. She pleaded her case with Father O'Reilly, and predictably, he had his usual quiet persuasive chat with the nun, and she relented, allowing Sheila to move forward.

There was another pig killed just before Christmas. It was not as traumatic this time, and I didn't pay much heed as the animal's head laughed out at me on a table inside the scullery door.

Jimmy Kiernan came and went, helping with the harvest, and Peter Johnson had to listen to Uncle John rant on again to him about all the petrol he had stored before the war at the big house. As usual, he ignored such remarks, and handed over a horse to Jimmy to help with the harvest. Uncle John was going to wait until the spring before taking Magic back to the fields again, as he was afraid she might be just a bit too giddy. By spring the foal would have been taken away from her, and she would have no other focus than the farmwork.

Maureen was getting a bit fed up with Uncle John's ravings about lost land and entitlements going back to the mid-1600s, and lately his being caught up in the petrol-storing rumours concerning Peter's wheeling and dealing across the border. Most people paid no heed to all this, but one morning as John broached the subject again, she turned on him.

'Will you quit that nonsense, John Costello, for good and all? The whole parish must listen to all this ranting and raving. Leave the man alone. Hasn't he suffered enough of late? And if he can afford to gather a few creature comforts in these troubled times, so what. I'm sick listening to it. Just bear in mind, you might open that mouth of yours just once too often.'

Uncle John didn't answer her, but taking an enamel bucket and his pipe, he headed out to do the morning milking.

We didn't see as much of Bartley as we used to, but it wasn't unusual to see him sitting on a wall on an autumn evening, courting Esther Kerrigan. On the nights when he arrived to our farm alone, Uncle John would advise him on the ins and outs of courtship.

Then Martha would take him to task, saying, 'What do you know about love, John Costello? Stick to what you know. Are you an expert on affairs of the heart? You never married.'

'I never married, but I might as well have been; sure haven't I the two nicest old maids in the whole county of Westmeath looking after me? I never needed to marry.'

Then Martha hit him with the tea towel, knowing she was getting nowhere with him in the argument, and he acknowledged his victory over his sisters by winking over at me and taking another long puff from his pipe.

At Christmas there were no raisins or currants to be got, but Mother came up trumps when a consignment arrived at the shop in the village. She was allowed to purchase a few pounds of muscatels for well over and above the normal price. It was one advantage of her working there that she managed on many occasions to take home an extra ounce of tea or sugar.

She also traded surplus produce such as butter and eggs from the farm for commodities such as flour and paraffin oil.

For the first part of the autumn, when night fell by the light of the fire, I had to make a special effort to have my homework done just before dark. When the oil arrived, there was only one lamp lit, which was put on the table, and everyone sat around it, reading and playing cards. The aunts and Mother began knitting – jumpers, mainly, as well as gloves and socks, to replace those now beginning to wear a bit thin. Martha knew where to get cheap wool in the town. It came from the west of Ireland, mainly brown in colour, as it had been dyed with peeled onion skins boiled on the fire. I didn't mind the colour in the least, as what my mother and aunts produced kept the cold away during the long winter days.

When it was time for bed, Mother took the lamp upstairs to show me the way, and she'd light a small candle stub on a sconce on the mantelpiece. Then she'd take the lamp back downstairs again. In this way, they were able to conserve the paraffin oil and put some extra by for a rainy day.

Fritz was a regular caller when he was away from school, and time passed quickly when he was around. Sometimes he took me to visit Sheila, and he was now under another promise to return to the lake when summer came. I enjoyed the visits to Johnsons' to see his grandfather working. He was in his early seventies and very fit for his age. His fall off the horse didn't hinder him in any way, and it looked as if it had never happened.

He was getting so much work repairing carts and traps that he opened a shop in one of the stables and enjoyed an increasing market in wood products, from furniture to smaller kitchen implements such as breadboards, butter pats, and salt and pepper canisters. The work he did was simple, but the wood looked beautiful and fresh, and the items he made could not be purchased in the town shops. He was happy to do all this. He was able to keep an eye on the smooth running of the farm while Peter was away as well. The house itself was run with precision by Jordan the butler.

Peter's main concern was what was going to happen when he came to the end of his days. If the estate was still in his possession, who would be his heir? As he was an only son with four married sisters, which of his sister's children would he leave the place to? But such matters were at the back of his mind now, as his life was focused on his beloved Georgina.

*****

Spring had arrived again. It was my second one at the farm, and we had a few back-breaking days of sowing potatoes as well as getting the extra crops sown. It was hard to believe that we were well into 1942 and the war was three years old. There was no end in sight for it. All my childhood memories before the war were fading, and I wondered if I would recognise Father, were I ever to see him again. Mother told me I was growing fast, and I made my confirmation before Easter in the parish church. It was a very long tiring day. I was called upon by the bishop to have my catechism examined, and Mother nearly had a seizure.

I was given a yellow card for being so good, and I prayed on that day that my diligence and prayerfulness would be rewarded with Father returning safely to us. I would then be moving into sixth class in July, just before the school closed for the summer.

I could feel that childhood was beginning to pass me by. But I was yet to suffer more loss and carry responsibility far beyond my young years. I'd have to grow up too quick. With the coming of Easter, though, there was something else to look forward to in the parish.

Old Father Tom would be fifty years ordained in April 1942, and the parish decided to pay tribute to him for all his years of service to the community. Most ordinations took place in June, but at the time of Father Tom's, he was being sent to the American mission. When the time came, however, the bishop asked him to remain in the diocese. He came to the parish in the spring of 1911, having served as curate in two previous parishes. He declared always that he was a true Meath man, but his first love was the town of his birth, Navan. As he said himself later at his jubilee celebrations, this was the parish of his adoption.

Uncle John was one of the people selected to form a committee to gather money to buy something for him and to make a presentation to him at a concert in the parish hall on Easter Monday night. Father Tom was a keen gardener, and he loved to grow his own vegetables as well as flowers. The orchard at the back of the parochial house had a bountiful supply of apples each autumn. Billy Bryce and Father O'Reilly lent a hand in keeping things under control, and the produce from the garden was the envy of the parish.

The committee decided that with the £120 gathered from the people, they would employ a local carpenter to build a new lean-to greenhouse against the orchard wall. The old greenhouse had collapsed with the weight of snow in the harsh winter of 1932. It had never been replaced. The new building would be announced at the concert on Easter Monday night.

To provide entertainment for this concert, Father O'Reilly was directed to the convent national school and the boys' national school for entertainment. Working as a unit, the nuns and the two schoolmasters decided on a programme for the night. The boys' school would produce two short plays by P. H. Pearse, *Íosagán* and *Eoin*, as Pearse had written the plays at St Enda's School in Rathfarnham, Dublin, in the years leading up to the Rising in 1916.

The convent school was to produce a programme of song and dance. The person in charge of music production was Sister Berchemans. She taught sixth class and was a very talented piano and organ player. Her choir from the boarding school sang at early mass each Sunday, while her parish choir sang at a later mass. Together with the other nuns, they designed a series of period costumes for the older girls in the boarding school, who would perform a medley of Strauss waltzes in song and dance, accompanied on the piano by Sister Berchemans.

She searched also for fifth- and sixth-class girls to sing individually onstage between performances, so as not to stem the flow of the night's programme. Each person selected had to sing two songs, and auditions were held in the school hall for this.

Mother told me the day before to put my name forward, as I was such a good singer.

'I'm not a great singer, Mother. Where did you get that idea?'

'Remember when Nana used to teach you songs at the fireside back home in London?'

'Stop that, Mother. I don't want to think about those days. It makes me sad.'

'Think of how proud she'd be if she saw you onstage singing your heart out.'

'I haven't been chosen yet,' I answered.

'Give it a try anyway. You have nothing to lose.'

We were all summoned to the convent hall the next day at two o'clock. Sister Berchemans and Reverend Mother adjudicated the auditions as each child volunteered to sing. Every candidate was asked to sing a song, and among those chosen, many of them sang rebel songs and a few Irish ballads.

Carmel Daly was up next, as I knew she wouldn't be left out. She sang very well and had quite a sweet voice. She did two verses of the ballad 'Killarney'. It brought back a sweet memory to me, of Nana playing the music of John Count McCormack. She loved those special moments listening to music on her gramophone, and 'Killarney' was one of her favourites.

Carmel sat down when she was finished, and Reverend Mother told her it was just lovely. I could hear murmurs of disapproval from some of the other girls who had not been successful, which brought Reverend Mother to shout, 'Quiet please!' to the disgruntled young audience.

'Margaret Kerr, will you step forward, please?' said Sister Berchemans.

I did as she asked and joined my hands, one linked over the other in front, the way I had in my school choir in London.

'Tell me, child,' said Reverend Mother. 'Have you sung in a choir before?'

'Yes, Sister. Our school choir used to perform in summer concerts.'

'Where were they held?'

'We were in a large concert hall a few times, but since the bombs came, I think all of that has stopped.'

Then Reverend Mother turned to the other girls and said, 'You see the way Margaret is standing. That's the proper way for a young lady to stand when she's performing a song.' Then she turned to me and said, 'Will you proceed.'

She sat down again and looked on with intent. I was quite nervous, but Reverend Mother's remarks to the rest of the class about my posture gave me an extra bit of confidence. I proceeded to sing the folk song 'The Lass of Richmond Hill', the one I'd sung for the wren-boys on my first Christmas at the farm.

Midway through the first verse, Sister Berchemans stopped me and said, 'Hold it a minute, please!'

She jumped up from her seat and ran to a press at the back of the hall. She rummaged through the shelves, and from the old oak cupboard she pulled out a large music book. She thumbed through the pages, then shouted, 'I've found it.'

She went to the piano, and placing the book in front of her, she called me to stand beside her.

'Now I have that song here, I'll play the introduction, and try and sing with the piano.'

'Yes, Sister,' I answered.

She played the introduction, and I sang along with the piano. Occasionally she smiled up at me, and when I had finished, she played a few bars to conclude the song.

'That's fabulous, child. Just wonderful.' The rest of the girls present applauded in appreciation.

'Tell me, have you another nice folk song like that?' she asked.

'I know 'The Ash Grove', Sister.'

'Oh, it's a lovely little Welsh folk song, and in fact, I have the music here too.'

She thumbed through the book and began to play again, and the song echoed through the walls of the hall.

The ash grove, how graceful, how plainly 'tis speaking
The wind through it playing has language for me
When over its branches the sunlight is breaking
A host of kind faces is gazing on me
The friends of my childhood again are before me
Each step wakes a memory as freely I roam
With soft whispers laden the leaves rustle o'er me
The ash grove, the ash grove alone is my home . . .

The girls applauded once more, except Carmel. It seemed I had stolen her thunder again.

'Will you sing those songs at the concert?' asked Sister Berchemans. 'What do you think, Reverend Mother?'

'Certainly. Well done, Margaret.'

'Thank you very much,' I answered. 'I'll do my best.'

'I think it will be a great concert, Reverend Mother. What do you think?'

'I certainly hope so,' Reverend Mother said, as she turned to the rest of the girls. 'And I would hope that our girls will respect their school, their community, and their parents, by being of their best behaviour on the night. Remember, you will be grown-up young ladies in a few short years, meeting the world and all its ups and downs. Just remember too, never let a day go by when you don't kneel by your bed and thank the good Lord for keeping you safe.'

When I returned to my seat, Carmel gave me a stare, coupled with a frown, which I depicted as being jealous and envious. I did not realise that over the next few weeks, I was going to have to deal with Carmel and her jealousy.

The boy who'd sung 'The Last Rose of Summer' with the wren-boys on St Stephens Day, whose name I remembered was Shawnie, was selected to represent the boys' school. He arrived with his friend Tommy. Shawnie was going to reprise with 'The Last Rose' again, as well as a song I'd never heard before, called 'Come Back, Paddy Reilly, to Ballyjamesduff'. Tommy was sent over, as he played an accordion and the master wanted to see if he was good enough to meet Sister Berchemans's standards. He played first, and it was a set of jigs and hornpipes, which everyone clapped to. Sister Berchemans gave her approval instantly. She had the music ready for Shawnie to sing, and he still had that beautiful male soprano voice. I didn't know then that in a year or two that voice would fade, but he would always have a good male singing voice.

When he was finished, she told him he was very good, and the two boys returned to their own school up the street.

There were still murmurings and whisperings among the girls in sixth class because Carmel had been chosen. Their thoughts reflected that she was selected because she was the doctor's daughter, a privileged child. They had no problem with me being chosen, as I was a complete outsider and I'd won my place fairly. I tried to point out to them that Carmel had been chosen fairly as well, but some of them disagreed, stating that this sort of thing had happened before.

In the heel of the hunt, rehearsals went ahead after school, and I was late home each evening, just before dusk, tired and hungry. Mother no longer had worries about me going to school. I had adjusted to the bicycle, and I was progressing well in my work. Occasionally, Reverend Mother paid a visit to the shop to place orders for goods needed at the convent. She was the only member of the congregation of nuns who appeared every so often in the village, and it was usually on official convent business. The rest of the congregation could be seen only if one were visiting the primary school or the secondary school. So Mother got to know her quite well, and she would always sing my praises regarding my manners, my behaviour, and my schoolwork.

She passed a comment one day. 'You know, Mrs Kerr, Margaret would be an excellent student to enrol in the secondary school. You'd never know, she might make a fine member of our congregation someday as a nun.'

When Mother related this to me one evening at tea, I was flabbergasted. What had possessed Reverend Mother to make such a statement? I was horrified. I could not envisage myself entering a convent and spending the rest of my days floating around in a black habit, winter and summer.

'Mother, no way would I ever become a nun. Just don't even think about it.' But she was in the mood for teasing me that evening, and she kept the thing going, supported by Uncle John.

'Your father would be so proud of you.'

'Mother, please!'

'Not alone that,' said Uncle John, 'we'd have someone in there in direct contact with God, praying for our mortal souls.'

'Stranger things have happened,' said Martha. 'I will continue praying for you, and give it time, you might have a vocation in the convent. Wouldn't it be just wonderful?'

'No thank you!' I declared, looking from one to the other. The hunger had been leaving me since this conversation began. I wasn't happy the way it was going.

'Whether or not you become a nun, sweetheart, remains your choice,' said Mother. 'But on a more serious note, if this war continues the way it does, in another year we must think of what you will do when you leave primary school. I don't want you leaving school and working in shops or domestic service; you need an education. It's going to cost money, which is why I'm working to try and provide for that day.'

With that, there was a series of protests from the aunts and Uncle John.

'No relation of mine is going to work in domestic service,' said Uncle John. 'God knows we *did* see our poverty days when we were young. You see, we do have a comfortable bit of savings. We will never be millionaires, but life has taught us to be thrifty and not to be too extravagant. We will send you off to the convent as a day pupil, and this house will fund it. It is what you deserve. However long you spend here, we will take care of that.'

There were tears in Mother's eyes as he said this, and I thanked him by giving him a big hug, but Uncle John's stubbly old beard grated on my softer cheeks, and I remarked that it was time he had a shave.

'Sure it's only Wednesday,' said Martha. 'He always waits till Saturday.'

*****

Carmel Daly was to enter my life in a big way because of the gala concert on Easter Monday night. She was, to all intents and purposes, a very clever girl. She was top of the class in all subjects, but for some reason I couldn't put my finger on her isolation, her unhappiness, and the selfishness she demonstrated when someone did better than her in school. She never smiled, and she publicly expressed how much better she was than the rest of her class.

In the little village community, where poverty abounded, most of the children came from large families. Parents were about able to eke out an existence in small houses and cottages, where illness was rife. Most families would have lost a baby or two – or for that matter, a parent; generally, a mother died because of giving birth to too many children. Those who survived were educated not by the great schools and universities, but to be good wives and mothers, to be able to cook, to sew, and to provide for a small farming family or to make a living growing vegetables, keeping a cow and a pig, and being as self-sufficient as possible. The war years weren't helping, and the Free State was only just managing to keep everybody alive. Most of the children in the convent school wore hand-me-downs from older siblings or clothes made from pieces of cloth bought cheaply at the market. That first year at the convent school, I was horrified to find that some of the girls started arriving barefoot to class by around May. The boots they were provided with each autumn were beginning to not fit anymore, and they would hold on to or endure the old ones if they could, till they were given new footwear going back to school in September.

This was not the world Carmel lived in. She wore the best of everything. She turned up at school each day in the best of clothes and had a well-prepared lunch too. It seemed she was happy with her isolation and in her privileged place. She was the youngest of three children; her two older brothers were away at a large public secondary school in Kildare. Carmel always exuded a strange coldness, and she had no friends. Even though she took part in our games, she was often last to be selected, or she was not chosen at all.

Sister Philomena told us that it was mean and sinful to exclude any of our classmates from games in the playground. I tried as much as possible to comply with the nun's request when it came to Carmel, but most of the time I met with a blank wall.

It was just before the Easter break when Carmel showed her true colours. The finishing touches were being made to rehearsals on Easter Tuesday and Spy Wednesday. The school would then close, as the solemnity of the Easter season was to be observed. We would return to the school for a final dress rehearsal on the morning of Easter Monday.

On Tuesday morning, we were all lined up in the convent hall to perform our songs, and I stood onstage and sang mine perfectly with Sister Berchemans playing the piano. She then called Carmel Daly to come to the stage. There were four or five steps down off the side of the stage, leading into the hall. The audience was shielded by a curtain in front, concealing the way upwards to the stage. One had to step carefully coming down, as it was dark until the curtain was pulled back, flooding the entrance with light from the hall.

I stood to one side and waited for Carmel to come onstage first. She smirked at me as she passed, and I turned to go down the steps. I placed my foot on the first step, and I could hear her whisper, 'There'll be no concert for you!' As she said this, she gave me a push, and I fell headlong down the steps. I screamed as I tumbled helplessly through the curtain onto the floor of the hall.

Carmel began shouting as I fell. 'Oh my goodness, help! Margaret is falling. I think she might be dead.' I fell, banging my head, and I remember very little of the commotion that followed, as I was hoisted up by three or four adults who were preparing the hall for the event. They carried me off to the convent parlour. My forehead was bleeding, and I had turned on my ankle.

Rehearsals were suspended for the morning, and classes resumed. Someone was sent to find Dr Daly and to tell Mother in the grocer shop what was happening. Billy Bryce was dispatched off to Dairy Hill to find Uncle John.

Reverend Mother could not have been nicer, bathing my head and telling me I would have to be brave, as the doctor might need to put a few stitches in my forehead. I was not one bit afraid of what the doctor might have to do. I was given weak warm tea, but I didn't really want it. She sat there while we waited for the doctor, telling me that I was a very brave young girl and that if it were anyone else, they'd be making a right fuss.

Dr Daly arrived in his car a little later. He was a well-dressed man in a grey suit. His hands were white and unblemished, not like Uncle John's or those of any of the other local men, whose lives were spent out of doors in all weathers, and the test of time could be seen in their wrinkled skin and worn coarse hands. He was in his early fifties and had a young face. His bald head shone in the sunlight, and it looked as if he polished it, as it had a great clean shine.

He peered at me over his spectacles, which sat on the middle of his nose. 'Well, young lady, what kind of acrobatics have you been up to?'

'I fell down the stage steps, Doctor.'

'Could you not see where you were going?'

'I just don't know. I fell.'

'I never saw any pupil in this school since I came here fall down those steps,' said Reverend Mother. 'Surely you must have done something silly or stupid.'

I hesitated to answer as the tears slowly came into my eyes. I was reluctant to say what had happened to me, as I didn't want to get Carmel into trouble. Then I didn't want to tell lies as well, as Mother would kill me if I told a lie. She would say always, 'Tell the truth and shame the devil.'

'It was an accident, Doctor, really it was.'

'What sort of accident was it?'

'I was pushed!'

'But there was no one on the stage,' said Reverend Mother. Then the penny dropped with the nun. She knew that Carmel had just gone onstage to sing after me.

'Be careful what you might say, child,' said the nun. 'Do you understand?' I knew she was relaying a message to me: if I was to tell the truth, I was to be certain of my facts.

'Reverend Mother, is it a sin to tell a lie?'

I was now putting her in a spot, as she knew what answer she must give to the question.

'It is, child! But if you need to be truthful, then tell Dr Daly who it was.'

I turned to him and looked into his eyes, and through my tears, I said softly, 'It was your daughter Carmel.'

'What?' he bellowed.

He sat down like a ton of bricks on the chaise longue by the window.

'Oh my God, I'm so sorry,' he said. 'I never brought my daughter up to do things like this.'

'I'm sure she didn't mean it,' said Reverend Mother softly. 'You know Carmel is very high-spirited.'

'High-spirited, my eye,' he bellowed again. 'No person wants his child to be cruel to others, and she really has got worse of late. The sooner we pack her off to boarding school, the better.'

He then examined my forehead, looked into my eyes with a bright light, and checked my pulse and heartbeat.

'Have you any pain in your head? By the way, I forgot to ask you your name.'

'I'm Margaret Kerr,' I answered.

'The little girl from the Blitz. Now I know who you are.'

The he asked me again if I had any pain in my head.

'My forehead is just sore where I banged it off the wooden floor.'

Then Mother arrived from the shop. She hadn't been able to leave until she got someone to take over for her. It had been an anxious few moments waiting for someone to relieve her. When she arrived, Dr Daly reassured her that I would survive. She sat down beside me and hugged me, saying she was so proud of me for not kicking up a fuss. Then Dr Daly told me what he was going to do.

'I am afraid you will need a few stitches, my dear. It may hurt a little, but I know you will be strong and brave. Are you injured anywhere else?'

'I hurt my ankle.'

'Can you stand up? Let me see if you can walk.'

I stood up and found it painful to put my foot down. I leaned on Mother as I tried to walk. I sat down again, and he examined my foot to see if there was anything broken.

'There's good news and there's bad news,' he said. 'The good news is that there are no bones broken. The bad news is that it's a bad sprain.'

'Does that mean I can't take part in the concert?' I asked.

'I don't see why not, but you will have two special friends to help you over the next few weeks.'

'Who are they?'

'A pair of crutches. You can't walk on that foot till it's better. I'll put a nice bandage on it and get your mother to bathe that foot every day and keep a bandage on it for support.'

Uncle John arrived then, and he was quickly relayed the ins and outs of what had happened. He sat shyly and quietly at the back of the parlour with his hat in his hand, his balding head shining as well in the light of the sun beaming in through the window.

'My poor little pet,' Mother kept saying.

'Mother, I'm fine. I don't know what all the fuss is about.'

Dr Daly then put three stitches in my forehead. Mother held my hand, as I flinched a little, absorbing the pain into myself, not wanting to show any sign of discomfort or hurt.

'You're a brave young lady,' Dr Daly said. 'You will heal just fine. Now on your way home, will you call to the surgery, John, and collect a pair of crutches for this young lady? She must take it easy for the next few weeks.'

There was silence in the room as he packed everything into his medical bag. Then, turning to Reverend Mother, he said, 'I want you to do something for me, Reverend Mother.'

'What's that, Doctor?'

'I want you to exclude my daughter from the concert for what she's done today. It's only fair; I will deal with her later.'

'There's no need to do this, Doctor,' exclaimed Reverend Mother. 'I'm sure she didn't mean it.'

'I need to see this through,' he said. 'She needs to learn her lesson. What message is it giving to the rest of the children if she gets away with it?'

I then tugged at Reverend Mother's sleeve and said, 'Reverend Mother, is it all right if I speak to Dr Daly alone?'

'Why do you need to do that, Margaret?'

'Please, Reverend Mother, I need to talk to him.'

'All right then, only if you let your mother stay with you.'

'That's fine. Thank you, Reverend Mother.'

She glided across the room and beckoned for Uncle John to follow her. When the door closed, Mother sat on one of the dining room chairs while the doctor sat on the chaise longue.

'Why do you need to speak to me, Margaret?' he asked.

'I don't want you to stop Carmel singing at the concert.'

'I can't do that. She must learn her lesson. What will the other children say if she's let away with it? It will be a free-for-all. They too will think it's fine to injure someone, the way it happened to you.'

'Nobody else saw her, Doctor. No one saw her do it. They all think that I fell by accident myself.'

'It still doesn't give her the right to hurt others. I don't know what has become of her. I can't put my finger on it. She must learn that the whole world doesn't revolve around her.'

'Doctor, I came from London nearly two years ago. I was so sad and heartbroken. My father is away in the war. Mother was injured in the Blitz, and my wonderful nana was killed when the bombs fell. I have every reason to be sad, but I will not let it happen to her. If she is not allowed sing at the concert, then neither will I.'

'I think that's said it all, Doctor,' said Mother. 'My wise little daughter has spoken.'

'You're mother should be very proud of you,' he said.

'I am, Doctor. She has just been wonderful.'

'So I have no choice in the matter then, have I? The great doctor has been beaten in his wisdom. All right, Margaret, you win. But I must deal with this some other way.' He shook both our hands and left.

A few minutes later, Reverend Mother returned and smiled at me.

'You are a very kind young lady.' While she was saying this, Uncle John swept me up in his arms and carried me to the trap.

'Now the first thing I must do is go collect these crutches for you. I seem to be always minding injured women in my house.' He winked at me and deposited me in the trap like a sack of potatoes. Mother retrieved my bag and coat from the school and placed them in the trap. Then she went to get her bike at the shop and cycled home in front of us.

Chapter 14

Easter was a quiet affair, and I spent my time resting. I did not attend any of the Easter ceremonies, but Mother and the two aunts went to Holy Thursday mass. On Easter Sunday we had two hard-boiled eggs each for breakfast. There was plenty of activity in the hen enclosure, as the eggs were coming fast and furious from the hens. On Good Friday, Martha brought in fifteen fresh eggs and set them aside separately for Easter Sunday.

'Good Friday eggs are special,' she said. 'It is the day our Saviour died on the cross. The old word for these eggs is a *clúdóg*. They are blessed, and we will eat them on Sunday morning.' Then Maureen pulled the crane over the fire to boil the big black kettle and said, 'If you're awake early, Margaret, get up at dawn if the skies are clear and see the sun dancing in the sky.'

'What do you mean, Aunt Maureen?'

'Because our Saviour has risen from the dead. It is a very happy time. Spring is here, and there's new life everywhere.'

Uncle John found that one of the hens was brooding, and he placed her in an old half barrel in the shed.

'A clucking hen doesn't lay,' he said, 'so she is put to good use for the next few weeks. She'll have some chickens in about three weeks' time.'

He placed a dozen eggs under her, and she sat on them. Mother Nature had told her it was her time to sit and hatch out a young family. The half barrel was lying on its side, and he placed some water and food beside her. He covered the opening with a makeshift door made from wood and chicken wire to keep out the two dogs, especially Shep, who was still showing a little puppy naughtiness, even though he had grown into a fine, lanky young dog.

'Have you not enough hens?' I asked, standing on one leg, propped by the crutches.

'I hope there's a good few cocks,' he said.

'Why?' I asked.

'Plenty of chicken stew during the winter.'

'So this was where last winter's chicken stew came from.'

I was now growing so used to farm life that it didn't bother me, and I enjoyed the chicken stew when we had it.

The sun did shine that morning, and I watched as it peeped above the horizon. It was cold outside. The ground was dry, and there was a white frost in the fields. The hens were calling from the henhouse, and the animals were letting us know that it was time to be fed.

'Now watch for the dancing sun,' said Martha. It glowed red as it lifted slowly above the horizon. I pretended to be excited about it, knowing that its shimmer was the same as on every dawn, but for Martha, it was because Jesus had risen from the dead. It was a lovely thought, and I knew then that this was another custom, and something that should be cherished for the future.

*****

I was brought to mass that Sunday, and I sat with Mother on the women's side of the church. The sun beamed brightly in the stained-glass windows, and gone was the purple colour of Lent. Daffodils glowed in vases on the altar, and some of the more well-to-do ladies of the parish displayed fine hats for the occasion.

Sister Berchemans lit the whole church with her music. The parish choir sang the Easter hymns as old Father Tom celebrated this Easter mass. The boarders' choir was not present, as the girls had gone home for the holidays. Some of them would return tomorrow for the concert.

There was a great feeling of new hope in the air, and I prayed to the risen Jesus to end the war and bring Father home safe to us. I gathered that Mother's prayers were the same, and I felt a little tearful in my childish supplications.

After mass I was confronted by an elegant, well-dressed lady on the steps outside.

'Margaret, I'm Nuala Daly, Carmel's mother.' She took my hand in hers, and she shook Mother's too. She wore white gloves, and her fingers were long, thin, and delicate.

'I'm so sorry about what happened at school the other day. I've had to punish Carmel for what she did.'

'Oh, please, Mrs Daly, there was no need for that.'

'I hope that's the end of it. I would like you to come with me.'

When we reached the car, the doctor was sitting in the driver's seat, and Carmel sat at the back, between her two older brothers.

'How are you today, Margaret?' asked the doctor.

'I'm fine, thank you,' I answered, as I stood there like a flamingo on one leg, propped by the crutches.

'Carmel, will you step out of the car, please, and do the right thing?' said Nuala.

Carmel stood in front of me, a little tearful, and she swallowed deeply as she tried to speak.

'Margaret, I'm truly sorry,' she said.

I dropped the crutches and threw my arms around her.

'There's no need to say sorry, really.'

'I've been mean. I really have.'

'You're not mean. I know something makes you sad, and you won't tell me.'

'I'm so sorry,' she said again, and handed Mother a box tied with fancy ribbon.

'This is for you all for Easter,' she said.

She got back into the car with her brothers, and Nuala handed me my crutches.

'Have a very happy Easter, everyone!' she said.

Nuala got into the front seat, and the doctor waved at us as he drove slowly down the village street. Black fumes ejected from the exhaust, filling the air with dark, pungent smoke, which dissipated quite quickly in the cold, frosty air.

'It's not every day the well-up people like that humble themselves to poor mortals like us,' said Uncle John. The aunts were sitting on the trap waiting for us, but Mother was a little rattled by what Uncle John had said, and she was a bit abrupt and cross with her reply.

'People like that know how to conduct themselves and eat humble pie on occasion. They accept that they were at fault; in this case, it was their daughter. They have a bit of breeding and a thing called education. You should take a leaf out of their book sometime, John Costello.'

Mother walked away, and taking her bike, she cycled home. Uncle John raised his hat and, scratching the front of his head, said, 'Well, sorry for living. I will have to take out my words and look at them before I speak ever again.'

'Will you all stop this right now?' said Martha. 'It's Easter Sunday morning.'

Uncle John looked at me, and I smiled, not knowing whether it was the right thing to do or not. I said nothing but hobbled along on the crutches to the waiting trap.

Back home, when mother opened the box, it was a fruitcake covered in marzipan.

'It's a simnel cake,' said Maureen. 'It's like the Easter version of the Christmas cake, except without the white icing.'

'That was really nice of Nuala Daly,' said Mother. 'She didn't have to do that, but I think we'll enjoy it just the same.'

*****

Mother dressed my foot each morning, and Aunt Maureen insisted on putting a poultice with goose grease on it before the bandage went on. It had a vile smell, but she swore by it. Mother didn't object, as it was something she carried in her own memory from her childhood days. She knew that either way, it wouldn't do any harm; if anything, it would do some good. Much to my protestations each day, the goose grease went on, and I continued to move around slowly on crutches.

The concert and presentation to Father Tom took place on Easter Monday night as planned, and the hall was filled to capacity. We were joined at the concert by Fritz and Manfred. There was a great festive atmosphere, and the bishop had given all the nuns permission to attend. The programme of events went according to plan, except there was one change: I sang my two songs together, as no one wanted me struggling up the steps onto the stage too often.

There was applause for everyone. The two short plays went down a treat, and one could hear a pin drop, as the audience was so intent on the drama. Carmel sang her two songs very well, but even with a very appreciative audience, she bowed at the end and exited the stage without even a smile.

It didn't go unnoticed. Aunt Maureen remarked, 'That's a very sad little child.'

Carmel returned to her seat and sat with her parents. I tried to find her after the concert, but she must have gone home.

Father Tom was overawed by the presentation of a scroll of appreciation, and when he heard about the greenhouse, he remarked, 'By dad, you had better get working at it soon, lads. I want to get some tomato plants in before the middle of May.'

'Where will you get them, Father? Even tomatoes are scarce because of the Emergency.'

'I have my sources,' he replied.

This brought a laugh from the audience, and a further one when Uncle John shouted up at the stage, 'The black market, maybe!'

Mother gave him a dig in the ribs as he said this, and he turned and winked at me. She was still a little cross with him for his remarks outside the church on Easter Sunday morning.

Tea was served in the secondary school after the concert. Mother sat beside Uncle John, and he whispered over to her, 'Any chance of us calling a truce?'

She was eating a sandwich when he said this, and she burst out laughing. She nearly choked in the process. 'You have never changed, Uncle John, have you? I don't think you ever will.'

Fritz came and sat beside me.

'I didn't know you had an accident,' he said. 'It gave me a shock when I saw you on the crutches.'

'It's a long story,' I answered. 'It happened at school. I'll tell you another time. Now, what has been happening with you?'

'I haven't heard anything about my parents in a very long time. Grandfather has contacted some of the Jewish refugees in Northern Ireland, and he asked them to send a message out to Germany. There is a secret network of people who are smuggling messages in and out, and there might be some hope for some news about them.'

'I will do a novena for you, son,' said Martha.

'What's a novena?'

'It's a prayer for a special intention, said over a period of days. Please God it will help.'

'Please try not to be sad,' I said. 'I don't hear anything about Father. I know he's in Egypt. Mother always says no news is good news.'

'I hope you're right,' said Fritz. 'I really hope it's true.'

*****

I was at home from school for a week following the holidays, but before long I was cycling to school in the village in the early morning. I had finished with the crutches, but I took it easy for a while when playing games. I didn't run too fast or exert a lot of pressure on my foot.

On fine mornings when the sun was up, it was a pleasant journey. Nature was fully awake, and the buds had begun to burst forth on the trees.

Rabbits scurried across the road in front of me, and the birds were busy building nests. But at times like this, I hoped that these quiet pastoral scenes would flow on the breeze to Father somewhere in the desert and turn his head in our direction again. I continued to worry that I might forget what he looked like. I had grown a lot since he left. I wasn't the little girl he'd said goodbye to at the station in London two years previously. Would we be strangers to each other? I had grown so close to Mother too. How would I adjust to having him around me again?

But the pleasant May morning as I made my way to school softened my worry pangs, and the bobbing white tail of a little wild rabbit on the road in front of me cheered me up no end.

Then, back in class again, Sheila was glad to see me. I hadn't seen her since the day I'd fallen down the steps into the hall. She had been in bed for most of the Easter holidays, and none of her family had attended the concert for Father Tom.

She leaned over to me and said, 'There's another little nest again this year. Wait till you see where it is!'

After school, I went with her to her garden again, and she brought me to a corner away from the hedge. There was a small hazel tree in the ditch next to the field.

'I made a babby house here last summer,' she said. 'I used to play under this tree.' *Babby house* was the local name little girls used when they pretended to have their own little home, which was furnished with odds and ends thrown out of their own place. Pieces of broken pottery were used as plates and dishes. Such pieces were collectively called *chaneys*. Small twigs and sticks were spoons, knives, and forks, and cakes were made from clay mixed with water and placed on jam jar lids to dry. This was the cooking. Sheila spent any day she felt strong playing babby house, and when the autumn came, it was abandoned until such time as the weather and her health allowed her out once more.

One of her treasures was a large old blue metal enamel teapot she'd gotten from her mother. It had seen its day, and had been used for many years in the Bryce kitchen. It had been fixed twice with pot menders she'd bought when she was in town, but when a third leak appeared, it was time to let it go. Sheila cherished it, and she hung it on a small branch of the hazel tree just above her head.

It was here that the little robin had nested this year, and it brought great joy to her once more. The bird had five more little eggs, and they were safe from attack, especially from cats. Sheila sat on a large log she used as a chair, as her breathing was laboured, and her mother warned her that she wasn't to stay too long in the garden.

When I was leaving, I promised her another trip to the lake this summer, and she giggled with glee.

*****

Mother had an unexpected letter in the post the next morning, and she didn't get it till she came home from work. It had a stamp with a picture of a map of Ireland on it, which made her wonder who was writing to her in Ireland. She would have been happier to see the head of King George, as it might have been a letter from Father, but she was in for a surprise. Not only that, I was in for a big surprise as well.

She opened the letter and read it aloud. It was from the dispensary in the village. We had not yet returned the crutches, and I thought maybe it was reminding us to do so, but I was wrong.

Dear Mrs Kerr,

I hope this short note finds you well. In view of the awful injuries inflicted by my daughter on your little girl before Easter, I feel we need to do something to make amends for this incident. With your permission, I would like to invite Margaret to tea at our residence in the village on Saturday next May 9th at around half past five in the evening. You need not worry about getting here, as my husband will collect her in the car and leave her home afterwards. I know you are helping in the grocery in the village. If you could just drop me a note before or after work, I would very much appreciate it. I am looking forward to Margaret's visit, and I know it will do Carmel good as well, as she is going through a difficult time now. I look forward to hearing from you.

Yours sincerely,

Nuala Daly

'That's a turnup for the books,' said Uncle John.

'Be quiet, you,' said Martha.

Mother looked at me with a light smile on her face and then said, 'What do you think, Margaret?'

'I don't know,' I answered. 'What if she tries to push me down the stairs or something?'

'That won't happen, I can assure you. I think that little girl has learned her lesson.'

'I'm not sure whether I should go or not.'

'It would be very impolite not to. They're putting themselves out in a big way because of what happened, and I think you should go. If you're not happy there, just ask the doctor to leave you home.'

I reluctantly agreed to go. Mother wanted to ensure I looked my best when I went there. I had not yet put a summer dress on. When she took down the two from last year from the wardrobe, she was horrified to discover that they were a bit too short, since I had grown so much in a year. Maureen took them from her, and she let the hems down. Mother said that this would be the last year I would get to use them. She would have to make a visit to the dressmaker next year.

'You don't need to do that,' said Maureen. 'I'll get the machine out and run two of them up for her. All I need do is get a few patterns when I'm in town, and sure you can help me make it, Margaret.'

'I'd love that,' I said. 'I have never seen a dress being made before. We could get Uncle John to model it for us when you're pinning up the hems.'

'And you can try on my new drawers to see if they fit,' he laughed.

'No thank you,' I said, running out the door. I'd decided it was a great time to go for a walk with the two dogs in the field.

*****

I was ready on Saturday afternoon at four thirty, and Dr Daly arrived just after five to collect me. He was in a hurry as well, as he needed to visit someone who had taken ill in the village that day. Mother, of course, gave me the usual orders to be mannerly and to behave myself. I sat in the front seat, and the doctor did not delay in driving back to the village.

The Daly family lived in a fine house at the edge of the village. It had been built as part of the dispensary unit sometime in the nineteenth century. It was a two-storey-over-basement building, with steps leading up to the hall door. There was a fanlight over the front door, which lit up the reception hall inside. There were five Georgian windows to the front, with shutters like little doors that opened back against the insides of the windows. It was an elegant and cheerful place. The house fronted onto the street and was set back from the road, with a short drive to the gates. Each side of the drive had plantings of trees, such as lilac, laburnum, a monkey puzzle, and a few varieties of holly, which in winter displayed excellent crops of berries on green and variegated stems, not to mention a yellow-berried variety, which added to the winter display.

The dispensary was a smaller two-storey building attached perpendicularly to the main house and extending to the rear. There was a separate entrance to the dispensary from the road. There was access to the building from the main house, but it also afforded privacy for the resident doctor and his family. The front hall led to a fine stairway, which turned and divided halfway up, showing a large window with a rounded top that lit the upper half of the house. To the right of the large hall was a drawing room with fine furnishings and a piano. To the left was a dining room, and to the rear were two other rooms, which were used for official business and guests.

The basement contained the kitchen, with a fine Aga cooker, a larder, a toilet, and a room for the maid.

Upstairs were four bedrooms, as well as a bathroom and toilet. The water supply came from a large tank mounted at the upstairs level next to the dispensary, which gathered rainwater from the roof. Down at the back of the house was a well, where drinking water was carried by bucket every day to the kitchen. The doctor and his family were among the few lucky people, apart from the nuns and the priest, to have running water in their homes. The system worked quite well until there was a dry summer, when the tank went low, and come winter, frozen pipes blocked the passage of water from the tank for long periods.

I thought how lucky they were to avail themselves of such luxuries, as I'd had to get used to a tin bath by the fire upstairs in my bedroom on a Saturday night, as well as the yard pump and an outdoor privy, which did not smell very good at the best of times.

Nuala greeted me with a warm welcome and brought me to the drawing room.

'You are very welcome to our home,' she said. She hung my coat on a hall stand and called up the stairs as she was doing it.

'Carmel, dear, Margaret has arrived.' She directed me into the room in front of her and asked me to sit down. 'Carmel will be here in a few minutes,' she said.

I looked around at the beautiful bright furnishings and the elegant marble fireplace.

'You have a beautiful home,' I said. 'I love the piano.'

'Do you play?' she asked.

'I don't. I was going to take lessons in London, but the war happened, and that was that.'

'That's such a pity.'

'My nan could play the piano,' I sighed.

'That's your father's mother, isn't it?'

'Yes! I loved her very much. She died in the Blitz.'

'I know that, my dear. I am so sorry. You have been through a lot.'

'I'm very happy at Dairy Hill with Mother, Uncle John, and the two aunts. But I don't know where Father is. He's away in the war somewhere. We haven't heard from him for a while.'

Carmel was standing in the doorway listening when her mother caught her eye.

'Come, Carmel dear, and join us.'

She sat on the chair opposite me, but she did not speak.

'Isn't Margaret so nice to come join us for tea?'

Carmel hesitated, and without a smile on her face, she answered with a short but curt 'Yes.'

'I'll leave you both to chat, and I'll go see has Molly got the tea ready yet.'

As she was leaving, the doctor returned, carrying his medical bag.

'I'll be back soon,' he said. 'I have just had a call from the convent; old Sister Ann has had a turn. They may have to move her to the hospital.'

'Poor old Sister Ann,' said Nuala. 'She's a lifetime at that convent. She must be ninety or more.'

'Don't worry, Margaret, I'll be back to take you home.'

'Thank you, Doctor,' I replied.

When Nuala and Dr Daly were both gone, I sat and looked around me at the pictures and the paintings as well as the big mirror over the mantelpiece. It had a large porcelain clock centred in front of it.

'Carmel, you have a lovely home,' I said. She made no answer but just sat staring at me with an expressionless face. I paid little attention to her stares but continued to praise her house.

'I could only dream of a house like this,' I said.

Again, there was a silence. Then out of the blue, she said, 'Why did you come here?'

'Pardon?'

'I said, why did you come here?'

'I was invited!'

'Who invited you?'

'Your mother invited me.'

'I did not tell her to. She is all the time arranging my life for me.'

'I'm sorry, Carmel, if I upset you, but I thought you would like to have someone to come and keep you company.'

'I do not want to make friends. I do not have friends. I do not have friends at school. I just want to be left alone.'

With that, the door opened, and Nuala peered around the corner.

'Come along, girls. Tea is served.'

I was glad she appeared when she did, as I was none too happy with the way things were going. Nuala directed us to the dining room, to a feast fit for a king. She had lots of white bread, sausage rolls, jam and apple tarts, and a large bread-and-butter pudding with loads of raisins and fruit.

Little was said during the meal, as I was ravenous, and Molly kept coming with more pots of tea. There was little rationing in the Daly household. Nuala kept asking me many questions about life in London, about school, the city, the coming of the war, as well as the circumstances of my arrival at Dairy Hill.

'You poor thing,' she said. 'Hasn't Margaret been through so much, Carmel?'

'Yes, Mum,' she replied.

'You have great colour in your cheeks now. It must be the soft Irish air.'

'No! They spoil me at Dairy Hill. They have never had anyone so young staying there.'

'Isn't that just lovely, Carmel?'

'Yes, Mum, it is,' replied Carmel.

'Well, as soon as you are finished, you should take Margaret up and show her your room. I'd say she would like to see your collection of dolls and other things.'

'Come along, Margaret. I'd better do what Mum says,' grumbled Carmel.

'Now, be nice, dear,' said Nuala.

'I *am* being nice, Mum. Can you not see that I am?'

I was beginning to feel uncomfortable in this situation. I felt I was being pulled and dragged between mother and daughter. Nuala was being sweet and genteel, showing a welcoming side that was too sweet to be wholesome. There was something not right about her welcoming ways. It felt as if she were covering something else up in her own life. Her smile was not a gentle one; it was more like an agonized grin. There was pain, loss, or even illness behind the facade. Then I noticed that she was sporting a nervous shake in her hands.

Carmel was reluctantly following her mother's orders, resenting my presence. If I could have left there and then, I would have. But I began to piece together that Carmel's behaviour at school and at home had something to do with her relationship with her parents. Her older brothers were away at boarding school for most of the year. Maybe she missed them.

I followed her up the stairs to her bedroom. It was very neat, with a well-made single bed covered with a coloured patchwork quilt, a large wardrobe, a dressing table, and a chest of drawers. There were five large porcelain dolls dressed in their late-nineteenth-century clothes on the window. Their faces peered through their bonnets, displaying pudgy rosy cheeks that prevented them from smiling, or the porcelain would crack.

'They are so beautiful,' I said. 'You are so lucky to have such nice things.'

'I don't really like them. They can't talk; they can't be my friends.'

'I want to be your friend, Carmel.'

'Is that because my parents asked you to be?'

'No, that isn't true. I have tried to be your friend at school, and you won't let me. Then your mum thought it was a nice idea to invite me to tea.' I didn't tell her about her mother's letter. I didn't know whether Carmel knew about it or not.

'Would that be because she was feeling sorry for you, because I pushed you down the steps?'

'Carmel, will you ever stop this? It's hurting me that you think such things.'

'You always seem to do better than me at school. You make friends. That sick girl Sheila likes you. So does that German boy, and the nuns think you can sing better than I do.'

I ran to her and took her two hands. I looked into her face, and I could see tears in her eyes. I said nothing but kept staring at her, and then I said, 'Are you lonely, Carmel? Do you miss your brothers? Tell me what's wrong. I think you need to let people be your friend. You walk away. You look down on the poorer children because they're poor. They can't help that. Be nice to them. Be nice to Sheila. Did you ever invite any of them to visit you?'

'No, I didn't. I don't think Mum would let them.'

'Did you ask her?'

'No, I didn't. I'm afraid to say anything to them. I don't want to say a word. I really don't. I'm afraid.'

'Why are you afraid?'

'Now, please, Margaret, don't say anything to my parents.' There were more tears in her eyes when she said this. I wondered what she was afraid of. What could be wrong in this perfect house? I needed to get under it. I had to find out.

Carmel ran to the window and picked up a large velveteen soft toy. Her expression changed immediately, and she faced me with a smile on her face. I knew it wasn't a true smile but a forced one. She wanted to change the subject.

'This *is* my friend,' she said. 'I got it from America. My aunt sent it to me for Christmas. It's Mickey Mouse. There's a film called *Fantasia*, and he's dressed as the Sorcerer's Apprentice. See, he has a wizard's hat on his head.'

'He's really beautiful,' I said.

'Aunt Noreen sent it to me from New York. It was a great surprise at Christmas.'

'He has a happy smile,' I said. 'And you know something, Carmel, you have a happy smile now.' With that, the forced smile became real, and Carmel opened up to me for the first time ever.

'Please don't say anything to Mum or Dad.'

'I won't, but will you play with us on Monday at school and don't go off on your own?'

'Margaret, I'm glad you came today.'

With that, her mother called up to her, and she placed the toy in the window and we went downstairs.

Nuala made more tea, and there was nothing but small talk until the doctor returned. Carmel showed her coldness once again, but when I was leaving, she just gave a gentle wave and said, 'Goodbye!'

Chapter 15

When we were all sitting around the paraffin lamp at the table that night, Mother asked me how my visit had gone. I told her all that had happened. Maureen was at the table reading some *Ireland's Own* magazines a neighbour had given her. Martha was darning some stockings. Where holes appeared, they were mended, and the stockings were in good use for another while.

'She's a strange child, isn't she?' said Mother. 'But as you say, Margaret, something is not right in that house.'

'She's lonely,' said Maureen. 'She misses her brothers.'

'There's more to it than that,' I said. 'But, Mother, I will find out somehow what's wrong with her.'

'Maybe she's a changeling,' said Martha.

'A changeling? What's that?' I asked.

'She's a fairy child,' said Maureen.

'I don't understand what that is.'

'She's not the doctor's real child. She was left with them by the fairies, and the fairies took their real child when she was a baby.'

'That's ridiculous!' I said, with a hint of sarcasm and disbelief. Then I knew I was going to be immersed once more in the mystic world of the two great-aunts.

'No, listen, Margaret,' said Martha. 'Ireland is full of tales about children being stolen by the fairies. They leave one of their own in their place. The child that's left is usually weak, ill, or strange in many ways. They steal little boys, mainly, but they have been known to steal little girls too.'

'That's not true, now, is it?' I laughed.

'In days gone by, mothers found ways to fool the fairies,' said Maureen. 'They had to find ways to hide their little boys from them. They made them

244

wear a dress or a petticoat until they were a few years old. Your Uncle John wore a petticoat until he was five.'

I laughed when I heard this. Mother too had a smile on her face. She said nothing but let the aunts continue with their old wives' tales.

'My mother used to tell us tales about such things when we were young,' said Maureen. 'And there *is* a story she told us about a family in Wicklow who discovered that their little baby boy was a changeling. Would you like to hear it?'

'Go ahead,' said Mother. 'I'm all ears, I'm just fascinated.'

So Maureen continued with the story.

'My mother told us that Wicklow was a county rich in stories about the fairies, and that she knew a family whose baby was taken by them. My mother came from Wicklow, you know. She married my father when they were young, and they had a very successful business in the town, until they fell on hard times and had to sell up and move. They bought this place, and this is where we have been ever since.

'Anyway, there was this young farming couple that she knew, and they were looking forward to the arrival of their firstborn child. Everything was busy in their little house, and they were both waiting for the arrival of the little baba. Thankfully, it arrived on time, and the father was so happy to hear the baby's first cries in the next room. When the midwife called him, he was handed a little bundle wrapped up in a small blanket. It was a strong, healthy little boy, waiting for its first feed from its mother. They were overjoyed with their luck, and the little boy thrived.

'When he was nearly a year old, things began to change. He grew sickly. He would not feed, and he was forever crying in the cradle. During the day when the father was down the fields, the poor distracted mother didn't know what to do about him. Wherever she was in the house or outside on the farm, she could hear him wailing nonstop.

'One morning while she was milking the cow, a strange silence fell over the place, and the wailing ceased. She feared that the little lad was after dying. She stole back to the house and peered in the kitchen window. A very strange sight met her. She gasped in horror at what she saw. The little crying baby was out of the cradle. He was leaning into the skillet pot which lay one side of the fire. It contained the remains of the morning's porridge, which would later be given to the pigs. He was scooping it up with his hand and gulping it down in mouthfuls.

'She dashed into the kitchen to catch him, but in that few seconds, he was back in the cradle, wailing and crying. She knew there was something not right with her little offspring. She thought he was possessed by the devil. She didn't tell her husband, or he'd think she was losing her mind.

'That evening, she left her husband caring for the baby and went to visit a local wise woman. She was a person who had many cures, and she was closer to God and the spirits than any of us. The local priest said she was a witch, but that didn't stop them from calling on her for help.

'She lived alone in a little thatched cottage beside a stream, which flowed into a larger river. She could be often seen in the early morning out in the fields and woods gathering plants and herbs for her own remedies. They said that she understood the birds, and in fact just like St Kevin, when she called from her cottage door, some of them came and ate from her hands. She also had a pet fox which followed her everywhere, and when winter came, the fox went back into the woods to find a mate. It was a she-fox, a vixen. She would return in the late spring with her brood of young cubs, and as the year wore on, they went their way one by one, back into the woods and mountains.

'The young wife knocked on the little door, and the old lady let her in. She sat down on a small stool which rested under the chimney breast, beside the fire. She told the old woman the story about her strange little baby boy.

'"You do have a problem," said the old woman. "That is a fairy child, a *sheera*. They stole your baby, I'm afraid."

'"What's going to happen with this one?" asked the young mother. "What about my little baby boy?"

'"As far as I know," said the wise woman, "this strange baby is an old fairy disguised as a baby, and it will eventually die. Your stolen baby will remain with the fairies as one of them.'

'The mother asked, "Is there any chance of me ever getting him back? My poor little baby boy, he doesn't deserve this."

'And she began to weep and moan and wring her hands in despair, but then the old woman said, "There is a chance, but you will have to trust me and believe me, if you want to see your little boy again."

'"What must I do, then?" asked the mother.

'The wise woman said, "Come with me on the eve of the first of May to where the two rivers meet, and throw the sheera into the water."

'"Oh my God!" exclaimed the young woman. "You want me to kill the baby."

'"Do you not trust me?" shouted the old woman. "I told you already I can do nothing unless you place your full trust in me."

'The mother said, "Yes, I do trust you."

'The wise woman told her, "You must not tell your husband. Promise me that." The mother promised, and the wise woman said, "That's good; now you must bring the baby here on the eve of the first of May, and I will help you."

'May Eve was about a week later, and the young woman could not sleep at night at the thoughts of what she was about to do. As well as that, the fairy child was getting weaker, and she knew it could die.

'On the evening in question, the sun was going down and a golden sunset told the world that the first of May was going to be a fine, warm day. She wrapped the baby in her shawl, carrying it close to her. She went quickly to the old woman's cottage, unknown to her husband. He was out in the fields, moulding the potatoes, covering the young shoots from the early-morning frost.

'The old woman led her to a point where the two rivers met. She took the baby from the young woman, held it above her head, chanted a prayer in some old lost tongue, and flung the baby into the air. It seemed to float in midair, and as it slowly landed on the water, the young woman waited to hear a splash. But as it landed on the water, a great big wave rose and swallowed the baby. At the same time, it turned into a little old man sitting on top of the wave, chanting some old fairy song and playing a fiddle. The wave carried him away, and he disappeared into the evening mist.

'The old woman turned to the young woman and took her two hands.

'"What about my baby?" the mother sobbed.

'The wise woman told her, "Don't worry, my child. Take yourself home, and everything will be all right."

'The young woman ran through the heather and grass. She didn't stop until she reached her little farmhouse. The first thing she noticed was a great silence. There was no baby crying. She walked quietly to the half door and peered into the kitchen. Her own little thriving baby was fast asleep in its cradle, and her husband was sitting by the fire.

'He knew something had happened, as he could see guilt and joy written all over his wife's face. She lifted the smiling baby from the cradle and held him close to her. Her husband gazed in amazement at her, and she took his hand and told him what she had done. He told her that if he had known what was happening, he wouldn't have allowed her to do what she did, but he praised her for her faith in the old woman.

'As the little boy thrived and learned to walk, their neighbours wondered why the young couple dressed him in little petticoats. This was the way he lived and played till he was ready to go to school. Indeed, they reared a large family and were blessed with three more boys and three girls. Each little boy wore the petticoat until school-going age, and they all grew up healthy and strong.'"

A strange silence fell over the room as she finished the story. The knitting continued, and no one made a comment till Mother spoke.

'I suppose you could write under all of that,' she said.

'What do you mean?' asked Maureen.

'I don't believe a word of it.'

'It's up to you, dear, to believe or not to believe,' said Martha, 'but it *is* a story told at our mother's knee. *She* believed it.'

'The winters are long, you know,' said Maureen. 'We were told many tales and stories, but it's up to each person to accept them or not to accept them. What our parents told us explained many truths. So believe them if you want to, but they often contain hidden lessons we can't learn till we gain wisdom from life, and that comes with age as well.'

'We didn't have a great education,' said Martha. 'Not like your late grandfather, Margaret. He was the oldest of us. He was educated, and whatever bit of learning we got at primary school, we use it as best we can to explain this world we live in, and by the grace of God, I don't think we've done a bad job.'

It was in later years that I understood what the great-aunts spoke about. Their world was their heritage, and the stories and tales they related to me during those years were old, and this was their folklore. There was a lot of truth in what they said. Some of it, though, you had to treat with caution and take it with a grain of salt. Their story about the little changeling boy was no more than a story, a fairy tale in a world of Celtic mysticism. As far as I could gather, Carmel was no changeling. She was lonely and lived in an insecure world. I was soon to find out what was bothering her, and it would begin when I returned to school on Monday.

*****

At playtime, we ran to our various corners where we gathered to play games, and as it happened, Sheila was not at school that day. When I'd called to see the little robin's nest the day before, she hadn't been at her best. I decided I'd call on the way home again and see how she was.

I found Carmel reading on the bench in the colonnade, and I took the book from her and said, 'Come on, now, you promised to play with us.'

She turned with a smile and said, 'Ah, maybe not.'

'Why not?'

'I don't know, but I'm happier here.'

'All right, then, I'm going to stay with you.'

She put the book down, and I began talking. She listened. I told her that I was calling to see Sheila on the way home to see how she was and to see how the little robin was coming along with her little blue teapot nest.

'May I come with you?' Carmel said. 'May I see it too?'

I wasn't sure whether I should let her. I didn't know how Sheila would react. But then I said yes, and Carmel was very happy.

'Wait for me after school. I have my bike today. I will cycle with you.'

'What about your mother? Will she not be expecting you home on time?'

'She's in town and won't be back till five o'clock.'

'All right, then! We won't delay.'

*****

Sheila was sitting outside the front door of the cottage when we arrived. Her mother was in and out doing her daily chores. She turned suddenly when she saw us approach the gate on our bikes. She was astonished to see the doctor's daughter with me, and she said quietly to Sheila, who was drawing on an old school copy, 'Look, Sheila, we have visitors.'

Sheila looked up when she saw us. Her face lit up, but then it changed to an expression of surprise when she saw Carmel.

'Sheila, Carmel came along to see the little teapot nest,' I said.

'Yeah!' said Sheila, a little dismayed.

'You are welcome, girls,' said Mrs Bryce. 'And a very special welcome to *you*, young lady,' she said to Carmel. 'But I don't know what your first name is.'

'It's Carmel,' she answered. 'Is it all right if I see the little nest?'

'It is, of course, but you must go easy. Sheila hasn't had the best of days today. She's only after coming out in the afternoon sun, and she won't be out for long.'

We let our bikes down and opened the little wooden gate. Sheila put her copybook and pencil down and came slowly with us. Her breathing was very heavy, and her mother walked slowly, linking her arm to offer support. When we got near to the babby house, Mrs Bryce made Sheila sit on an old broken kitchen chair. Carmel gazed in amazement at Sheila's little play space.

'What's this?' she asked. My heart missed a beat; I was afraid that she would say something that would hurt Sheila's feelings, as she had done so often before, not just to Sheila, but to some of the other poorer children as well.

'It's the babby house,' said Sheila.

'What's a babby house?' she asked.

'It's my little place to play when the weather is fine.'

'Sheila makes her own toys from little odds and ends. She has great fun doing so,' I said.

'You mean you have no toys at all,' said Carmel.

'I don't need any. I pretend. I love to pretend. It takes all my sickness away.'

Carmel turned to me, and she had tears in her eyes. Something was changing inside her. She was a little uneasy, and I didn't know whether she was going to say something hurtful or run away. Then she said, 'What about the little nest?'

'The little ones have just hatched,' said Sheila. 'She's flying in and out all the time now. We will have to wait and see.'

We kept our eyes focused on the little teapot, and before long, the little robin flew into it, and there was a short caterwauling of little voices screaming for food. Then it all went silent as she flew out again.

Sheila remained seated as Mrs Bryce let Carmel peer into the little blue teapot.

'Give a gentle whistle,' said Sheila. Carmel gave a little whistle and the beaks opened, shouting up at us for food. Carmel laughed gently through her tears, and then Mrs Bryce spoke.

'Now come away, girls. We don't want her abandoning her little babies.'

Carmel turned from us and went to Sheila. She threw her arms around her and said, 'Thank you!' Then she burst into tears and ran.

I ran too, calling her to see what was wrong. Carmel was finding it difficult to pull the little bolt on the gate leading to the road, and when she did, I said, 'What's the matter, Carmel?'

She turned to me and said, 'Now I know what I need to do.'

'Where are you going?'

'I'm going home.' She took her bike and headed back into the village. Mrs Bryce and Sheila had followed slowly back from the garden.

'That's a very strange little child,' she said. 'I don't know if we will ever make her out.'

'Mammy, that's the first time she was ever nice to me,' said Sheila.

'I hope it won't be the last,' answered her mother.

*****

I went straight home, and Maureen had one of her specialities ready, the memory of which always remained with me: fried potatoes with onions and bacon. The aroma met me at the gate when I arrived. The two dogs came quietly wagging their tails, and they flittered around me with great excitement.

Uncle John was mending a harrow in the shed, and he called to me, 'You're late today.'

'I called to Sheila,' I said, 'but a very strange thing happened.'

He was all ears, and he followed me to the kitchen to hear all about Carmel and her visit to see the robin's nest in the teapot.

'I still think she could be a sheera,' said Martha.

'Stop saying that,' I said. 'That is not true. But she is changing, I know she is.'

'She's growing up and getting sense,' said Maureen.

'The track of her father's hand across her backside might have worked wonders,' said Uncle John. I thought it was a terrible thing to say, but knowing him, that was something he would never allow. He was joking, as usual.

'I pray for her every day,' said Martha.

I was just finishing my dinner when the dogs began barking, and we could hear the noise of a car driving into the yard to the back door. When we looked out, it was the doctor and his wife, Nuala. She was in tears, and he was quite worried looking.

He stepped out of the car and said, 'Is Carmel here?'

'No, she's not,' said Uncle John.

'She was late home from school, and she was in tears. She went upstairs, and in a short while, we couldn't find her. We looked in her room, and her soft toy she got last Christmas was gone, as well as a delft tea set she got for her birthday. What's going on, do you know?'

I explained what had happened, and how Carmel had been upset after seeing the bird's nest at the Bryce cottage.

'Where is she now?' asked Nuala.

'I have a fair idea,' I said. 'May I come with you?' When I heard of the missing soft toy and the tea set, I knew that what she'd seen at the cottage, the poverty as well as the illness, had gotten to her so much that it upset her.

Was it pangs of guilt regarding her previous behaviour? I didn't know. Maybe it was a good thing.

'Where are you going?' asked Dr Daly.

'Bryces' cottage!'

I got into the back of the car, and he drove quite quickly towards the village. When we reached the cottage, Carmel's bike was leaning against the hedge. They had failed to see it when they were passing earlier.

'What is she up to?' asked Nuala.

'I think I know,' I said. 'Let's wait and see.'

When we got to the cottage door, there was nobody inside, so I took them to the garden. Sheila was sitting on the broken kitchen chair, and Carmel was seated on an upturned bucket. There was laughing and giggling between them. Mrs Bryce stood some distance away, pretending to remove weeds from a young cabbage patch. She was keeping an eye on the proceedings. She was mesmerised, just the same as we were.

'What's going on here?' asked Nuala. The two girls stood up and went silent. Sheila was clutching the velveteen toy, and the tea set was arranged on an old log. The broken pieces of chaney had been swept to the ground. Sheila's face was alive with a smile, but Carmel suddenly changed.

'Go away, Mum and Dad. Why did you come here?'

'What are you up to, child?' asked her father.

'I'm playing. That's what I'm doing. Sheila has no toys. So I brought her these.' I could see the doctor's face melt when she said this. He was seeing a side to his daughter he'd never seen before.

'I need you to come home *now*,' said Nuala. She spoke in a more abrupt manner than I had ever seen before. As Carmel stood up, Nuala called her over and slapped her across the face.

'Nuala!' screamed the doctor. 'What are you doing? This is uncalled for.'

'She needs discipline, David; she must get that.'

Carmel ran to her father, who held her close to him as she wept bitterly into his fawn woollen overcoat.

'That's enough, now. It's time to go home. There's a lot of talking to be done.'

'She needs to be taught manners . . . ,' Nuala was saying.

'Stop it right now,' Dr Daly said. His wife turned from him and headed back to the car. 'I'm sorry, Mrs Bryce, for intruding on your premises like this. Please accept my apologies.'

'No harm done,' Sheila's mother said. 'She's a nice little girl.'

'What about your toys?' the doctor asked Carmel.

'I gave them to Sheila; she can have them.'

'Thank you very much!' said Sheila.

The doctor embraced his daughter again, and turning to me, he said, 'I will leave you home first, Margaret, and I'll collect the bike later.'

Carmel was in tears the whole way back to Dairy Hill. I'd seen a side to her mother that I hadn't seen the day of my visit. Her sweetness to me and to Carmel on that day, as well as the fine spread for tea, was an outward show. I could see as well that the doctor had not been aware that his daughter was being treated like this. Was Nuala ill treating and beating her, unbeknownst to him? Was Carmel's behaviour at school over the past two years a reflection of life at home?

I knew the doctor felt that the sooner she went to boarding school, the better. The day I had my injury, he was aware that something was wrong, but he didn't know what was going on in his little girl's life. Sending her away was his way of shifting responsibility onto someone else to change her behaviour.

But inside, Carmel was screaming, and nobody noticed. She was aware that I knew something was the matter. She was afraid to say anything for fear of what might happen to her. That was why she'd pleaded with me not to say anything to her parents the day I visited her house.

'Why did you do that?' exclaimed the doctor to his wife again.

'She has no manners, David. That's all that's wrong.'

'May I say something?' I asked.

'Yes, Margaret.'

'I think Carmel is lonely. Aren't you, Carmel?'

'Dad, I had a lovely day, and Sheila made me laugh.'

'You should have told me first what you were doing,' said Nuala.

'And then I know you wouldn't let me go.'

The car turned up the avenue and stopped at the back door. Then the doctor said, 'Thank you for your help, Margaret.'

Carmel had to climb out of the car to let me out, and just as she was about to step back in, her mother pushed her roughly, saying, 'Get back in there now, and stay quiet.'

'Nuala!' exclaimed the doctor.

With that, Carmel took off running down the back into the haggard and across the gate into the fields. I ran as fast as I could after her. She wailed and screamed her head off as she went.

Her father followed on foot while Nuala stood at the car door, weeping into her handkerchief. It was an acute family drama being enacted at the house of Bethany.

John followed the doctor to the field gates in pursuit of two athletic girls running as they'd never run before. I shouted and called after Carmel, but she kept going. She made for the ditch so she could climb over into the next field. Then she screamed and fell on the headland.

When I reached her, I could see her leg was bleeding. She'd cut herself on some sharp briars, and blood was flowing down her leg. She was crying her heart out as she screamed, 'I hate her! I hate her! I hate her!'

'Shh! Shh,' I said softly. 'It's all right, Carmel.' I tried to stop the bleeding with my handkerchief, but she just kept sobbing.

'It's all right, Carmel. I understand. You are my friend, and Sheila's as well.'

'I don't want to live there anymore. I hate that house.'

By now, the doctor and Uncle John had reached us, and Carmel's father stooped down and cradled her in his arms. He brushed her hair back and kept saying, 'It's all right, my sweet little girl. It's all right.'

He could see I wasn't able to stop the bleeding, and in an instant he had his coat off, then his blazer. Yanking off his sparkling clean shirt, leaving him with only his vest to cover him, he tore the sleeves into strips and began tying them around Carmel's bleeding leg.

'That's quick action,' said Uncle John.

'Any port in a storm. I did this on numerous occasions during the great war to help stop bleeding. But in your case, Carmel, the good news is you're going to live. May I use one of your rooms, John, to fix this little lady up?'

'Certainly, no problem,' said Uncle John. 'Now tell me, Carmel, where in the honour of all that is sacred were you intending to go?'

'I don't know,' she sobbed. Then Uncle John, who had this uncanny knack of bringing laughter from tears, often referred to as reverse psychology, said, 'Now before we go back to the farmhouse, little woman, I want you to do something for me.'

'Okay,' she sobbed softly.

'I just don't want you to laugh.'

Carmel looked into his face with a puzzled expression.

'Don't even attempt to.'

The doctor caught on at what he was doing. Then Carmel giggled.

'What did I say? You are not to laugh!'

With that, the tears turned to laughter, and I joined in. Any pain Carmel had seemed to go away. The doctor put his blazer and coat back on, stuffing the remains of his shirt into the deep pocket of his coat. Then he picked her up in his arms to carry her.

'It's all right, Daddy, I can walk,' she said, as her sobs began to subside. He took her by the hand, and we walked slowly back to the farmhouse.

*****

There was hustle, bustle, and fuss as the aunts began making tea and boiling water for the doctor to bandage Carmel's leg. Nuala was sitting by the fire, holding her handkerchief to her nose, sobbing silently.

Maureen broke the silence. 'Can anyone tell me what is after happening or what's going on? You know, Margaret Kerr, we never had any excitement in this house till you came around here. Now we have the whole medical profession here today, and my little kitchen has become a hospital.'

'I'm so sorry, Maureen,' said the doctor, 'but we will be out of here soon.'

'Take as long as you like,' said Martha. 'Our door is always open.'

'May I say something?' he said. 'But I don't know what's going on. Nuala, tell me what's happening.'

'I don't want her to grow up to be a useless article. She needs to get an education to make her way in the world. She needs discipline.'

'Well, as far as I can see, Mrs Daly,' said Uncle John, 'you're going about it in a very strange way.'

'Daddy, I don't want to live at that house anymore. It's a lonely place. Mum won't let me have friends. When Margaret came over to visit, I thought it was because I tripped her on the stage. I am very sorry for that, but nobody will listen to me. Margaret knew there was something wrong, and I didn't want to say anything in case Mum started shouting at me. The day Margaret came, it was like a big party; Mum wanted to show all the nice things we had and the nice food, and that I was a very lucky girl.'

'I only want the best for you, dear,' said Nuala.

'I don't want that, Mum. Why don't you let me bring friends to the house?'

'Well, they wouldn't be the type I'd like you to mix with.'

'They are poor, Mum. Some of them don't even wear shoes in the summer. They stay away from me because I have everything I need. I don't want that. I want to run about in my bare feet and roll in the grass down the hill. I can see them from the house. Today, Margaret brought me to see Sheila. She's sick. She sits in her babby house, playing with broken plates and cups. Her friend is a little robin in her nest in an old teapot. Mum, I want to be able to play. I'm going away to boarding school in September, and I'm afraid I might not have a friend.' She started sobbing again into her father's shoulder.

He sat her on the table and took a seat on the chair to dress and clean her wounded leg. Then Nuala got up and came over to her. I knew she wanted Carmel to be what *she* wanted her to be. Carmel had no choice in the direction she wanted her life to take.

'I'm so sorry, Carmel. Please forgive me.'

'That will do for a start,' said the doctor. 'We'll continue with this at home.'

'Now I think a nice cup of weak tea will do for everybody,' said Martha. 'I know *I* could do with one after all this excitement.'

Carmel turned to her father. 'Daddy, is it difficult to become a doctor?'

'Yes, love, it's not easy. It takes many years' study.'

'I want to be a doctor just like you. People like Sheila need doctors to cure them. I want to be a doctor someday.'

'That will be up to you, but you'll have to study hard. But don't do it because you want to please me or your mother.'

'No, I'll do it because I want to.'

*****

The upshot of it all was that, amongst other things, Nuala was suffering with her nerves. It had been going on for quite a while, on and off for about two years. The long hours the doctor spent away from the house had left her with no other focus but her daughter when her boys went to boarding school. She'd had this idea that Carmel was wild and needed discipline. Carmel in turn had courted attention negatively, boasting about all she had and the places she went as well as how good she was at her studies and her singing, as these were the things she concentrated on at home, having nothing else to occupy her.

The doctor had been unaware that the bubble was about to burst within his household until I told him what Carmel had done on the stage. He hadn't been able to put his finger on what was going on, and Nuala had kept an outward barrier between him and her own problem.

News reached us a few days later that Nuala had gone to Dublin for a well-earned break. We knew that she had gone for treatment for her problem. It emerged, too, that she had been taking some of the medication from the surgery, unbeknownst to the doctor.

He felt guilty about it all. He had been so busy dealing with all those who were ill about him that he'd been unaware that there was illness in his own house too.

Then one Saturday afternoon about two weeks later, he arrived in the car with Carmel, and she ran to me and embraced me. Martha invited him in for a cup of tea, and nothing would do her but for her to take him and his daughter to the parlour.

'The kitchen would have done fine,' he said.

'How is all in your own household?' asked Uncle John.

'I presume you know all that's happened. There are no secrets around our little village.'

'I just want to know how you're keeping yourself.'

'I'm just getting over the shock of all that has happened in the past two weeks. It's made me do a lot of thinking about the future.'

'Don't say you're going to leave us,' said Mother. 'We do need a good doctor in this area, and there's none better than yourself.'

'That's just it. I've been doing a lot of thinking. I've been so busy in the past two or three years that I've overlooked the issues in my own family. It all began when the boys went away to boarding school. Now I need to take a few steps back and consider my options.'

'You're not retiring from practise,' said Mother.

'On the contrary. I am going to ease the work burden on myself.'

'How are you going to do that?'

'I need someone to do some secretarial work. I have been making enquiries.' Then he turned to Mother. 'I have learned that you did some office work in a past life.'

'I did indeed. I worked for a while in a law firm till I got married, and then I had to give up work to mind my little girl. I haven't done that sort of work for more than twelve years.'

'Would you come work for me? I know you're helping to provide for your little girl. There should be a British army income for you, but I presume that's all in a mess over in England.'

'We are refugees from the war, Doctor.'

'Now in the house of Lazarus,' joked Uncle John.

'I would have to give notice to the shop first,' said Mother.

'I won't be ready to take you for a month, as I have to get some adjustments done to the spare room at the dispensary to turn it into an office.'

'Thank you very much, Doctor. I really appreciate that.'

'I can't thank you enough for all you've done,' he said.

'I did nothing, but you can blame someone else for most of it.'

'Yes, that's what I mean. Thank you very much, Margaret. I'm organising a picnic at the lake in July for you and all your friends from school. I hope Nuala will be better by then. It would do her good to get out into the air as well.'

Carmel stayed that afternoon, and we ran through the fields, crossing gates, and the dogs ran with us. She met all the animals on the farm, and she hugged Paddy the young colt, who was now turning out to be a fine animal. We sat for a long time on the big rock at the top of the farm. She loved the view of the lake.

Already, Carmel was blossoming. Today she was happy. She stayed for tea, and her father collected her just before eight o'clock.

I'd never seen such a great change in anyone. At school, she could run faster than any of us in the playground. She told us that she was going to a boarding school in Navan, and that she was going to work very hard to become a doctor like her father.

The picnic did go ahead as planned. We made it our day of promise to Sheila. We were joined with other company that day, as the lake shore was crowded with children and parents. The sun shone for us all. Fritz had returned from school, and I had so much to tell him. The summer of 1942 was one of the happiest times I spent at Dairy Hill, but the war was never far away from us.

Part 8

Germany Calling! Germany Calling!

Chapter 16

It was in the autumn of 1942, just before the end of September, when on a Saturday evening, Fritz arrived unexpectedly. He rode a bicycle, and when I looked at it, I knew it was Esther Kerrigan's. He was white in the face and breathing fast. He passed Uncle John by and came into the kitchen.

'Shouldn't you be at school?' asked Mother.

'I got leave of absence,' he said. He was visibly upset and on the verge of tears. Something was happening, and it was a few minutes before he was able to compose himself to tell us.

'What's wrong, lad?' asked Uncle John. 'Is it your grandfather?'

Fritz was so mixed up and upset that he spoke in German. 'Nein! Es geht ihm sehr gut, Gott sei dank.' He spoke as if he was winded.

'I don't understand what you're saying,' said Martha.

'I am so sorry. My grandfather is fine; thank God he is well. May I sit down?'

'Of course!' said Mother. 'Sit down by the fire here, and take it easy. Now tell us what the matter is.'

'It's my father,' he said, and then he burst into tears. Mother pulled one of the kitchen chairs beside him and held him close to her as if he were her own son. He wept into her arms, and after a moment, he composed himself. Looking into her face with glassy red eyes, he said, 'Dear lady, my father is dead.'

'Shh! Don't cry, love,' she said, and she held him close to her again. I ran to Maureen, and I too was in floods of tears. Nobody said a word, as we didn't know what to say. Through his tears, he began to apologise.

'I'm so sorry, but German boys don't cry.'

'Stop that now,' she said. 'Any boy should cry. It is no shame to do so. It means that you loved your father very much and you need to grieve his loss.'

'I will never see him again,' he sobbed.

'What about your mother?' asked Martha.

'There is nothing about her. There is no trace of her; maybe she is dead too. But I know my father is dead.'

'How did you find out?' asked Uncle John.

'Peter got news from refugees in Northern Ireland. They were smuggling letters and information in and out of Germany as well as many other occupied countries. Father and Mother were helping some Christian organisations to smuggle people, mainly Jews, out of Germany. But they were discovered, and they too were sent away to one of those camps. Herr Goessler and Father were sent to one camp, and my mother was sent to another. That is why we know nothing about her. Father was not content to be locked away, and there was a plot to escape. I do not know what took place, but during the escape attempt, several men were shot by guards. Four of them got away, unknown to the Germans. My father was killed. Herr Goessler saw him with a bullet through his head.

'Herr Goessler got to the big river, and he tried to swim away. He was lucky to find a large piece of wood, and it carried him downstream. He got away, and through some of the people he was working with to help people escape, they managed to get him out as well. He reached Northern Ireland, and it was there Peter found him. He's with my grandfather now.'

Fritz began to weep again, and Mother sat with him and comforted him. He continued to sob for a few minutes, and nobody spoke. Then he peered into Mother's face and said, 'Oh, Mrs Kerr, I am ashamed to be a German boy. My people are doing terrible things.'

She patted him on the shoulders, and he continued sobbing. Then Martha arrived with her usual cure for all ailments: her cup of weak tea.

'Get this into you, lad. It will help calm you down.'

He took the mug from her and drank some of it. Then taking a handkerchief from his pocket, he wiped his eyes. Nobody bothered him, but we all waited for him to relax.

'I'm so sorry,' he said again.

'Will you whisht now. It's all right,' said Uncle John. 'You don't need to apologise.'

Mother took him in her arms again, and he continued crying for another ten or fifteen minutes, until he was nearly hoarse.

'They are not my people. I do not want to be part of a Germany that would do such things. Nazis are evil.'

There was silence in the kitchen, and I went to him. I took his great big hand, and I realised that he had grown so much in such a short time. Then Uncle John found words to comfort him in this hour of despair.

'You are a brave young man, you know. You have a heart of gold. You get it from your parents and your grandparents. Someday, please God, this damn war will be over. The Germany you once knew will come back. It will need bright young people like you to make things right again. You have seen the terrible things, and it will be young people like you who make sure it will never happen again. I won't live to see it, but *you* will, and so will your children. It's time to be sad but be proud you had such wonderful parents, and we pray the rosary every night. We pray for Margaret's father, that he will come back from the war; we will pray for your mother too. It's all we can do. Remember, no matter what, there are people who care for you, and they always will.'

'Thank you, Mr Costello. You are all such kind people. I always find peace in this house.'

'You are always welcome here, you know that,' said Martha.

'I do,' he answered. 'When I came back to Johnsons' this morning, I did not know what to say or do. I had to tell someone. Esther gave me a loan of her bike to come here.'

'Stay as long as you need,' said Maureen.

He sat by the fire, wringing his hands, and the tears came again, and went. Mother sat with him, and soon darkness began to fall. After another cup of warm weak tea, he calmed down, and he smiled over at me.

I could see that his boyish looks were going away, and his face seemed longer and thinner. There was a hint of soft blond fur under his chin, indicating he was on the cusp of adulthood. I knew he had just turned fifteen. There was a deepness in his voice too. I did not realise that my little twelve-year-old world was set to change soon, and I found myself wanting to be with him. He was ever so handsome, and in my own little secret universe, I was falling in love with him.

When he gathered himself together again and calmed down, I knew he was embarrassed by his outburst of emotion. He sat quietly staring into the flames of the fire, and they reflected on his face as he sipped his mug of tea.

An hour later, Peter's car arrived, and its lights reflected in the darkening kitchen as it pulled up beside the back door. Manfred Von Gebler peered into the kitchen, apologising for the intrusion.

'Mein lieber Junge, ich dachte du wärst weggelaufen.'

'Nein! Grossvater, es tut mir eid, aber ich musste mit jemandem reden.'

Then Martha wanted to know what they were saying.

'Can you talk in plain English? I don't understand what you're saying. I don't know any German.'

'I'm so sorry, dear lady,' said Manfred, 'I thought my grandson had run away. I do not want to lose him the way I lost my son. Our hearts are broken.' For an old man, he was very composed in such a sad situation, but that might have been the German discipline he'd grown up with, having come through the Great War as well. He embraced his grandson and said, 'I need you to be strong, my boy. You are all I have in the world now.'

'I'm sorry, Grossvater. I won't go away like that again.'

Then Peter stepped in the door. 'I see he has found refuge in Bethany.'

'He's always welcome here,' said Maureen, 'no more than your good self.'

Uncle John gave a sarcastic gasp, which brought a stare from Mother that would cut you in two like a knife. He thought it better to say no more.

Manfred led his grandson to the car, and as Peter was leaving, Uncle John said, 'Will you for God's sake mind that gossoon. He needs a lot of love and care.'

'He knows where to go to get it,' said Peter, reversing the car, and saying no more, he sped down the avenue.

It took Uncle John a few minutes to realise Peter was passing him a compliment.

*****

That night Bartley had the excuse of taking Esther's bike back to Johnsons', and he cycled down the avenue, wheeling her bike parallel to his own, holding the handlebars of hers with one hand and steering his with the other.

The house was silent, and we didn't know what to say to each other. I didn't eat anything, and I went out into the haggard. Sam followed me, and I threw myself against a cock of hay and sat down with my thoughts and my grief. Old Sam sat beside me, and soon Shep joined us. He sat nuzzling his head under my arms, and I stroked his beautiful shiny coat. He was now past the point where all puppies play bite, and all he wanted was to seek attention and be petted. Sam sat quietly, scratching himself, and then he curled up and went to sleep. All that was worrying Shep was when to eat, when to sleep, and the odd bark to remind us that strangers were around.

I sat there stroking his head, and every so often he cocked an ear as he picked up a strange sound that came to him on the darkening autumn breeze.

Then Mother called me from the back door, and I came to her at once.

'It's time for bed,' she said, and I went quietly upstairs.

During the night, I had a nightmare. I couldn't for the life of me remember what it was about, but I'm sure it concerned Father. Mother came to me when I cried out, and she held my hand. I was sobbing.

'It's all right, pet. It's only a nightmare. You were thinking of Fritz and his father.'

'Mother, I hope Father isn't in a prison camp.'

'I don't know where he is, love, but all we can do is pray that he's safe.'

'Will we ever see him again?'

'Let's pray that we will, dear. It's all we can do. It's like this: if something happened to him, we'd probably hear about it from the Home Office. If we hear nothing, we know that he's safe. Just keep remembering that.'

Then I settled into an uneasy sleep. My world that had become so secure at Dairy Hill was now becoming quite unstable again.

*****

One Saturday just before Halloween, Uncle John took Mother and me to town. The surgery was closed for the weekend, and Dr Daly took emergency calls from the house. Mother was glad to take the trip, as she had been working very hard as the doctor's receptionist since early summer. She bought me new shoes for the winter to wear to school. They were fur lined inside, and they laced up the front. She bought me a blue pixie hat that tied around my chin to keep me warm on my journey to the village school each day. I was no longer alone on my morning journey, as she cycled with me to open the surgery and prepare for doctors' hours.

On this trip to the town, Uncle John left us and went off on his own. He was to meet us at Keenan's pub, as he planned to have a few pints before taking us home again in midafternoon. He wasn't worried about being out in the dark, as the carbide lamps attached to the front of the trap would light our way home.

When we met up with him, he wasn't quite finished with his last pint and was chatting with a few other farmers whom he met on occasion at the fairs. Mrs Keenan beckoned my mother to follow her, and we were directed away from the bar to the snug.

Uncle John had preordered tea and sandwiches for us, and Mother was delighted to see that the sandwiches were made with white-batch loaf bread and not bread made from dark-black flour, as it was called, which we had all become used to.

'You must have searched high up and low down, Mrs Keenan, to get that bread,' said Mother.

'Let me put it this way, love: when you're in business, you have your sources. I got a great supply in this morning, but the problem is, it will be gone stale by Monday. Would you like a few loaves?'

'I would love some,' said Mother. 'How much are they?'

'I'll give them to you as a present. John Costello is a good customer of ours over the years, and it's time to reward him for his loyalty.'

'You are ever so kind,' said Mother.

'When you're leaving, come into the kitchen, and I'll have them tucked away in a large sackcloth shopping bag. I don't want anyone to see them. You can drop the bag back to me when you're in town again.'

I tucked into the sandwiches. They were a mixture of ham and cheese, and there was no sparing the tea leaves or sugar, as there wasn't a profusion of milk, and the tea was darker and sweeter than normal. Mrs Keenan didn't seem to be concerned with the emergency rationing, as what Uncle John had ordered was very generous indeed.

When he finally came to bring us home, he was carrying a large cardboard box, and it was quite heavy. He wouldn't tell us what was in it.

'You'll find out in due course,' he said.

The carbide lamps were lit on the trap as we headed home, and by the time we reached the farm, it was black dark. There was an overcast sky, and it began to rain softly just as we reached the avenue.

The evening chores were finished, and the lamp was lit. The open fire in the kitchen was welcome, and Mother and I sat on each side of it.

Uncle John put the heavy box in the parlour and still wouldn't tell anyone what was in it.

The aunts kept questioning him about it, and he warned them not to touch it.

'Curiosity killed the cat, and information made him fat,' he said as he headed off out into the darkness to unyoke the jennet and let him out into the pasture.

We had to wait until after tea before he decided to open it. We had relished some of the white-loaf bread that evening with butter and gooseberry jam. We felt it was a nice treat.

Then the kitchen table was cleared, and when all the delft was washed and placed on the dresser, he brought the box to the kitchen and set it down on the table.

'Now we can find out all the happenings in the world on our own doorstep,' he said.

'What are you talking about?' said Martha. 'Are you losing your sanity or something?'

'No, I'm not. I've just bought a wireless for you all.'

'What did you buy a contraption like that for?' asked Maureen. 'What would we be doing with a wireless?'

'It was far from a wireless you were reared,' said Martha. 'We have done without it up till now; I don't see any need for bringing contraptions like that into the house.'

'I think it's marvellous,' said Mother. 'We haven't heard the radio since we came from London. We might be able to get the BBC news on it.'

'I only hope it doesn't do my head in,' said Martha.

I helped Uncle John open the box, and the wireless was packed in wood shavings, which looked like straw. He was careful taking out the battery. It was what was called a wet battery, and he said it had to be taken occasionally to the garage to be charged. It could be done in the village without any need for going to town.

There was a long, thin, green wire, which he fed out through the open window, and he fastened it to a nail high up on the wall outside. He then closed the window, as the wire was thin enough to allow the window to stay shut.

'That's called an aerial,' he said. 'It finds the wireless signal from the air, and it comes down into the wireless for us to hear.'

'What is the world coming to at all?' said Martha. 'It's sinful. If the good Lord wanted us to listen to the wireless, he would have allowed us to do it centuries ago.'

'It's called science,' said Mother. 'Man is only learning to do all these great things. He has even learned how to fly and drive cars and talk to each other on telephones. These things can only help us and to make life easier for us.'

When Uncle John was ready to switch on the radio, he placed it in the window and connected the wet battery to it.

'Now where am I going to put the spring flowers when they come?' asked Maureen.

'Don't worry,' said Uncle John, 'I'm going to get a shelf put up on the wall beside the window, and it won't be in anyone's way.'

'You think of everything, Uncle John,' I said.

'Sure, aren't I a Costello?' he said rather wryly, which made Martha throw her eyes up to heaven. Wiping her hands in her flower-stained apron, she sat down beside the fire to watch the switching on of this new contraption.

'Now are we ready?' he asked.

We gathered in a half circle around the window as he turned the knob, which gave a little quiet click. A gentle yellow light lit up on the channel deck, but nothing happened.

'That's a great yoke,' said Maureen. 'It only lights up.'

'It has to heat up first,' he said.

'I hope it doesn't set the house on fire,' said Martha.

Then he turned up the volume, and the machine began to whistle and squeak.

'My God, is this what we have to listen to from now on?' grumbled Martha. 'I think I'll go and book myself into a home for the retired.'

She turned around and began to stoke the fire. Uncle John began moving the channel dial, and suddenly there was Irish music playing.

It seemed to be a céilí band. Uncle John grabbed a hold of Mother and began waltzing her round the cement floor. The two aunts sat down, and Maureen took her apron in her hands. I thought she was weeping into it, but in fact, she was breaking her heart laughing. Martha turned from the fire, and she followed suit.

Uncle John then bowed to Mother and began waltzing with me. Mother dragged Martha out and waltzed with her as well. It was a regular hooley. Then the music stopped, and a man spoke.

'Now we're bringing strangers into the house as well,' said Maureen.

'It's Radio Athlone. It's broadcast from Dublin to a transmitter in Athlone, and that's how we receive it.'

'When is the rest of the man going to appear?' said Martha. 'I can only hear his voice.'

'That's all you will hear,' said Mother. 'It's called radio. You will grow to like it.'

It wasn't long till the aunts accepted the radio, or wireless, as they called it in the house. Having not had such new technology in their quiet, sheltered lives, this was the first innovation of the twentieth century that they had encountered. Their initial shock was amusing, to say the least, but after a short while, when the rosary was said, the wireless was turned on for any news that was available. During this period of the war, little news reached us through the radio, as it might be heard by the enemy, but what little there was brought listening ears each night.

Then one night the following week, when Uncle John was trying to find new channels, especially the British ones, to see if there was any news of the war, a voice spoke in a very cultured British accent.

'Germany calling! Germany calling!'

The speaker began to relay details of failed bombing raids and sunken British ships, and Mother declared, 'John, who's that?'

'That feckin' bastard!' he exploded.

'Watch your tongue, John Costello,' shouted Martha. 'This is a good Catholic home, and there will be no language like that here while I'm alive.'

'Who is it?' asked Mother once again.

'It's that get broadcasting from Germany, Lord Haw-Haw!'

'Turn him off, turn him off,' said Mother, and she disappeared upstairs.

'Go after her!' said Maureen. 'She doesn't need to listen to that fellow after all she's been through.'

Mother was crying in the bedroom. She was inconsolable, and I hugged her and held her. It was all coming back again, the horror of the Blitz, the fires, Nana's death, and Father being away. Even though she had found peace and refuge in Bethany, the war was never too far away.

'Will it ever end?' she sobbed.

'It will, Mother!'

'No, it won't. It's getting nearer to us. It has even come into our homes with that person, whoever he is; he's teasing us and boasting about Germany, and he wants to make little of what we're doing to keep our freedom and dignity.'

'Stop, Mother! Please stop!' I pleaded.

'I'm just heartbroken, Margaret, and you too have had to give up so much. We are here in this house, depending on the goodwill and good nature of my aunts and uncle. I often feel that we're a burden on them, and we shouldn't be sitting up on them.' Then we were startled by a voice at the bedroom door.

'Kitty Costello!' It was Uncle John. 'Do not let me hear you say things like that again. This is your home, and it will always be your home. Come hell or high water, Hitler, or Lord Haw-Haw, if they come here, they will have to drag us all out fighting. Get any notions about being a burden on us out of your head; we have never been as happy since you both came. You have made us young again. We love you both to bits, and we now worry about the day you may have to leave us. Come here and give your auld uncle a hug. I think you need one badly.'

She embraced him and cried into his shoulder, and soon she was laughing through the tears. I put my arms around his waist, and he pulled me close to him as well with his other free arm.

'You are the kindest person I know, Uncle John, and so are Maureen and Martha.'

'Kindness is not the word. Blood is thicker than water, and no one is going to see any relative of mine, the few that I have, living on the side of the road. Now come on downstairs to the fire, and I turned off that auld wireless. I think I will pack it up and bring it back to the shop.'

'Do nothing of the sort,' sobbed Mother. 'I just don't want to hear that Lord Haw-Haw again. I hope he will get his comeuppance someday.'

Martha had made us all some hot cocoa, it being a cold, frosty night outside. Even though there was a shortage of sugar, she made it hot and sweet and with lashings of milk.

'Now get that into you, Kitty love. It will warm the cockles of your heart on this cold night.'

'Forget about that auld German fellow with the English accent,' said Maureen. 'We all know he's just a liar.'

In the months and years that followed, if we had gone to bed early, Uncle John would sneak a quick listen to Lord Haw-Haw, so much so that eventually no one passed any remarks on hearing his broadcasts. If Mother happened to be within earshot, she'd quietly slip away into the evening, if it was still bright, and take a walk on the avenue, or she'd make herself busy with some knitting or needlework in the parlour till the broadcast was over. I couldn't fathom out how someone who might have been English was betraying his country with such propaganda on the radio. Mother said that maybe he had been taught English by an Englishman and as a result had a distinct English accent. Fritz spoke German very well, but his accent wasn't English.

It was only some years later I learned that Lord Haw-Haw was an Irish American, William Joyce. He was captured after the war and was hanged for treason. But the propaganda broadcasts brought the war close to our doors, and it upset Mother if she had to listen to it. Uncle John told her that he would not switch the wireless to that frequency, but she pointed out to him, that we might learn some information in relation to the progress of the war, so she stayed away and let him listen.

*****

Things began to happen with Bartley and Esther. There were rumours afoot that he was going to pop the question and ask Esther to marry him. Being such a shy man, he decided to consult with Uncle John on the matter, and he arrived one foggy night in November. It was not usual for him to call at night, and Uncle John knew there was something in the wind when Bartley arrived out of the blue like that. It happened that Martha and Maureen were making the Christmas pudding that night, so the house was full and busy. I had just finished any homework I had to do, and Mother sat at the fire, knitting a pair of gloves.

Bartley sat in front of the fire to warm himself, and in a few minutes the big black topcoat was off. He had very little to say, as Uncle John spoke about the price of pigs and sheep at the fair in Kilbeggan, as well as the harvest that had just been saved, and the crop of wheat that had been taken away as part of his compulsory tillage. Then Bartley decided to broach the subject.

'John, I want to ask your advice on something.'

'That's all right. Are you buying a new cow or a few sheep?'

'No, a different subject altogether. I'm thinking of settling down, you know what I mean?'

'You're going to make an honest woman out of her, are you?'

'I didn't know Esther was a thief,' I said. 'What did she steal?'

'Margaret!' exclaimed Mother. 'Watch your manners.' The kitchen erupted in peals of laughter, and that included Mother, who saw the funny side of my remark.

'If someone isn't honest, they are probably a thief or a liar,' I said, defending my earlier statement.

'Bartley means he is thinking of getting married,' said Maureen. 'That's what he means, love.'

'Oh!' I answered, then seeing my folly out, I began to laugh too.

'I'm not getting married just yet,' said Bartley, 'but I want to make the first step.'

'You want to pop the question,' said Uncle John.

'I do! I need some advice.'

'You're coming to the wrong person if you're asking John Costello for advice. He never asked someone to marry him, ever,' interrupted Martha.

'Or for that matter, neither did you,' said Uncle John.

'It's a man's job to do the asking,' she said.

'Will you stop arguing, both of you, and let the man speak?' said Maureen. 'He's about to make a very important decision, and don't disturb his thinking.'

Mother was smiling to herself, taking it all in, and the work on making the pudding stopped while this conversation was going on.

'I don't know what to say or do,' Bartley said. 'I might say the wrong thing.'

'First thing you'll do,' said Maureen, 'sell that engagement ring you have at home. It's stale, second-hand. It was used before, and it was not lucky.'

'Use the money to buy a new one,' said Martha. 'She deserves that much, at least.'

'Aye, all right!' he said. 'That's good thinking.'

'Then take her out somewhere, to a teahouse in the town, and buy tea and buns or maybe some ham sandwiches, and then ask her to marry you,' said Uncle John.

'But what will I say?'

'Say, "How would you like to be buried with my people?"' joked Uncle John.

'John Costello!' exploded Mother. 'Will you stop?' There were peals of laughter again.

'Would you stop making a joke out of it and be serious?' continued Mother.

'Well, try this, then.' By now he was lighting his pipe, and we had to wait for his next statement till after he had taken his first puff and it hit the darkened ceiling with a cloud of blue smoke.

'How would you like to make my breakfast, dinner, and tea for a very long time to come?'

'Stop this charade now,' said Mother. 'It's getting out of hand.' There was a smirk of amusement on her face. She was enjoying the banter, but she felt sorry for Bartley at the same time.

Then, holding his index finger in the air, Uncle John went on to say something else. 'Say to her, "How would you like me to take care of you for the rest of our lives?"'

'That sounds better,' said Mother. 'In fact, it's a nice thing to say, but why don't you just ask her to marry you? It's as simple as that. All she can say is no. But I don't think she will.'

'I think I'll do just that, then,' said Bartley.

Uncle John kept smoking away at his pipe with a smirk on his face, and as usual, he turned to me and winked. He was making light of the situation, and he knew Bartley didn't take him seriously anyway.

A week later, Bartley was back again. He looked happy and smiled as he came in. Sitting at the fire, he told us he'd taken Esther to the hotel in town and they'd had afternoon tea. They both cycled there, and leaving their bikes in the bottle store of one of the pubs, they settled into tea and sandwiches. There was no pomp and ceremony, but he asked her to marry him, and she said yes straightaway. He had previously taken the aunts' advice and sold the old ring, but he didn't tell Esther he had done so. When the afternoon tea was over, they went to the jeweller's and he bought her an engagement ring, a simple diamond well embedded in the gold. She was elated, and he too was very happy. Being such a shy man, he hadn't thought he could do it. But the sky didn't fall, and they went home happy. Bartley had taken a big step forward in his life.

Chapter17

I did not see Fritz again until Christmas. The Johnson house was deserted for the festive season, as Peter was spending his time in Dublin to be close to Georgina. As usual, he left the place in the tender care of Esther. She would stay and cook dinner for the Von Geblers. She had no near relatives to go home to, so it was the same to her. Then Uncle John had an idea.

'We will invite them here for their Christmas dinner, and Bartley will be coming as well.'

'Now you leave well alone,' said Martha. 'I don't want you teasing the poor man; you give him a hard time as it is. What about the Von Geblers?'

'We'll invite them too.'

'Oh, right! We might as well invite the whole parish,' grumbled Maureen. 'And who will do all the preparations? It's us. You do all the inviting, and we do all the work while you sit back and do all the entertaining.'

'Aren't there enough of you to cope anyway?' said Uncle John. 'Wait till you see – Esther will take over and run the whole show.'

'You have a point there,' said Martha, 'but it's not younger we're getting, and I'm not able for a big crowd.'

'Well, so much has happened in the past year, and that unfortunate gossoon losing his father, it will be very lonely this Christmas for him. It's the least we can do.'

'Everyone wants to find refuge in Bethany,' said Mother, with a smile on her face.

'If you put it that way, Kitty,' said Uncle John, 'then why not?'

There wasn't another word said. Preparations went ahead for the Christmas, and we had a full house on Christmas day. We dined in the large kitchen. The table from the parlour was brought into the kitchen as well, and we all sat down to eat in front of the great big open fire.

When Esther and the Von Geblers arrived in the little sidecar, I could not believe my eyes. Fritz was growing taller by the day. When Uncle John saw him, he viewed him up and down.

'What age are you now, son?' he asked.

'I'm fifteen,' he replied.

'You're a big lad for fifteen. You must be heading for six feet.'

'He has a very good appetite,' said Manfred.

'Yes indeed,' said Uncle John. 'He's getting so tall, he could eat hay off a loft.'

This brought a burst of laugher from everyone, and Fritz explained to his grandfather what Uncle John meant. Then the old man followed with a lone belly laugh that reached to the rafters.

'Yeah! That is good, Herr Costello.'

The day passed quickly, and following the meal, which was enjoyed by all, Manfred brought out a shopping bag he had with him and handed me a parcel.

'For you, little girl.' Then he spoke to Fritz in German, who translated what he said back to me.

'Grandfather wants to say thank you again for saving his life. It is two years now since it happened, and it's only a token for all you did.'

I told him thank you very much and gave him a gentle peck on the cheek.

When I opened the package, it was a wooden sculpture, six to eight inches high, carved from black wood. I thought it might be made of ebony. It was an open hand holding a little baby cradled on the palm.

'I know where you got that idea,' said Martha. 'It's part of an old Irish blessing when going on a journey: *May the good Lord hold you in the hollow of his hand.*'

'It's beautiful,' I said.

'Peter said it was made from bog oak,' said Fritz. Then Uncle John explained what bog oak was. It was thousands of years old, having lain preserved in the bog for a very long time. It turned black with age. Manfred had carved it and turned it. Then he'd covered it with beeswax to enhance the blackness so that it did look a little like ebony.

'I think she will cherish it always,' said Mother.

When all the eating and celebrating was over, Uncle John stood up and drank a toast, holding up a great big glass of stout.

'To absent friends,' he said, 'and to those we love so dear.'

Then Mother began to cry. But suddenly she hiccupped, and Martha told her she was drinking too much sherry. This cheered her up no end.

Bartley was quiet through the afternoon, and he sat beside Esther. They talked softly together, and she made sure he got the best of everything.

Then Maureen asked her a question.

'Where is the lovely ring that Bartley bought you?'

'It's in my handbag.'

'What's it doing there?' asked Martha. 'You should be wearing it.'

'I didn't want to damage it when I was helping with the cooking.'

'You should really wear it,' said Mother. 'You have a greater chance of losing it by taking it off. That happened to me a few years ago. I couldn't remember where I put it. I found it eventually in a silver cup on the sideboard. I take it off at night, and it's ready on the dressing table in the morning.'

'Go on, then; let's have a look,' said Maureen.

Esther took the ring out and placed it on her finger, and there was a sparkle on the diamond, reflecting in the dancing flames of the fire.

'God give you both luck and many children,' said Maureen.

'Well, when are you going to name the day?' asked Uncle John.

'Oh, not yet,' said Esther. 'It's only right to have a reasonable time after an engagement before there's a wedding.'

'Don't leave it too long,' said Martha. 'It's not younger you're both getting.'

Bartley refrained from drinking much that day, having only one glass of stout with his dinner. Even when Uncle John offered him more, he refused, while Esther sipped a glass of sherry. But Uncle John gave me that impish wink a few times, which said a lot. Then late in the afternoon just before dusk, they excused themselves and went walking in the cold evening air.

Fritz decided he wanted to get away for a while, and we walked together through the frosty fields. I hadn't talked to him since his father's death, and I didn't want to say anything unless he wanted to say something himself. He was quiet for a while, and I took him to the rock at the top of the farm.

'Everything changes all the time,' he said.

'I know,' I answered. 'You have changed so much.'

'How have I changed, then?'

'You are so tall; your voice is changing; you are no longer a boy.'

'You have changed too; you are growing as well. Your face is longer.'

'I have not a long face,' I said rather crossly.

'I don't mean it that way. You have become more like a woman.'

'I won't be thirteen till April.'

'Thirteen, fourteen, it doesn't matter,' he said. 'We all change.'

'If the war doesn't end, or if Father doesn't come home, I will be going to secondary school in September. Uncle John is going to pay for it. Mother and he had an argument about it one night. She wanted to pay for it, and he told her that with the wages she gets from working at the dispensary, it wouldn't pay for even the half of it. He was going to do it if she was under his roof.'

'What would happen if you didn't go?' he asked.

'I'd have to go working in one of the big houses or work in a shop.'

'Would you like that?'

'Uncle John is a proud man, and he wouldn't want to ever see me work in domestic service. He didn't like to see Mother work in the shop in the village, but when Dr Daly gave her the job at the dispensary, he was happier about that. It makes Mother happy to be a breadwinner and to help pay for some of our keep. Her money helps to buy food. We get very little with the ration books, but those extra pleasures like paraffin oil, tobacco, and tea can be got on the black market, and they cost dearly. While she can help somewhat, he's prepared to go along with that.'

'When this war is over,' said Fritz, 'some people are going to be rich out of it. '

'Yes, at the expense of everyone else.'

'I wish I could have lived in another time. I hate this war. I hate myself. I hate everything. I hate everyone . . .'

'Does that mean you hate me?'

'No! No! No! I do not mean it that way. I do not know if I want to live the rest of my life. I have lost everything. When this war is over, where do I start? My grandfather is all I have. He is getting old. I will never see my parents again. Where do I go when I have nothing? You have your mother, your uncle John, and your aunts. This is a lovely place, and they will help you and look after you. What am I going to do?'

'Don't say that,' I said. 'We'll have to find a way. I too have lost a lot. You are my friend. I know I can share something with you. Whenever this war is over, things will never be the same again. You know they won't. We will just have to forget . . .'

'I will never forget my father and my mother.'

'There is still hope for her, Fritz. Don't give up yet. I still have nightmares worrying about Father. Reverend Mother told me that he will never go to heaven because he's a Protestant. I know she's wrong, but sometimes it frightens me to think that it could be true.'

'In our war, we do not fight people, we fight ourselves. We are fighting to hold on to what we have. It is a private war, which is worse.'

'Don't worry,' I said. 'We will fight it together.'

'You're a good friend, Margaret, the best I've ever had.'

He took my hand in his. It was warm despite the frost, and we walked through the fields back to the farmhouse as the evening turned to night. Another Christmas was fading into memory. It was a different Christmas, though. I knew for the first time that I'd found a friend who shared the same troubles as mine, and that we could fight it together. We were allies now in our own private war, and there was no way any great army was going to stop us.

*****

Mother went back to work in the dispensary the day after St Stephen's Day, and when she came home in the late afternoon, there was a note from Dr Daly inviting me to afternoon tea the following day. Carmel was home for Christmas from boarding school, and she wanted to see me.

There was snow threatened for the afternoon, but the doctor said he would collect me and leave me home. Afternoon surgery was set to go on longer than usual, due to the winter coughs and illnesses. Dr Daly took a half hour off around midday and collected me. He told Mother he would take us both home when surgery was over.

When I arrived at the house, I was taken to the glow of a warm fire in the parlour. I once again admired the porcelain clock on the mantelpiece and its lovely tinkle on the hour, beating out the number of bells denoting what time of the day it was.

Carmel greeted me with a smile, and she gave me a little peck on the cheek. She too was taller, and her hair flowed in waves down her back. She was a different person, and she looked to be very contented.

'I am so glad to see you, Margaret. Had you a nice Christmas?'

'It was lovely. But enough about that. How are you getting on at school?'

'I don't like the idea of boarding school, but I've made many friends, and I'm on the junior hockey team. There is so much to learn as well, new subjects like domestic science, science, bookkeeping, French, and even German.'

'I would love to learn some German,' I said. 'I'm going as a day pupil to the school in the village in September. They only teach French.'

'I know you want to learn German because of that German boy that you know.'

'It would help, all right, but he has very good English. As soon as the war is over, he will be going back home to Germany.'

'What about you? What will you be doing?'

'I don't know. Hoping that Father will return, we'll go back to London. I don't really know what's happening.'

'And I think of how cruel I was to you. I'm so sorry for that.'

'Don't be sorry! I love to see you happy again.'

'My mother is better again, and my father keeps a fair eye on things. With your mother working in the dispensary, it takes a great burden of paperwork away from him. But he was still so busy during Christmas. On Christmas night, he was called to Sheila's house. She was very ill, and she is now in a hospital in Dublin.'

'Oh my goodness,' I said. 'I didn't know that.'

'The news today is that she has improved a little. Her breathing was very bad.'

'Let Mother know when she's home, and I'll go to see her.'

I could not believe the change in Carmel. She was not the same person I'd known at school. Even though she said she didn't like boarding school, it had helped her confidence, and she now had a smile on her face. We sat down to afternoon tea, and this time she tucked in as well. Her mother left us alone, and she was much quieter too. The lady who'd greeted me earlier in the year and the little girl with the sad and dour face were gone. It was a normal family home now.

When we went upstairs, her room had changed. The dolls were gone, as well as the soft toys and other toys she'd had on display. Carmel told me she had given a lot of them away to children in the village for Christmas. She felt she was past them now.

'I don't need all these material things. I have plenty. I am one of the lucky ones, you know. If you look at yourself as well, you are lucky too. We have warm clothes, a bed, good food, people who care for us, and we are getting a good education. Lots of children from the village don't have that. Even in summer, they don't have shoes to wear. I went out with Dad several times last summer when he was visiting sick people out the country. They're poor. Some children are hungry. The men get little work, and there is little or no money going into the homes. We are children of privilege, Margaret. We are just that.'

I sat listening to her, wondering where this had all come from. Carmel had just turned fourteen, and gone was the strange, selfish child I'd known at school. Even now, I thought it strange the way she was looking at the world. There was precious little in her room except for her bed, a wardrobe, and a dressing table with just a few little objects such as a hairbrush, a comb, and some ribbons and hair slides. On the window was a statue of Our Lady and a string of rosary beads in a little purse beside it. Was this the result of the teaching she was getting from the nuns? Why had she changed so much? She was denying herself the things all girls of her age should have.

'I know you're wondering why I'm saying all this,' Carmel said, 'but I feel that someday I want to help those who are far less off than we are. It's not fair how some people are rich and some are poor. My father is a doctor, and he isn't poor. He works very hard, though. Maybe I'll become a doctor. I don't know. I'm still only in first year. What would you like to be, Margaret?'

'I have no idea,' I answered. 'I'm only going into first year in September, and I don't even know how long I'll be at school here in Ireland. I'm watching how the war is progressing. Did you see the fields? In places they have large poles dug into the ground. Uncle John said they're to prevent enemy aircraft landing. There are blackout blinds in all the windows so they won't see any village, town, or other lights from the air.'

'I saw this huge balloon near the town way up in the air. Dad said it was to prevent aeroplanes from flying low.'

'Uncle John calls them barrage balloons. They're filled with some kind of gas to keep them up in the air. So this war isn't ending for a while. I'll be here for a few years yet.'

We continued talking until around five p.m., when I heard Carmel's mother calling us. Mother had arrived, and it was time to head home. Carmel gave me a hug as I was leaving, and Mother stood in awe looking at her, seeing a different girl from the one she'd seen last summer.

The doctor had put Mother's bike in the boot of the car outside the front door, and the engine was running. It was starting to snow, and he declared that we might have a white New Year.

That night I told everyone about the changes that had come over Carmel, and the aunts sat listening intently. Mother couldn't believe the difference that had come over her. Then Martha said something that set me thinking.

'I know what she's going through now,' she said.

'What do you mean?' asked Mother.

'That girl is going to be a nun.'

*****

On New Year's Day, I rode on the slushy road towards the village to visit Sheila. I heard she was home from hospital. Mother had baked a small Christmas cake with leftover fruit and spices the night before and wrapped it in brown paper with old newspaper to protect it. She'd put it in a sackcloth shopping bag and told me to be careful with it.

The whole Bryce family was home for the new year. Sheila was in bed, and her father brought me down to see her. She was sitting up, surrounded by toys I'd never seen her with before. The velveteen toy was sitting beside her on the pillow. I knew that Carmel must have given some of her other toys to her as well.

'You're a great girl to come to see her,' said her father.

'Mother baked this for you all and said to wish you a happy New Year.'

'You are all such good people,' said her mother. 'Now you're going to have a cup of tea and a slice of cake, because you came all the way in that cold weather to visit Sheila.'

Sheila was excited to see me, and she leaned forwards in the bed to talk. Her arms were so thin, and I could see her bones through her flesh.

'You promised me you would eat more,' I said.

'I'm feeling a lot better, and I'm eating quite well now.'

'She's going to come down to the table now and sit with you for a cup of tea by the fire,' said her mother.

I didn't realise how weak she was until they brought her down. She could barely walk, and her brother Conor swept her up in his arms and carried her. She sat in a chair next to the fire, and indeed, she did eat a fine slice of cake with some warm, milky tea.

'Will we go to the lake this year?' she asked.

'That will depend on you,' I answered. 'You're not well enough to go outside the door. You must do your best to get well again, and when the summer comes, we will go there. I think Dr and Mrs Daly intend having that great picnic once more. Carmel told me you were not well and that you were in hospital.'

'She has been so kind to me. She brought me more of her toys at Christmas. Now I have too many.'

'You have more than I have. But that's not a bad thing; you have plenty to do now when you're at home sick.'

'I would like to get back to school for the spring and summer. My reading has improved. Conor brings me books from the library in town.'

'Well, get plenty of rest as well,' I said.

'You know, you have wisdom beyond your years,' said Fintan. 'She will listen to you, and she won't listen to us. You will have to come here more often.'

'I will hurry from school each day,' I said, 'and I'll drop in for a few minutes each evening. The days will start getting longer, and it will be easier.'

'That's great,' Sheila cheered. 'I will look forward to that.'

When I left her, she was eating another piece of cake and sipping her cup of tea. There was a frost looming, and the slush on the road was freezing. I walked most of the way back, as it was too slippery to ride the bike.

When Mother realised it was getting too dark, she went walking down the avenue to meet me. When she began walking, she realised how icy the roads were. But it wasn't long till she saw me coming home, and she was relieved to see me.

I sat and warmed myself by the fire, and everyone wanted to know how Sheila was. When I told them about her and how she was still weak and ill but slowly improving, Maureen said, 'I don't know if that little girl will ever survive. She is getting it so hard to recover from that auld TB. I fear for her future. I don't know if she is meant for this world at all.'

With that, I exploded in anger at what I was hearing.

'Aunt Maureen, what are you saying? She is not going to die! She's going to get better. I know she will.'

'Margaret, do not speak to Aunt Maureen like that. Apologise right now.'

'I'm sorry!' I blurted out, and I ran upstairs to my room. I lay on my bed, crying on my pillow, and in a few minutes, Mother came to me. She sat beside me and placed her hand on my shoulder.

'Margaret, please don't cry.'

I sat up in the bed, and turning towards her, I said softly through my tears, 'She's not going to get better now, is she?'

'I don't know, sweetheart; I really don't. Aunt Maureen didn't mean to upset you. She speaks her mind out, speaking from the heart, and you can't fault her for that.'

'I know that, Mother. I know it myself, and think it myself, but I don't want to even say it.'

'I know what's on your mind right now. You're thinking of Nana and your father.'

'And Fritz!' I began again to cry into her shoulders, and she hugged me to console me.

'Times are cruel, my little girl, and you're one of the bravest people I know. You have kept me from losing my marbles, and you've made me laugh. I have seen how kind you are to others, to Sheila, to the aunts and Uncle John. Look at Carmel, see how she has changed.'

'I'm no miracle worker, Mother.'

'Yes, you are. You are a very caring young lady. You remind me of your late grandfather. Pity he didn't live to see you; he'd spoil you rotten.'

'The way Uncle John does now.' I smiled through the tears.

'I want you to promise me something.'

'Yes, Mother?'

'I want you to stop thinking of people dying. It all rests in the hands of the Lord.'

'Mother, I made a promise this evening. I told Sheila I would call to see her for a few minutes each evening on my way from school.'

'That's a very good idea. But don't stay very long, as darkness comes early.'

'I won't. But the days will be getting longer.'

'They will, but we will have dark evenings for a long while yet. Now come on down and don't stay up here.'

'No, I think I will go to bed.'

'All right, love.'

'Good night, Mother.'

'Good night, Margaret.'

Part 9
The Mother-of-Pearl Pendant

Chapter 18

The New Year came and went. The days became longer, and the nights dwindled to those few short hours that saw the sun set and the sky darken only to carry an early summer dawn back to us again. As promised, I called on Sheila each day, and her hope of seeing me saw her health improve, and she kept talking about a visit to the lake again.

As promised, Dr Daly and his family hosted a summer picnic in July, and Fritz took us both in the little sidecar to the shore. The sun shone on the day, and there were races and games for the parish children. The local shops donated what they could in the line of confectionery and soft drinks, even though such commodities were hard to come by. Sheila was not able to take part in the sports activities, but she went with me to the shore, and she talked again about sailing away on a cloud to see the world and to look down on the fields. I didn't like the way she said things like this, but she stared out across the lake and watched two swans bob up and down on the water, quiet and calm, completely undisturbed by the revelry on the shore. The day ended, and again Sheila was disappointed that it was all over, but I promised her she could come and visit during some of the warm days, and this cheered her up no end.

But life moved on at its own easy pace at Dairy Hill. In September 1943, I began as a day pupil in the secondary school. I was one of fifteen day pupils from the parish, while twenty boarders from all over the county and beyond were in the same class. I settled into a new routine, and just as when I'd arrived three years earlier, everything was all new. As Carmel had said, the challenge of new subjects was a great adventure. I wore my grey uniform dress and blue cardigan, each bearing the school crest, and a blue beret when we attended services such as choir or stations of the cross in the church.

It wasn't long before I found myself in my fourth year at Dairy Hill. Uncle John declared that I was going to be as tall as Aunt Maureen. He said I should be called Mairead óg, or little Margaret. I told him not to even try.

But Mother declared that I would always be her little Margaret, no matter how old I got or how tall I grew. Mother was quite content to see me attend the convent school, as the nuns were determined to make young ladies out of us. Whether they ever succeeded or not, I don't really know. Fritz came into our lives at holiday time and went again when those worthy days of rest passed away so quickly.

With the passing of time, Uncle John was beginning to show his age. He was now approaching his sixties, and when needed, he employed teams of local labourers to help with the sowing and harvesting.

Paddy and Moonlight soon became a great pair in front of the plough or pulling a mowing machine. Paddy spent a short while up at Johnsons', as Uncle John didn't want a hot-blooded stallion out in the fields.

'How can you stop that?' I asked.

'I need to intervene in Mother Nature's plans and call a halt to his gallop.'

'I don't understand.'

'The same as what happens to the bull calves. You're a big girl now, and I suppose you should know. He's going to be castrated. A vet will do it. He will never sire any foals.'

'Ah, the poor thing.'

'He'll be all the better for it. He will be quiet and placid, just like old Paddy.'

'Will he know what happened?'

'He will be sore for a while, but all that will worry him then will be his food, his work, and any attention we might give him. Just the same as a bull becomes a bullock, Paddy will be a gelding.'

My years at the farm made me more accepting of this news. If I had heard it when I first arrived, I would have been devastated. Mother Nature's secrets were still being revealed to me. Though it sounded cruel, I knew Paddy would have no worries for the rest of his working life. Even so, because of this revelation, Paddy got a lot more attention from me after that.

*****

We'd seen very little of Bartley since he'd gotten engaged. He was a busy man. His tumbledown house was undergoing big changes. It was now shining with a sparkling coat of whitewash, and in the summer of 1944, the roof was reslated. There was always a line of washing out to dry. The cobwebs had never appeared again, and Uncle John said you could eat your dinner off the floor. Then one evening, Bartley and Esther announced that they were getting married the following June.

'When you marry in June, you are a bride all your life,' said Martha.

'What do you mean by that?' asked Esther.

'It means you'll have good health and youthful looks for a very long time.'

'I'm a bit long in the tooth for youthful looks,' she said.

'You're still a young woman in your prime,' said Maureen. 'Embrace it, love; you have a good man, and I know you will be happy.'

The announcement ended with a toast to absent friends as well as the future bride and groom.

Sheila didn't go to secondary school; her family couldn't afford it. There was talk of starting work in a shop in the town, but her health failed again, and she remained at home. Billy Bryce kept me informed of her health, and I made it my business to visit her on the weekends. I came home from school late each evening, as I stayed back for study, but I was out on time to cycle home with Mother. I knew deep down that Sheila was losing the battle for life. Her face was growing thinner, and she wasn't eating again. She spent a few weeks away in a sanitorium in Dublin, but when she returned, she was worse than ever.

Then come summer, she bounced back, and with the fine weather, her health improved. It was the wet, damp winters that were draining her life away.

In June 1944, the Allies landed on the coast of Normandy, and there was hope that the war would be over before Christmas. I was so excited by the news that I thought that within a few weeks, we would be going home to London again, whenever Father returned. We had received a short note from the Home Office at Easter, confirming that he was alive and well. Mother had requested the information from them, as she hadn't heard from him for quite a while. All she was told was that he was stationed overseas.

Sheila was very disappointed when she heard I'd be returning to London as soon as the war was over, but I didn't realise that the war in Europe would last for nearly another year. We got used to listening to Lord Haw-Haw, and even Mother ignored his rantings, as she deemed him to be a lunatic. From information in newspapers, I began to map out for myself the advance of the armies across Europe, and I wondered how long it was all going to take. Their advance wasn't half quick enough for me, and I waited with bated breath for the great day to come.

Night after night, the radio was our link with the war and the outside world, and a change came over me. This was going to become a greater part of our lives. God only knew what way the world was going to advance in the coming years.

Each weekend I visited Sheila, charting our progress through the war, and I failed to realise that I was her lifeline. She was beginning to fret that I was going away from her forever. She showed a brave face through it all. I was too preoccupied to realise that she was losing her battle for life, and if I had been more careful, I might have been able to do something about it.

*****

One morning in December 1944, there was a knock on the classroom door, and when the nun answered it, she called my name, as there was an urgent request for me. When I got there, it was Billy Bryce. He was pale as death, and he was in a hurry.

'Margaret, she needs you,' he said. 'She's poorly.'

With that, he handed me a little brown envelope and said, 'She told me to give you this. She said you will know what to do.'

I opened the envelope to find the mother-of-pearl pendant and chain I had given to her at Christmas 1940, as well as the little card that went with it.

'When did she give you this?' I asked.

'A little while ago. I came straight here with it. We were up all night with her. She took bad late last night. Dr Daly is with her now, and so is the priest.'

I said nothing more but dashed back into the class, and grabbing my books, I excused myself with the nun, telling her that my friend Sheila was terribly ill. She hadn't time to enquire further into her circumstances, as I was gone. I told Billy to tell Mother at the dispensary, not realising that she had been informed a little earlier and was making her way to join me as well. I knew that Mother would deal with any complaints from the nuns about me absconding during class time. But we'd bridge that gap when we came to it.

It was a cold, wet morning, and I hadn't even time to button my coat. I threw my bag around the handlebars of the bike and cycled hastily to Bryces' cottage. My coat flew open in the wind, but I was oblivious to the fact that the wind and the rain were penetrating my clothes. My only concern was to reach Sheila, to be with her. She needed encouragement to keep her fight for life going, and I wanted to be there.

When I reached the house, there was a crowd of relatives gathered in a group outside talking, huddled in heavy coats and caps from the rain, as there was not enough room in the little cottage for everyone.

'How is she?' I asked.

'Just waiting for the last,' said a man with a shiver in his speech. 'The poor little pet.'

The rosary was being recited, and I edged my way through the crowded kitchen to Sheila's room.

She was propped up on pillows, breathing heavily. Her face was as white as the sheets on the bed. She was conscious, but very weak. The hum of the rosary pervaded the room, and she saw me as I came in. Her mother made room for me, and I sat beside her at the head of the bed.

I took her hand and placed the little pendant in her palm and closed her fingers. She lifted her hand up weakly and looked at the pendant. Then she dropped her hand slowly and smiled. She could only whisper.

'I knew you'd come,' she said.

'I should've come earlier,' I said, as the tears came.

'I was waiting for you. I wasn't going anywhere till you came.'

'You're staying here,' I sobbed. 'I'm not letting you go anywhere.'

'Ah, but I am. I'm taking that trip on the cloud.'

'You will not. You will come back to the lake with me next summer.'

'But you'll be gone back to London.'

'No, I won't. I'm not leaving you, ever.'

'You must go your way. You are not to cry. Can't you see? I'm not crying. Mammy is crying all night. There is no need to cry.'

'You're my friend,' I sobbed. 'Why shouldn't I cry?'

'We'll always be friends,' she said. 'We have our own little place on the lake shore, with the wind and the waves, and the swans are our own . . .'

Then she began drifting into sleep. At least I thought she was sleeping. Her mother wiped her face, and we each held a hand. The rosary continued for another half hour, repeatedly. I had never seen anyone die before, but I was glad that when I looked across the room, Mother was standing among the quiet relatives at the door.

At about noon, the priest returned and gave Sheila the last rites, and the rosaries continued into the afternoon. She never woke again, and she faded away with the daylight. Her long-suffering body rested now, for the first time in her life, just after five o'clock.

We all left the room, and Mother was there for me. She held me as I poured my grief over her shoulders. Sheila's mother, now composed and relaxed, took my hand and said nothing. I knew she was glad I was there. I too was glad to be there, but it didn't make parting with my friend that much easier.

Mother took me home, and we sat by the fire all evening, peering into the darkness of the kitchen to conserve the light. I had no homework to do, and it was the last thing on my mind. All that was bothering me now was the next few days and the funeral.

People came and went to the Bryce wake, but they did not delay very long, for fear of contracting TB from the house. It was a quiet affair, which was quite unusual for Irish homes. The night before Sheila's body was brought to the church, Uncle John was called upon by several men from the locality to go to the house and read the office for the dead over the corpse. This was something the men of the area did at wakes, and things were then set in motion to bring the body away for burial.

I went to the funeral feeling miserable and hot. One minute I was warm, and the next minute I was cold. The whole affair was a nightmare to me. Fritz was away, and it would have been much better if he were with us, but he was doing his Leaving Certificate Exam the following June, and there was no way he could take time out to be with us.

We followed the coffin from the church to the grave and stood in the rain to pay our last respects to Sheila, my best friend. There was a great sense of loss as we stood there looking on. Just before the coffin was lowered into the ground, a little robin alighted on it, looked around for a few seconds, and flew away. This was too much for me. Then, when the coffin was lowered into the ground, the local men spat on their hands and began shovelling clay on top of it.

Mother held my hand, and I was glad she was there. Uncle John threw a heavy raincoat over us and stood there with his hat off as the rain pounded and pelted all of us. It was punishing us sinners. We were here at the funeral of a little saint. It was warning us to pull our socks up. All sorts of strange thoughts like this rolled through my head.

Then a thought struck me. The little robin was Sheila's guardian angel, and it had come to tell us that its job was done. Just before the funeral concluded, I said to Mother that I wanted to go.

'I don't feel well,' I said.

She felt my forehead and saw me shivering.

'You have a temperature.'

She beckoned at Uncle John to come, and he took us home in the trap. I was wrapped in an old coat to try to keep me warm.

I was put to bed, and there I was to stay. Dr Daly was sent for.

'You're a lucky girl,' he said. 'You are not very well now. Plenty of bed rest for you for a week or two.'

'I think I might be getting TB,' I said.

'It's pleurisy, love. That's what it is. You're strong and able to fight it. But you will need plenty of bed rest. I'll drop in to see how you're progressing.'

I hovered between wakefulness and delirium for several days, fighting the demons that were attacking my body. The nightmares that came with it were of Sheila floating away on a cloud, followed by Nana, Fritz's father, and my own father. I was losing everyone I ever cared for. Was this the road my life was going to take? Everyone I loved was either missing, dead, or dying. I told myself in those dreams that I would be better off dead. Then I'd set sail on a cloud and follow Sheila. Fritz was standing there, screaming at me to come back.

It was at times like this that Mother was there. The room was dark, but there was a warm glow from a fire lit in the little grate in the bedroom. I thought the darkness would last forever. But it was the wet, dull days, coupled with the curtains drawn to keep out the draught, that made my passage to recovery so long and painful.

When my temperature went down, I was more lucid. Mother was wonderful, and she kept giving me fluids to drink. When Uncle John appeared, his entrance was always foretold by the sweet smell of pipe tobacco.

I wasn't able to eat anything, but there was beef tea, and the soup from the winter stews, with well-mashed vegetables, gave me encouragement to strengthen up again.

Then, when I heard that preparations were being made for Christmas, I made a greater effort still to sit up and eat.

Mother told me we were going to have a crowd again this year, and I looked forward to seeing Fritz.

But before that, I had a very unexpected visitor. I was sitting in the soft chair by the fire in the kitchen when Dr Daly's car pulled up to the back door. He was on his usual rounds and had decided to call to see how his patient was coming along.

When Martha opened the door, Carmel accompanied him. She was home for the Christmas holidays. Mother had told him that morning that I was on the mend and sitting up at the fire. He'd asked Carmel to go with him, and he would let her stay for a few hours while he finished his rounds.

When Dr Daly finished examining me, he said, 'I'm afraid I have bad news for you, young lady.'

'What's wrong, Doctor?'

'You're going to live. I want you to stay close to the fire, stay in out of the cold, and eat and drink plenty. I think before too long you'll be on that bike again, heading off to school.'

'Thank you, Doctor,' I said, rather relieved.

Then he was offered the usual cup of tea and sweet cake, but he declined and rushed off to visit people in other areas of the parish.

Carmel sat beside me, and she didn't refuse the tea and cake. She was sad and tearful when she heard about Sheila's last days. She was fascinated when she heard about the little robin landing on the coffin.

'That's amazing,' she said.

'When I was very ill, I was thinking that the little robin was her guardian angel. It was never far away from her.'

'When she showed me the robin for the first time, it changed me,' said Carmel.

Then Martha spoke from the table, where she was putting together the ingredients for a Christmas cake.

'The ways of the Lord are strange and amazing. Maybe it *was* a little angel. It could just be a coincidence, but then, she was a very special little girl.'

'She saw good in everyone,' said Maureen.

Carmel was now in tears. It was only now that she was coming to terms with Sheila's loss. She had been alone and away from home when Sheila died, and this was the first chance she'd had to grieve.

'Don't fret for her, child,' said Martha, embracing her and comforting her. 'She is with God and the angels now. She has no more illness or pain. Think happy things, and think about those lovely visits to see her little garden friend. Pray for her and ask her to pray for you. We all have great loss in life, but we must move on and leave everything in God's hands.'

Carmel sobbed for a few minutes, then she smiled through her tears and said, 'I'm glad to see you getting better. It must be boring sitting there. So, I brought you these. I have finished reading them, and you can have them now. Happy Christmas.'

She handed me a large paper bag, and when I opened it, out popped three hardbound books. When I looked at them, I knew I had plenty of reading material during the Christmas period. She'd given me *Heidi*, *Little Women*, and *Jane Eyre*. I hugged her and declared that I had nothing to give her in return. But she said that the best present she could get was to see me on the road to recovery.

When her father collected her, he told me he wasn't coming back anymore and he didn't want to see me very ill ever again.

When Carmel had gone, Martha declared once more that she had the makings of a very good nun.

*****

Fritz arrived on Christmas Eve, and I was sitting by the fire in the parlour. For the first time we both had shoulders to cry on, and our main topic of conversation was Sheila and all she had said about floating away on a cloud. We both had known when she said this that she would never get better. Yet we had been in denial and hadn't let ourselves say anything about it.

Sheila herself had known it as well. She had poured her whole life into those few short hours each summer, and we had been there to help her do

304

so. I took Fritz's hand in mine and we talked for ages, until Mother arrived with slices of Christmas cake and hot tea.

This was like coming home for Fritz. He knew we sensed it. The aunts doted on him, as usual, and treated him as if he were the son they never had. On Christmas day they presented him with knitted socks and a jumper to keep him warm. Christmas came and went, and we passed into another year, and the spring of 1945 arrived without ceremony. Returning to school in the middle of January, I put Sheila's death behind me, though I remembered her each week with a visit to her grave.

It was on one of these visits that I met Billy Bryce. He had come to pray. I was placing a bunch of daffodils on the small mound of dark earth when he spoke behind me.

'You miss her, don't you?'

I was startled when he spoke, and he stood there, gazing down at the small grave.

'I do,' I answered. 'I will always miss her.'

'I miss them all, you know. I'm alone here now.'

'When did they go?'

'Last weekend they shut up the house and left. There was no ceremony about it. They left everything behind them. There's a gardener's job at a big house on the south side of the city, and Fintan got it. Peter Johnson recommended him highly.'

'Will they ever come back?' I asked.

'I doubt it. There are too many sad memories for them.'

'As long as I'm here, I'll come to visit her,' I said.

'You're a good girl, you know that, Margaret? You deserve to do well in life.'

'I would like to have said goodbye to them.'

'Maybe it was better this way; there might have been tears all over again. Anyway, I was told to give you this.'

He took from his pocket the brown envelope he had handed me at the school the morning he came to fetch me. I knew what was in it.

'That's for keeps. You'll remember her with it.'

'I'll always cherish it,' I said.

'I don't go near the house now since they left. It's going up for sale soon, and it's full of disease. They should knock it down, you know.'

'They won't do that,' I said. 'It'll be sold.'

'I hope not,' he continued. 'Some other little girl or boy will be cursed with that terrible disease once more if it goes on the market.'

*****

One Saturday morning at the end of March, Mother had a telegram in her hand from the Home Office. I knew the worst news had come. It was the news I feared, and I began to scream. She began shaking me and shouting at me.

'He's not dead, he's not dead. He's alive, just about.'

'What happened to him?' I sobbed.

'He was wounded, and he's in hospital. His back and his leg are injured. They fear he might never walk again. He's being taken back to London next Friday, and they're going to operate on him. There's a bullet lodged close to his spine. They removed one from his leg as well.'

'Oh, Mother,' I sobbed, 'please don't let him die. Please go to him and bring him home. Don't wait, just go!'

'I'm leaving in the morning; you'll have to stay here.'

'I'll be all right; he needs you now. I know he does. Just when this bloody war was about to finish, he had to go and get himself shot.'

'Don't cry, and don't swear like that. This war has just left us beyond crying.'

'It will be a miracle if we survive it at all.'

'Please don't give up, not now. These are the hard times, and we should hold on as long as we can.'

We spent that evening packing her case for her and making sure everything was in order. I heated the irons on a bed of coals on the fire and replaced them whenever the one in use began to cool down. Martha ironed her clothes, and there was a fresh smell of laundry all over the house.

I gathered a bunch of wild violets from the ditch and wrapped them in damp paper. I told her to give them to him. They were the first of spring, and they might brighten up his day.

Uncle John brought Bobby into the shed for the early-morning trip to the town so that there would be no rushing at the last minute. I insisted on going with them. Mother said I was to go to school, but she gave in when I said I wanted to see her off. I didn't want her to be lonely on her journey, so at least I'd keep her company as far as the station in Mullingar.

In the morning, the air was dry but frosty. We had a good breakfast. Mother said goodbye to two very tearful aunts, and we made our way out on to the main road. It was amazing how quiet the countryside was at this time of the morning, except for the occasional wood pigeon clattering its wings high up in the branches of the trees.

When we got to the town, things were different. The new cathedral stood elegantly in the early-morning sunshine, reflecting the eastern sunlight back into the landscape. It was now nearly six years old. It had been consecrated when the war broke out in Europe, and I prayed that maybe now we were in the last days of this terrible event.

At the station we sat on the cold platform, waiting for the great train to come through from Athlone. When it thundered slowly to a halt, I knew it would be the last I'd see of Mother for some time. I knew she would stay with Father and help him to recover, or maybe she would send for me. By the time she'd gotten the telegram, he was on a hospital ship somewhere in the Mediterranean.

We embraced on the platform, and she joined the other passengers on the train bound for Dublin. Uncle John and I followed her until she found a place to sit down, and she kept waving at us until she was out of sight. Then Uncle John took my hand and squeezed it.

'It's time to go home, love,' he said. His great arm stretched around my shoulders, and we moved out of the station back to the trap.

*****

A week later in early April, I had a letter from Mother. She said she had so much to tell me. Father had been working in a military office in Cairo for the duration of the war. There had been no other information given to us, as he was involved in intelligence work. It was then that I realised why his post had been so secretive and why we had gotten very little information about his activities during the campaign.

Mother had so much to say, she wrote, that she couldn't put it all down on paper now. About a week before he was to return to London, she said, Father had been caught in the cross fire of some criminal activity in Cairo and was shot in the back and leg. So much for the wounds of battle and fighting for your country; it happened that he was just in the wrong place at the wrong time. He'd gone down to the market to purchase some little trinket for me when it happened. He was rushed to hospital, where they found that the bullet was lodged quite close to his spinal cord. His leg was injured badly as well, but they managed to remove the bullet there. There was nothing they could do for him until he was taken back to London.

He had undergone an operation when he arrived, and they had successfully removed the bullet from his back. At this stage, he was out of danger. He was conscious, and time would tell whether he would ever walk again. Mother reassured me that he would get well again and that he was not going to die.

Quite a lot of the city was in ruins, she said, but the people were beginning to pick up the pieces again. She was staying at Felicity's house; despite the war, her family had never gone to Scotland at all. The ruins of our house were gone. In fact, the whole street had been cleared away, and there was nothing left but wasteland, waiting for development whenever the war was over. According to the news and the papers, it now looked as if the war would be over soon, but only time would tell.

In my return letter, I told Mother that invitations had arrived for us to attend Bartley and Esther's wedding. The wedding was to take place on the last Saturday in June. They were going to spend their honeymoon with a friend of hers in Wicklow. Uncle John had promised to look after the farm while they were gone.

Meanwhile, all the crops were sown, and when Fritz came home, I wished him well on his final term before his exams.

*****

I walked with Fritz to the lake that weekend, and we had time to talk. It was the first bit of breathing space we'd had since Sheila died. It was evening, and the April sunshine was telling us that showers weren't too far away. Indeed, there *was* a shower, and we stood in the shelter of a large alder tree on the shore. The sun was at our backs, and a rainbow stretched across the lake.

Then again, I heard it: a cuckoo. It was telling me that times were about to change, or so I thought.

When the hail shower was over, Fritz took my hand and showed me how to skim stones on the water. He was much better at it than I was, but all the same, it wasn't long before I had the knack of it.

'What is going to happen to us?' he asked.

'I don't know,' I said. 'I will be returning to London soon. Father is recovering. He's in hospital with spinal and leg injuries from two bullets. Time will tell whether he'll ever walk again or not. But he's alive. I must wait for Mother to return, whenever that will be.'

'Will I see you again?'

'Yes, you will,' I said. 'I'll see you when your exams are over, won't I?'

'I suppose. Then what?'

'I don't really know.'

'Grossvater is not going to return to Germany, but Peter has asked him to stay and manage the estate for him when he's away. He is very happy here. He has lost so much; he feels it's better to stay. Too many sad memories. There will never be a Germany like the old one.'

'Wait till you see, it will grow from the ashes. It will never give up, will it?'

'Ireland will be a great place to live. It has survived the war, and there are no ashes from which to build. It is all there.'

'I must return to London. Mother said that great areas of the city are in ruins.'

'No matter what happens,' he said, 'I will always love you, no matter where I am.' He hadn't the words out of his mouth when he planted a soft kiss on my face. I put my hand up to my cheek, and of course I blushed. He had taken me quite by surprise.

'I'm sorry,' he said. 'I didn't mean to be so forward.'

'It's all right. I don't mind.'

'I have no other way of telling you this. You have made me very happy these last few years. You were my friend when I needed you, and made all the loneliness go away. We had fun and we had laughs.'

'It's not all over yet. Promise me you'll come to Esther and Bartley's wedding.'

'I will. When is it exactly?'

'You mean Esther hasn't told you yet?'

'She's in Dublin now for Easter with relatives, probably preparing for the wedding.'

'Well, it takes place the last Saturday in June.'

'I will be just finished my exams.'

'Then let's not say any farewells at this stage. We have lots to do, and if you don't stop kissing me, Fritz Von Gebler, I'll tell Mother, and you know how good she is with shotguns.'

As I said this, I pulled up a few handfuls of clover and threw them over his head. Then I ran screaming into the woods, knowing that he'd catch me before I got to the gate.

Part 10
The Fires of Hell

Chapter 19

When Fritz returned to school, it was time for me to do so as well. In the last term, there was talk of preparing for the summer exams. So it wasn't long before I had to knuckle down and forget all that had happened. Everywhere I went, people were asking me how Father was, and there was a new spring in my step. Uncle John knew as well that soon he might have to say farewell to us, and he grew quiet once again.

One evening when I returned home from school, he was gone somewhere with the jennet and farm cart. I asked Martha if anything was the matter.

'It's the gates. He's gone with them to the forge. He's getting them repaired at last, and it's not before his time.'

I knew that on an occasion like this, Uncle John wouldn't return until the early hours of the morning. He'd end up drinking, and old reliable Bobby knew the way home.

This trip was no different, but it would be Uncle John's last trip of its kind, due to the events of the next few days.

In the evening, I helped with the cows and put them out into the pasture. In fact, milking them was second nature to me now. Minnie had just had her first calf, and she was a quiet, placid animal. Her offspring was just like her. She was going to replace another cow who was coming to the end of her working life on the farm.

I was beginning to feel lonely now that I knew I'd have to leave soon. But I didn't want to think about it. I took a walk across the fields just before I sat down to study for the night, and Martha followed me.

'We had better make a May bush,' she said.

She cut a blackthorn branch that was laced with milky-white blossoms, and we twined it with primroses, daisy chains, and little bunches of violets. I gave her a hand, as it was a job we had done every year since I'd come to the farm. We placed the bush in the hedge in the front garden. Within

313

the next few days, the harsh winds of May would dry up the flowers, and someone would remember to remove the branch sometime in the summer when the hedge was being trimmed.

She took the last few daisy chains with her into the house. I followed her to her bedroom, where she twined them round the veil of the Blessed Virgin that stood on a chest of drawers. I'd come with her at times when she was praying, and she'd say who the prayers were for as she prayed out loud. Tonight she sat on the side of the bed and recited a decade of the rosary. Ever since Mother left, she'd prayed each night for my father, that he would have a speedy recovery. During the winter, these prayers were said after the rosary in the kitchen, but as the days grew longer, it was left until dusk, when everyone was in for the night, and just before bedtime.

Because of my galivanting in the fields with Martha, I was late starting my homework, and I sat close to the fire, listening to the crackling of the logs and the turf, which carried sparks up the chimney in the dying spring twilight.

Then Maureen lit the lamp and placed it on the table. She knew I'd need it, and she'd trimmed the wick beforehand to let it give a newer and neater light.

At about eight o'clock, the aunts made some tea and we all ate slices of brown bread, hot and fresh with pats of homemade butter. When I had finished my homework, I decided I'd had enough and kissed them both good night.

I knew they were anxious for Uncle John's safe return, as there was no stopping him when he wanted to go out. They were on a vigil till he returned safely from his adventures. When he returned, they'd have to put him to bed, as his drunken condition would leave him unable to undo his bootlaces. They'd unyoke Bobby from the cart and put him in the shed for the night. When Uncle John woke next morning, he'd have a very sore head, but he'd marvel at the miracle of his safe return, having no memory of the events of the previous evening.

When I went to bed, I couldn't sleep for thinking about him. If he hadn't returned by one a.m., I was going to go after him.

It was a dark night at first, but a waxing gibbous moon began to glow on the horizon, and the night became a bit brighter. My thoughts wandered to Mother and Father and then to Fritz. What would Father say when he heard I'd been kissed by a German boy, after he had spent more than five years fighting them? But he wasn't a true German; he was born in Limerick, and his mother was Irish.

I giggled to myself, knowing that it was an unusual situation and that there was plenty to talk about whenever we got together again. I knew that the bombing was long over and that the Allies were on the outskirts of Berlin. It was only a matter of time now.

Then suddenly, the whole countryside around us was rocked by a great explosion. The sky lit up, as if by a great flash of lightning. But whenever there is lightning at night, darkness follows it. But now the whole place was awash with light, and there were explosions one after another for about two or three minutes, followed by a raging fire, which lit the place like day.

I thought we were being bombed, but experience told me that there was no whistling sound to denote that bombs were falling. What was this?

I shivered with fright as I searched the night landscape from my bedroom window to see what this was. There it was, down the main road, about two miles nearer to the town.

I ran downstairs to Martha and Maureen.

'What is it at all, alannah?' shouted Maureen.

'It's Hitler, he's here,' cried Martha.

'Definitely not!' I exclaimed. 'There's only one thing that it could be, but I hope I'm wrong. Remember Uncle John saying that Peter Johnson had stored barrels of petrol in a large shed? If that's it, he must have stored a lot of it, and it was a very stupid thing to do.'

'Jesus, Mary, and Joseph, protect them,' said Maureen, blessing herself as she spoke.

'By the cross of Christ, I have never seen such a thing in all my life,' said Martha. 'What can we do?'

'There's nothing we can do,' said Maureen. 'Only pray that everyone is all right there.'

'I'll get my bike and go there to see if there's anything I can do.'

'You will do nothing of the sort, child,' gasped Maureen.

'But they could all be dead.'

'Dead or alive, I'm not letting you outside this door. What would your mother say if she heard you went on your own off out into the night to fight a fire? You are in our care, and we promised her we'd watch over you, so you're not going anywhere.' Maureen was in a bit of a panic, as she ranted on, but Martha calmed the situation when she spoke in her quiet way, gentle as ever.

'Leave it so, child. There's not a neighbour from here to Mullingar that you'll find hasn't gone there tonight to help. I only hope that the nice big house is all right. Just let's all wait for this devil of a brother of mine to come home, if he ever does. We'll know soon enough what's happened.'

We sat downstairs in our nightgowns by the fire, waiting, for another hour and a half.

Uncle John arrived home at half past one in the morning. He was nearly asleep with drunkenness, and he was wet to the skin.

We helped him into the kitchen and sat him down at the fire. There was a very strange smell from him, and it began to pervade the kitchen. There were two smells, actually; one was bog or ditch water. To my horror, I thought the other was petrol.

'What happened to you?' asked Martha.

'I don't know,' he said. 'Those bloody Germans must have dropped a bomb. The jennet bolted, and I ended up in a drain. I had to follow him back nearly to the village before I got him.'

'Lord save us, you smell of petrol,' said Martha.

'Did you burn down that barn?' asked Maureen, rather crossly.

'What the hell are you talking about?' protested Uncle John.

'The petrol. You reek of it,' said Maureen.

'I was running past the Johnson place after the jennet and cart. There was a fire there; the whole place was lit up. Someone jumped off the wall and ran straight into me. He was carrying two buckets, and when he bumped into me, one of them spilt all over me. Whoever he was managed to save the other one and escaped into the field across the road, and he made good his escape into the darkness. I continued and managed to catch the jennet. For Christ's sake, don't let me sit too near that fire, or this house will go up in flames as well.'

'Well, let's get you out of all this and into your pyjamas,' said Martha.

I went outside and released Bobby into the shed. I shoved the cart against the wall, and there was a dreadful smell of petrol from that as well. I only hoped Uncle John was telling the truth. But I knew he was a very honest man and would tell no one any lies.

When I got in again, he was in the back room, washing himself with soap and water to remove any traces of petrol from his body. Before too long he was sitting at the fire in his pyjamas, drinking a hot cup of tea. The shock of it all had left him stone sober.

'Never again will I go off like that,' he said, 'I got such a fright.'

'I should jolly well hope not,' said Maureen. 'You have us demented worrying about you all the time.'

'Maybe now, as you're approaching old age, you might get a bit of sense,' said Martha.

'I hope they're all right up there,' he said. 'The Johnsons. I hope nothing happened to them.'

'Morning will tell, wait and see,' said Maureen.

*****

Morning *did* tell. At eight o'clock, I was getting ready for school when we heard a car. I knew it must be the Johnson car, and I ran to see if what I had said was true. To my horror, it wasn't Peter Johnson but the sergeant from the village with two other guards from the town.

He stepped out of the car, carrying himself as if his shoulders were rigid at the top of his body, carrying his head straight. Then he approached me.

'Is John Costello in?' he asked.

'He's in bed,' I answered.

'Will you tell him that we'd like to speak to him, please?'

I ran inside, and as I did so, Martha ran up the stairs, calling him. When I went back outside again, the other guards were examining the cart, and one of them was smelling it. They looked from one to the other and then to me.

'Why is he in bed so late?' he asked.

'It's only eight in the morning,' I said.

'Well, a man who has cows to milk shouldn't be in bed at this time. Why is he not up yet?'

'I'll not answer that. You can talk to him yourself; he'll be down in a few minutes.' In fact, I hadn't the words out of my mouth when he appeared at the door. He was in his shirt sleeves, wondering what had brought the guards to his doorstep so early in the morning. Then the sergeant spoke.

'I would like you to tell me of your whereabouts last night between the hours of eleven a.m. and twelve thirty a.m.'

'What do you want to know for? If it's that fire you're talking about or whatever happened, I had nothing to do with it.'

'Don't beat about the bush, now; just answer my question.'

'I was on the road, on my way home from the town. I left the gates at the forge, and then I went to the pub. I nearly broke my neck when there was a great explosion. The jennet reared up, and I fell off the cart into a drain. I had to follow him nearly all the way to the village.'

'Did you see or meet anyone?'

'I did. In fact, someone bumped into me after the explosion. Whoever he was carried two buckets of petrol. He spilled one of them on me accidentally and kept running. He climbed a gate and disappeared into a field.'

'What did you do with the bucket?'

'I kicked it into the drain.'

The sergeant reached into the car and took out a silver-coloured galvanised bucket. It had traces of dirt from the drain on it.

'Would this be the one?'

'It could be. I don't know.'

'But you said you threw the bucket into the ditch. So you should know what it was like.'

'How the hell am I supposed to know what it was like? It was dark.'

'Mr Costello, had you any motive for burning down Johnson's shed?'

'I didn't burn it down, Sergeant,' answered Uncle John angrily.

'Just answer my question and stick to the point.'

'I had no motive to burn it down.'

'Are you sure?'

'I'm certain, as God is my judge.'

'Well, we have sources who say that you constantly referred to the petrol which Peter Johnson had stored. You asked him on many occasions whether it had burned down or not.'

'Peter Johnson and I have been bantering at one another for years. I won't let him away with the fact that he owns the lands of all the dispossessed local people around here. There's no harm in it. I wouldn't hurt a rib of hair on the man's head. In fact, he saved my life several times in the past few years, when I had no horses to sow the seed or save the harvest. I wouldn't burn down any man's property, not even if you paid me.'

'Well, this story of another man throwing petrol on you sounds as if it's a real cock-and-bull story,' said the Sergeant.

'He didn't throw petrol on me; we bumped into each other. The bucket hit me in the chest when we collided. It spilled all over me, and he kept running. I couldn't make out who it was. My clothes were soaking.'

Maureen went to the shed and brought Uncle John's petrol-stained clothes to the Sergeant.

'Right, John Costello, I would like you to come with me to the station, as we need to investigate this incident further, and I'd like you to help me with our enquiries. I want to see if this bucket has any fingerprints on it.'

'Do you mean you're arresting me?'

'Mr Costello, you are not under arrest.'

'Well, then I don't have to go.'

'If you don't come with us, then maybe I will have to arrest you.'

'All right, then, never let it be said that I've resisted the law. I've been a law-abiding citizen all my life. I owe nothing to no one. I go to mass on Sundays. I've even done my part during these terrible years, and here I am, heading off to the garda station, number-one suspect in a crime I haven't committed. This will be the death of me, and it will be on your head it will hang, Sergeant, if anything terrible happens.'

'Don't be so melodramatic, Mr Costello. The sooner we get going, the quicker we can clear all this up.'

Uncle John turned to his sisters and said, 'Make sure you look after everything.'

They were, in fact, a little amused by it all, thinking that this might put an end to his foolish behaviour.

'If I don't come back, alannah,' he said to me, 'will you try and help me?'

I gave him a big tearful hug, and he turned from us and got into the squad car. It seemed like the exit of a great actor from a theatre for the last time, and we watched as the car headed down the dusty avenue on its way to the town.

*****

But the matter did not end there. We got word that evening that they were detaining Uncle John for further questioning. There were no fingerprints on the bucket except Uncle John's, so he was given free board and lodging at the station in Mullingar.

Maureen and Martha would make no response to the news but sat by the fire, crying into their aprons. It was then I decided to do something about it.

I got my bicycle and headed for Johnsons'. I was on an errand of mercy again. But I wondered how I'd be received. After all, Uncle John was being accused of causing grievous damage to the private property of a man who had been more than kind to us over the years. If he decided to turn me out and send me back down the road I came, he'd be within his rights to do so. But I wanted to get under what this was all about. Was Uncle John's story of a mysterious man running from the scene a credible one, especially when they'd bumped into each other in the darkness? Then, from what I could remember, a near full moon was just beginning to show some night light into the spring air, and maybe it was possible to avoid someone running from the scene of the crime. Could it be that Uncle John, in a drunken stupor, goaded by idle chat at the pub about the ancient land war and all that, had been so stupid as to set the shed on fire?

But I knew in my heart that he was by no means a malicious man and that anything he had said in the past was in jest rather than having any grudge in it. Then again, he always maintained that he'd never shake the hand of a landlord, even though we knew that the landlord system in Ireland was long gone, and gladly so. But for some people, old wounds take a long while to heal, and in Uncle John's case, it took many generations. Even though he was back making a living on some of the old ancestral lands, it seemingly wasn't enough.

Peter Johnson was at home, and he took me to the drawing room. He was openly upset by what had happened, and he had lost the flamboyant lustre he usually expressed in dealing with people.

'I'm very sad this has happened, Margaret. It's a sorry state of affairs.'

'I know Uncle John wouldn't do such a thing,' I said tearfully, with a shake in my voice, 'but I don't know where to turn. Mother is in London with Father, and the two aunts just can't cope. They're at home and won't stop crying. I just don't know where to turn.'

'I don't believe it myself. I know he has always teased me about the petrol I stored in my shed here. People around here know I've always been dealing in contraband; I have made a career out of smuggling across the border. I never kept much stock, as I had it delivered immediately to my customers. I began storing petrol when the war approached, as I knew there would be a shortage. I could find no customers for it. People reverted to the old horse traffic again. So I used it myself. Dr Daly got some from me on occasion, especially if he was taking a pleasure trip with his family away from home for a few days. I used it too, but I drove as little as possible. I was down to ten barrels.

'I've been storing it since 1938. The oil lorry came every month. It came from across the border, and I filled a barrel. I warned my men to stay away from there. The barn was locked always. It was lucky it was far enough away from the house and the farm buildings. It was at least one thing I did right. Whoever got in there climbed in through the high wooden window over the door, where hay and straw were stored on a loft for animals in the winter. It was thrown down on to the ground from that opening. I know John Costello wouldn't be able to climb that wall and get in through the opening. It was a much younger and fitter man who did it. The culprit got in on the loft and climbed down into the lower part of the barn. He must have lit a lantern or a candle and dropped it on the loft, as there was still some hay there. The whole place went up like matchwood, and he just managed to escape. He was lucky he wasn't blown to kingdom come himself.'

'Uncle John was drunk when he got home,' I said.

'Yes, I know the whole story. John Costello is no liar, Margaret. He's an honest man.'

'Can you not get the guards to let him go? Tell them what you've told me.'

'I cannot interfere with the work of the law. They will have to release him sometime tomorrow or charge him. But I tell you, I will speak up for him, if necessary. I promise you that.'

'Why then does he go on about the land war and landlords and all that?'

Peter got up from the fire and went to one of the big bookcases. Opening the glass door, he took out a large black book, which looked more like a register than anything else. 'Come here. I want to show you something.'

He opened the book to reveal tables and lists of townlands, people's names, and dates from the seventeenth century.

'This book was compiled in the last century. What it is is a list or survey which was done in the last half of the seventeenth century, sometime in the 1650s. It was known as the Down Survey. When Oliver Cromwell carried out his campaign in Ireland, it was funded by moneys given by wealthy individuals in England and Ireland. When the campaign was over, more than two and a half million acres of land, which were confiscated during the rebellion, were distributed among some of Cromwell's creditors. The lands belonged to the defeated Confederate Catholics who supported the Royalists in England. Cromwellian soldiers who served in Ireland were entitled to an allotment of lands here in Ireland as wages for their involvement in the campaign. Those who lost their lands were transported across the Shannon to Connaught, or shipped off to the colonies. Obviously, they didn't all go. If you look at this page here, you'll see what I mean. The townlands of Carrickloman, Esker, Dreel, Ridgeway, and Ballinciggill were given to a Sebastian Johnson, Esquire. He was an ancestor of mine. The Johnsons have been here since then. The lands of Esker and Carrickloman were taken from a man by the name of Walter Costello. It is clear, then, that some of the Costellos stayed on, as they're still in the area. The Costellos didn't get some of their lands back until your uncle John's father bought Dairy Hill early this century to provide for your granduncle and his sisters. Your late grandfather, as you know, had his own profession, but unfortunately died a young man, and the rest is history.'

'I wish he'd stop this nonsense,' I said.

'I'm afraid I can't help you there, Margaret. He knows as well as I do that we are the legal owners of the lands around here. He has no sons or daughters to leave it to. Believe me, Margaret, look ahead several years: Who is there left to take over Dairy Hill farm only you? Maybe fate has done the right thing for you. Do you really have to return to England?'

'Whenever Father is released from hospital, I know I must return with them,' I said.

'Maybe you will, but I know in my heart and soul you will be back. I know you love this place.'

'Meanwhile, what are we going to do about Uncle John?'

'Leave it to me. There's nothing we can do till morning, and maybe a night in the cooler will do him a world of good.'

'I feel sorry for him,' I said.

'I know what you mean. He is your pride and joy, isn't he?'

I didn't answer him, but I knew he was right. I left and went home.

Next morning, Uncle John was brought home, and the first thing he did was go to his room. We were back to the days when old Paddy died, and he wouldn't get up out of bed.

'He'll do that again someday,' sobbed Maureen, 'and there he'll remain till he's brought out in a coffin.' She said it loud enough that it would reach his ears upstairs. He didn't heed her, and we carried on with the chores, inside and outside.

People were calling to the house, wondering if he was all right. It was out of curiosity more than anything else, just probing to find out if he was the real arsonist or not. Uncle John would languish in his room for quite a while before coming to his senses, even when the mystery was solved and put to rest.

*****

Early next morning, Peter Johnson stopped his car at the back door. He still had a drop of petrol somewhere. He came into the house and sat down. Maureen, as usual, did the needful and offered him a cup of tea.

'I will, thank you,' he said. 'How is John?'

'Upstairs,' muttered Martha. 'He has taken to the bed.'

Maureen interrupted the proceedings by dropping a hot cup of tea on the table in front of him and offering brown bread and butter as well, apologising that she had no buns or sweet cake. When he had taken a few sips of the tea, he decided to respond to what Martha had just been saying.

'He can get up; John Costello didn't do it.'

'Who did it, then?' asked Maureen.

'I don't know. It's still a mystery. But there has been another fire.'

'Where?' exclaimed Martha.

'Bryces' cottage was burnt down last night.'

'Uncle John was here all night,' I said.

'Yes, I know. The guards kept a watch on the front gate last night, and no one came or went.'

'Good God, is all this burning going to continue?' grumbled Martha.

'I don't know,' he said, 'but we will have to find out.'

Suddenly, a thought struck me. I remembered the day I'd met Billy Bryce in the graveyard when I was visiting Sheila's grave and he'd told me that the house was going up for sale. He didn't want to see it happen. It was still full of disease and some other little girl would come to live there and get TB, just like Sheila.

I turned to Peter Johnson and said, 'I think I know who might have done it. Will you bring me to the village? We have no time to lose.'

When we got into the car, I told him why I thought it might be Billy Bryce, and he said very little. He just looked ahead, keeping his concentration on the road. Then despite all that had happened, he was ready with a smile on his face, and it wasn't long before he told me why he was happy.

'No matter what has happened, dear,' he said, 'there's always light at the end of the tunnel. My rather smug old Anglo-Irish pride has been hurt. I can replace that old shed, and I will have plenty of help to do so.'

'It shouldn't have happened, though – this war, all the dying, the TB, my friend Sheila dying. It's just like one long nightmare.'

'Ah, but you have the reassurance of a home and happiness through it all from the folk at Dairy Hill Farm.'

'That's why I'm so upset,' I said. 'Uncle John wouldn't harm a fly.'

'Well, maybe we can do something about it, then.'

The village was quiet. There was mass on in the church, yet life was slow in stirring. We stopped at Billy Bryce's cottage just opposite the church, and there was no sign of life anywhere.

Peter Johnson knocked on the door, and it seemed empty and quiet inside. He looked at me and knocked again. There was still no answer.

'See if the door is open,' I said.

He lifted the latch and slowly opened the door. As was usual with Billy, I expected to see the light from his fire through the darkness of the kitchen, but the fire wasn't lit. The kitchen was cold, and the house was abandoned. His bed hadn't been slept in. It seemed there had been some great rush on, as the wardrobe door was open and it lay empty.

On the mantelpiece in the kitchen, I found an envelope. Written on it was:

Whoever finds this envelope, please open it.

Peter asked me to do so. There was a letter inside, and I read it aloud.

Dear Finder,

I want you to take this letter to Mr Peter Johnson, and he'll know what to do. I'm so sorry I have left everything in such a state. I didn't mean to burn down the shed. I lit a yard lamp inside the shed, and it fell on the hay. I was lucky to get out of there as the whole place went up so quick. All I wanted was some petrol to burn down my brother's cottage. I didn't want any other family to live there in case they got that dreaded disease. So, there was no way out. It was being auctioned next week.

I'm so sorry to have offended John Costello. He had nothing to do with all of this. He's an innocent man. I only hope Peter Johnson can pick up the pieces and rebuild that fine shed. It is something that shouldn't have happened.

By the time you get this, I will be more than likely halfway across the Irish Sea. I'm going to England with a friend of mine. They say they will need a lot of help to rebuild the country, as soon as the war is over. I cannot stay here and face a jail sentence for something that happened quite by accident. But I want to point out, that I regret it ever happened.

God bless you all

Billy Bryce

I began to cry when I had finished, and Peter consoled me by telling me that it was all over.

'All we can do now is return home and let things settle down again.'

'What about Billy?' I asked.

'What about him, then?'

'Are you going to have him brought back here to face trial?'

'No, I don't, unless you do. The Bryces have always been good, honest people.'

'I want to forget it ever happened, and I'm sure Uncle John will do the same. We'll have to tell the guards, though, to have his name cleared.'

'Let's go home,' he said. 'I'll show them the letter this evening sometime. It'll give Billy enough time to get clean away.'

We left the village that quiet morning and returned home to a relieved and rather saddened pair of aunts, who brought the news to Uncle John.

His return message was that he'd never be able to hold his head high in the village again.

Martha came down the stairs with a rather angry face on her, wondering how they'd get Uncle John back to his old self once more. Peter Johnson mentioned the big event of the season, namely, the wedding of Esther and Bartley at the end of June, and said he hoped to see John there, as he knew he wouldn't miss it for the world.

There was a great sense of relief on the farm that day, and the neighbours arrived in dribs and drabs to find out if there had been any more developments since the burning of the cottage. We had little to say about it, as we were waiting for the all clear from Peter, which he gave us later that evening.

Through all the excitement and activity, we missed all that was happening elsewhere. We hadn't listened to any of the news on the wireless relating to events in Europe. I didn't know about it until the next day. Hitler was dead, and the war in Europe was over.

Part 11
The Gates

Chapter 20

The day I'd been looking forward to for a long time was approaching. It was the event of the year in the area, and the war and all that had happened had paled into insignificance. Bartley and Esther were tying the knot.

Martha and Maureen yoked Bobby to the trap one day in late May, and we drove to Mullingar. They bought me a beautiful new summer dress for the wedding, and a hat with lace just covering the top of my forehead. I felt like Greta Garbo or Joan Crawford. I wasn't a little girl anymore; I was a young woman.

Mother had written a few days earlier saying that Father was recovering well, but it would be some time before she'd get back to Ireland. If all came to all, she'd send for me when she was ready, when Father was due to come out of hospital. I was resigned to the fact, then, that I'd be staying at Dairy Hill for a few more months. The summer was ahead of me, and I was looking forward to the big day.

The only blot on the landscape was Uncle John. He stayed in his room, languishing in his bed or sitting staring out the window. He wouldn't even get dressed but wallowed there in the darkened room, his grey beard getting longer every day. As Maureen had said, the time would come when he took to the bed and the only way they could take him out of there was in a coffin. It looked like no coaxing would ever get him up again.

It got to a point that I'd had enough. His two sisters were suffering, and I could see their distress, which was affecting their health too. Even Bartley couldn't persuade him to come out. I began to see that maybe he was playing on his sisters, and now I would have to take drastic measures to deal with it. At fifteen years of age, I would have to place an old head on young shoulders and try to resolve the situation. Maybe if he had married when he was a young man, the firm hand of a woman would have done him good and kept him from such moods. As far as I was concerned, Uncle John was acting like a spoilt child.

The incident regarding the burning of the barn had been well put to rest, and Peter wasn't short of petrol. He had his sources, and the hum of his car could still be heard on the main road. There was still a petrol shortage, and it would continue for several years to come.

It was early June. I had gone to Uncle John's room most days, but he'd only just grunt at me or tell me to leave him alone in peace. For all the world he looked like he was sleeping, but in fact, he only pretended to do so when he heard anyone coming. He was usually lying with his head facing the wall. He couldn't lock the door, as Martha had asked Bartley to remove the bolt recently, much to Uncle John's anger and protests. When he went to get the key to lock himself in, it had conveniently disappeared too. He tried, then, to block the door with a chair. It worked for a short while, until the doorknob fell off and vanished into the darkness somewhere. He wasn't getting things his own way. It was time for action.

When I peered into the dark room, Uncle John made no move to wake up. The curtains were still pulled, and it was after midday. There was a stale smell of tobacco in the place. The blackout blind was down as well, and I rolled it up, filling the room with pools of early summer sunshine. I opened the casement window, and the weights rattled inside the wood as they held the window open. There was a fresh breeze from the east, and it freshened the room immediately.

'Close that blasted window,' he shouted.

'Oh, you're awake, then,' I said. 'I thought you were asleep.'

'Get out of here, you young cheeky little strap.'

'Not until you come with me and get up. There is nothing wrong with you. The whole thing is over. You know right well it is; you are just boiling over with self-pity.'

'You're not too old to get across my knee and get my belt to you.'

'You'd have to catch me first,' I said, with a smirk on my face.

He sat up in the bed and threw a pillow at me. There was a hole in it somewhere, and feathers began floating around the room. I flung it back at him with such force that it burst, sending clouds of feathers everywhere. He slumped back in the bed and was immediately covered in feathers.

'Get out!' he shouted.

'I will not!' I roared back.

'If you don't, I'll make you.'

'Get out of that bed and go wash and shave. You are a holy show, and Bartley's wedding only a few short weeks away.'

'I'm not going. The whole parish will be talking about me.'

'Well, just to let you know, that's just what they're doing *now*. They're calling you a coward and a waster, hiding away from the truth, giving up on life, just because you had to spend a night in a cell at the barracks. You are innocent, and well you know that. Now they're talking about John Costello, the man whom everyone respected, becoming a strange little self-pitying wretch, unable to face up to the truth.' Before that moment, I hadn't known I had such complex words in my vocabulary. It must have been all the reading I was doing. But anger is a strange ally at times.

'You know the truth of what happened,' he said, a little calmer.

'We all know it, and *you* know it. You are an innocent man. People want to shake your hand. Peter Johnson wants to talk to you and shake your hand as well. But then you won't get up and be there to shake the hand of your best friend on the happiest day of his life.'

'I won't shake that Johnson's hand, if you ask me. He's just a land grabber like all his kith and kin before him.'

'Go on, admit it. He's your friend, isn't he?'

'I tolerate him. I must, as a neighbour.'

'Don't tell me that, Uncle John. You know as well as I do that the land he has is legally his. Just because your ancestors and mine were lords over all this country doesn't mean we have any claim to it. Forget it. Forget about the land war you were part of when you were young and when your father was alive. It's past and gone. You have turned out to be a bitter and cantankerous old man. It's a pity to look at you. Your beard is growing long. You are dirty and smelly. You are a pitiful sight to look at. I feel now that I should never have come here. I don't want to see you again, ever. If people ask me about Uncle John, I'll tell them that I haven't got one. I don't know him.'

I was flaming with anger. My temper was at a boiling point. In one fell swoop, I let go of all the negative energy – the war, Nana's death, Mother and Father far away in London, Sheila my best friend, and the loneliness I'd felt when I'd come here at first. It all seemed to mushroom like a great cloud from a volcano, and the object of it all was the only man in my life I loved next to my father, kind and generous, if not a little eccentric at times. I shouldn't have said all those things to him. I began to cry, and turning to him once more, I screamed at him.

'Goodbye! I hope you rot in here.'

*****

I turned on my heels and slammed the room door behind me, leaving him to languish in the silence. I ran to the gate leading into the cow pasture. I forgot to notice that Maureen and Martha were sitting on each side of the fire with tears streaming down their faces. I kept running till I reached the highest point on the farm at the large rock. I sat down on the fresh green clover, my back resting against the rock, and sobbed bitterly to myself. I didn't notice when Sam and Shep came to me and began nuzzling at me, looking for attention. Whether they sensed my sadness or not, maybe they were trying to comfort me. I held the two of them close to me, and they began licking my salty, tearstained face.

I had said too much, and I wished to go home. I wouldn't enjoy Bartley's wedding now, after all that had happened. I sat there with the two dogs listening to my sobs, hoping that it was all just a bad dream. I'd wake up back in my bedroom in London with the red eiderdown and the people rushing past my window in their early-morning passage to work. There would have been no war, and I would never have had to come to this place.

After about twenty minutes, Sam and Shep began silently wagging their tails as something shaded me from the warmth of the sun. Then a voice spoke softly.

'Margaret!' It was Uncle John. I turned around, and he stood there, silhouetted against the sun. I stood up and faced him. He was wearing his overcoat over his drawers, and he had stuffed his feet into his dried leather boots. He hadn't even bothered to lace them. There were feathers everywhere in his hair, in his beard, and all over his clothes. Even though I was so upset, a strange feeling came over me, as if I wanted to explode laughing, but I composed myself, not knowing what was going to come next.

'Forgive me, Margaret,' he whispered.

Of course I'd forgive him. He had come out. He had risen. He was Lazarus rising from the tomb. I ran to him and threw my arms around him. I was sobbing again.

'I'm so sorry,' I said. 'I shouldn't have said all those horrible things to you. You are the kindest man I know, and I will never forget that as long as I live.'

He held me close to him there, and we just stood, saying very little, just knowing that the past was behind us and the war was over.

'I went that day to do something for you,' he said.

'It's all right,' I answered. 'Forget about it.'

'I did it for you. I brought the gates to the forge. Have they come back?'

'They're in the shed, I think. The blacksmith left them back. They're all covered up with sacks. I haven't looked at them.'

'That's good,' he said. 'You see, I'm a lonely man, Margaret. I know you must go. Between the fire and knowing that you'd have to leave made me act the way I did. I'm a stupid old get, and I'm stubborn. I've always told you that. I can never see further than my nose. I suppose I wanted a part of you to stay forever. That's why I got the gates done. Come on, and I'll show you.'

'I'm so sorry again,' I said, a little twitch of a sob there still. 'You can get me across your knee if you want to.' I didn't know why I said that, but he always joked about doing such a thing if I teased him.

But he answered as he always did. 'Any man who'd do a thing like that is a coward. What about that pillow? It burst, you know.'

'It was good enough for you. Just look at the state of you.'

'Still as cheeky as ever. Now come on till I show you this.'

We went to the shed where the barley and oats were stored during the winter. It was a place I seldom visited; I also didn't have any interest in the gates. He pushed back the sliding door, and the rollers overhead creaked as it opened to allow the daylight in.

The gates were covered in sacks to protect the new coat of paint the blacksmith had put on them. They were a dark blue in colour. They were against the wall, one facing the other as they would be when they were swinging from the piers at the roadside. He pulled down the sacks to reveal that the blacksmith had made some letters and welded them into the top of the gates. The left-hand gate had the letters *B E T*, and the right one had *H A N Y*. When the gates closed, they'd reveal the word *Bethany*.

'Dairy Hill Farm no longer exists,' he said. 'From now on it will be known as Bethany, and Lazarus has risen from the dead to tell you.'

'It's wonderful!' I exclaimed, with tears in my eyes.

'I want you to remember this. I know this place has been Bethany to you since that morning I brought a little shy waif of a thing and her poor distressed and injured mother from the train. If I don't get to tell you this, I fear you could be called away quickly. There will always be a place for you here, girl. This is your home. There's no one else for it. After our day, it will be yours to do what you please with. My wish would be for you to come back and make your home here.'

'You know I'll come back. I'll be waiting for the day when it's possible for me to return. My heart is here, but my duty is to Mother and Father.'

'They're roots are in England now,' he said, 'but I now know that yours are here.'

'I love you, Uncle John, and always remember that.' I hugged him once more, and then I said to him, 'Listen, will you do me a favour?'

'I'll try.'

'Will you go in now, and we'll get a bath ready for you in the back room. The water is boiling on the fire. You smell like ten pig houses.'

He grabbed me and threw me across his shoulders, tickling me as he did so, and headed back into the house. The aunts were still crying, but this time it was with joy. It was a strange place indeed, a house of contrasts. An hour before, I had been screaming at him. Now he was playing with me as if nothing had ever happened.

*****

I was up at dawn the morning of the wedding, helping with the milking and making sure that all the animals were right for the day until we returned that evening. Martha asked two men from the village to do the evening chores so that there would be no rush for us to return.

The fire was lit all night, and there were pots of water boiling so that I could have a bath in the back room. Uncle John announced that as soon as he could afford it, he would get the water into the house and make a bathroom out of that room. All it was ever used for was to hang geese at Christmas or to store the salted bacon during the winter. When I had finished outside, Martha and Maureen had a bath ready for me. You would swear it was *my* wedding we were preparing for.

The ceremony was to take place at nine o'clock in the village church, followed by a breakfast in Johnson's hay barn. It was at the other end of the farmyard and well away from the burnt-out shell of the horse barn. Peter had had it cleaned out and decorated for the occasion. He'd had some electric lights put in and redirected some wiring from his generator to provide light for the dance that night.

He paid for Esther's reception as a gift to her. He said it was the least he could do after her twenty years of working for him in the big house. She'd come there when she was thirteen, when she had just left national school. She in return had been a very diligent worker, and over the years, she'd made sure the place was run and managed properly, even when he was away on business. His only regret now was that he might not get anyone of the same calibre to replace her. But that didn't stop him giving her a good send-off.

We set out on the jennet and trap just after eight o'clock to the village. It ordinarily would take nearly an hour to get there, but in the morning, Bobby was frisky, and he'd make the journey in nearly half the time and then relax for the rest of the day.

It was a bright June morning. There was a soft breeze from the west. Whenever the sun disappeared behind a cloud, it was much cooler, but that was for short spasms only, and we knew that the day would stay dry.

When we arrived at the church, all the neighbours and friends were arriving at the same time. Bartley stood at the door, all dressed up and nowhere to go. When the week's beard was shaved and he was clean and all spruced up, he was quite a handsome man at forty-two years of age. There was just a hint of silver threads among the gold, as the first traces of grey were beginning to appear on his temples. His hair was shining from a good helping of Brylcreem, and his best man, Jimmy Kiernan, was dressed the same. They were two different men when they were cleaned up, with all traces of farm life gone from their bodies for the day. Everyone was shaking hands with Bartley.

Uncle John was a new man too. He had lost the washy appearance he'd had when he arrived out of the room a few short weeks previously. But today, dressed up, he was a king. He had a pin-striped suit and a new hat. He looked like Lionel Barrymore or Edward G. Robinson, and I was proud to see him looking so well.

At a few minutes past nine, everyone went inside, but I decided to wait for Fritz, and Uncle John said he'd stay with me. Martha and Maureen had left us much earlier before the congregation went into the church, as they wanted to pray the stations of the cross. They were dressed in their usual black clothes and their hatpins glistened in the sun as they went into the darkness of the building.

Esther was only five minutes late, and Peter's car looked good when it was washed and polished. Manfred Von Gebler was driving, and she'd asked

Fritz to give her away. Her father had been killed during the Great War at Passchendaele when she was six years old, and her mother had died of the Spanish flu in 1919. She had been reared by her aunt until she left national school, and then she'd made Johnsons' her home. She would have liked to have Peter do the job; Peter was a good Christian and had a very generous heart. But in fact he was delighted that she asked Fritz to do the job.

Peter stepped out of the car to open the door for Esther, and as he did so, Uncle John burst past me and made straight for him. Before he knew it, Peter stood with his mouth wide open in shock as Uncle John took his hand and kept shaking it without letting it go.

'It's good to see you, neighbour,' said Uncle John.

'It's good to see you too, John,' said Peter.

'We have a lot to talk about, you know,' said Uncle John.

'I know we have, and a lot to share. Maybe this evening. Unfortunately, I must take Manfred to Dublin on some important business today, but we should be back this evening, and we can talk into the night.'

'Right you be,' said Uncle John. I knew that the great land war that had lasted for centuries was now over, and I took his hand when he returned and squeezed it.

Fritz stepped out of the car. A more handsome man you might never see in a lifetime. Taking Esther's arm in his, he led her to the door. She wore a bright-blue summer dress with a white hat covered in lace. One of the girls who worked at Johnsons' was her bridesmaid, and she shivered with nerves. Someone had a small box camera, and there was a bit of running here and there to position it so that the person taking the photograph stood with their back to the sun to make the best use of the light. Then we all went inside to wait for the bride to enter.

*****

It was a quiet ceremony. A lot of the village people had gathered to see Bartley tie the knot. It was a nine-day wonder. There were whispered remarks among those gathered that the couple were made for each other.

He was nine years older than Esther, and he had worked that farm since he was in his teens. They knew that she would be a welcome addition to his life and that he was a lucky man to have met her. If it hadn't been for his time in hospital getting his appendix out, it might never have happened.

Afterwards, we threw rose petals on them, as there was no confetti or rice, but they did the job well. The box camera came out again, and more photographs were taken. I stood in the background, looking on, as all and sundry talked among themselves. Then someone tapped me on the shoulder. It was Fritz.

'You did a great job giving your daughter away,' I joked.

'It was my privilege. I can always boast that I gave a lady away to her groom when I was only seventeen.'

'Are you enjoying the day?' I asked.

'I am. Will you stay with me?'

'I will,' I answered.

'Peter asked Grandfather to go to Dublin today with him on business. He said he'd tell me about it later.'

'Do *you* want to leave?'

'I don't know. I have been here so long, it's difficult to leave now.'

'I know how you feel. I'm waiting for Mother to call me back to London as well.'

'Let's not talk like this,' he said. 'Let's enjoy the day. I heard you are very good at drinking some black stuff from a big jug. I want to see you do it again.'

'Fritz Von Gebler, who told you that?' I gave him a thump on the arm and began to blush.

'Wait till I get Uncle John.' Fritz was laughing. It was nice to see him laugh again. I joined him on the little sidecar as we left the village and made our way to the farmyard of the big house.

*****

As the wedding party moved along the gravel road, someone played the concertina, and Shawnie, whom I'd heard singing with the wren-boys when I'd first arrived, had now grown into a fine young man, with a lovely tenor voice. He lifted the air with his singing, and the only sound otherwise was the gentle trundle of cartwheels on gravel and stone.

The dust rose from the avenue as we made our way to the farmyard, and we settled into a morning of feasting, which lasted into the afternoon. It was a day to remember. It was a time of hope for everyone, knowing that things could only get better. I was happy that day, happier than I had been in a long time.

When the feasting was over and the wedding cake was cut, everything was cleared to one side and the floor was swept. Some of the men who worked on the land brought in great planks of wood nailed together and laid them down on the floor for everyone to dance on.

The music began about four o'clock, and the barrels of Guinness were opened. Fritz offered to get me a glass, but I thumped him on the arm once again and I decided to sample Esther's homemade lemonade. I don't know where the lemons came from, but we never questioned where Peter had sourced all his merchandise.

Soon the music began, and away the people went, into a frenzy of dancing, which would last late into the night. We joined in, jumping and dancing in our own crude way, but nobody minded in the least. Esther looked like a queen as she moved quietly through the crowd, bringing her new husband with her. I knew Bartley felt a little awkward following her around, but that would change. This was the first day of their lives together.

Later that night, Bartley and Esther left the party to go to their house. They were followed from the place as the pony and trap brought them back to Carrickloman by all the men on bikes.

Nobody came any farther than the gate, and the men waited. Bartley and Esther closed the door behind them. During the day, one of the wedding party had managed to climb in a window and tie a spring-mounted butler's bell to the springs underneath the bed. As soon as one of them climbed into bed, the bell began to ring, causing all those listening at the gate to raise a glorious cheer, like one would at a football match when a goal was scored. It was followed a minute later by the window being opened and the bell being flung unceremoniously into the yard. Another cheer went up, and the house went silent.

When the wedding escort returned to the barn, we were all dancing on the floor. Peter parked the car in the darkness close by, and nobody passed any remarks. They knew he too would join the wedding party for a while.

We were dancing the siege of Ennis when Fritz stopped suddenly as his grandfather appeared into the light of the barn. There was a lady with him. She was thin, worn, and bedraggled, carrying the scars of suffering. Fritz stood with his hand gripped tightly around mine. His face became a frenzy of excitement and tears. He began shouting at the top of his voice in German. The music stopped, and the crowd looked on in dismay. He ran and left me standing there.

He ran to her, shouting. 'Mutter! Mutter! You are alive. Mutter! Mam!'

He swept her up in his arms, carrying her like a baby and swinging her round in a circle. She was light as a feather and undernourished from years in a prison camp. She was crying with joy, and so was he.

'Fritz, my son,' she kept shouting. 'Fritz is now a young man.' The silence lasted for nearly ten minutes as Fritz and his mother were reunited. Manfred stood close by, and she reached for his hand to bid him join them. When they composed themselves, Fritz swept her up in his arms again and carried her to the waiting car. Then the crowd cheered and applauded the great happy event.

I stood there alone, not knowing whether to laugh or cry. Fritz was lost to me now. He had found his family again. He had no need for me anymore. I was standing in a tearful trance on the floor when Uncle John put his arm around me.

'There goes one very happy young man tonight,' he said.

'I know,' I answered. 'I know.'

*****

I didn't see him for about a week. He arrived one morning in early July, and I knew by the way he was dressed that he was leaving. He was a different person altogether with a glint in his eye, happier than I had seen him for a long time.

He was leaving that afternoon, and we walked through the field of oats around the headlands as the green heads were beginning to turn colour, gently moving back and forth in the soft breeze. He took my arm, and we walked slowly together.

'We are going to England first,' he said.

'What about Germany?'

'Mother doesn't want to go back there.'

I thought I might be able to visit him if he was in England. 'Will I come and see you there?' I asked.

'Maybe. I'm not sure what's happening. But we will probably return to Germany when things settle down.'

I buried my head in his chest and sobbed quietly. He held me close, saying nothing, but feeling awkward in breaking the news to me.

'I'll never see you again,' I said.

'Don't say that. You know I will.'

'Will you write, then?'

'I will, and tell you everything.'

'I love you, Fritz.' I sobbed.

'I love you too, Margaret.' Then it happened. He kissed me. It was my first real kiss, not like the one on the cheek he'd given me when I was twelve. We stood there looking into each other's eyes, and then we kissed again. We smiled together at once, knowing that we'd both wanted that more than anything else in the whole world. We walked arm in arm around the field, cherishing our last moments together.

Then we stood on the rock, looking across country to the lake. It was just the same, with its islands, clear blue water, and a lonely boatman out fishing. It was a place of peace, a getaway from the troubles of our times. It was there that I'd first encountered Manfred when he fell from his horse.

'We have great memories of this place,' I said.

'And Sheila.'

'She shouldn't have died,' I said, rather quietly.

'Our lives are going to change again,' he whispered softly.

'Will we ever be as happy as we are just now?' I asked.

'Of course we will. But we have wonderful memories from here.'

'Then we had to grow up.'

'Let's not look back now,' he said. 'It's time to look to the future.'

'We wouldn't have met except for the war, and now it's going to make us drift apart.'

'Don't let's look at it that way,' he said. 'It happened, that's all, and now we must go.'

'I don't want you to go now,' I answered softly through tearful eyes. 'You could stay. I could stay. We could go on like this together.'

'I have found my family again. I have found my mother. I have never been happier in a long time.'

'Then I was just good enough for you until you found her,' I said, turning away from him. 'Now you can go away and leave me behind. I was your pawn, and now you can throw me there.'

'Margaret, you know that's not true.' He grabbed me and swung me around so that I looked straight into his face.

'I *do* want you. If I could stay, I would. You know now that my duty is to my mother. She has suffered enough in this conflict. I thought I had lost her. You know right well that I must go. I'm not dumping you. I love you. I think you know as well as I do that this day was going to come. Dreams do not last forever.'

'They do if you want to make them last.'

'Don't dream, then, Margaret; this is reality. We must go, and I don't love you any less. I'm just seventeen and you are fifteen. We still have long roads ahead, and we can meet again.'

'Then reality is a cruel monster,' I sobbed. 'It shouldn't happen. It puts us together and then separates us. That's why I want to live in my dreams.'

'All we can do is live the memories,' he said softly, and then he kissed me again. We stayed there in that moment with the breeze catching us and waving us along with the ripening fields of oats, beckoning us on to an uncertain life ahead.

I wanted that afternoon to last forever. We were alone, hemmed in by the hawthorn hedge laden down with rosy ripening haws as the clouds rolled above us eastwards towards the Irish Sea. Maybe Sheila was with us, telling us that this was the end and that the future was good. But I thought of her then, with all her troubles over. Maybe ours were just beginning.

We walked back to the farmhouse, and he said farewell to everyone. Martha and Maureen had their aprons out, wiping the tears away.

Uncle John remarked to him that if they needed anyone to make hay in Germany, he should apply for the job.

'Goodbye, sir, and thank you,' he said.

'Don't leave it as long before you return,' whispered Uncle John with a shiver in his voice.

'I'll try,' he answered, and he made his way on the trap down the avenue. I went with him for those last few moments. The gates were now installed, and it gave the entrance a new sense of identity. For the passing stranger, they gave the impression that the farm belonged to some country gentleman or squire.

Fritz stepped down, and he embraced me once again.

'Why do you have to go?' I sobbed.

'I must go, you know I must.' He kissed me one last time, and with tears in his eyes, he sat back on the trap and waved.

'Goodbye!' I shouted.

'I love you,' he answered back, as he rounded the bend on the road.

I ran after the trap to the turning and watched him go. His blond hair was shining in the summer sun. He didn't look back but kept going, the pony trotting at a gentle pace on the gravel road. As he rounded the next bend, he didn't turn around, but he knew I was watching, and he raised his hand in the air and waved. Then he was gone.

I turned and walked slowly to the farmhouse, greeted by the two dogs, who came bounding to me as I moved along the avenue. Uncle John was waiting at the gate. He could sense that someone needed a shoulder to cry on, and I did just that. I wept loudly and bitterly, as if the whole world were going to end. He said nothing for a while but held me close to him. I knew by the way he comforted me that I was his granddaughter, the one he'd never had. Inside, he too was feeling lonely. He'd have to let me go too.

'You love him, don't you?' he asked.

I didn't answer but nodded my head.

'That's what it's all about. It's something fantastic, but something we must often let go.'

'Why am I so sad? This place has made me so happy, yet I have to say goodbye. I might never see him again.'

'You know something? He was your first love. Always remember that.'

'I will, but I knew this was going to happen.'

'I know, but these were great years despite the war and all that people have lost. We must move on, and things will change. How that will happen, I just don't know. We will need to trust in the good Lord himself for that.'

'I would like it all to have been a dream and let it start all over again,' I said. I was thinking of Mother and Father and when I'd be with them again. I didn't know when that was going to happen. Overall, I was in a very happy place, but my sadness at losing Fritz confused me and left me uneasy. I knew it was time to move on, as Uncle John had said. I was afraid of the future, but Uncle John, as usual, had the kind words that eased my distress.

'We could all do that. We could all be dreamers. But because of that, we'll never grow up. Maybe that's what happened to me. I had the dreams of my ancestors, and the return of all the Costello lands to our name. I hoped that justice would be done for all the generations before me, who suffered because of it. That's what dreaming is, and it can lead you astray from what is real. I was such a fool. I know that now. If you live that way, you might never get anywhere. But that shouldn't ever stop you from having dreams of a better life. I have only one dream for you, Margaret, and you know what that is. I would like to see you return to Bethany someday.'

I looked up at him and smiled.

'It's my dream too, and I know it's up to me to make it real.'

He placed his arm around my shoulder, and we went back to the farmhouse for dinner. The aunts were quiet, but they too knew that soon they'd have to let me go. When that day would come, they didn't know, but I could read their minds and wondered when my day to leave would arrive.

*****

But I hadn't long to wait. On Sunday morning a week later, we returned from early mass in the village. When all the morning chores were done, I decided to go out into the front garden to read a book. The bees were very active on the hollyhocks and the evening primrose. There was a great strength in the sun, telling of a fine summer day ahead.

I was aroused from my book and my thoughts by a car coming up the avenue. I thought that Peter was arriving on a social call or to borrow a hay bogey to help with the harvest at his place. It drove to the back of the house and stopped. Sam gave his usual little yelp of welcome, and Shep began barking. I stayed where I was and continued with my book. About five minutes later I could hear footsteps on the gravel path at the side of the house, thinking it was Martha or Maureen calling me in for dinner. Then the footsteps stopped, and a voice said softly, 'Margaret!'

I looked up.

It was Mother. I dropped my book and ran to her. I threw my arms around her neck and began crying and weeping into her hair.

'It's all right, my darling,' she said softly. 'We're back.'

'What do you mean by *we?*'

Then I looked behind her. There stood Father, smiling at me with tears in his eyes. He was moving slowly towards me on crutches. He was walking. I couldn't believe it. He looked quite well too, and his smile said everything about his slow progress back to good health again.

I left her and went to him.

I didn't speak but held him gently, sobbing into his white shirt. I didn't know what to say. Mother came to us, and we stood there in a ring, holding each other, together for the first time in several years. We had been divided by a bloody, bitter war but were now united here in a place where we had sought refuge from the terrors of our time, to find peace and understanding and to learn to live once more.

*****

The day before I left, I walked the fields again, ending my journey on the lake shore. It was still the same. It hadn't changed from that day in winter when I'd first come here to feel the freshness of the wind on my face. These were the last few hours I had to think and reflect on this place. I was leaving, and I knew things were going to change again. This time around there wasn't the fear of loss, as when Father had left to go off to war or when Nana had died so tragically. This time around the changes in my life were going to be for the better. But deep down, just as on that last day with Fritz, I still didn't want things to change.

Then a thought struck me. This was a place that never changed. If I returned here in five years' time, I would still find Uncle John feeding the animals and talking to the ones he wanted to keep, giving them names, thus establishing that they'd have a long and fruitful life on the farm. Maureen would be going through the ritual of making a Christmas pudding, or you would find Martha flitting around getting a stew ready for a cold winter day. There was a great sameness about life here, a place where peace could be found. It was a peace that came from within, that had been locked away by the hustle and bustle of a busy life. To come here opened truths about yourself, truths you'd never known existed. This peace was an inner blessing, a prayer, something that would come back to me in times of need. It was here I'd found my sense of place, my past, my ancestors, which would root me to the very rocks that bound me to the earth.

I walked back through the fields again and climbed to the highest point on the farm, onto that big rock, the pedestal of my heritage, which gave a panoramic view of Carrickloman right down to the lake shore. It was here I'd walked with Fritz in the ripening field of oats. I knew he would always be here. This was a place for him as well, where he'd touched my life for a few short moments. I'd discovered then that these were much more than my own selfish needs. His hair, like the ripening corn, had caught the sunshine, and his smile had reassured me that come hell or high water, we'd return to this place. It was here we'd learned to laugh and cry, and where I'd discovered at a very young age what it was like to love someone, even though that love was only a few mild kisses in a field of ripening oats.

The hastening days of summer held a chill in the evening air, and I could see the whole place alive, as if I had never seen it before. This was my home as well. I knew there was always room at the table for me, and a place in the hearts of three special people who'd brought me in from the cold and loved me as if I were their child. I wondered if my journeys as I grew older would lead me back here. I knew I would come back at the earliest opportunity, but that lay at the hands of my parents, in whose trust I was being placed again. But there were great memories here that would remain with me, whether I ever came back or not. They were rooted in the landscape as well as their gentle and prayerful life. They gave a lot of their time as well to helping those who were less fortunate than themselves. They were going to continue with their simple lives for many more years. In the times that followed, wherever I was, when I wanted to dream, I'd think of Dairy Hill, and the smile would return to my face. I knew that when the right time came, I'd pack my bag, and make that journey along the road to Bethany.

About the Author

Danny Dunne is a historian and retired School Principal from Mullingar, Co. Westmeath. He has ten books to his credit including, The Little Silver Bell (1995), a book of poetry Along the Gravel Road (1996) and compiling and editing eight books documenting the local history of communities in the Mullingar area. He is married to Betty and they have three adult children.

In 2018 he published *The Spindle Tree - A Story of Lost Childhood and Redemption in the Irish Midlands.*

The Spindle Tree

Sarah knows what happened to the Larkin children. They were spirited away somewhere, because their father had abandoned them when their mother died. Her own mother too is very ill. What will happen if she dies when her father is away working in England? But then, her mother dies suddenly and there is no sign of her father returning. She has to take drastic measures, and hide her body to pretend to the world that nothing has happened. Life on the outside must go on as normal. When her Dad comes home, he'll know what to do. But as the days wear on, there is no sign of him. Meanwhile, she and her brothers are led into a maze of events outside their control, which will draw them back many years later to confront their past. What will they find there? Will the whole house of cards come crashing down on them, or will they find redemption?

Please Review

Dear reader,

Thank you for taking the time to read my book. I would really appreciate if you could tell others about it if you think it is something they would enjoy to read. If you purchased the book online, you could leave an honest review of the book on Goodreads or on whatever online bookstore site you purchased it from?

This matters because most potential readers first judge a book by what others have to say. Thanking you in advance.

Danny